Make Me

ELITES OF CHESHIRE SHORE BOOK ONE

CAROLINE MASCI

Caroline Masci

Make Me: Elites of Cheshire Shore (Book 1)

Second Edition

Copyright ©2023 Caroline Masci

All rights reserved

First Published 2023

This book is a work of fiction. Names, characters, places and incidents are products of the author's imagination. Any resemblance to actual events or persons, living or dead is entirely coincidental. All activities portrayed in this book are a work of fiction and may not be replicated in real life.

No part of this book may be reproduced, stored in a retrieval system or transmitted in any form or by any means, without prior permission in writing of the author, nor be otherwise circulated in any form of the binding or cover other than in which it is published, and without a similar condition, including this condition, being imposed on the subsequent purchaser. The only time content from this book may be reused is in the case of a brief quotation in a book review.

18+ content not suitable for younger readers

Structural Edit: Creating ink

Line Edit: Creating ink

Proof Reader: Creating ink

Cover Design: Books and moods

Formatting: Books and moods

Published by: Date night Diaries

Authors note

Dear Readers,

please be advised that on- page panic attacks and anxiety are portrayed within this book which may be triggering to some. As someone who has suffered from anxiety, depression and panic attacks, I hope that I have given the subject matter the sensitivity and care it deserves. Also portrayed are toxic parental relationships.

To those that hold our hand extra tight when they know we need it most.

Founding Five Families
CHESIRE SHORE

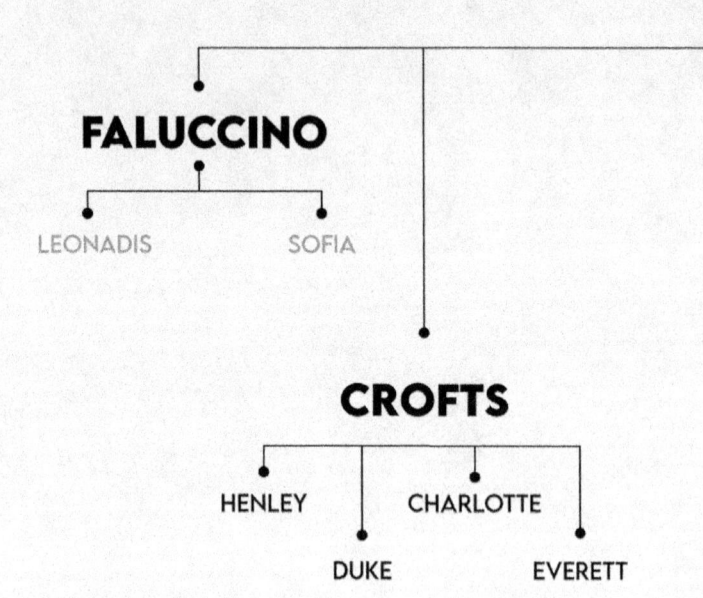

FALUCCINO
- LEONADIS
- SOFIA

CROFTS
- HENLEY
- DUKE
- CHARLOTTE
- EVERETT

■ COUSINS
■ SIBLINGS

FALLINGTON
- RYDER
- ZANDER

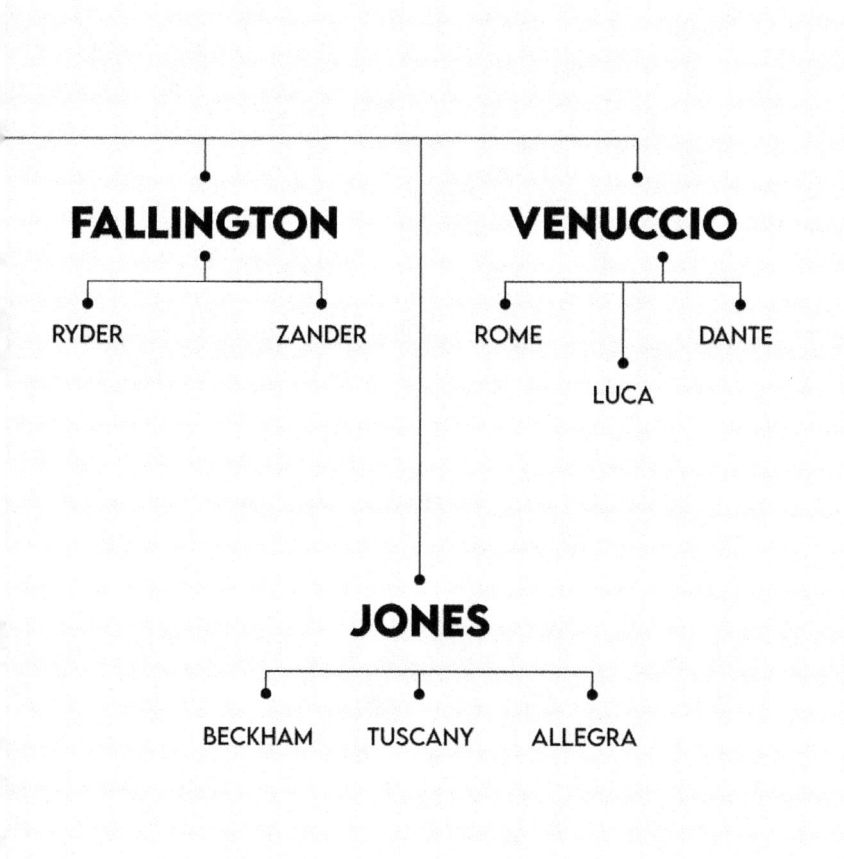

VENUCCIO
- ROME
- LUCA
- DANTE

JONES
- BECKHAM
- TUSCANY
- ALLEGRA

CHAPTER ONE

Livvy

"Remind me again why you agreed to go out with him tonight?" my best friend, and roommate Kendall leans against the door jam, crossing her arms over her chest.

"Not this again," I blow the strands of hair that have come loose from the roller out of my face. According to Kendall I've seriously broken a cardinal rule in the girl code.

"You've barely started dating the guy, and he gets dibs on your birthday," she grumbles.

I internally groan. "Kenny, you already decided you wanted to do something with me next Saturday night," I reply. "Besides, I'm hoping this will give Kyle the push he needs to take our relationship to the next level." Dabbing the cream highlighter, my family's make up company – Glam Co – is currently testing on my cheekbones, I lean into the bathroom mirror and scrutinize the application. So far, I'm liking it. I think it's ready to move phases.

"Pa-the-tic. Not you, just your taste in men." Her top lip curls in disgust, to say she isn't a Kyle fan would be an understatement. Personally, I believe she's on more of a Kyle hiatus. She doesn't like him, and she has no problem making sure the world knows it. Kyle isn't a bad guy; Kendall just doesn't think he deserves me. While I may not be head over heels for Kyle, his goals align with mine, my parents love him, and we both have the same ambition. He's uncle also happens to sit on the Glam Co board, which only makes my transition to a more senior role that much smoother. I brace myself for the next guilt laced thing to come out of her mouth when a blur of brown and white fur skids past us with something hanging from her mouth.

"MoMo," Kendall yells, chasing after my Jack Russell. "If you see a shoe with the Fendi logo, you leave it the fuck alone."

I snort a laugh; shoe theft or destruction of property is a daily occurrence with those two.Unfortunately, the little furball seems to have an affinity for Kenny's designer shoes, hence her excessive hostility.

"You owe me a pair of shoes." Kendall directs this at me.

"Put it on my tab," I reply. It's not the first pair and it won't be the last. I'm almost certain Momo is up to three pairs of shoes, but who's counting.

MoMo is growing on Kendall like a fungus.

My gaze catches on my 'Livvy's way to achieve her dream' checklist pinned to the bathroom mirror, and I mentally go through it for the second time today.

Graduate summa cum laude in cosmetic science.
Check.

Make Me

11 million followers and counting on Make Me.
Check. Check.
Owning my Nanna's little black book of product formulas.
Check. Check. Check.
Work my way up from Glam Co intern to product development.
Check. Check. Check. Check.
Date the man who will be my equal in every sense of the word.
Check. Check. Check. Check.
Becoming CEO of Glam Co. *Not there yet, but soon.*

If only Nanna was here to see this. God, I miss her. She ascended to be CEO of Glam Co and my dad has been leaving really strong hints, that I'm following right in her footsteps. Most nannas pass down recipes for sugar cookies and apple pie. Mine passed down her original recipe for making moisturizer and her patented beta complex.

I know — by today's standards — a twenty-five female CEO is considerably young — even in the cosmetic industry. I knew I would need to be more than just good. I'd need to be outstanding! That's why I started my career early on Make Me – the world's hottest make up app –proving to the board of Glam Co I don't just love make up, I live and breathe it. I worked so hard and sacrificed so much, it's why I've thrown myself into everything Glam Co from the moment I learned what CEO stood for. Why everything else comes second to my academic achievements and professional goals. If I want this, I need, no, I have to be ready. And I am. I'm so ready, I'm practically bursting from it. Make up has a much deeper meaning, one over the years I've come to learn. It's about celebrating our femininity and beauty and learning how a little bit of lipstick or mascara can make us feel more confident in our own skin.

I stare at my scrawled formulas for the teen line I plan to launch– my constant reminder what I'm working for – stuck below my check list on the mirror. My stomach gives a flutter of excitement. This teen line is going to be my legacy at Glam Co and my way of ushering in the new era. "Twenty-five is going to be the best year yet," I whisper, running my hand over the pieces of paper.

"Are you nearly ready?" Kendall calls, shattering my moment. I add the final touch — my signature red lipstick — to my lips.

"Just a second."

"Can I borrow your blue The Row dress for my client dinner tomorrow night?"

I guess Kendall distracted herself from MoMo going through her closet by going through mine. "Sure, my closet is your closet, Babes." I reply, spritzing my perfume on my wrist and neck.

I glance briefly at the screen of my phone. *Shit*. I'm running late, I needed to be ready ten minutes ago. Kyle is going to be here any second and he hates it when I run late. I swipe the last few touches of blush on my cheeks and hustle out of my bathroom.

"Is he here?" my eyes scan our spacious apartment while I slip into a bright red pair of *Valentino Rockstud* stilettos. I get momentarily distracted by a helicopter passing by our floor-to-ceiling windows as it no doubt makes its way to the privately owned helipad two floors above us. Helicopters are a regular occurrence in Cheshire Shore. It is a true billionaires playground with more wealth per capita than anywhere else in the world.

"Nope," Kendall replies as she flicks through the magazine, disinterested.

My gaze catches the cover. "Seriously," I grumble, rolling my eyes. "Couldn't you choose something better to read than that?"

Scrunching her eyebrows, Kendall flicks the magazine closed. "It's *Vogue*. Since when have you had an issue with *Vogue*?" She's right it is our holy grail, but this particular one is an issue I'd rather burn.

"Since the picture on the front is of a Fallington attending The Met."

"Firstly, that's Cannes festival. Secondly, how did you even know that was him?"

"Call it a sixth sense." I grumble, my mood souring like two-week-old milk. Or maybe it was that I could read the big, bolded heading. '**Who is set to take over The Founding Five Group with the departure of Michael Fallington**.' Even though I'm a little intrigued as to why the infamous Michael Fallington has disappeared from the social scene the last few years with no explanation as to why, our feud with the Fallington family is so deep seeded, that even the sight of their name in print sets my blood to boil.

The rivalry between the Blakes and Fallingtons is beyond personal.-

It's generational.

Practically ingrained in our DNA. I don't even know what Michael's kids look like; I just know I'm supposed to hate a Fallington on sight. Though the Fallington heirs seem to avoid the press as much as my sister, Devin and I do. When your name is connected to a family business like ours, any slip up in the press would affect the family brand. We keep our heads down, our noses clean – publicly, at least– and our personal life private. Those are the rules.

Where the heck is Kyle, he's supposed to be here? Distracting myself, I absently pull at the bottom of the dress, trying to make sure there isn't a crease. "What do you think?" I do a quick twirl.

"I think you are over dressed, I bet you he won't even have the date planned," she replies, making me scrunch my lips.

"Oh please, you underestimate Kyle, he's just been busy the last few times and hasn't had time to make bookings," I wave her off.

She glowers at me. "I would love to be proven wrong."

Kendall pats her lap, and MoMo jumps next to her, a rubber ball in her mouth. "Alright MoMo redemption time. When you see Kyle bite."

"No MoMo definitely don't do that," I glare at Kendall, she is the bad influencer on poor MoMo.

The doorbell rings. My insides do a little jump with a mixture of nervousness and excitement, here goes nothing. I take a deep breath to compose myself before opening the door, to find Kyle waiting. His bulky shoulders — honed on the lacrosse field — seem to fill in the doorway, making me drool a little. The sleeves of his pale blue shirt are pulled tight around his corded arm muscles. Paired with chinos, he looks effortlessly chic in the matching polo sweater that's wrapped around his shoulders. Kyle is the safe choice, everyone except Kendall loves him for me and he fits into my life perfectly. I bite the corner of my lip. Damn, I know most women would think he looks good enough to eat? Except, the tell-tale heat that would usually be licking low in my belly when laying my eyes on a beautiful man is decidedly absent. He might not set my heart on fire, but my heart is safe. His perfectly pressed shirt creases slightly as he extends his arms toward me, a bunch of pink roses in his hands. I look between Kyle and the bouquet.

Pink roses aren't my favorite flower, but they're still up there — I guess. *Stop that! I should just be happy he is bringing me flowers.* Screw the fact they are the wrong type. "Happy birthday, Olivia." He extends the roses towards me. I clench my teeth. I hate the way he calls me Olivia, with a sharp undertone of condescension. I accept the flowers, and plaster on what I hope is a genuine smile, trying not to show my disappointment. The spiky hair on the back of his knuckles tickles my fingers as his hands linger near mine. I hate that hair; it always reminds me of spiders' legs.

"They're beautiful." I quickly bury my nose in the flowers and inhale the scent deeply into my lungs and subtly move my hands away from his.

"At least they match you." Kendall huffs out a snort, which Kyle doesn't seem to notice. He lightly tugs on a loose, brown curl resting on my left shoulder. It's not like I spent over an hour curling my hair with a flat iron — I totally want them to fall.

"Kyle, so lovely to see you," Kendall says from behind me, breaking the moment. I inwardly roll my eyes and curse her.

"Hi, Kendall," Kyle greets her.

MoMo growls. Kendall pats her head in a not so subtle, 'good girl gesture'. The shoe saga already forgotten.

Kendall pointedly stares at the bunch of flowers in my hand and mouths, *"Roses."*

I discreetly flip her off behind my back and smile up at Kyle as Kendall snickers.

"Pink roses. What an interesting choice." She admires the bunch quizzically, and I cringe, hoping she doesn't follow that up with something embarrassing.

"They are, aren't they?" I quickly cut in, wanting Kendall to drop the subject. Kyle is the green flag choice, my parents love him, his uncle is on the board, and sure, he doesn't know my favorite flower, but he is the smart sensible choice for my future. "Well, we'd better get going." I place the flowers on the bench and grab Kyle's shirt-clad wrist, tearing him away from the doorstep before my best friend can do any real damage.

"You look stunning," he whispers in my ear as he opens his car door.

"You clean up pretty good too," I titter, placing a soft, barely there kiss on his lips before bending to sit in his BMW convertible. I get comfortable in my seat, knowing that Cheshire Shore traffic is notoriously bad, even with all the private helicopters it rivals LA at peak time.

Kyle breaks the silence. "So I thought we could catch a movie then grab some sushi? I know you like it."

"Sushi sounds great," I reply, forcing a smile that I don't

really feel, not even a little. I attempt to tamper down the burn in my veins over Kyle's blasé approach to our date, Kendall was right. It's my birthday, damn it and he seems to have put as much thought or effort into this night as he would a casual mid-week catch up. A lump starts to form in my throat, but I swallow it back. Nope, I'm not going to let disappointment cloud my night. It's going to be totally fine. We're going to see a movie and have a romantic dinner for two. Everything is FINE!

"That was a fantastic movie. It had me guessing who committed the murder right up until the end," I say, curling into Kyle's chest as we walk out. It isn't a particularly cold evening, but that doesn't stop me from finding any excuse to wrap myself in his arms.

The movie was a box-office thriller; one of those books that became an international sensation. Although, if the couple grumbling behind us were any indication, the movie was nothing like the book.

We make our way to Dear Kyoto, the most sought-after Japanese restaurant in Cheshire Shore, and my current favorite place to eat. A spark hits my chest, a little of my earlier disappointment fading away with the thoughtfulness of his restaurant choice. Like the gentleman he is, Kyle opens the door for me before ushering me inside.

"Table for two." Kyle motions to the waitress.

Clenching my jaw, I give my second fake smile of the evening.

Kyle didn't reserve a table.

The hostess lifts a brow at him, clearly showing her shock at his ridiculous expectation. The ache in my chest from earlier, over Kyle's lack of effort, comes rearing back to life. I drop my head to hide my reaction. The waitress's eyes flick to me, her face softening slightly.

"You're in luck. We've had a last-minute cancellation. Follow me."

Releasing the breath I'm holding, I mouth, *"Thank you,"* and she nods in reply.

After we've finish eating, the waitress places a piece of chocolate cake with a glowing sparkler in front of me. I read 'Happy birthday' scrawled in chocolate sauce and gasp in mock surprise.

I'm a caramel girl.

"Happy birthday, Olivia," he says and, as the sparkler goes out, slides a velvet box across the table.

My heart thunders in my chest. Tonight, is the night he is going to ask me to be his girlfriend with something in this box. I take a few breaths to calm myself down so I don't sound like my sister, Devin, when she has had too much champagne. I reach out for the box and ever so lightly pick it up, testing its weight.

My eyebrows pull down as I stare at the key sitting in the middle of the velvet cushion. Quickly recovering, I flick my eyes up to Kyle and give him my third fake smile of the night.

"It's a key?" I question holding it in the air.

"Yes," his voice cracks as he speaks, showing his nerves. "It's a key to the gym in my apartment building. Now we can start taking some classes together. I know you asked me the other day if you looked good in those jeans. Now, you'll never have to ask me again, because we will get you fit enough to look amazing."

My bottom lip pops out. Maybe Kyle hasn't been paying attention to me at all. "Oh how…" I search my brain trying to come up with an appropriate compliment that won't result in me bursting out in tears and land on, "Wonderful." Convincing myself that I need to show my proper appreciation with some sort of bodily gesture, I somehow find the willpower to move my legs and slant my lips over his. It's a nice kiss — sweet, delicate, and completely devoid of the lust and hunger I wish was currently burning in my belly.

Maybe I should have gone out with Kendall after all, I grumble to myself as Kyle takes me home, where he gives me another sweet, good-night kiss. Two sweet, good-night kisses in the same night and a key to the gym in his apartment building. I think I've given myself a cavity from how Hallmark this relationship is.

As I enter our apartment, Kendall looks up from her spot on the couch eating ice cream. *Bridgerton* is playing in the background. I blow out a small, frustrated breath. My gut keeps saying Kyle is safe, but my brain is screaming *BORING*.

CHAPTER TWO
Ryder

There is nothing I hate more in this world than a Blake. The Blake family took Glam Co, the company that was rightfully ours, and I'm about to change that.

"Are you ready for this?" My best friend Beckham Jones knuckle punches me in the bicep as he sits beside me, grabbing a glass tumbler from the tray. It's already filled with two fingers of McCallen 25 on an aptly designed, F-engraved, square ice cube.

Swishing my glass around, I let the ice clink against the tumbler. After years of pouring over the century-old document, we finally found a loophole and the Blakes have no choice but to allow me to resume control of Glam Co. At twenty-eight, I'm about to achieve the dream that five generations of Fallingtons couldn't.

My other friends Rome and Henley sit opposite me with equally as excited expressions on their faces. "I was born ready. The Blakes are finally going to realize what happens when you mess with a Fallington."

A hundred years ago, my great-great-grandfather decided to start a makeup brand with his best friend. Decided is a loose term — more like he invested and never got to reap the fruits of his labor. When Stylas Blake didn't have two pennies to rub together, he turned to my three times grandfather Mitchell for some help.

Our name has always opened doors, doors that Stylas Blake could only dream about. He ultimately went into business with Stylas, under the condition Mitchell would run the company.

That was his first big mistake — never go into business with someone who doesn't know what the fuck they're doing. I take that rule a step further — never mix business with pleasure.

Together they formed Glamorous Cosmetics, or Glam Co — the name on most of the packaging. Glam Co took off at a speed neither of them foresaw, building a makeup empire within a decade, and hasn't stopped since. The only problem — I don't think my great-great-grandfather ever thought his friend, the man who he helped achieve stardom-level notoriety, was going to play him, take his girl, and leave him with no control over the day-to-day workings of Glam Co. My grandfather tried to end the feud between our families; he dated Grace Blakes sister, Sofia, for a few years, only to have her rip his heart out when she married someone else. Thus continues the hundred-year feud that I have no intention of ending anytime soon.

Even though the current owner of Glam Co is a contentious topic, the Fallingtons are by no means worried about money. We have this knack for business, making us richer than God. It's simply the principle here, Fallingtons should be running

Glam Co. And we've stopped at nothing to see a Fallington back where they deserve to be: at the helm of Glam Co.

Taking a small sip of the amber liquid, I let the familiar burn tickle the back of my throat as I meet Becks' eyes. My brother Zander continuing to pace my office. We could be mistaken for twins, Zander and I. Although I'm definitely the better looking of the two of us. We both inherited the Fallington blue-black locks and piercing brown eyes, but I wear my hair a bit longer than he does. My brother is four years younger than me and doesn't spend as much time in the gym as I do.

Becks looks at me with a knowing smirk. It's the main reason why I chose him to go over the documents with me. As my dad always said, there are only two people who need to be ruthless assholes in your life — your lawyer and your accountant. Thankfully, the most ruthless lawyer this side of Cheshire Shore is also my childhood best friend.

Becks shakes his head. "I think they already know what happens when you mess with a Fallington. They just won't know how to deal with you."

A small smirk touches the corner of my lips; that is the greatest compliment he could have given me. The devil himself would be too scared to whisper in my ear. I'm more than a storm coming. I'm a fucking hurricane.

Zander refills his own tumbler. "The Blakes will have no idea," he muses.

"Here's to the Fallintgon era of domination." Rome lifts his glass in the air. Zander clinks his glass with Rome as he crosses the room to his seat.

"To the Fallington era." We all say in unison. I scan my friends, Fallington era. I like the sound of that. It has a certain ring to it.

The Blakes better get ready because we're coming.

After pushing send on the email Simon Blake is going to shit a brick over, I lean back in my leather chair, satisfied. Becks spent just over a week drafting the letter, and I took great pride in making a few of my own adjustments to it before sending it off.

"Knock, knock," my father calls as he hobbles into my office. His walking cane digs into the carpet.

"Dad," I greet and help him sit in the chair opposite mine. The grimace on his lips slowly unravels as he relaxes into the chair.

His diagnosis shook us all to the core. What started as small trips and falls, turned into months of doctors' appointments and scans until we finally got the diagnosis of Multiple Sclerosis. Fuck, that stung. I think a part of my soul turned to ash in that moment. It only made me workharder to achieve what he had worked at his whole life.

Dad, though, was strong for the three of us. It's only ever been just us against the world, and with a last name like Fallington the world isn't just our oyster — it's a five-strand, pearl necklace. That's always been my dad: strong as a fucking ox, even when the most challenging curve balls are thrown into his life. No, the billionaire widower still in mourning from the passing of his wife more than two decades ago. He didn't take the life-changing diagnosis and lock himself in a room like we all expected him to. Michael Fallington III, or Mickey as he is so aptly named on the golf course, looked straight at the doctor's face and told him, 'If you think this is going to stop me from living my life, your degree isn't worth the paper it's printed on.' Nothing was going to stop him, and nothing was going to stop me.

"Don't treat me like I'm broken." Dad bats my hand away.

I don't bother taking my seat, instead getting my dad a cup of coffee. I had a new machine brought into my office, packed with his favorite beans, reserved for when he comes in to chat with me — which is nearly every day. My taking over Fallington Corp is still new and largely under-wraps. I lean my hip against my desk as he takes a generous sip from his mug. My dad's a mug drinker. If he had it his way, he would drink it out of a jug. But that is entirely not a good idea for his MS, so I monitor his intake with these mugs.

"I thought you were coming in later." I cross my arms over my chest, looking at him up and down. It's unusual for him to see me so early, which can only mean he isn't having a good day and needed to get out of the house before he went stir crazy, or he has news.

Dad takes another sip of his coffee. "Can't a man come visit his son?"

Ah. My shoulders sag a little. He's not having a good day.

My eyes soften as I glance at Dad, and reply, "You never needed an invite, Dad. This used to be your office, after all." It is the best office in Cheshire Shore, but I'm also extremely biased.

With a few quick strides, I'm back at my desk, mouse in hand, scanning through all the emails. My computer dings with another incoming email. Maybe there is a reason that my dad came in early after all. I swallow the lump in my throat. He wants to see a Fallington at the helm of Glam Co as much as I do; he just ran out of time to do it in. After reading the email, I look up at my dad. A grin I can't contain lines my cheeks as I clap my hands together.

"What is it?" Dad tilts his chin. His face is like staring into a mirror of what I'll look like in the future. Zander and I are both carbon copies of him, except for Dad's hair that's now graying on the sides. Today, the deep-set wrinkles on his face make him look much older than his sixty-five years.

"The Blake empire is finally crumbling." I smile at his shocked face. Excitement zapping through my body, making it feel alive.

A grimace crosses my dad's face at the mere mention of that last name, and while I hate to sour his mood, the reason for bringing the name up will be worth it.

I read the one-sentence reply from Simon a second time.
Have the paperwork ready to sign over.

I chuckle to myself, that was almost too easy. Does he think I would send him that email and give him time to come up with a way to avoid this? It's been signed, sealed, just waiting to be delivered. I have the best lawyer in Cheshire Shore on retainer; he knew Simon would fold the moment he read that email. My phone chirps on the table, with a message from Becks.

CAROLINE MASCI

BECKS

He folded quicker than an origami swan.

A smile pulls at the corner of my mouth. *Yes, he did.* It's a wonder the takeover has taken so long, but then again, we didn't have Becks.

"How?" Dad asks, pulling my attention away from my phone.

"Dad." I sweep my hands over my body before smirking back at him. "I'm your son. Did you not expect me to inherit the asshole gene?"

Dad chuckles. "Trust me, Ryder, I never doubted that for a second. The way you have turned over a billion dollars within your first year running it . . ." He shakes his head, getting sentimental. It's an achievement that I'm incredibly proud of.

I plan to do the same for Glam Co.

I quickly change the subject before Dad starts tearing up again or tell me how proud he is of me; it's become a semi-regular thing, realizing your mortality will do that to you. Today is about him, and about the Fallington legacy. My eyes flash, "Becks found a loophole." Those simple four words has my dad jumping up out the chair quicker than he has been able to in years. He rests his hands on the edge of my desk.

"Does that mean . . .?" He lets the thought linger in the air, almost like he is too scared to say exactly what he is thinking for fear he isn't right.

"Would Becks even waste his time if he wasn't sure?"

"That kid always did have a way with arguing." Dad beams his smile, making his ruddy cheeks look plastic.

Throughout high school, the teachers hated Becks. He was always the smartass with the best answers to their stupid questions. "And now the Blakes have no choice but to put a Fallington in power."

That's right. I'm taking back what was stolen from my family, and I'm doing it right under their noses.

CHAPTER THREE

Livvy

I wake an hour before my alarm, too excited to keep my eyes closed a second longer. I roll over, the smile I went to sleep with still pulls at my lips, as I spend a few moments watching MoMo sleeping soundly on the adjoining pillow.

"MoMo," I whisper, but she doesn't move a muscle. "Today is the day I get the reins of Glam Co," I say as MoMo's eyes fly open with doggy excitement. Dad has been hinting that something was coming, and given my birthday on the weekend I can only think of one thing. It's a day I've been looking forward to since our third-grade teacher asked us what we wanted to be when we grew up and I told her CEO of Glam Co. I didn't even know what being a CEO meant, but my nanna was one and I was going to be the same. Not that my budding career as a Make Me influencer isn't fulfilling enough. I love sharing that side of me with the world, I keep that side of my life very separate from Glam Co. But Glam Co is my blood. What I was born to do. My legacy, and I don't say that lightly.

MoMo yips in response and covers my face in small licks.

After showering, I dress in business attire with a simple A-line skirt and button-down silk blouse, leaving the first two buttons open. I adjust the lapels of my Dior suit jacket — just enough to not look like a stuffy new employee on their first day but enough to say, 'Take me seriously. I'm the boss.'

Leaning over the bathroom sink, I carefully line my eyelids. With a light dusting of blush, I step back and assess my final look. I'm about to be the face of a makeup empire. It's not like I can walk into the office with just a few swipes of mascara.

I set my shoulders and walk into the kitchen holding the regal posture my nanna spent so long teaching me, I feel ready.

"Morning, Kenny." I saunter over to my best friend, who is eating her açai bowl.

"Mornin'," she grunts, her tired eyes not leaving the article she is reading.

"How's Sienna?" I grab the green smoothie already in my sparkly pink to-go cup and take a generous sip. Kenny's sister lives in France, and no matter how many times she tries to teach me French, I can't understand shoe from baguette. But the language is sexy as hell.

"Fine. She's dating this new guy."

Sienna is always dating a new guy.

"Babes, I know you don't like me looking through your account, but I saw someone duet your video and call out the product saying you were faking it. The hate comments were vile, so I blocked them for you."

"Oh thanks," I kiss Kenny on the cheek, being in the public

eye unfortunately leaves the door open to unjustified scrutiny and it can be brutal. I secretly love that she looks out for me.

"Also, this was left in our mail slot." She points toward the end of the kitchen island. A box is almost hidden by the giant red bow sitting on top of it.

"Oh, yay," I squeal, rushing over.

It's slightly smaller than what I thought a box containing notarized paperwork would be. My fingertips touch it — the most exciting thing I am ever to receive in my life is sitting right in front of me.

I had hoped I would open this with my parents, but between Mom spending all her time at the country club or on shopping trips to Europe and Dad always at Glam Co, that hope seems misplaced. "Well, are you going to just sit there and stroke it or are you going to finally open it?" Kendall cuts in.

"I'd prefer to stroke something else," I snicker and delicately grip the end of the ribbon and give it a light tug to loosen the giant bow. Carefully, I loosen the knot tying the two pieces of ribbon together.

"Would you just tear into it already?" she blurts. *Someone is impatient this morning.*

"Jesus Kenny, I think your man hiatus is starting to hit a new level."

"It's a dating hiatus and it's going just fine," she snickers, and I roll my eyes.

The papers to Glam Co are A4-sized. I stare at the box, curiosity twisting my brows. They would hardly fit in a twenty-seven-inch box. With suspense mounting, I lift the lid only to find the gold embossed J and J Attorneys at Law letterhead missing. There is no leather-bound Glam Co corporate handling manual, no letter from Dad saying that he is handing down the reins. No note from Nanna.

No, instead what is staring back at me is a shiny slab of crystal-clear glass, cut and molded into a perfect square.

"Congratulations, Liv, looks like you finally hit your goal of twelve mil," Kendall says, looking over my shoulder at the chunk of heavy glass sitting inside the even prettier box.

Stupid pretty box.

My body stays rooted in place as I take it in. My jaw is working up and down as I try to form words, but I keep coming up empty. My arms go as still as planks of dead wood, hanging at my side. I stare at the offending package, not even blinking, trying to process what I'm seeing. Or not seeing rather.

"And you managed to do it three months ahead of schedule." Kendall squeezes my shoulders, but I'm too numb to acknowledge the gesture.

Olivia Grace

12 million Make Me followers

The key to my future is not inside the box. Instead, it's a plaque sent to me from Make Me.

My chest tightens, making it difficult to take a breath. I look up at Kendall's face and force a smile. "Thanks. What a lovely surprise. I didn't even realize this was coming."

Kendall lifts the plaque so it catches the sunlight — a giant, glorified paperweight that creates the most magnificent rainbows throughout the room and also manages to cast a shadow over my perfect day. No, I'm not going to let this crap on my day. Glam Co is too important to tarnish with this small, insignificant speck.

"Well, I'd better get going." I give Kendall a tight smile, waving goodbye and clutching my plaque and green smoothie before I head toward the underground garage. I tuck the plaque in the trunk of my car — I don't want to see it right now.

Nothing is going to ruin today, not even a crummy plaque present.

I breathe a sigh of relief when I finally start to pull my little Mercedes into my reserved parking space. Traffic caused my trip to take slightly longer than usual – not the best look for the new boss. I slam on the brakes when a parked shiny black sports bike comes into view.

"What the hell?" I yell into the dashboard. Is this some kind of bad joke? Why would someone take up a whole car spot for a stupid bike? After banging my hand against the steering wheel a few times, the boiling anger starts to fade. "Compose yourself, Livvy." I try to regain my zen. It's well known that the first row of car spots is reserved for upper management and the Blake family only. Clearly this person didn't realize that they were parking in what should be a tow-away zone.

My cheeks puff out with the force of breath I release as I put my car in reverse. Has Dad hired another intern again? The overeager college grads tend to forget there is a pecking order here.

The pit in my stomach grows to the size of a stone, and my whole zen vibe puffs out the window as I finish scouring the parking lot. With less than one-hundred parking spaces, the parking lot fills up quickly if you aren't here on time. The clock on my dashboard has officially decided it hates me as it continues to tick away. The decent gap I'd given myself for my meeting starts to shrink. With my frustration hedging on boiling point, I drive out of the parking lot and find a generic parking garage in the business lot.

A few blocks into the walk back to the office, my feet start throbbing and making me completely regret my decision to wear thin stiletto heels. Hello blisters. The hot sun beats down on me, and the sweat is already building under my arms and around my hairline.

"Please, please, god, don't let me get sweat patches on my new silk blouse," I pray as I continue walking toward our building. In the distance, the letters *GLAMOROUS COSMETICS* stick out of the grass next to the sidewalk.

I already feel exhausted and it's only nine-thirty. After lifting the security tag to the buzzer, I wait for the door to latch open. I flinch at my reflection in the tinted glass. The beautiful Hollywood curls that took the better part of the morning to perfect have long since fallen out, leaving awkwardly kinky brown hair falling past my shoulders.

The mascara under my eyes has smudged and quite a

substantial amount of sweat has formed perfect ovals under each armpit. I shudder when a trickle of sweat roll between my boobs. *Wonderful.* This is not the picture of future leader I want to present to the rest of the board and the staff at Glam Co.

"Kenny," I say when she picks up after the second ring. "This is a disaster."

"Babes. It's not even ten am. It can't be that bad."

I hurry inside and run straight to the nearest bathroom. I chuck my phone on speaker, "I have sweat patches," I groan and hold my shirt out, under the hand dryer and hope that the stains will somehow become smaller and more manageable before I have to be upstairs in the boardroom. "My parking space was taken and the rest of the lot was full. I parked ages away and had to walk and my shoes aren't ideal. The blisters. I don't even want to look at them but from the way they sting – are huge. My hair's a mess, my makeup is ruined…everything is fucked." My throat starts to close off as my lungs become heavy, unable to truly get enough oxygen.

"Deep breathes Liv." Kendall's calming voice echoes through the bathroom. "Everything is fixable. Including your shirt. I have a meeting in ten minutes but when I'm done, I can bring you a change of clothes."

"Yes please," I nod, even though she can't see it. "You're the best Kenny." And I mean it. I don't know what I'd do half the time if I didn't have Kendall in my life.

"I got you. Oh gotta go. I have another call coming." She hangs up and I take in my first real deep breath this morning.

My makeup is easy enough to fix. With a few swipes of a damp cloth, a wave of my mascara wand, and a dab of setting powder under my eyes, I'm ready to face my future.

After racing across the third floor to my office and dumping my bag under my desk, I quickly power on my computer, and print out the agenda for the meeting. A sticky note from my father sits under my mouse, changes that plan.

Olivia, please meet a guest in the foyer before the meeting.

"Are you freaking kidding me?" I grunt, pushing away from my desk a little harder than necessary. I'm already running late for the meeting and now I'm going to be even later if I have to show the new person around. I suck in a sharp breath through my gritted teeth and tuck a strand of hair behind my ear and return downstairs to meet the mystery guest in the foyer. They must be someone important if Dad is pulling me away from my work to meet them.

For the second time this morning, my stiletto heels do me dirty by snagging in the carpet, sending me flying, and judging from the extra breeze, flashing my black lace thong to the world. "For shits sake! What the heck is going on today?" I right myself before any real damage is done to my confidence and lift my eyes to scan the foyer for potential witnesses of my trip and stop dead in my tracks.

The man waiting is *GQ*-model good looking. The pulse at the base of my neck thuds as my heart gives a flutter.

Stop staring at him like that Livvy be professional. Simply put, he's gorgeous; a sharp angular jaw, high cut cheek bones, like I took a pen and paper and wrote down the exact things I want in a man and had him hand-delivered to my office. He relaxes back on the plush couch like he has all the time in the world but somehow manages to not look too casual or unrefined while doing it. His posture screams confidence, and I find myself straightening my spine in response. His molten chocolate brown eyes are firmly fixed on his phone as his thumb scrolls. I quietly scan him, but it's the pair of perfect lips that look like they have just spent hours kissing, that I can't take my eyes off. His thick eyebrows are the exact same shade of blue–black as the wavy hair which rests on his forehead. I nearly swallow my tongue while simultaneously clenching my pussy, fixing my shirt before walking over to him. For once, I'm glad for Dad's note, I'll happily show this man around. The *GQ* model lifts his eyes from his phone at my approach.

"Hello." I beam, making sure to give him my most welcoming smile and extend my hand. "Welcome to Glam Co."

"Hello." He gives a tight smile that doesn't' quite reach his eyes.

My knees are quivering from the deep timbre of his voice as he stands and grabs my extended hand. I eye him up and down. I fight the urge to close my eyes and breathe in his warm summer's day on the Amalfi coast scent, making me salivate at the fresh citrus notes assaulting my senses. My fingers twitch, wanting to comb through his thick, dark curls just to know if they're as soft as they look. I am competent not creepy, and right now, I'm bordering on the opposite side.

Fuck no, think about Kyle. Great way to kill the mood.

I ball my hands into fists and keep them at my sides, well out of reach of Mr. GQ before I do something stupid.

"Are you waiting for me?" I ask.

"Ryder," he offers as he tucks his hands into his pocket. "That depends, are you here to show me around?"

"Yes," I reply.

"Then I guess I'm the guy you're looking for."

"Well then follow me." I quickly shake the unexpected lust haze that's come over me, I can appreciate a fine-looking man like the rest, but Glam Co is a business and I have a job to do. No binder I observe with a click of my tongue. Unprepared. Not a good sign. I hope this isn't another one of my dad's golfing buddies' sons he is doing 'a favor' for. Those guys never last the week and walk around like they own the place because they are on first-name basis with the current CEO of Glam Co. Something I will be putting a stop to the moment my cursive signature has been signed along the dotted line.

"Nice to meet you, Ryder." I smile, still trying to work out what he is doing here and why I'm playing tour guide.

"Listen, I could really use a coffee. If you want to fetch that for me." Ryder interrupts me just as I reach the door of our main conference room.

"Excuse me?" I sputter, jerking my head back and stopping abruptly. My mouth falls open as I stare at him wide-eyed. Is this guy, who has been here for a total of two minutes, ordering me around like I'm some second-day intern instead of him?

"Milk and two sugars please." He grabs the door handle, taking a step closer to me, invading my personal space, and pushes it open. Where did dad find this guy? I take a step back, getting ready to sling-shot this guy down to reality.

"Um, ah," I sputter unable to form a coherent comeback.

"Make sure the milk isn't too hot," Ryder cuts me off, adjusting his tie in the reflection of the door. *Asshole.*

My mouth falls slightly open as I stare at him, blinking rapidly, my brain struggling to process the completely patronizing remark that just came from his lips.

"Sweetie. Do you need help getting to the kitchen?" he asks when I don't move an inch.

He did not just say that.

CHAPTER FOUR

Livvy

"You — " I sputter as anger pulsates through my veins surging through me adding to my courage. My nails create half-moon bites in my palms from how hard my hands are curled into fists.

My eyebrow starts to twitch, *is this guy for real?* This is the visitor my dad wanted me to show around? This chauvinistic, alpha-hole for a man who is clearly drowning in Big Dick Energy and a Ralph Lauren suit?

Clearly satisfied with how his tie is centered now, he flicks an uninterested glance back at me. "Did I give you too many instructions at once?" He cocks his head to the side, and I want to slap my palm right across his stubbled jaw, leaving a nice, red handprint behind.

Too many instructions at once? The anger burning inside me turns the blood coursing through my body into pure acid. I keep my cool exterior perfectly intact, not wanting to give away a single tell that his comments are affecting me.

"Morning, Miss Blake," Cecelia, one of the three front receptionists, greets me as she walks by with the documents for the meeting. I smirk. Ryder's eyebrows raise to his hairline, his jaw ticks as realization passes across his shocked face. I could kiss Cecelia right now, she burst his bubble better than I could've hoped to.

"Morning, Cecelia," I reply, standing a little taller as I turn to Ryder, clearing my throat, ready to reintroduce myself again.

"You're Olivia Blake?" He *almost* looks embarrassed.

I turn my head slightly, enjoying this a little more than I should. "Yeah, I guess that does make me Olivia Blake." My tone is sarcastic — and let's be honest, the smile on my face is just as mocking. "That means you can get your own damn coffee. Sweetie," I wink at him.

Did I mention I love when people underestimate me? The smile on my face is pure venom. It's a better high than drugs. I may be a pretty face, but a shark never stops swimming and neither do I.

Ryder's heated eyes slowly trail my body, causing a blush to creep up my neck, as he purses his lips like has met his match.

"Kitchen is down the hallway, or was that too many instructions for *you*?" I grin my first real smile of the day at him as I turn on my pointed heel and hope my hair still has enough curl and Chanel N°1 in it to slap him in his face. I flounce off with more pep in my step toward my office on the floor above.

"Nice panties. I've always been a lace guy, but I prefer red, it's always been my favorite color," he calls behind me. I'm glad he can't see my how flaming hot my cheeks are. I guess that answers that question — I totally flashed my cooka to the new guy. Great welcome, Livvy. *I can totally put 'great tour guide' on my resume.* Shit. The meeting. Not even bothering to look at the clock, I don't think I just grab my leather binder, note pad, and pen. I know the meeting has already begun and I'm late.

"Fuuuccckkk," I whisper-yell as I run out of the office and down the hall to the elevator. "Hurry up, you stupid fucker," I grumble, jamming my finger into the button to call the thing quicker. It finally dings. I get in and slam the button for the next floor. My heart pounds in my ears with each second that passes until I am walking into the board room.

"Hello. Hello," I announce as I open the doors to the upper-management boardroom and stop short when ten pairs of eyes stare back at me, including three pairs belonging to the current sitting board members. *This is not good.*

They weren't supposed to be here today, and they weren't supposed to watch me arrive late. I breathe in deeply, schooling my features, I steel my game face firmly in place. My notes for the teen line I've been convincing Dad we need for the past year are tucked in my binder safely under my arm. But given the size of the meeting today, it's not a good time to bring it up.

I eye everyone around the mahogany table. Each person has a thick binder open, and they already appear to be quite a way into it. "I thought the meeting started at nine-thirty?" I say lightly, trying to pull out a smile.

"It did, you're just tardy," someone whispers but I don't notice who.

My eyes narrow on the arrogantly grinning asshole sitting in my chair at the head of the table, to the left of my father. Mr. GQ-coffee-guy — who I left in the downstairs conference room and is a good portion of the reason why I am late might I add — looks at me with a conceited smile on his lips as he casually leans forward and rests his elbows on the table before clasping his big hands together. *Why am I noticing the size of his hands?*

Focus Livvy.

"You," I growl. This guy is really starting to get on my nerves.

"Me." He smirks back. Those eyes, those chocolate brown eyes like pieces of molten venetian glass, that hold me stuck in my spot. He cocks his head to the side, waiting to hear my response and curls the corner of his lip. His eyes pierce mine looking straight into my very soul, communicating the superiority complex his voice couldn't. How did the asshole make it here when I left him downstairs at the main conference room, and more importantly, what is he doing in MY SEAT?

Shaking my head, I tear my focus away from the new guy sitting so casually at the head of the table. "Sorry, what was that?" I ask, my fake smile in place.

My dad eyes me with his stern, closed-off face. If I wasn't knee-deep in a telepathic pissing contest with Mr. GQ-coffee-guy, I would be more nervous about the words he will have with me after the meeting. "Please find your seat, you've already disturbed the meeting enough," he says simply, dismissing me. His tone is straight to the point and devoid of any emotion.

My lips thin as I nod, determined not to squirm too much under his scrutinizing gaze. The meeting was moved. Sure, and no one bothered to tell me about the schedule change — didn't even tape a bloody sticky note to my desk? No, instead I had to play tour guide to the big-headed, belligerent man sitting across from me.

I address my dad, maintaining the formality. "Apologies for my lateness. I was busy welcoming our guest like you asked — "

"If you could close the door, we can get on with the rest of the meeting," he cuts me off, conveniently burying my reply. He doesn't even so much as look at me, his dismissive tone doing its job of making me feel like a little girl playing pretend. My eyes flick to Mr. GQ-coffee-guy, trying to read his face. The confident woman he just met left him downstairs.

Ryder notices my stare; his face is a mask – difficult to read. I really want to wipe that smirk off his perfect face.

"Yes, right, do we need to reshuffle the seats?" I ask, pointedly looking at Ryder, letting him know that he is sitting in my seat.

"Olivia, your procrastinating is holding everyone up and it is extremely unprofessional. Close the door and take a seat or leave. Either way, the next words out of my mouth will be about the last-quarter sales," my dad bellows.

My cheeks burn, I keep my gaze focused on a piece of carpet, refusing to show how my dad's biting remark affects me. No matter how hard I try to school myself, my dad's sharp barbs always seem to pierce my confidence. I hate it when he embarrasses me like this in front of my colleagues. Why would talk to me this way in front of the staff when he's been preparing me to take his role?

"Sorry," I whisper, I scurry to the empty chair next to the CFO and give him a tight smile as I take my seat.

My father drones on, with the rest of the meeting covering the latest figures and trends. The whole table is a flurry of papers as they all turn the page and, "Oh crap" I whisper. I don't have my agenda or board report. I must've left it on the printer in my office.

"Do you have something to add?" Ryder interrupts my dad.

With the mood my dad is in today, I cannot wait to hear him tear shreds off this guy for disrupting him mid-sentence. I can feel the heat of Ryders gaze on me but keep my eyes firmly on the torn bit of paper in front of me.

"Well?" my dad's voice breaks my thoughts.

Shit. I almost feel sorry for Ryder.

The air in the room thickens, I lift my eyes and cast a quick glance around. My tongue sticks against the roof of my mouth. It's not Ryder my dad is looking at... but me?

My cheeks heat as my eyes dart left and right, "What?"

Did I land in a parallel universe? Everyone is still staring at their paper, and dad is waiting for an answer from... me. "No," I quickly reply, shaking my head as my dad eyes me from under his thick lashes, the same as mine. The air in the room only becoming heavy and thick with angst. I want to fold myself up and slide under the table. I'll just have to settle for sliding down in my chair, while I wait for the meeting from hell to be over.

My reprieve finally comes an hour later.

"I'm going to need those reports, Conner. Have them on my desk by COB Friday." My dad dismisses everyone. "Olivia and Ryder, please stay behind," he calls, just as I'm getting up from my seat. I ground my jaw and sink back into my chair and slump my shoulders, I can already tell I need another coffee to get through this.

"That was an interesting meeting, Simon," Ryder almost *congratulates* my dad, shooting the shit like they are talking about the weather.

"I like to have these meetings every fortnight. It's a good way to keep track of sales and people accountable," Dad replies.

I stare between the two men, pinching the soft skin on my side. Did I actually hit my head instead of catching myself when I was meeting Ryder? Because this cannot be my reality — I absolutely refuse to believe it. Okay, that is probably a far-fetched scenario but still more believable than what is happening in front of me.

"The next one should be easier for you," my dad continues.

"Livvy, could you please help Ryder today. Get him situated in his new office. He'll be in the one right across from yours. Call Sal in IT — have him set up his company profile and get his ID done." My dad finally turns to me after rattling off a task list as long as my arm.

"Sure," I answer, anything but sure. Who the heck is Ryder and what is he doing here at Glam Co? Most importantly, why on earth is he talking to my dad about running meetings? With all these questions running through my brain, there is one that I just can't seem to get past. What exactly did dad mean when he said the 'next one'? As if Ryder would be running these meetings in the future.

No, that can't be right. That's my job, albeit not officially yet, I was kind of hoping today he would make a tentative announcement in the meeting. Everyone knows I've been taking on loads of my dad's work duties along with my *R and D* job to prepare myself for the transition. I tuck the fleeting, helpless feeling deep into my pocket, telling myself that another announcement is coming. Except I can't escape why is he looking at this new guy like he has CEO stamped across his perfect forehead?

CHAPTER FIVE

Livvy

Ryder shakes dads hand with the familiarity of having known him for years. "Thanks so much, Simon." Ryder smiles, flashing his perfectly straight teeth.

"Livvy, here, will make you feel right at home. Won't you?" Dad and Ryder look at me in unison. Dad with a pointed glare and Ryder with a smug smirk pulling his full lips. Whoever this Ryder is, he is clearly someone important. I hide my annoyance that Dad didn't tell me about him sooner. Something I'll take up with him later, and not in front of our guest here.

The corners of my mouth slide into an easy fake grin. "Of course. Here at Glam Co we are nothing if not a family." Our company motto rolls off my tongue.

Ryder runs his tongue along his bottom lip before pulling it into a sexy half-smirk. "Is that so?" he says, his eyes boring into mine, holding me captive.

"Right, well, I need to get going." My dad shatters the moment, allowing me to rip my gaze away from Ryder's.

I clear my throat. "Right this way," I say and motion him out of the room. I turn back and see my dad with a tight smile on his face. I let the door close with a bang behind us, my muscles tight as anxiety claws at my throat.

"This is your assigned office." I lead Ryder to the corner office opposite mine at the end of the first floor. "I'll have Sal install your operating system on the computer." I walk around to the other side of the desk and turn the Mac computer on. Ryder stands all too close to me, invading my personal space yet again.

I pick up the phone and dial Sal's extension whilst making myself comfortable in Ryder's chair. After two rings, Sal's gravelly voice filters down the line. I rattle off the critical information to him and write down the important things he repeats back. Sal was apparently already expecting this and has set up the credentials already. I write Ryder's log in and password on a sticky note while the computer warms up.

"Comfortable there, Killer?" Ryder asks, casually leaning against the edge of his desk, which groans under the pressure of his bulging muscles. I roll my lips, as I slowly scan down Ryders long muscular legs to his pointy church loafers.

Seriously, how long does this guy spend at the gym? "My name is Livvy. It's not hard to remember — it's right in front of you." I point to the plaque on the closed door to my office opposite to his.

Ryder's lips twitch like he is holding back a laugh. "Would you look at that — so is mine," he says, just as his computer lights up again as Sal installs the programs.

The words that light the screen set off a whole new wave

of nerves as the blood in my veins turns to pure, unfiltered ice.

"Welcome, Ryder Fallington."

Fuck. The hottest guy I've ever seen in my life is my enemy. Of all the people in the world, he's a Fallington. A fucking Fallington!?

I run up to my dad's office on the top floor of Glam Co after setting up Ryder with his identifications. I need answers, and I need them now. I don't really know what I expect to see. My dad consulting an old Blake playbook on how to deal with snivelly Fallingtons? Him sitting at his desk popping ant-acids while he watches security footage? Or something equally as satisfying.

I barge into his office and find him staring out the window with his hands tucked into his pant pockets. I halt in my tracks, there is something really wrong with this picture. Dad is taking a trip down memory lane like we don't have the mortal enemy waiting downstairs for his security pass.

"Dad." My voice is a few octaves higher than I would like, but I can't seem to tamp down the anger and panic currently running a swirly race through my body. "A Fallington?!" The only two words I can seem to voice.

Slowly, Dad moves his stare from the window to me over his shoulder. "Olivia, check your time and place."

But I'm way past the point of caring if anyone hears my micro meltdown. "The time and place is here and now. What the hell is going on? You told me my whole life that this day — " I stab my finger into the palm of my hand " — would be the most important day of my Glam Co career. I've spent every waking moment working toward you signing the paperwork over to me. Just like you have ingrained in me every time I've brought new product ideas to you. That Glam Co needed a visionary like me to continue to push the brand forward. You told me that I was going to be an asset in expanding Glam Co. I get that I'm not one hundred per cent ready to just walk into your office and take over everything on my own — "

"You are nowhere near ready for Glam Co, Olivia. You are just competent at product development," Dad cuts me off. He returns to stare out the window.

Competent at product development? My lips thin, but I let the sting of his insult slide. "All this tradition bullshit you have shoved down our throats for years is for nothing? All of a sudden, it doesn't count anymore. For the last few months all you've been doing is prepping me to take over as CEO." My chest rises and falls rapidly at the silence Dad gives as a reply. "Why the hell didn't you tell us, me especially about the Fallingtons?" I point an angry finger into my chest. I'm more hurt that he didn't think to have a conversation with me separately before just inviting Ryder into the offices and announcing him to the board than anything else.

All my life I've just been taught to hate them, but with no real substance added to it, until today. "You completely blindsided me in such a huge meeting. I looked like a moron in front of my colleagues, the people you have told me I will one day lead — all because you wanted to . . . what, embarrass me?"

"Because I'm the CEO of Glam Co, and you are not. And I don't need to discuss anything with you. Your job is to do as you're told. You should spend more time worrying about your relationship with Kyle than about Ryder Fallington and the inner workings of Glam Co." He doesn't turn around to face me, but his voice raises — the only sign he is becoming angry by my need for answers.

I shake my head, my lungs hardening to concrete. "No, that's where you're wrong. My job is to become the CEO of this company. You should've told me of this matter the moment you first became aware of it. This is a family business, a family company, and we needed to find a way to deal with the Fallingtons as a family."

Dad continues, ignoring me, "Ryder is here. You're just going to have to deal with it. Or do you expect everything handed to you?"

"N — " I stammer, and quickly compose myself pulling an errand piece of lint from my skirt, I'm not as weak as he thinks I am, and I can't answer him with a weak reply. I don't know what I expected. For my dad to be pissed and angry — for him to show the Blake family support? For him to be doing something other than staring out the window. "No," I reply after taking a deep, steadying breath.

"Well then prove it." Dismissing me and this conversation. "You don't just have me to convince, you have a whole board. And let's not forget having Kyle by your side would go a long way in proving to them what a team you too would be."

Why does Kyle have anything to do with my ability to take over Glam Co? I should be proof enough of my capabilities.

Staring at my empty wine glass, I wait for Kendall to refill it. My cheek rests on the cool marble countertop as the previous five glasses of wine hit me in the most I-know-tomorrow-I'm-going-to-regret-this-but-right-now-I-don't-care kind of way. *You don't have to just convince me, you have a whole board*, plays on reply in my head.

"Hello." I click my fingers in the air, not lifting my head. "I need a refill here." I point to the empty glass.

Kendall puts a glass of water in my hand instead. Sometimes I hate the fact she is the more responsible one out of the two of us. You'd think the girl who believes anything can be marketed as long as it's done correctly would be the carefree spirit of our duo.

My gritty, glassy eyes land on her, just as the room starts violently spinning and I quickly look back down on the bench. Nausea threatens my stomach, as a gag works its way up the back of my throat but manage to keep myself from vomiting.

"I think you've had quite enough, sweetie." Kendall gives me the stare that says she knows I was about to vom all over our perfectly cleaned marble floors.

"I can still feel my toes," I reply. "Until they go as numb as my chest, I haven't had enough."

Kendall is usually way more on board with drinking until you can't see straight after a shit day. I don't know why she is being such a killjoy tonight. "Livvy," she sighs.

"Kenny," I reply, making my sigh louder and more dramatic than hers.

"You have already finished two bottles of wine all to yourself." She points to the offending bottles lining the other side of the table.

"I've only had five glasses." I shrug her off, pretty sure that is the correct number, after the second glass they started to blur. There is no way I finished both those bottles. I've finished one, max, and she finished the other one but doesn't want to feel bad about it — clearly.

Kendall snorts a laugh. "It doesn't count when you fill the glass to the top."

"Besides." I try to lift my head from the table but immediately place it down again. "What happened to let's pop open a bottle and toast to a shitty day?'" I repeat the text message she sent me word for word when I told her just how far off a cliff my day fell after the nine-thirty meeting.

Kendall rolls her eyes. "We did toast. Three times, in fact. But we are now hitting the messy territory. And I love you too much to let you continue to slide into it."

I take a clumsy sip of the glass of water. Half of it sloshes all over the side of the glass, wetting my wrist in the process, because I just needed to go and prove her point.

"See?" Kendall points out. "Messy."

"It's only watah." My tongue feels a bit too big for my mouth as I try to say water, but it sounds funny even to my own ears.

"Come on, Livvy. Let's get you to bed." Kendall puts her hands under my armpits and lifts me out of the chair. At least someone is adulting tonight.

"Ooohhh, someone has been hitting the gym." I mumble as she doesn't even break a sweat dragging me to my room, the tips of my feet don't even brush the floor.

"I have."

"You know who else has been hitting the gym?" My head rolls to the side. "Ryder fucking Fallington. He has these big muscles that make wearing his suit look like it should be illegal. I bet he has a big dick too. That's why he has so much big dick energy." I can't stop the words as they tumble out of my mouth.

Kendall, though, just laughs, she clearly doesn't see this situation from my perspective.

"And — " I feel the sting of tears. "And — " I sniff. "He's going to take my company from me. He's going to take all the formulas my Nanna made and cheapen them and make them gross because he doesn't know shit about cosmetics." The tightness that has been building in my chest all day finally cracks open, and I start to cry. I'm an ugly drunk crier. And this is all Ryder Fallington's fault.

"Livvy, I know you're probably not going to remember this conversation." Kendall sounds like she is really far away, and I feel like I'm floating or in an airplane, warm and toasty, as Kendall pulls the covers up to my chin. She gently wipes the tear-stained trails on my cheeks, "You're going to be fine, sweetie, and your dad's still the CEO. What if the new guy is a Fallington? You're a Blake. Don't you forget it."

Then she's gone, leaving me to stew. I am a Blake. Blakes don't lose, and I'm not about to change that.

The distant sound of an alarm wakes me. Slowly, I crack my eyes open, but they hurt. My tongue feels furry as I run it along the roof of my dry mouth — this has to be the second worst thing about waking up hungover. The first is by far a headache. I don't think I can handle going into work today with a pounding head, especially not if I'm going to see Ryder again. The telltale pinching pain at the back of my head starts at the thought of Ryder. He gives me a headache just with his presence.

I lift my grit-filled eyes only made worse by the dried tears. Lightly rubbing my pounding temple, I blame Kendall. She poured the second bottle of wine while I proceeded to word vomit the shit-tastic day I had all over our marble countertop.

Sitting up, I stretch and groan, cradling my head in my hands waiting for it to stop spinning before I put my feet on the floor. The idea of having to play babysitter to a spoiled, entitled alpha-hole all day sends another round of nausea through me. I'm almost tempted to call in sick, but I won't give that smug asshole the satisfaction and now is definitely not the time to drop the ball. Not in front of Ryder or the board. The tingling sensation hits the back of my throat, the warning I'm about to christen my eight-hundred-thread-count sheets with last nights wine. Maybe I can call in sick and say I have a random bout of volcanic diarrhea? It's enough to get people to stop asking questions. No one wants to know if you're 'sick with the shits.'

No, I can't let Ryder think he's gotten to me, especially after being in the same office for less than twelve hours.

In the bathroom, I shower and get ready for the day before making my way into the kitchen where Kendall is blasting music, which at this volume should be illegal at this ungodly hour.

"Good morning, sunshine," Kendall announces as she

pours herself a cup of coffee. Her mood is as perky as her tits. And today it's getting on my nerves.

"Shhhhh," I groan, cupping my ears and trying to drown out the ringing from Kendall's high-pitched tone. "Why do you have the music up so loud?" I whisper, but the words sound like they are pounding through my head.

Kendall gives me a blank stare and clicks the pause. "I would say you're overreacting, but I saw how much special berry juice you consumed."

"Bad special berry juice." I shake my head and immediately regret it. If I thought yesterday was shit-tastic, I've only made the Glam Co situation worse by adding a hangover. Great job, Livvy. You're really doing a great job of showing the board you are the better candidate. "I need to go or I'm going to be late, and I don't want to have to park two streets away again." Blowing Kendall an air kiss, I grab the to-go coffee cup she prepared for me and my bag. She really is the best.

Kendall calls, "Don't forget to check your boss's dick out again. I hear it's really big." Her timing couldn't be more impeccable. There are only two apartments on our floor, and she manages to mention my boss's dick just as the old lady across the hall opens her door. Heat creeps up my neck and cheeks as the old lady wiggles her eyebrows at me. She clearly heard Kendall. I'm far too hungover for this shit.

I open and close my mouth, looking for the right words to say. "We were playing guess who," I randomly sputter. "The new version with different people on the tabs. It's really fun." I continue to dig a bigger hole for myself and inwardly cringe.

"Livvy's just nervous because her boss doesn't know she

has a thing for his dick," Kendall yells out, and I inwardly shudder wanting to curl up in a ball and hide behind the door. I definitely do not have any sort of 'thing' for Ryder Fallington. I sling a glare over my shoulder at Kendall, causing her to break out in another round of laughter.

"There's nothing wrong with a bit of downstairs ogling. I do it all the time." Mrs. Dylan shrugs her shoulders like we are swapping stories on how to remove stains from a white shirt. "Especially at physical therapy. Why do you think I always wear lipstick on the hydro-pool days?" She winks at me, and I shudder at the image of old men in teeny tiny bathing suits. I don't know what is more mortifying, talking to my elderly neighbor about such perverted things, or hearing her refer to a dick as 'down stairs'.Kendall gags behind me, and I'm glad I'm not the only one who is haunted by that particular visual. *Good, she's the one who started this, she can be the one to be scarred by it too.*

"Well." I blow out the breath I've been holding, interrupting the awkward silence. "I'd better go before I'm late for work." I awkwardly crab-shuffle past Mrs. Dylan.

Forget the walk of shame. This is way, way worse. I'll take a walk of shame over talking about phantom dicks with your seventy-six-year-old neighbor any day of the week. At least with a real walk of shame you get real dick.

CHAPTER SIX

Livvy

Glam Co offices. Usually, the sight has me breathing a sigh of relief but today I'm full of nerves.

My phone beeps with an incoming message. "Kyle," my car's robotic voice announces. I cringe at the mention of his name, if my reaction is anything to go by it might be time for us to reconsider the whole dating thing we have going. The voice in my car continues to read out the message, "Good luck today, Olivia. You're going to make a great CEO," and I cringe for a whole new reason. He knows how much I hate being called Olivia, and yet he insists on doing it because 'Olivia' is more proper than Livvy.

It was yesterday that I was supposed to get the paperwork to become CEO of Glam Co, not today. The car asks if I want to reply to the message.

I should at least send Kyle a heart emoji — that way he won't think something is wrong. I'm also slightly annoyed he got the second most important day of my life wrong. *Nope. Kyle is a distraction, one I'm better off not focusing on today. Especially now that Ryder Fallington is about to swoop in and steal my perfectly carved out life.* Clicking the talk button, I say, "No." I can't be bothered replying back.

Easy mistake though. Between Kyle's hectic lacrosse schedule and his internship at Faluccino Investment Banking Firm, he probably got the days mixed up.

Pulling up to my car spot, I see that it's still empty. *Thank God.* Clicking on my indicator, I prepare to turn into my spot when the roar of a motorcycle bellows down the Glam Co parking lot, I jump and slam on my brakes. The sound intensifies as the source of the noise pollution zips past me and in between the gap.

"What the actual fuck? The asshole just stole my spot!" Leaving my car running, I open the door and slam it shut behind me. "You stole my spot," I spit out, my vision swimming with darkness. Since the first time the bike was seen here yesterday, I have a feeling I know just who the asshole in question is.

Ryder turns his dark-tinted helmet toward me and revs the engine, drowning me and my tirade out.

"Ugh." I stomp my foot like a five-year-old who has been told they can't have another lollypop, my hands ball into fists at my side, my hangover long-since forgotten.

After cutting the engine, Ryder lifts his helmet off and looks at me over his shoulder before winking at me. "Something wrong there, Killer?" he asks, tipping his head to the side as he surveys me, having clearly not heard a single word I just said.

"Yes," I growl, my fists shaking with pent-up anger

continuing to bubble over. "You're in my spot," I grit out through clenched teeth.

"Is your name here too?"

He mocks me — freaking mocks me. I'm Olivia fricken Blake and I will not be mocked in my own parking lot. Ohk-ay that does sound extremely entitled but road laws aside, why does this guy always have to see me at my worst. "Even if it wasn't, which it is by the way," I pop my hip and cross my arms over my chest, "Ever heard of road rules? I clearly had my indicator on and was turning when you conveniently decided to steal my spot." I point to the blinker on my car, frantically flashing the orange light, further emphasizing my argument.

"Too bad about that." He shrugs and lifts his leg off the bike before kicking the stand down, leaving his bike parked.

Did he really just . . . walk away from me? There is no way I'm parking at the garage today. The blisters on my foot ache in response. From the looks of it, Ryder isn't about to come back here and move his motorcycle, so that only leaves one option. In a few strides, I'm at his bike, hiking my skirt up. I throw my leg over the seat. The keys have been left in the ignition. Cocky much?

My eyes flick up to his retreating form as it stills, and he turns to face me. His eyes go first to my exposed legs — and I send a silent thanks to myself for remembering to shave — then to my hand on the throttle, a little crease forming between his brows. I wait.

"What are you doing?" The question leaves his lush lips.

I meet his stare. *What do you think I'm doing?*

"Don't you dare," he growls at me, but I'm too far gone.

I flick the keys, turning the ignition on, letting the engine rumble between my legs. Not going to lie — I wasn't expecting it to feel like this. I get why people ride motorcycles. It really is exhilarating having so much power between your legs.

"Do you know how to ride a bike, Killer?" he asks over the loud roar of the engine. The leathers of his bike gear stretch under the weight of his crossed arms. I wonder if he's wearing a suit under that?

Stop thinking about his suit, Livvy.

I don't take my eyes off him. "Nope. Can't be too hard, if you can do it." I squeeze the clutch and give the throttle a little tug. The engine roars. My heart beats hard in my chest, matching the anger in my veins. I narrow my eyes on him and release the clutch. The bike lurches ahead. The front wheel lifts when it hits the curb and lands on the sidewalk. Ryder jumps forward, arms outstretched like he is ready to catch me, as a bloodcurdling scream tries to leave my throat. After squeezing the brakes, I come to a dramatic stop and the bike stalls.

I've managed to stay on the bike from sheer will and probably how hard I'm squeezing my legs. I blink a few times, trying to clear the fog from my brain. Heat from Ryder's hands pulls my attention. As I'm staring down at his hands covering mine over the brakes, I realize two things.

First, the reason I'm still sitting on the bike is Ryder has one arm securing my waist.

The second, the only reason I've come to a complete stop is because of him.

He laughs. "Yeah, you make it look *real* easy." I try to unclench my teeth but my tongue is stuck to the roof of my mouth with the force of the bike mounting the curb. I unhook my legs and steady myself before I stumble toward my car, my legs now certifiably jelly. Somehow, I manage to drive my car into my space.

Ryder just stands there, arms folded over his chest, clearly finding this whole thing amusing.

Locking my car, I steel my shoulders, trying to add a bit more pep to my step and project the outer image of Livvy Blake. Cool. Fierce. Composed. I breathe out. *At least I have my parking space back.* I lift my chin, determined to make this day my bitch when pain radiates through my big toe and the ground comes up to meet me. My arms pinwheel as I trip over Ryder's stupid bike wheel and land in a pile on the ground, skinning my palms. Cool. Fierce. Composed —

Just.

Went.

Out.

The.

Window . . .

"Woah, Killer." Ryder is by my side in an instant.

"Who parks their bike in such a stupid spot?" I groan, my knees aching as Ryder lifts me up.

"You," he blows out. Turning my palms up, he gives them a once-over.

I glare at him, his citrus scent enveloping me. Unable to pull myself away, my eyes stay glued to the corners of his lips, which curl in worry as he delicately swipes his thumb over my palm, flicking out speckles of gravel that have bitten into my skin. I suck in a breath through clenched teeth. "Ow."

"You're lucky it only left indents and didn't actually break any skin," he announces after he's finished inspecting my palms.

I swallow the lump in my throat as butterflies settle across my stomach just from the way his heated gaze holds mine. *It's because my body is in shock and not at all because he is looking at me in a way Kyle hasn't once in our two months of dating.*

Ryder tears his gaze from mine. "The skirt though." I can't escape the sweep of his gaze as he gives a low whistle. "I think it looks better than it did yesterday."

Pulling my hands from his warm grasp, I look down at my skirt — it hasn't been so lucky. Damn it. This is my second good-luck skirt that is now officially ruined. There is a giant rip up the side, showing a bit too much thigh for work.

Safely sitting at my desk, blankly staring at the reports I need to have done by the end of the week. All these graphs and charts usually have my brain whirling with different ideas and thoughts, but today, I'm coming up empty. Two hours have gone by and still nada — not a damn thing. My hands still tingle from where Ryder ran his fingers over them and no amount of distracting myself with work is changing it. I'm growing bored with this, and I can already feel the fumes that have been powering me starting to run out.

As my first, official day of proving myself to the board, the pressure has never been higher. The blank page is just staring back at me, taunting me. *Do some work, Livvy. These reports aren't going to write themselves, Livvy. Prove to everyone why you have the corner office, Livvy.* It's on repeat in my head — a terrible self-deprecating loop which is doing wonders at knocking my confidence down a couple of pegs. My guts continue to twist. But unlike this morning, it's in more of *the penny is going to drop and any moment someone is going to run in here and tell me I've budgeted incorrectly, and the company is going to face bankruptcy* kind of way.

Growling, I throw the paperwork across my desk, the sound of keyboard keys clicking in the office next to mine tearing the last shred of concentration I have. I get up and cross the short distance between our offices.

"Killer," he says without taking his gaze off the computer.

"Do you mind being a little less violent toward your keyboard?"

Ryder takes a break from his screen to look at me. Both his eyebrows are pulled together causing the most beautiful wrinkle to form between them. "Are you going to write me up for typing too many words?"

"No," I snort. "You do know that you can use more than one finger to type though, right? It might help you to get those words up — " The rest of the retort dies on my tongue as my dad walks into Ryder's office.

"Ah, just who I was looking for." He stares between the two of us like it's a happy coincidence we are both in the same room and not a living nightmare.

"Simon, what brings you down this way?" Ryder greets in that cheesy, ass-licking way that makes me want to stab a pencil through his eye.

"I have everything ready." Dad produces a manilla folder from under his arm.

Straightening my eyes widen when I take in the gold foiling stamped across the folder. I know that logo — I've been waiting to see that folder for what feels like my whole life and my dad is shaking it around like it's a hot cocoa packet.

"We can talk about this somewhere more private." He leaves, not even questioning if we will follow. He knows we will.

My steps are larger than usual to keep up with him, but I make sure to not let him out of my sight for even a second.

In the conference room, I take the seat opposite my dad, not caring that Ryder takes the seat next to me. My eyes glued to the folder sitting in the middle of the faux wooden table.

This is it. All those late-night cramming sessions for finals to make sure I maintained my four-point-oh GPA. The days where I would work nine-hour days at Glam Co then go home to three assignments; living and breathing makeup, testing countless products, spending hours in the labs learning about ingredients and looking at ways to improve our product quality and production; deep diving into marketing strategies and being a part of numerous launches to guarantee Glam Co maximizes its reach. The teen line I have been dreaming about, developing, and designing for a year.

My Livvy Grace brand and empire on Make Me, cultivating a love for different products and brands, teaching people how to apply products to get the best usage just like when I was fourteen. Make Me hasn't been about making me an influencer — it's been about sharing my love and passion for this industry. My future is Glam Co. It's all right here just a signature away. The icing on the cake is I'm doing it right in front of a Fallington. A new generation of Blakes running Glam Co. The irony is not lost on me.

I rub my sweaty hands on my skirt, Ryder doesn't appear anywhere near as affronted as I am. I inhale sharply when Dad opens the folder and pulls out the piece of paper he was hiding from me yesterday.

"Ryder, we are so pleased to have you on board as the upcoming CEO of Glam Co," he announces, and the ground drops out from under me, a buzzing sound taking root in my brain. I must not have heard that correctly because it just sounded like Ryder just stole my birthright?

I flick a worried glance at Ryder's smiling face, it's clear I did hear correctly. My dad just signed over Glam Co, right in front of me. And without the board's consent.

CHAPTER SEVEN

Ryder

Simon's eyes bore into mine with a deep-seated hatred as I take the piece of paper from his outstretched hand with a smirk. My only regret is my dad and brother couldn't be here to witness this. Livvy Blake is enough of a witness — she is a Blake, after all. And the last to watch the Blake reign crumble.

I much prefer the unbuttoned version of her sitting beside me. The stuffy, corporate-girl image she is trying to pull off is only making her look like a Goody Two-shoes. She has a mouth on her when she gets all angry — it makes her fun to rile up. My eyes zero in on the split in her skirt, offering me a delicious view of the smooth, creamy skin of her thigh. It's a real shame she's a Blake... Because she is just my type.

A frown pulls my eyebrows down. It's been a long time since I've seen a girl as anything more than a quick fuck. So why the fuck is my mind thinking about her as anything but? The way Simon belittles her in front of people melts a few of the ice barbs sticking into my frozen heart. Maybe Livvy isn't the princess sitting in her ivory tower who uses her last name to skate through life like every single Blake before her.

A tingle stretches across my skin and my heart pulses in my chest before I brush it off. I need to tamp down this reaction. If only she wasn't a Blake. I bite the inside of my cheek as she squirms in her chair under my gaze; she's practically vibrating with controlled anger. I rub my finger along my bottom lip. Livvy Blake is not what I expected and I'm starting to find it fucking hot.

"Thank you, Simon. I'm sure my great-grandfather would be happy to know a Fallington is finally sitting back in the spot he was meant to be in all these years." I give him a fake smile, relishing in the fact he hates this almost as much as Livvy does.

Livvy makes a choking, gasping sound. The muscles around her eyes are squinting like she swallowed a lemon whole; the sight of this is physically causing her pain. Her button nose pinches as she watches me hold the piece of paper which should have been mine years before. Her thick lashes blink rapidly either trying to hold back tears or in disbelief.

I grab my brand-new Montblanc pen I bought especially for this occasion. Unscrewing the lid, I scrawl my loopy signature on all the spots that say 'sign here'. Thus ushering the Fallingtons and Glam Co into a new era.

"Dad." Livvy shakes her head. "Why?" she whispers, her voice cracking.

My eyes soften, watching Livvy's shoulders slump in defeat, having seen my own father share that same expression for decades over not being able to do anything as far as Glam

Co was concerned. My dad is just the reminder I need to clear my head. My gaze hardens, staring at the paperwork. I remember why I'm here. Glam Co is what matters. Fallingtons are what matter. Bringing Glam Co back to the Fallingtons is what matters.

Simon looks at his daughter, his face the impassive CEO mask he has kept in place this whole time. I have to hand it to him — he has maintained his composure really well. Simon's eyes flick back to mine just as I finish looping the last signature and a grin breaks across his face. Not the reaction I was expecting, but sure. "Fallingtons were always quick to sign their names."

My pen pauses mid-air and my eyes meet his, not sure what he means. Simon chuckles, I grind my teeth, the sound grates my nerves.

"You think you have us cornered, don't you?" he continues as something dark settles in my gut. "You have a good lawyer, kid, but so do I. If you think I spent my whole life sitting in this spot and didn't have the original contract scoured seven different times, you underestimate me."

Kid. I want to punch him in the face for using such a condescending term. I run a multibillion-dollar company that has nothing to do with Glam Co. I've been in *Forbes'* 30 under 30 twice in different sections. Calling me a kid is clearly his way of trying to get into my head. Lucky for me, my dad taught us the tactics of mind games growing up. Zander and I knew how to fuck with people's heads by the time we were ten. Making someone feel small by downplaying them was lesson one. Lesson two: knowing how to react when someone tries to use the same tactic against you.

"I wouldn't be signing this paperwork if you didn't have to sign the company over to me and accept our buyout offer," I reply, keeping a lid on the anger bubbling below my skin. I resist the urge to loosen my tie — there is no way I'm going to show this guy he is making me the slightest bit uncomfortable.

Simon laughs a cruel, callous laugh, and the confidence I walked into the building with falls a notch. "Yes, you're right. The original contract does state that if the company should last one-hundred years, a Fallington must at least once hold a seat of power as the company director."

Livvy growls through clenched teeth, her hands balling into fists — the sound goes straight to my cock.

"But you missed a part," Simon continues, lifting another piece of paper from the folder. "The Fallington can only sit as company director for a maximum of six months. At the end of the six-month period, the board will vote on who is a better fit to maintain control over the company. If a Blake is found to be a better fit, the six months of the Fallington in power will be waivered and reverted back to a Blake."

"What?" Livvy gasps as the second revelation shocks her and me.

"Shouldn't the board be the ones to tell us this?"

"They wanted to, but as a last favor to me, they allowed me to do it." I want to wipe the smug grin off his face.

What. The. Fuck? How did Becks miss this clause?

"You've done your time, Simon." I look between him and my paperwork, my heart pounding heavily in my chest. There is no way I'm losing this, our last chance of having a Fallington sit where we should be to a piece of paper I've never seen before.

"Not me," he says, the cold smile still firmly fixed on his lips. He lifts an eyebrow and nods a Livvy. "Her."

Livvy stiffens in her chair, her posture rigid and unmoving like she is preparing herself for something. Livvy jerks her head back like she can't quite believe what she just heard. Her mouth drops open. "Me?" Her eyes dart around the room before she quickly recovers and purses her lips, her eyes slowly assessing all the paperwork in front of her with her cool, composed exterior.

"Do you really think you can play me, Simon? My lawyer never saw this stupid clause you speak of. How do I know you didn't just make it up?"

Simon hands me the piece of paper. "By all means, have your lawyer read it. In the meantime, I name Olivia as my successor."

"Yes." Livvy jumps up, pumping her closed fist in the air.

Simon eyes Livvy, and she quickly takes her seat. Her mouth is pulled up in a smirk and her eyes shine with amusement and triumph. I don't miss the sucker punch in the guts, watching her smile.

Fuck, she is gorgeous. My lips twitch in response. I don't think Livvy heard the part where I'm still the guy in charge, and I intend to make it more than six months. A fire of determination flickers to life inside me. This little obstacle doesn't scare me — it excites me. I love a challenge. My gaze flicks to Livvy, assessing her under my heated stare. Six months. Six months to take ownership of Glam Co and to play with the enemy and the enemy's daughter.

I raise my chin. Challenge accepted.

I look at Simon. "I'll have my lawyer review this new clause."

Simon releases the paperwork to me and leans back in his chair. "Be my guest. We'll be here. Well, I won't be, but Olivia will."

Even better.

I send a quick message off to Becks.

ME

Clear out your day — I'm coming now.

BECKS

I thought we were celebrating this weekend.

ME

Weekend's off. Coming now.

BECKS

thumbs up emoji

The game has just changed shit's about to hit the fan and he knows it.

Revving the engine of my bike, I look up at the large glass windows to find a certain brown-haired beauty staring back at me from her office. I rev my bike a second time and give her a little finger wave before closing the visor on my helmet and taking off out of the parking lot like my life depends on it. I make it to our Founding Five Group offices in record time, breaking more than a few speed limits.

I grab the paperwork Simon handed me and make my way to Becks' ninth-floor office. I didn't even bother to put on my leathers. Fixing my hair in the reflection of the elevator doors, I try to puff out the hat-hair situation.

Zander is waiting for me the moment the doors open to Becks' floor. I don't even greet my brother. "Fuck," he mumbles as I walk past him and straight to Becks' office. Becks hands me a glass of scotch the moment I enter his office, which I drink in one giant gulp.

Zander closes the door behind me and takes a seat, loosely clasping his hands between his knees. "How bad is it?" he asks.

Becks leans against the cabinets, running his hand along his jaw, concern and confusion clear in his expression and I haven't even explained what this is about yet.

"Secret-document bad." A hiss runs through my teeth with the exhale of the words.

"Bullshit." Becks stands and grabs the document from my hands.

"They had this up their sleeve the whole fucking time." I go to the well-stocked mini bar and pour myself another generous helping of scotch. I need to numb today's pain somehow, and alcohol is the perfect way to do it. "What's going to be next? I marry his daughter in order to gain control over the company which has my fucking name on it?"

"If you're not up to it, big brother, I can always step up a little more — for the family business of course." Zander smirks, making me clench my jaw. The thought of having Zander anywhere near Livvy makes my blood run cold.

Becks continues to pore over the new piece of paper, and he shrugs. "As far as secret clauses go, this one isn't too bad."

"I've seen the Blake daughter, and I've been a part of my fair share of corporate mergers — " I rub my hands together, accidentally knocking my glass over and sending it crashing to the ground where it shatters into little pieces. "This one isn't going to be too hard."

"The cleaners are going to have a fit," Becks grumbles at the pile of glass dust lining the carpet, pulling me out of my rage haze.

I roll my eyes. "It's not like they said anything when you and Tiffany trashed the place with the sex fest you had in here."

"I wouldn't call it a sex fest," Becks scoffs.

"Bro," Zander interrupts. "Your ass was literally imprinted in the glass window; you could see the outline of her nipples. What did you use — fucking honey?"

A satisfied grin crosses Becks' face. No doubt recalling the event when his on-and-off girlfriend, Tiffany, visited him for a particularly special bout of make-up sex. Thank fuck they've stayed off — I don't think I can handle another make-up session. "It wasn't honey." Becks shakes his head and clears his throat, pointing to the piece of paper. "Basically, you need to prove you're a better fit to run the company than the Blakes."

"Livvy," I correct. Zander pulls his brows down in confusion. I roll my eyes and grab my phone from my pocket before clicking a few buttons and pulling up an article written about her in *Vanity Fair*. "His daughter is Olivia Blake." But the article isn't what makes my chest tighten. It names her, 'the makeup sensation of a generation,' which already means from the board's perspective, she is in front.

"So?" Zander lazily flicks through the article, unfazed. "Last I checked, brother, you took Founding Five Group to a billion dollars after only running it for a year."

"Yes, but it's not makeup. I don't know the difference between primer and moisturizer."

Becks barks out a laugh. "Don't look at me. I have no clue what those two products are."

Zander hands me my phone back, waving Becks off. "Don't worry about that man, you just have to beat her at her own game, bro."

He says it like it's so easy to do. I don't even know what her game is, and I'm already supposed to be two steps ahead.

Crossing my arm over my chest, I ask, "And how do you propose I do that?"

"Easy." He shrugs. "Let Glam Co fall under her reign — create a bit of chaos, maybe give her a little push too. When she starts to fail, sweep in and save the day like the hero you are. Just make sure the board sees it all. Get them on side and they will practically gift wrap the signed papers before handing them over and knocking the Blakes out for good."

Running my hand through my hair, I mull over exactly what my brother is proposing. Ruin Glam Co in order to save it. It sounds stupid, but it also might just work.

CHAPTER EIGHT

Livvy

Kendall twirls her forkful of sauce-covered spaghetti in the spoon, letting the noodles curl into an oval shape and leaving red tomato sauce stains on the white napkin she has tucked into her shirt like a bib. "Your dad finally named you successor?" she repeats for a second time, causing adrenaline to surge through me. Our Wednesday lunch date is filled with my saucy gossip — pun intended – although today its mostly mine.

He was less 'Congratulations, you did it' manner but more of a 'It's her you're fighting against and if she loses everything she's worked for also dies' kind of way to Ryder. I still heard the words and I'm going to take the win. *"Yes,"* I mouth around a mouthful of spaghetti, that elated feeling I was sure I was supposed to feel couldn't be further from how I feel right now.

Our favorite restaurant, Enoteca Ilaria, makes the best mushroom pasta, and it's my stock-standard order every time I come here. Kendall has an aversion to fungi and believes

Make Me

they're slimy tree growths and should remain in the ground.

"But you now need to prove you're a better candidate for the job than . . . who is it again?" She takes a sip from her acidulated water. She knows exactly who I'm referring to, she's just trying to tamper down his significance.

I swallow my mouthful of creamy deliciousness. "Ryder Fallington." AKA the new bane of my existence or BOME as I've nicknamed him. He's a Fallington and therefore my enemy by name and birthright. I didn't even know about the existence of a contract until a couple of hours ago, and now I'm catching my tail to bring myself up to speed. Everyone else seems to know what's going on before I do and it's becoming incredibly frustrating.

I should have known there was more to him than just a random guy who got the corner office next to mine.

"*The* Ryder Fallington," she emphasizes my enemy's name. The man with the last name I've been taught to hate without ever really knowing why…well, now I know why. He's after Glam Co.

My lips draw down as I turn my phone over and show her a few of the things I found about him online. "After scrolling through Facebook only to find him on private . . . booo . . . his Insta yielded the same results, and don't even get me started on what came up on TikTok. Unfortunately google only gave me one option. According to LinkedIn — "

Kendall snorts. "You went on his LinkedIn?"

Releasing a heavy sigh, I say, "Focus Kendall. I have to know who I'm up against." I roll my tense shoulders, trying to relieve some pent-up stress. "Unless I go down the creepy path of creating a fake account and sending him a friend request — "

"We've done that more than once."

"Yeah, we have, and I'm almost tempted to do it again. I'm sure we would uncover his dirty little secrets, but that's a little too eau de désespérée. For now, LinkedIn is all there is. I had to learn if he would qualify as CEO even if he only has six months to prove himself. I don't want Glam Co to be run into the ground by some shit stain, leaving it the laughingstock of the industry and I have to pick up the pieces of it."

Kendall points, laughing and shakes her head. "Don't forget he has a big dick too."

My nostrils flare. *She's never going to let that go.* "I can't forget it."

"Neither can Mrs. Dylan. She's asked me twice for an update or if I have any pictures of your boss's penis." She winks at me, and I shudder.

"Great, now I can never stop to have a conversation with Mrs. Dylan ever again." I plan to strategically avoid Mrs. Dylan at all costs, leaving poor Kendall to deal with our eccentric neighbor. In all fairness, she did instigate the whole penis-gate, so I don't feel sorry for her.

"Naw, come on. It's not that bad. At least she didn't show you her pictures."

A shudder creeps up my spine, imagining how gross those would have been. "Can we get back to these pictures?" I pull up another article about Ryder and his brother, Zander from a couple of years ago.

"And who is that delicious piece of hot sauce?" Kendall zooms into the blonde God standing on Ryder's left.

I have to admit his sea-green eyes are like blown glass — beautiful even in these pixilated photos. I swipe two fingers over the screen, bringing the tiny writing below the picture into focus and reading the description. Ryder is in between two men. The guy on his right could literally be his twin, so that would have to be his brother, Zander. That just leaves –"I think that's his friend Beckham Jones," I point at him. I intend to learn every single thing I can about this guy, including when he shits. His friends sound like the perfect start.

"Fuck, with friends like that, how could you be straight?"

I look at her out of the corner of my eye. This dating hiatus isn't paying off. "You really need to get laid."

She's not entirely wrong though. Beckham is worship-level hot. But given his friendship status with BOME, he has lost a few hotness pegs. Or he is just shit at choosing friends.

"I get laid plenty, thank you, Miss The-guy-I'm-dating-prefers-to-only-touch-me-from-the-neck-up."

"Jealous much?" I take a sip from my glass of white wine, because obviously red wine would not go with my lunch choice. In reality, the current status of my relationship — or lack of spicy time — is not something anyone would be jealous of.

Kendall takes my phone from me and continues to scroll through article after article, ignoring my comment. "I've got an idea." She snaps her fingers together and hands it back to me. "It's clear this guy probably knows what he is doing. Like, he can run a company if Founding Five Group are anything to go by, so you clearly won't be able to outmaneuver him when it comes to numbers and reports and shit."

I groan. She's right. FF Group is a giant conglomerate

which encompasses some of the biggest companies in the world. A couple of decades ago, some mega rich guys got together and thought, 'Hey, let's find ways to get even richer' and thus FF Group was born. To be backed by FF Group is like signaling to the world you're more than a triple-A credit rating, you're your own freaking currency. They invest in every signal aspect of business from property and racing to shipping and investment banking. There is no industry FF Group haven't put even the tiniest pulse into... except beauty. That was our industry. People would cut their arms off just to get an interview with FF Group. They don't just breathe business; they are business and I'm going to have to prove myself against the guy who makes the final yay or nay decisions for this global enterprise.

Holy Fuck.

There is no way a stupid profits projections graph or in-depth analysis on the sustainability of our ingredients suppliers or carbon footprint are going to impress or intimidate him. "Don't remind me he has a freaking MBA and experience running businesses bigger than Glam Co. My MBA is in molecules, Bunsen burners and acidic reactions. I have more than six years working at Glam Co. Sure, I've worked in production all the way to my current role of R and D. But is my experience in makeup, and my nanna's bible of formulations enough to compete with him?"

"Livvy." Kendall clasps my hand.

My voice cracks. "The board will vote in six months on who they want to run Glam Co. I don't know how to make sure it's going to be me." I pull my hand away, resting them on my lap.

Ryder made a single investment with FF Group in a multibillion-dollar empire — according to an article in the *Financial Times* — and probably has a few degrees under his belt.

What if he is better at running Glam Co than me?

Wringing my hands together in my lap, I try and hide my nervous tell from Kendall. Six months. That's right around the time we have our annual Glam Co charity ball.

Even though I've been dreaming of having the full reins of Glam Co, I envisioned a transition period — an extended time of my dad job sharing elements of his role with me until I'm confident enough to take over fully.

Pinpricks of light dance across my eyes. I dig my fingernails into the palm of my hand, hoping the pain can pull me out of the dark well my mind is falling down. I didn't expect to just walk in one day, sit behind a desk, and be given 'sign off on the summer collection today or else it won't run' kind of responsibility.

Then maybe you aren't ready to be CEO, the dark voice in my head whispers, and my mood takes a dive. The voice continues, feeding itself on the negative thoughts taking root in my psyche. *That's why Ryder is the better choice; that's why Dad didn't give it to you sooner; he knew you weren't capable; you're just a ditzy girl who can put makeup on; you're not fit for Glam Co.* The room starts to close in on me. My vision swims between color and darkness as the walls around me draw closer and closer, just before everything fades away.

"Livvy?" Kendall calls my name. "Livvy." She shakes my shoulders, and the darkness finally loses its grasp. I find her crouching in front of me.

Shaking my head, I separate myself further and further from the uncomfortable thoughts, simmering, waiting to grab a hold of me again. "Sorry, what did you say?"

"Are you okay?" she asks, worry causing the crease in her brow. "You went pale. I thought you were going to faint." Kendall hands me a glass of water, and I take a few sips.

"Yeah, I'm fine. I think I'm just a little bit dehydrated." I offer her a weak smile and take a few more sips, letting the iced water cool my overheating body. Satisfied that I'm not about to face plant into the remains of my food, Kendall releases my shoulders and sits back down.

"I need to go to the bathroom." I grab my Dior saddle bag before cutting through the restaurant to the restrooms. I splash cold water on my face, cooling my clammy skin. After a few deep breaths, I open my purse and fish out my nanna's book. My finger caresses her loopy writing. I've never needed a hug from her as badly as I do today. Slowly turning the pages of her book, I start to calm down. My semi-dry hands must have touched something because the page I thought was the last one curls slightly.

My mouth gapes open. *"What the?!"* I whisper, unsticking the page and reading the note in the middle.

> Never trust a Fallington, especially if they pretend to like you—they always have an agenda. My poor sister, Sophia, was left at the altar today and all because a Fallington wanted Glam Co. But it's the Blakes' livelihood. No Fallington will ever understand what the Blakes have done

> to keep this company afloat. My grandfather started it with his blood, sweat, and tears, and I plan to make sure it wasn't for nothing.

I scan the unseen paragraph two more times before I close the book and put it back in my purse.

"Maybe we should stop talking about this if it's too much for you." Kendall wrings her hands together when she sees me emerge from the bathroom.

"No, don't stop. I need to figure out a way to fix this," I tell her, taking my seat, my nanna's words swirling through my head.

Kendall nods and grasps my hand. "The best way to beat Ryder is by being Livvy Blake."

I roll my eyes. That is entirely unhelpful. How is being me going to compete with a guy who runs a billion-dollar company? Glam Co is all I've ever wanted and for him, it's just another little cog to add into his well-oiled machine. It's useful but not essential. For me, it's my entire world.

"Hear me out," Kendall continues. "Ryder doesn't know shit when it comes to makeup. He wouldn't understand the difference between contour and highlighter. You, on the other hand, have twelve million people who would put cow poop on their face if you told them it would make their foundation stick better. You have the edge, Livvy. You live and breathe makeup, and you have your own audience."

She's right. I nod as the vise-like hand gripping my throat starts to release and my swallows become easier.

I'm Olivia Blake — makeup is in my blood.

"This might actually work." I sit a little straighter. "I just need to show him how out of his depth he is."

"Exactly." Kendall winks at me.

I grab my wine glass and lift it to her waiting one. "I knew you were the smart one. To Livvy Blake finally being CEO of Glam Co," I toast.

"To Glam Co."

We clink glasses and I feel lighter than I have all day.

Wednesday night equals family dinner. Cue the serotonin decrease. Attendance is non-negotiable, and a shitty week is definitely not on the list of reasons we're allowed to skip it. I resist the urge to slump against my steering wheel. Devin and I have a love-hate relationship. Sometimes I blame my parents for that part — my biggest rival in life is the woman who shares my last name — while simultaneously wishing we could be like Kendall and Sienna. My parents have spent our whole lives pitting us against eachother. The only difference is that I have three years on Devin, which in her eyes means I got an unfair head start. Even though she has expressed she doesn't want to take over Glam Co, she views herself as unimportant because she hasn't received an upper-management role yet.

"What?" I bark out at my sister a little harsher than intended as I get out of my parked car. I just hope Devin isn't waiting here to tell me Dad decided to have the Fallingtons over or something.

"A little birdy told me Dad named you Glam Co's up-and-coming CEO." The false smile on her lips should be enough of an indicator she isn't out here to congratulate me. Not that there really is much to be congratulated on. Should I expect anything but fake sincerity from Devin? Our sisterly bond purely exists on paper — all we have in common apart from the same eye color is our last name.

"What's your point, Devin?" My patience is shot today.

"Nothing." She shrugs her shoulders, and I start to breathe a sigh of relief. Maybe she doesn't know about the Fallingtons attempted takeover yet and how they want to take back power of Glam Co, and I hope to keep it that way for as long as possible. I turn my back on her, intending to leave her standing there in the garage on her own. I don't want to entertain wherever Devin is going with this conversation. Mentally, I'm so drained I just want to cuddle MoMo and collapse in my bed — in that order.

"Too bad Ryder is going to take away Glam Co from you then, huh?"

My body freezes, and there it is. I slowly scan her, trying to keep the disgust from my gaze. "And you too, wiseass, or did you decide not to spend your future at Glam Co?"

Devin levels me with a bored expression. Seems she didn't realize that if I lose Glam Co, so does she. "Don't you have a hole to crawl back into?"

She shrugs her shoulders. "Probably, but then where would the fun be in that?"

"You're right. It is way more fun for you to pester me with stupid shit." Leaving her, I walk inside the house, ready for this dinner to be over.

My phone buzzes in my pocket. I fish it out, reading the message.

CAROLINE MASCI

MOM

> Sorry Darling. Have to cancel dinner. Dad and I are at the country club.

Can this day just end already?

CHAPTER NINE

Ryder

Club Trix, our usual Saturday night spot, is wall to wall with sweaty, horny patrons.

"I got four numbers," Zander mumbles as he sits beside me in our private booth, putting the four crumpled pieces of paper on the table. I can barely hear him above the loud vibrations as the DJ gets ready to drop the beat. He's some famous Spotify dude who gained a giant following for his mixes. The club has him on a standard Saturday night booking and he never fails to draw a crowd.

"I got five numbers and a pair of panties." Becks throws his collection of numbers and neon-pink thong to the mix.

"I would like to know exactly what it is you say," Henley Croft – head of Croft racing and another member of the FF group – side eyes me and sits down. I'm guessing that means he got zero numbers again.

"You gotta give the ladies a bit more then 'Hi I need your number for a competition'. No woman is going to want to do shit for you then." Rome Venuccio – Head of Venuccio industries sector in the FF Group – taps Henley's shoulders a few times before taking his own seat. "I only have two."

"I do not say that," Henley gasps in outrage.

"I guess that's why you are the only one with none then," Leo, the final member of the FF Group sits and flashes his two numbers.

"You really need to up your game man, or Fallington here will be buying for the rest of our lives," Rome points at me, and the group laughs, except for Henley who noticeably slides down in his seat.

The only thing that makes our night more interesting is the longstanding bet of whoever gets the most numbers after two songs is paying for drinks the whole night. Zander and Henley the unlucky bastards, have never had to pay for a round. Becks usually gives me a good run for my money, but it's my credit card that carries the weight of most of our Saturday-night adventures.

Tonight, though, is not his night.

Despite the numbers he's pulling, his attempt to steal my throne is about to be thwarted.

"I win." I grin at everyone, throwing down the ten numbers I collected walking across the dance floor over to the offices to see Matt, the owner of Club Trix.

"There's a shocker." Zander rolls his eyes.

Straightening my legs, I pull out the thong an overexcited woman shoved down my pants while cupping my junk as her friend grinded against my leg.

"Really?" Becks blanches.

"One more," I say, digging my hand deeper into the front of my pants.

Zander snorts. "If you're just using this as an excuse to touch your dick, the dance floor is that way and by the looks of things you will easily find someone to do it for you."

"Trust me, I don't need to stroke my cock." I level my brother with a shit-eating grin as I pull out a hotel-room key card and chuck it on the table.

"We know, you do it all for yourself." Rome throws his head back and roars with laughter. "That settles it. Drinks on Ryder."

I wince, jostling myself in the seat trying to get more comfortable now that I'm not packing. "I think that thing cut my dick."

"You're not getting out of buying drinks tonight." Leo deadpans.

"Wouldn't dream of it."

Our booth has a waitress who comes by and eagerly takes our order, her eyes surveying Becks as she licks her lips with a hungry look.

I hand her my Centurion Amex card. "Put it all on my tab."

Her eyes widen. "Yes, sir." She nods and leaves.

From our booth, we can see right out onto the dance floor below us. But because of the shadowing and darkness of the club, it makes it hard for the people dancing to see us. Feeling myself relax for the first time this week, I lean heavily into the padded couch, glad I didn't bail on our night out.

The waitress arrives with a bottle of vodka with a sparkler

shooting fireworks out the top. Placing our shot glasses down on the table, her eyes stay fixed on Becks. "What are we celebrating?" she asks, her voice taking on a husky tone as she eyes my best friend hungrily.

"Life." Becks shrugs as he gently runs his teeth along his bottom lip for her benefit. Yeah, he is totally about to get laid.

"I've never heard a better thing to celebrate," she replies like they are the only two people in the room. The sparkler has long-since blown out. Becks pulls the useless sparkler from the lid of the Grey Goose vodka bottle pours a shot for all of us and offers her one.

"To life," she whispers, clinking her glass with his before putting it in her mouth bottom-side up and using her tongue to turn the glass around and down the shot.

I clear my throat. It's not that I want to be a cockblocker, but I'm not the one about to get laid, so I don't really care.

"To life."

We all say in unison and drink our shots, ready to get shit-faced drunk.

Becks looks at us. "Surely that counts toward my tally."

"Hotel key card." I flash the card between my index and middle fingers. It's the biggest trump card I've ever received. Becks grumbles something under his breath and downs another shot — no doubt pissed at losing his two-week streak.

Three shots later, I'm loosening up watching the club member below from my spot perched on the rail. I'm nowhere near as buzzed as I want to be tonight but I'm well on my way. Zander, Henley and Leo are lost somewhere on the dance floor, and Becks escaped with the waitress during her 'break', leaving Rome and I at the booth. The music continues to pump through the club as more and more people flood the floor — if that's even possible.

From the corner of my eye, I spot a familiar brunette walk in. Her long, tressed hair is slicked into a high ponytail and she's wearing a short, skin-tight black dress that finishes just below her ass cheeks, putting all that soft, creamy skin of hers on show.

What the fuck is Livvy doing here? I track her movements as she weaves her way to the bar. I never would have picked her as someone who would frequent Club Trix. Not that Club Trix isn't the place to be, but because Livvy is Livvy. Another girl wraps her arm around her waist as they wait by the bar, trying to get the bartenders' attention.

Since she's here, let's have a little fun. I signal the security guard holding the rope sectioning off the private-booth area. I down another shot as the security guard taps Livvy's shoulder and indicates for her to go upstairs. Even though I can't hear the exchange, Livvy shakes her head 'No' as her friend jumps up and down and bounds toward the steps. Livvy hunches over, her gaze darting between the bar and her friend's retreating figure, before she decides to follow her, who is already halfway up the stairs. I chuckle under my breath. If I'm going to take Glam Co, I think I need to get to know my opposition a little better, and what better way to do it than with alcohol and the façade of a truce?

"You must be Ryder," the bubbly friend extends her hand out to me.

Laying the charm on thick, I take her extended hand.

"And you are?"

"Kendall." Her pupils blow out the moment my lips touch her wrist, and her voice takes on a breathy note.

I don't collect random numbers and panties for nothing — being charming comes easily to me. Livvy clears her throat. I release Kendall's hand, watching her golden curls swish against her shoulder as she looks behind to where her friend is casually stepping from foot to foot.

Livvy is loosely holding her clasped wrist in front of her body, acting almost like a shield against her insecurity. She has no clue that she is a fucking smoke show and is outdoing nearly every single person in this club. Her brown eyes look more hazel underneath the dark eyeshadow lining the lids of her eyes. She stares at me head on, not backing down from my gaze. That red lipstick should be completely illegal — it makes her lips look puffy and entirely too kissable, and I imagine what it would look like coating my cock.

"Livvy." I dip my head in greeting at my little nemesis in training.

"Ryder." She steps forward, like she's going to extend me her hand but instead she reaches past me and pours a shot into one of the empty glasses and downs it.

"Thirsty there, Killer?" I stare at her, one eyebrow raised, the corner of my mouth lifted into a half-smile.

Livvy pours herself another shot and downs it, wiping the drop of vodka that escapes the corner of her lips with the back of her hand. Nodding her head, she places the glass on the table. "On the contrary," she replies. "I'm entirely too sober to be dealing with" — she motions to the empty booth —

"whatever this is."

Kendall gives a little growl from beside me.

"Oh?" I question. "And just what might *this* be?"

"Do you always sit alone in booths on a Saturday night? Or is that just how you make yourself feel like you have four hundred of your closest friends around you while still being above them?"

That tongue.

Becks laughs behind Livvy, making her jump slightly and grasp her heaving chest. I wrinkle my nose; he smells like cheap perfume and sex. Becks downs another shot. The light isn't dim enough to hide the pink tinge on the tips of Livvy's ears.

"And who might this be?" Becks turns his attention to Kendall. In typical Becks fashion, the waitress is long-since forgotten.

"I'm Kendall," she introduces.

"Kendall." Becks tests her name on his tongue, pouring another round of shots. "And how do you feel about vodka, Kendall?" he asks, winking as he hands her a glass.

"Love it," she replies.

My eyes flit back to Livvy, only to find her gaze unwavering from mine. I step closer invading her space, enjoying her squirm.

"Where's your brother?" she asks.

"What makes you think I have a brother?"

Ah. Someone has been doing their research.

Livvy snorts and turns her head, her eyes scanning the dance floor. "I do my research."

"Where's your sister?" I counter.

"I would say probably buried under a pint of ice cream and drawing X's in her hit lists."

A deep chuckle escapes my lips. It's the way her nose is scrunched like the thought of her sister is the equivalent of stepping in dog shit and dragging it behind her with every step she takes.

"I'm guessing you don't get along well with your sister?"

"I didn't take you as much of a guesser, Mr Fallington."

The corners of his lips curl. "What brings you here on a Saturday night?"

"Actually, this jerk decided that he wanted to contest the company I work for, effectively trying to stop me from inheriting it, and my BFFL is sick of seeing me mope around — her words not mine. Her solution was to get shit-faced drunk and dress me up like some go-go dancer." She points to her outfit.

I blow out a whistle. "Wow this guy sounds like a total jerk."

She looks at me out of the corner of her eye as I cage her into the rail, a half-smirk tugging the corners of her lips. "He really is."

"Do you think the jerk will win?"

Her heated gaze holds mine captive. "Losing isn't in my vocabulary," she replies.

"Nor in mine, Killer."

"Don't take it too personally when I wipe the floor with your ass," she breathes, patting my chest. Oh Livvy... *let the games begin.*

I swallow, trying to keep my voice from cracking. "I guess

we will just have to see who comes out on top."

Something unreadable dances in her eyes before she leans in close. Her hot breath tickles the shell of my ear as she whispers, "Between you and me, I love being on top."

Olivia Blake is really making it hard to be her enemy.

CHAPTER TEN

Livvy

I have officially had too much vodka — that or the shots were laced with something. Some sort of top-shelf, high-proof, only-available-in-three-bottles-a-year kind of stuff. There is no other way my intoxicated brain would've gone and blurted shit I want to keep buried in a locked box at the very deep recess of my spank bank otherwise.

I'm mesmerized by the five o'clock shadow that clings to Ryder's jawline. The tip of my tongue has a mind of its own as it licks across my bottom lip.

Ryder's eyebrows are still raised to his hairline in surprise. His Adam's apple bobs with the force of his swallow. "Lucky for me, Killer, so do I," he finally says.

Biting my bottom lip, to hide the excited shiver runs through me as his eyes track the movement of my tongue. I stop myself from word-vomiting excuses and trying to cover up the fact that I just flirted with Ryder Fricken Fallington while my situationship is at home watching sports on TV. Leaving me conveniently on 'read' after his 'We need to talk' message after I told him about the six months deadline and whole Ryder situation might I add. Tonight is about letting off some steam and celebrating my birthday, I should not be thinking that Ryder looks even hotter with a black silk shirt, with the first three buttons undone showing the expanse of his slightly tanned chest.

"Birthday shots," Kendall calls, saving me from my reply, the air between us thickening with something I'm not sure I'm ready to admit yet.

I stiffen before moving back a fraction, adding some much-needed space between us. I suck down a sharp lungful of breath, needing the oxygen to cool my heating libido, one hundred percent laying the blame on the vodka coursing through my veins.

"Whose birthday are we celebrating?" Becks asks, his eyes trailing slowly over Kenny.

"The one and only Livvy Blake." My so-called best friend points at me.

The heat of Ryder's stare intensifies. "I guess it's only right we celebrate with a shot then?"

"I guess so," I reply. My four-shot pre-game whilst getting ready are now well and truly buzzing through my body. Ryder leads me back to the booth and places a shot in my hand. Becks and Kendall are already clinking their glasses together when Ryder lifts his glass to meet mine.

His stare deepens, as he leans across closing what little distance I'd created between us, his hot breath curling around the shell of my ear, "Happy birthday, Killer. I hope you're ready for a fight."

I swear his lips ghost my earlobe with a feather-light kiss before he downs his shot in one quick swallow. I quickly follow, needing the liquid to cool my dry mouth.

"Ryder?" a male voice calls, completely shattering the moment. A man who could be Ryder's twin is standing behind us looking rather pissed off.

Then it clicks. "Ah, this must be the brother."

"I didn't realize we were bringing chicks up here?" Zander replies.

A shiver runs down my spine at the thought of just what they do in this booth. Zander's eyes slowly survey my body, his gaze narrowing on how close Ryder is standing to me as his upper lip curls in disgust. I raise a brow at the brother and cross my arms over my chest, but all that does is rub my over-sensitized breasts so I drop them back to my sides. *Stupid libido.*

Ryder's eyes flick to me then to my chest, clearly seeing the outline of my nipples through my dress and smirks.

Asshole.

He tips his chin to the side, eyeing Zander. "Never really stopped any of us before?" Then he casually leans back in the booth.

I take a deep breath, the smell of citrus-still strong in the air-wrapping me further under its spell.

"Zander, this is Livvy."

Zander doesn't move an inch, his biceps flexing under his shirt.

"Hi." I give Zander a weak smile and wave my hand, heat flooding my cheeks.

Zander eyes me one last time and takes a seat opposite Becks and Kendall. I think I have an allergy to siblings.

Ryder's brows pull down in a frown as he watches Zander.

"Siblings, huh," I mumble. I don't think Ryder hears me though. Instead, he's pouring another round of shots into the empty glasses.

Go out, Kendall said. *It will be fun*, Kendall said. *You look like shit*, Kendall said.

Glaring at Kendall sitting on the opposite side of the booth sharing shots with Becks, I start to wonder if maybe she chose Club Trix for a reason. One that didn't include 'Let's celebrate your birthday and forget this shitty week and let your hair down a little' and more 'I stalked Becks' Instagram and I know where he will be tonight.' Eyeing Ryder out the corner of my eye, I take in his easy, laid-back smile. He wants a challenge. Lucky him because Glam Co is mine.

"Hashtag regret," Kendall groans when I open her curtains. Usually, it's the other way around — Kendall is the cheery one and not hungover in the slightest and I'm the one completely regretting my decisions.

"Hashtag your idea," I reply smugly and laugh. Surprisingly, I didn't wake up the slightest bit hungover this morning. Kendall, on the other hand, looks like she could stand in for Bradley Cooper in *The Hangover*.

"Can we please stop talking in hashtags," she grunts, throwing the pillow over her head. "Fuck, I'm never drinking vodka again."

We've all made that call — it never seems to stick.

I snicker. "You were the one who went to their booth."

"Not my fault Becks is so fuck-me-hot it's not even funny."

Ah, there it is.

"He's no good for you." Partly because he is Ryder's best friend, who also happens to be his lawyer, and he is trying to take Glam Co from me. Which is more of a reason why both Ryder and Becks are no-no's for either of us. Plus, she is on a dating hiatus.

"How would you know." Kendall lifts the pillow slightly so she can glare at me with one eye.

I pretend to wobble on the spot. "Because he's friends with Ryder, who is a walking red flag in every sense of the word. Did you now see how much of a playboy he was. Yep. Nope. Kenny, Becks is a one-way ticket to the heart-break hotel."

Kendall mumbles something that sounds like, 'Why isn't she running in fear from my stink eye?' Little does Kendall know Devin makes giving the stink eye an Olympic challenge, winning the consecutive gold medal every single time.

Pulling the pillow off her face, I make sure to return the extra cheery favor she bestowed on me earlier this week. "Up and at 'em, sweet cheeks. We have brunch in twenty."

Unease bubbles through me at the prospect of seeing Kyle. I haven't really spoken to him all week, and I don't really miss him. Last night with Ryder had more emotion attached to it, then Kyle has this whole two month of 'dating' – I use that term loosely.

"Why the fuck are you so cheery?" Her eyes are barely slits as she blinks through the onslaught of bright light I just allowed to pour into her room.

"Oh, I don't know." I shrug, my mood is riding a serious high and it really shouldn't be, especially when our girls' night was completely crashed by Ryder and his merry group of douches. "Don't forget we're meeting Kyle for brunch," I remind her.

"Ugh," she gripes. "What do you even see in that guy?"

Pursing my lips, I mull over her question, not really sure how to answer that and closing the door just in time to miss the thud of her pillow. Kyle is the complete opposite to the red flag that is Ryder Fallington. That's why he is the sensible choice.

In her still hungover state, Kendall decided to opt for oversized Prada glasses to cover the dark circles ringing her eyes. "I'm never drinking again," she mumbles, sliding farther down in her seat. Even the green vitamin shot I blended and made her drink before we left hasn't really done much to perk her up.

"Yeah, yeah, we know. I've heard it all before." I wave her off, searching for Kyle in the crowd.

ME

> We're sitting outside. Kenny needed the sunlight x

Not so much Kendall needed the sunlight as I just didn't want to be in an enclosed space if she decides to hurl her guts out. I click send on the message as I hear, "Hello, Olivia." Kyle, dressed in his usual polo shirt with a sweater resting on his shoulders, stands behind me. *Boring*, my mind screams at me, but I quickly shush that voice.

"Kyle." My arms reach around his shoulders and pulling him in a tight hug.

Kyle places his hands on my hips, making sure to keep a respectable distance between us. Our hug lasts for a whole three seconds before he pulls away and dots a kiss on my cheek. "How was girls' night?" he asks as he takes the seat next to me.

"Good." I nod, fixing the napkin on my lap. "We danced, we drank, we sang." I conveniently leave out that we found Ryder and he and I loved the same songs — we stood on the balcony screaming along to Katy Perry blasting through the speakers. Kyle hates pop music. He prefers podcasts. Every time he is in my car, he hooks up the latest podcast he's listening too.

"Yeah, just fan-tastic," Kendall murmurs. "We saw — "

I kick Kendall under the table.

"Ooof." She bends to rub her shin, glaring at me over the rim of her glasses.

"How was the game?" I quickly change the subject. I don't really care how 'the game' went, but I feel I should at least pretend to be interested in what Kyle loves.

"We won." He smiles at me. He has a nice smile. I almost wish it made my stomach quiver the way it does when Ryder smiles. It's one of the things I find most attractive about him. Shit. No, Livvy. What the fuck am I saying? Nothing about Ryder Fallington is attractive. He is the poster boy for red flags. Stick with green.

"Woo-hoo." Kendall gives a less than enthusiastic cheer, raising her fist in mock excitement, and I have to agree with her.

"Ready to order?" The waitress arrives. Kendall and I put in our brunch order, while Kyle spends a bit of time humming and hawing over the menu before deciding on the same thing as me. For some reason, that frustrates me. Normally it wouldn't, but today it does.

"How's work been?" I ask Kyle.

"Really busy. I'm hoping the Faluccinos will keep me on permanently. Then I intend to climb the corporate ladder and hopefully get invited to FF Group. The only worthy companies in Cheshire Shore are run by FF Group." Kyle flashes his overly whitened teeth. His aspiration should make me proud, but it just rubs me the wrong way.

"Ass licker," Kendall coughs into her fist. The feeling is mutual.

"Kendall looks like she had fun last night." Kyle eyes Kendall as she lifts her glasses and uses them as a headband to pull the hair from her face.

"Yeah, she got well acquainted with a bottle of vodka," I tell him.

"Hey, it wasn't my fault; it was free, and vodka is, like, zero calories," Kendall replies.

"Yes, but it's not zero hangover, or was that a new kind of vodka?" I singsong.

"I hope you weren't drawing attention to yourself to get free drinks, Olivia. You know that's beneath you. It's not like you aren't capable of paying for them yourself," Kyle grumbles.

The high I'm riding slowly starts to fade.

"Ew, Kyle. Gross. That's a bag-of-dicks thing to say. No, the booth had a tab going, so it was all good," Kendall replies.

Kyle freezes as he looks between the two of us. "You two got a booth?" he asks, ignoring Kendall calling him a bag of dicks. I kind of agree with her — he is totally acting like a bag-of-dicks right now.

"No," I rush to input.

As Kendall replies, "Ryder and his friends had the booth and he lost some bet, so he was paying the whole night."

"Ryder, as in Ryder Fallington the new chairman and all the top board members of FF Group, including my boss, Leo?" Kyle clenches his jaw. He still hasn't elaborated on what exactly he needs to talk to me about, and now he is coming at me with this knuckle-dragging crap. To say he wants to be Ryder would be an understatement. I give him the *CliffNotes* version of what happened and he is more pissed that I'm spending all this time with Ryder than he really should be. What happens at Glam Co isn't really his business — at all. Clicking my tongue against the roof of my mouth, I eye Kendall, her *oopsie* look isn't going to get her out of this. There is a reason I didn't want her to bring Ryder up, and she just did the opposite.

Kyle's eyes stay fixed on mine. "I thought we decided you were going to avoid Ryder Fallington, unless I was with you. And now I find out you were making a fool of me with my boss and his friends present. This is my future now you're playing with." His words come out clipped.

I stare at him, forehead wrinkling. His jealousy toward Ryder confuses me. I doubt Ryder would even know his existence. Besides, we aren't even official yet and we're becoming less official by the day, I don't care if my dad keeps pushing me in his direction. We have been on a handful of dates; he hasn't even felt my boobs for Christ's sake. Yet he wants to control aspects of my life?

The waitress returns with our food, giving me a few seconds reprieve from Kyle's scrutiny.

I wait for her to leave before confronting Kyle. "Well, I can't avoid him or his friends completely. I have to work with Ryder for the next six months, I might run into his friends on occasion."

Kyle grunts, aggressively cutting into his oat pancakes. "That's working with him. There is no need to socialize with him or his friends outside of office hours. We don't want him to get the wrong idea about me because of my association with you." Kyle's worried I'm going to somehow damage his potential career with FF Group, but all I care about is mine with Glam Co.

"We weren't socializing. We just happened to run into him, and he happened to invite us up to his booth. That *is* it." I grab a sip of water, trying to quench the dryness that is taking over my mouth. My mood is well and truly soured like the buttermilk cream on my oat pancakes.

"Glam Co means too much to us to have you lose it."

To us? Shouldn't it be Glam Co means too much to me? It's my name on the piece of paper.

CHAPTER ELEVEN

Ryder

I turn the dial up on the hot water, allowing the scalding temperature to slowly turn my skin red. My head falls back against my shoulder, the burning sensation of the hot spray relaxing my tense muscles. Livvy's seductive voice whispering in my ear she 'likes to be on top' has been on repeat in my brain all night. My cock has been at half-mast ever since as a new plan starts to formulate. I run a hand through my damp hair. Livvy Blake is not easy to read. She keeps her face as a blank canvas, but when the canvas slips, it's like a clear window peering straight into her soul.

My ego appreciated the stroking, just as my cock aches from the lack thereof. Closing my eyes, I reach down to palm my aching cock, trying to imagine it's a smaller, more delicate hand stroking me, but give up just as quickly as I start. I can't be led around by my cock; I'm determined to not make the same mistake as my great grandfather.

Finishing my shower slower than I usually would, I get

dressed and grab my coffee on the way out as I head down to FF Group offices. I need to prep Zander to look after operations while I focus on taking over Glam Co. Six months with me in the shadows is going to be a huge test for Zander — one I'm not willing to risk. I love my baby brother, but it goes without saying that I shield him from a lot of shit, especially where FF Group is concerned. The group wasn't struggling before I took over, but I don't want to see it lose one second of its momentum. It's only going to get better when I add Glam Co to the Fallington portfolio at FF Group.

Zander meets me in the foyer of our office, the sullen scowl from last night still present today.

"Bro, what the fuck is up with you?" I press the button on the elevator, not bothering to wait for him to get in. If he left a chick in his bed to come here — tough shit. Since losing our mom, Dad and I have babied Zander more than we maybe should've. But it's now time to take the training pants off. He is going to need to start being more present in the group and worrying less about partying.

He works his jaw aggressively. "Since when do we get so chummy with the enemy?"

I narrow my eyes. "Chummy?"

"You were practically humping the girl into the fucking booth."

Ah, now we understand the true issue — Livvy. Rolling my eyes, I release a calculated breath. "So?"

Zander is overreacting, I wouldn't call us sitting next to each other dry humping. I got more action walking the dance floor of the club than with Livvy.

"So?" Zander jabs his finger into the emergency stop button, causing the elevator to groan and come to an immediate halt. His voice lowers to a barely audible growl. "Did you forget that if she wins, you will lose the only shot we've had in one-hundred years to take back what is rightfully ours?"

I'm almost hurt that he would imply I'd let my cock dictate such an important business choice. "No, I didn't forget, brother." I eye him carefully. "If it wasn't for me, you wouldn't have even known about the loophole." I tuck my closed fist into my pocket to stop myself from punching my brother in the face for even suggesting something so stupid.

We both want to see Glam Co back in Fallington hands. A piece of ass isn't going to change that.

"Let me tell you something, brother." I press the button, releasing the emergency stop and letting the elevator whirl upwards toward our office. "One way or another, I will get Glam Co, and if it means I have to sleep with the enemy to do it . . . I will," I announce as the doors open.

I step out of my Aston Martin DB11, which I've conveniently parked in the spot I assume to be Simon's, leaving Livvy's space free. Still pissed that my brother would think I'd let a woman – especially a Blake woman cloud my goal, our goal. I click my door shut, Livvy zips her car down the small parking lot. I snort at the sight of Livvy giving a little fist pump after pulling her car into her space.

"Ryder." She nods at me as she gets out of her car, straightens her suit jacket, like she wasn't just a backup dancer in her car concert and walks into the building. I shake my head and grab the special parcel from the passenger seat and follow her, not bothering to take my key card out and swipe my ID. There is a certain receptionist I need to see. Livvy smiles at Cecelia before pressing the button for our floor. Even though, technically, Simon's vacated his office on the top floor next to the board-members offices, keeping tabs on Livvy will be a lot easier if she is across the hall rather than two floors below me.

I wait for Livvy to step into the elevator before turning to Cecelia.

"Good morning, Mr. Fallington," her voice quivers.

"Cecelia." I flash her a smile that usually wins me the bet most Saturday nights.

"Y-y-yes."

"Please call me Ryder."

"Oh, okay, R-R-Ryder." Her whole body is rigid, like she's worried about where this conversation is going.

"I was wondering if you could do me a favor?"

Her pupils blow out, "A-a-anything, sir."

"I heard you are a giant Sarah Franetico fan." *More like I eavesdropped when you and Livvy were talking in the hallway about this book a few days ago.* It was something to do with a thriller movie Livvy had gone to see and she was asking Cecelia for more book recommendations. Livvy kept referring to Cecelia as a 'booktoker', whatever the fuck that means, and Cecelia was going on and on and about Sarah Franetico.

Sarah doesn't realize it, but she just became my lucky gold bar.

"Yeah, she's my favorite author." She fiddles with her ring.

I smile. "You don't say?" Pretending like this is some happy coincidence and not something I meticulously planned out, I continue, "I happen to have a full set of first editions of the *Neverworld* series, hand signed by Sarah . . ." I trail off, and the look of awe that lights Cecelia's face makes me internally chuckle. *Got her.* "But I was thinking if you're such a fan, I would love to give them to you."

"Really?!" she shrieks and jumps up, knocking her chair over and mounting the desk to wrap her arms around my neck. This is not the reaction I was expecting, but I'll take it. "Thank you, thank you, thank you." She goes to plant a kiss on my cheek, and I quickly pull away from her. That's a bit too far.

Maybe the books were a bit too much. I hope I didn't accidentally sign some sort of blood pact without realizing. Do people really have this kind of reaction to being gifted their favorite books?

I grab the bag with the set Becks gave me yesterday and hand it to Cecelia. "I just need to ask you for a favor?" I stress.

"Anything." She snatches the bag from my hand like a rabid dog eating its first meal in months. A smile pulls at my lips. *Exactly the answer I was looking for.*

I'm glad Zander talked me out of having Sarah show up at Glam Co offices. I think Cecelia would have fainted, but that does give me a good idea. If she is this popular with a die-hard following, Glam Co should do a collaboration with her. I shelve that little idea for the moment.

Lightly rubbing my knuckle where Cecelia scratched me, I clear my throat. "Can you please have a comprehensive product guide of everything we sell at Glam Co put together, including a detailed description of uses, price points, and levels of importance?" I don't know anything about makeup and I can't turn to Livvy for this stuff — not when she could use it as a way to prove I'm incompetent to run the company.

Cecelia snorts but doesn't take her eyes off the book she is flicking through. "Isn't that what the Glam Guide is for?"

Ah, the Glam Guide. That's what I need. "I suppose it is."

Did she just . . .? Yep, she sniffed the pages.

Cecelia's focus stays fixed on her books, flicking slowly through the pages. "You know the online guide we have to view all our products. Do you want me to send you the link?"

I let an easy smile pull at my lips. "Yes, that would be great."

"I can also create a spreadsheet of all our upcoming products which aren't on the guide yet?" She puts the book down and picks up another one before repeating the process and sniffing it deeply into her lungs.

Distracted, maybe this gift is a bit too much. I should've gone with a book plate like Sarah's agent suggested. I mutter, "Yes please,"

and somehow refrain from gawking when she pulls her phone out and starts snapping pictures of the books tucked against her chest. Cecelia looks up at me, blinking, waiting for me to reply.

I blink rapidly, "Sorry, what was that?"

"I asked when do you want it by?"

"ASAP," I reply.

"No problem." She nods, flicking through another book. "Oh, my shit. Inserts?!" she gushes, staring at something in the book.

It took Becks two days to get Sarah's location from her agent and it did involve some serious sweet-talking from him. It didn't help that his usual method of extracting information wouldn't work. Sarah's agent is a sixty-five-year-old man with a balding patch and didn't really care that Becks could fuck him pretzel-style across his desk. In the end, Becks parted with a bottle of one of my dad's top-shelf scotches, one that is reserved for special occasions only. But given the stakes, I was willing to hand a brand-new bottle over to the guy. At the end of the day, a fifty-thousand-dollar bottle of scotch means nothing when comparing it to Glam Co.

"Oh and can you keep this just between us?" I don't need Livvy getting wind of this.

A guy carrying a bunch of peonies stands beside me. Jerking back, I roll my eyes over him. Something about the guy is familiar. I think I've seen him before with Leo Faluccino, one of FF Group's investors.

Where the fuck did he come from?

"Morning, Cece." The guy knocks on the counter once then saunters off, whistling some dumb-ass tune as he catches the elevator.

"Hey Anders," she replies.

I snicker at the suited-up dickhead. His slicked-back hair screams try hard.

Cecelia has already started typing on her computer. Completely unbothered by the guy, she replies, "Keep what between us?" without even looking at me.

"Exactly." I nod and leave her to email me the guide. I click the button on the elevator and smile to myself.

Making Glam Co ours is going to be a piece of cake.

I'm already congratulating myself as I step out of the elevator.

I freeze when I notice the guy from downstairs is fucking hugging Livvy in the doorway of her office. My gaze narrows on the way Livvy is happily squished against his chest. My jaw ticks, all the muscles tighten, readying themselves, and I tuck my clenched fist into my pocket to hide that this bothers me more than I care to admit. She's the enemy, I should feel nothing but contempt towards her, and it bothers me I don't. My angry strides falter when he pulls the bouquet of peonies from behind his back and hands them to Livvy.

This is not fucking happening.

CHAPTER TWELVE

Livvy

I smile into the camera. This is my happy place. Not the mountain of PR behind me, most of that will be donated. It's that I get to try on these products and explain how best to use them to the world. I grab a parcel, my eyes flick to the monitor sitting beside it, checking everything is in the frame how I like.

The light rap of fingers against my door followed by, "Knock, knock," pulls my attention away from my video. I click pause, cross my office in a few strides, excitement buzzing through my veins — I already know who is waiting on the other side from the timbre of his voice.

"Anderson Davenport, when did you get back from London?" I squeal, wrapping my arms around his broad shoulders and embracing him tightly while burying my nose straight into his neck.

"A day ago. I had to do something in Havenville before I could get down here." Anders laughs and wraps an arm around my waist, pulling me against him.

"Our Facetimes have been way too infrequent for my liking," I grumble, already feeling the built-up stress roll off my shoulders.

"Me too." Anders gives me a sad smile. "The time difference between here and London doesn't make it any easier."

"Or is there a certain someone who has been taking up all your time?" I ask, wiggling my eyebrows as I pry into his love life.

Anders groans, resting his thumb and forefinger on his nose. "No, not this again. You are not setting me up again. The last woman brought cue cards with our kids' names and astrological signs on them."

"Wow." My mouth falls open and I wiggle my eyebrows in excitement. My childhood best friend has a notoriously bad dating life, and I've taken it upon myself to remedy it. "It must have gotten far if she already had the cue cards written up."

Anders squints at me, his lips set in a grimace. "We hadn't even reached the appetizers yet."

The secondhand awkwardness overcomes me, and I shift from foot to foot. "Ouch." Nodding, I venture, "So less crazy next time. Got it," and wink at him. Not the slightest bit deterred from finding him a girlfriend –its what best friends are for. Ander's is undeterred about choosing the right woman therefore, he needs a gentle push in the right direction and who better than me to be the one to do it.

"Vivi." Anders' eyes flash in warning, using my childhood nickname.

"What?" I shrug, heat filling my neck. "I was thinking

Kenny's sister. She is in France; you spent most of your time in London . . ." I trail off.

Anders rolls his eyes and says, "Sienna and I don't need you to set us up. Can we please get off the topic of my love life?" before pulling a giant bouquet of flowers from behind his back. "Someone turned twenty-five. And I wasn't here for it."

A soft gasp escapes my lips, as I grasp the bouquet. "Ande, this is too much. You already sent me a giant bunch of flowers on my birthday."

"Yes, but those were from Ares too. These are just from me. Plus, these are hand delivered — they must count for something." Anders dots my cheek with a kiss.

Snorting, I lightly tap his chest. "You're such a marshmallow."

"Shh," Anders whispers, resting his arm comfortably around my waist. "Don't tell anyone — it will totally ruin my street cred."

"And just who the fuck are you?" a low growl from behind Anders has us breaking apart.

"I think the better question is just who the fuck are you?" Anders' eyes roll up and down Ryder, surveying him. There isn't much height difference between Anders and Ryder. Although Ryder has a couple more pounds of muscle compared to Anders.

"Umm, so" — I clear my throat — "I think I might need to catch you up on some things. That's Ryder, as in Ryder Fallington. Ryder this is Anders as in Anderson Davenport."

Anders jerks back like I've slapped him.

I nod. *Yup.* "And he is here because the board is going to

decide between the two of us who is going to run Glam Co."

"Fuck, Vivi." The mutual hurt in his voice sends warmth through my chest. *At least someone is sharing in my pain.* "Talk about catching up. I feel like I've missed a whole fucking season."

"Vivi?" Ryder interjects. My muscles tighten, hearing Ryder use my childhood nickname only reserved for Anders and his brother Ares, it should make me mad, but I actually like it.

Out of the corner of his eye, Anders gives Ryder a tilted look. "If you know, you know. Clearly, you don't." Anders turns his attention back to me. "Listen, I know I've disrupted filming. I do have another reason for this visit."

Ryder's gaze is fixated on Anders' arm around my waist, a low growl escapes his throat. I stare between Anders and Ryder, both eyebrows raised. *What. The. Fuck.* The testosterone in the room is so thick, it's difficult to breathe. If I'm not mistaken it seems Ryder is… jealous?

Ryder crosses his thick arms over his chest, almost blocking the doorway, "And what's that?" he asks before I can.

"Congrats on twelve mil, Vivi. I know you already received the plaque, but Ares and I had something special made for you." Anders pulls a little box from inside his suit jacket.

"Anders," I gasp, taking the present from him because, duh, who doesn't love a present? My gaze flicks to him and I try to hide my grimace. "It's not a key to your gym, is it?" I've had a bad experience.

"Fuck no, that would be a really thoughtless gift," Anders laughs.

I breathe a sigh of relief and open the small, rectangular box. "Is that — ?" My eyes widen as my jaw practically falls to the floor as I stare between the present inside and Anders.

"Yup." Anders nods as Ryder peeks over his shoulder, curiosity clearly winning out.

In the box is my favorite Chanel N°1 perfume, my breath catches as I run my finger over my name engraved in the bottle.

The back of my throat burns. "Thank you," I whisper.

"Naw, Vivi." Anders slings his arm around my shoulders and pulls me into his chest for another hug. His phone starts buzzing in his pocket, cutting through our moment. Without looking at who is calling, he says, "I have to go — that's Ares. We're having a few issues with our new program, and you have a strict schedule to uphold," and releases me.

My bottom lip pops out, clearly pouting but also not ashamed to admit it. I hardly get to see Anders his career is really thriving, but sometimes I just miss being able to hangout together. "Okay." I drop another kiss on his cheek. "But promise we will do something with Kendall this weekend, and you can finally meet Kyle."

Anders pushes past Ryder, exiting my office. "Is this the same guy Kendall messaged me about?" He pauses, his finger calling the elevator.

From the way he said it, it doesn't sound like a good thing. "I think so?"

"Can't wait." Anders' eyes flash as he steps into the elevator, but the look that passes across his face says the opposite.

Out of the corner of my eye, Ryder picks up one of the parcels from the pile behind my desk.

Make Me

"Can I help you?" I ask, placing the flowers and present down.

"What did Anders mean about your schedule being strict?" he surveys the PR wall before flicking his eyes to me.

I grab the parcel from his hand and return it to the pile. "Anders is talking about my Make Me schedule."

His eyebrows draw down as he runs his index finger over his lip. "Make Me?"

"It's only the hottest app to hit twenty-first century screens," I snort. "It's like a hybrid between Instagram and YouTube but only for makeup and skincare." I purse my lips and cross my arms, stopping myself from saying duh.

"Interesting," Ryder replies, sitting in the seat looking at the parcel I'd started to open. "Is Glam Co on Make Me?"

Shouldn't he know if Glam Co was on it or not? Maybe he hasn't done as much research as he thinks.

"No." I shake my head and take the seat next to him. "Just me, Olivia Grace. I have a strict routine posting two videos a week and once a month a new makeup PR unboxing."

"Interesting," he replies, still holding my package. "Why Olivia Grace?"

"Grace was my grandmother's name. She's kind of the reason I love the industry. She took this insecure girl and made her into the woman you see standing before you today." I fiddle with the hem of my top. "I wanted to have a piece of her with me as I share things she has taught me on Make Me."

Ryder's throat bobs. I must've hit a nerve. "I'm sure she would be very happy." His husky voice makes the hairs on my arms raise.

Damn it, why did I have to notice that?

"Yeah, she would get a real kick." My voice catches. "Besides, if I use my name Olivia Blake, I lose instant credibility. People online just see me as this privileged rich girl who just sits in front of my phone and pretends to put makeup on and lives off daddies' money. And I get it. I get that people wouldn't take the time to get to know me and just take me on face value."

"You sound like it's something you've experience a lot."

Suddenly I'm swamped with bad memories, high school was hard, and college was no better, luckily, I found Kenny. She's the first real friend I've ever had.

"Yeah." I run my tongue along the back of my teeth. "In high school I thought my friends were my friends, until they leaked a photo of me passed out on my lawn with my top pulled above my bra, and I know it didn't get there on its own. That's why Kenny and I are so tight. We've kinda both had similar shitty experiences. I guess it was what we bonded over."

"I didn't realize—"

"That women can be brutal to other women? Shit yeah. Sometimes you need to have a thicker skin with your own gender. Add in the fact my family is a Blake… I'm automatically hated. But as Olivia Grace, my voice and my opinion suddenly means more than just a rich girl who is bored."

"And Olivia Grace was born."

"Olivia Grace was born." I nod. I don't know why I decided to share so much with him, most people think having a privileged last name automatically means my life is all rainbows and roses. "Now, if you wouldn't mind, I need to get back to filming." I sniff pointedly, looking between Ryder and the door, hoping he takes the hint. I lift the remote and press play.

"Not really, no. As current acting CEO, I'm happy right here."

My eyes almost bug out of my head. Acting CEO. Since when? If anything, it should be acting Co-CEO. I don't think Ryder Fallington has had to share anything in his life – Let alone a job title. Placing the half-open PR box in my lap, I say, "Do I look like I'm doing something that requires the imaginary CEO to be involved?"

Where is my stress ball when I need it?

Lifting my chin, I meet him dead on as I try to ignore the flutter in my stomach from staring into his chocolate eyes. This never happens around Kyle.

"There is nothing imaginary about me, Killer."

I shrug. "About certain parts of you, maybe not. Now do you mind? This video is already going to need some serious editing." I brush him away with a flick of my wrist.

Only, he doesn't listen and instead loosens his forest-green tie, runs a hand through his styled yet disheveled locks, and smiles at my camera like he was meant to be here and was just running late.

"What're you doing?" I ask.

"Trying to make sure the camera has my good side — what does it look like?"

My lips form an O shape and my body goes on high alert at his closeness, but quickly recovers. "It looks like you might be high on something," I mumble out of the corner of my mouth.

"What was that?" he asks.

"Nothing," I reply, pinching the bridge of my nose and

already feeling the low thrum of a headache forming behind my eyes.

"You have a bit of lipstick — " He circles the side of his chin.

"What, where?" I flick my eyes to him.

Oh no, it's like video three all over again. I thought over-lining my lips with red lipstick would look totally amazing, but all it did was make me look like a drunk clown.

"Here." Ryder swipes his thumb just below the corner of my lips, his touch surprisingly gentle.

"Thanks," I whisper, my lip tingling from the feel of his thumb.

Ryder has made it clear he isn't budging, so after clicking play, I pick up right where I left off. I can always just edit him out.

His brows lower in a frown. "How does that work?"

Rolling my eyes, I draw in a breath, here we go. We're going to have a big problem with Ryder running Glam Co if he doesn't even know how to send a parcel. "This here is my address." I point to the sticker. "Other companies put together these boxes and send them to me and other influencers — that is called PR." I make sure to annunciate the *P* and *R*.

"I get that, Killer, but I mean with you working for Glam Co — isn't it a conflict of interest?"

I swallow the lump in my throat, it can be, I just had hoped he wouldn't have thought so. As the Co-CEO he is well within his rights to impose a no-Glam-Co rule, which I hope he doesn't. My dad never did as long as I never explicitly dropped trade secrets on camera — which so far, I haven't. I don't want to give up Make Me. I've been on it for so long, it's almost like an extension of who I am. "No one online knows anything about my involvement with Glam Co. *I keep Livvy Blake separate from Olivia Grace.*"

If I expected Ryder to have a profound reaction, like I'd just told him my biggest secret — which I did — he doesn't. His face remains the same impassive mask as he slowly nods, tucking that card away for later.

I fool myself for a second into thinking maybe I can actually trust Ryder and what I initially thought of him may be all wrong. He isn't such a bad guy. After all — we just want the same thing, which has accidentally put us on opposing sides. Crossing my fingers under my chair, I hope that means he will keep my secret.

"Do I just hand you the parcels?" he asks, changing the subject.

"You're not going to leave, are you?" I run my tongue along the back of my teeth.

"I'm really not," he replies.

"That means you will be in the shot. You know that, right?"

He smiles and winks. Fighting him on this is futile. "Make sure you catch my good side, Killer."

"Yeah," I breathe. God he's sexy when he winks. No. Livvy. Stop. you can't think of him in that way. "If you want, you can open them so it's easier for me to just pull the product out and talk about it." I hand Ryder the small box cutter I keep in my desk drawer.

"Can do." He grabs a few parcels and lines them up on my desk before cutting into them, while I turn back to the camera with a smile on my face.

"Hey, Gracites, I have a special guest joining me for the rest of the unboxing. This is . . ." I look at Ryder. Definitely not my boss. My work colleague? Yeah, no. Given no one knows I'm going to inherit Glam Co, it's essential I keep Olivia Grace the Make Me sensation and Livvy Blake the soon to be CEO of Glam Co separate. Clearing my throat, I turn back to the camera. "This is my friend Ryder, and he is helping me today with all the hard labor of cutting open the packages." I nod, trying to convince myself of the excuse.

After taking the first box Ryder hands me, I select one of the lip glosses and excitedly sniff the doe foot brush. "Ooh, this one smells like cherry." I swipe it along my bottom lip and smack my lips together in an overexaggerated gesture, trying to get a feel of the gloss.

Ryder's nose scrunches. "I hate glosses — it makes kissing feel tacky." He clasps my wrist in his much bigger hand and brings the brush to his nose before giving it a sniff. "The cherry smell isn't bad; I've smelled worse on other girls. There was this one girl, Colette — " He shudders. "Now that lip gloss smelled like straight-up chemicals, but this one I could get around."

I sit rooted in my chair; arm frozen still holding the gloss to him.

When Ryder sat down to be in the video, I thought I could get him to just hand me the packages and cut him out when I do the editing. But to hear him actually review product? My body starts to feel all warm and fuzzy, and I find myself holding back a smile that's trying to break free. Kyle would never. The corners of my lips start to pull into a grin as excitement bubbles in my stomach. Is it me who's high, not him?

Ryder hands me more packages and gives more of his brutal opinions, and somewhere between all that I start to have fun. Kyle never wants to be a part of my videos; in fact, he gets mad if I ask him. He says Glam Co should be my priority, not being Olivia Grace. That an 'influencer' isn't even a real career, and I shouldn't waste my time on it. But with Ryder, it's easy to be Olivia Grace. I have more fun testing makeup than I have had in a long time.

"Last one." Ryder holds up the package from Glam Co excitedly. I wipe away the bit of concealer on the side of his cheek — the gesture is so intimate I don't realize I'm doing it until I finish swiping the makeup wipe. Ryder's eyeline dips to my boobs pressed against his forearm before looking back up at me, his stare heated. My body lights up under his gaze. For a second, the camera melts away and all that exists in the room is him and I. Casually crossing one leg over the other to stop the throbbing between my legs.

My leg grazes his under the table. "Sorry." I jump away like I've been electrocuted. *Stupid body overreacting.* Well, that's what I convince myself it is.

Ryder's throat bobs as a weak smile crosses his lips. "This Glam Co one looks interesting." His gaze darts toward the camera and he opens the parcel, while I take a deep breath and try to compose myself.

Ah, poo. It seems Ryder Fallington is taking over my company as well as my body.

CHAPTER THIRTEEN

Livvy

They love him.

Like *win the Make Me award for creator of the year* kind of love him.

Like *if he doesn't turn up in your next video, we will boycott your channel* love him. My brain stutters struggling to process what is happening.

My audience.

My people.

My Gracites.

The channel which I have spent countless hours culturing, sharing, and nurturing LOVES RYDER FALLINGTON.

This has to be a bad dream.

More comments continue to pour in. I didn't really expect the video with Ryder to do that well, but its already surpassed five million views in four hours. None of my videos have ever gone this viral. And the comments — the comments. I rest my forehead in the palm of my hand. They're wild.

Ryder honestly makes this video.

We need more Ryder.

I'm totally buying that gloss purely because Ryder said he liked it.

Olivia, you've been holding out on us!

Ryder's opinions are actually the best.

Can we have a Q and A with Ryder?

I need this lip gloss now.

Where the fuck has sexy Ryder been this whole time?

That comment has four hundred likes. Every time I refresh the page, the counter climbs higher. My phone buzzes on my desk with Kendall's name flashing on the screen.

KENDALL
Girl, you're going viral.

I want to write back *yeah, but not for the right reasons.*

Followed by a message from Anders. Since he and his brother, Ares, created Make Me, it's not surprising he would know when I went viral.

ANDE
Vivi, look at you go. Ares and I will need to get you a new plaque soon.

The comment would usually have a smile pulling at my lips. But this is all for the wrong reasons — for the wrong Fallington reason.

ME

LMAO

That's all I can think to reply back. It sure beats Crying My Ass Off.

The next comment pings through Make Me.

Can we make Ryder a regular for unboxings?

Second that.

This is unbelievable.

My phone flashes with a message from Kyle. My spirits already begin to lift at the sight of his name.

KYLE

Can't. Have lacrosse.

I close my eyes and rest my head against the chair as my mood takes a dive. *Could the day get any worse?*

Powering off my computer — I need to stop looking at my comment section or rather the glowing praise Ryder is receiving — I hit dial on Kendall's name.

"I think I need to close down my Make Me account," I say the moment she picks up the phone.

"Don't be silly," Kendall replies.

"They love him, Ken." I whack my palm into my forehead. "And now I'm going to lose Glam Co and my channel and everything I've worked hard for and that leaves me with nothing. You know what that makes me? Washed up at twenty-five. But hey, at least I know how to apply winged eyeliner well . . . I have nothing." I sniff tears already building behind my eyes, my breaths shallowing out as an invisible hand feels like its tightening around my throat. "I'll have to move in with Devin. Can you imagine? She will treat me like I'm Quasimodo's uglier cousin — only allowed to come out for an hour every second weekend." I blink rapidly as the burn of tears sting the corners of my eyes.

"Woah, woah, woah. Back it up a second there. Since when did you lose Glam Co?"

"I don't know, somewhere in my melt down." I exhale, wiping the snot ball running down my nose on my sleeve. I'm being dramatic, but right now I think dramatics is warranted. "I haven't…yet."

"So then why are you telling yourself you have? That thought process isn't going to help you."

I nod. *She has a point.*

"And who said anything about you moving in with Devin?"

The hand around my throat begins to loosen as I start taking deeper breaths.

"And why would you close down your Make Me channel? You've spent years building it. Your community loves you, Liv," she continues, debunking my worries.

"But they think Ryder's hot." My throat hurts as more silent tears trail down my cheeks.

"Sweetie, he is hot."

Her bluntness shocks me. I need more kid gloves and less reality check at the moment, but Kendall is serving it to me how it is. "I just feel like my walls are already closing in on me with all the pressure surrounding Glam Co. I don't want to lose Make Me to him too."

"It's not necessarily a bad thing — it helps you to get more views."

"Why does he have to be so hot?" I grumble into the phone.

"Karma," she replies, and I agree. It has to be Karma. Having a hot enemy who you work with has to be Karma's finest form of revenge.

I've been sitting in my car for a solid five minutes trying to compose myself as I teeter between having a giant, ugly cry moment or screaming and raging against the steering wheel. *They don't love you anymore, Livvy. The instant you show up without Ryder in tow you will lose your whole audience.* The dark voice in my head continues to grow, making itself louder and louder with each horrible thought. *Ryder is everything you aren't — it's clear from that one simple video. You could never go viral like that.*

"Ugh." My cheeks burn as I try to quiet the voice — the death grip it has on me makes my body shake. "I can do this." I take a few deep breaths, softening the voice with each exhale. "I can do this." I say with finality and the voice becomes silent.

I fix myself up, wiping the streak of mascara that is smudged under my lashes and fix the loose strands of hair that are sticking up around the crown of my head. "I can do this," I repeat with more force helping push me out of the car and inside our apartment.

My phone rings just as elevator doors open to my floor.

"Fricken hell," I groan, I don't need a psychic to tell me who it will be. "Hello, Dad," I answer. He's calling for his weekly update and I don't have the energy to talk to him, but

I know if I don't answer he will just call again. At least if I'm going to cry, I can do it in my own house.

"How are things going at Glam Co?" Dad asks. Early retirement or, rather, forced retirement doesn't seem to be suiting him very well. He won't stop pestering me for updates.

"Fine." I shrug, opening my door and immediately dropping my bags to pick up MoMo.

"Just fine?" He presses for more information.

"I mean, nothing has burned down; Ryder doesn't know contour from concealer, so I would say it's not going too badly."

"Wonderful. Remember, if Ryder Fallington wins, you can kiss your teen line goodbye." His voice makes my nerves tingle and not in a good way.

I harden my stare; it's not the first time Dad has used my teen line as a way to control me. It's like a dangling carrot he keeps over my head because he knows just how much I want it.

"Hopefully the board will come to their senses and in six-months' time, they will name me CEO." Cutting the conversation short, I say, "I've got to go. I'm meeting Anders for dinner."

Lucky for me, Dad doesn't know Anders is in Havenville.

"Liv?" Kendall calls, pulling me away from my train of thought. Since the call from my dad, I've been more distracted than I care to admit, and buried myself in Glam Co work.

"In here," I call, sliding farther down the couch. After opening the proofs for our upcoming product launch, I freeze. Scanning the document twice, my eyes tighten as my nostrils flare — someone fucked with my product launch. These are not the designs we spoke about three months ago when I created this special-edition collection. My eyebrows pull down farther than my preventative botox should allow as I continue clicking through the report. My lips pull into a tight line as I read on. Why are we changing our packaging printing house?

Kendall appears next to me. "What, huh?" I say, shaking the fog from my head.

"I said is Anders still in town? We should go to Club Trix together Saturday if he is? Ooooh" — she claps her hands — "let's book a booth next to Ryder."

I shake my head. "No, he messaged that he had to go back to London," I reply, only half-listening to her.

"I can't believe he came to visit you at Glam Co and didn't see me." She pouts.

Wiggling my eyebrows, I tap my finger to my chin. "Hey, didn't you say something about your sister being in London this weekend?"

Kendall snickers. "One of these days, Anders is going to actually tell you to shove it with the crappy dates you set him up on."

"Hey," I reply, resting my hand on my chest in mock hurt. "He's the brother I never had. It's only fair I do my duty in finding him the perfect woman."

Kendall pats me on the head, "If you say so," and walks away.

I turn my attention back to the email from Ryder. My muscles tighten scanning the message. He has tagged half the marketing team in this email.

@Olivia These proofs are to be approved through me before we send them to the printer. We need a new quote; I believe this is too high.

@Cohen this collection needs to be rethought before we commit to it. All future collections must first be signed off by me.

"Are you fucking kidding me?" I growl, the vein pounding at the base of my neck. "He wouldn't know a good collection if I painted his ass with it."

Ryder has only been with Glam Co a couple of days and he's already stopped production on our collection, beads of angry sweat form on my brow.

The collection the team has worked on for months has just blown up in a puff of smoke. This is really, really bad. This is going to cost the company hundreds of thousands of dollars and potentially our contracts with Kosmedika.

That absolutely cannot happen.

Not on my watch.

Going to the company directory, I cross my fingers and hope his details have been uploaded. Without giving myself time to think about what I'm doing or the consequences, I plug his number into my phone and shoot off a message.

ME

> Just what the fuck do you think you're doing?

CHAPTER FOURTEEN

Ryder

Facing the log-in screen for Make Me, my eyes flick to Becks.

"Once you do this, there is no turning back," he reminds me for the second time. I rub my temple; well aware this could be bordering on creepy.

A few hours ago, I didn't know what the fuck Make Me was.

"I'm in too deep now to back out."

"I'd imagine she's going to be out for your blood. You've completely fucked with her launch schedule and then this."

"Yeah," a satisfied smile tugs at my lips. When I happened across the email from Cohen this afternoon, I realized what a missed opportunity it would be to not flex my muscles a bit more. "I can only hope she is."

"Glam Co is one thing, Ryder. But Make Me is her domain," Becks stresses to me again, because apparently, he doesn't think the message is getting across. I need to figure out what makes her tick, and I can't do that unless I really get to know her, and from what it looks like Make Me is a huge part of her personality. I roll my eyes, "It's not like I'm going to start making videos. I'm using this purely for the purpose of monitoring her videos."

"Isn't that bordering on weird?"

I hold my hand up to halt whatever he's about to say next, "Don't give me the lecture on creepy. Should I remind you about the cart girl? You're the reason we can't go golfing at the Cheshire Shore course every second Saturday."

"Hey, that was a misunderstanding, and you know it."

"Doesn't matter what I think." I shake my head. "There is video evidence of you fucking her in her cart, violating the number one club rule. Both the board and her manager agreed. Your kids are banned from ever getting a membership and they aren't even born yet."

Becks grumbles and crosses his arms over his chest.

I start typing in my — I'm calling it my pen name. *Midnight Crystals*. Isn't that what people do in these situations to remain anonymous?

Becks squints as he watches me type in the name. "That sounds like a stripper's name."

"And?" I stare at him with one eyebrow raised. "Are strippers not allowed to have Make Me accounts?"

Becks snorts. "No, I'm just saying if you're going for under-the-radar vibes, all you need is to add a profile photo of My Little Pony and we will have the FBI on our door wondering if you're a child groomer."

Stabbing my finger into the delete button, a little harder

than necessary. I purse my lips into a hard line. "Okay, Mr. Expert, what name should I use then?"

"How about Rachel Fallout? That way it's similar to your name without being too out there."

I type the name and stare at it for a few seconds, testing it out. It's not bad. Not over the top and just subtle enough — it could work. In a new tab, I open Pinterest and write 'girl makeup' into the search bar. I click on a photo which shows half a torso and glossy pink lips. Perfect. It's anonymous without being weird. I check with Becks to make sure the photo is 'Becks approved', before I tick activate. Then I go on Livvy's channel and hit the little 'follow channel' button.

Becks blows a sharp whistle. "She has a huge following."

The knot of my tie feels like it's cutting off my air circulation. Hooking my finger inside, I loosen the silk noose.

He's not wrong — I know nothing about makeup and I know the kind of influence her large following would have. Bigger than I thought when I sat down to be in her video. *Fuccccckkkk*. I always knew she was going to be a fun challenge, but this does add another layer to her. Well played, Livvy. Well played.

"What's this video?" Becks points to the computer screen to her latest video which is sitting at more than six million views.

My eyes practically bug out of my head reading the number.

"Is that you in the photo?"

Hovering my mouse over the video enlarges the thumbnail photo, and yep it shows me and Livvy. My lips part. "She uploaded it?"

I thought she would edit me out before posting it.

"What do you mean she uploaded it?" Becks questions, eyeing me.

"I found her with a mountain of boxes in her office, and I just kind of sat down and started opening them." I shrug.

"You just sat down?" Becks repeats, and I nod, unsure why he thinks it's such a strange thing to do.

"Yep, it was actually fun." A grin pulls across my lips before I can stop it remembering filming with her. "I learned a bit about makeup. Concealer goes under the eyes and contour goes on cheekbones," I report, proud of myself.

"Click," Becks announces excitedly as he moves my hand onto the play button.

The intro to Livvy's video blares through the computer speakers. Every few seconds, a little text box comes up with comments from her followers.

"Dude, they love you."

"I know." I laugh, eyes widening as comment after comment pops up mentioning me.

"I think you're also the reason that gloss is going to sell out the moment it hits shelves," Becks laughs, clapping me on the shoulder. I didn't even realize I had influence, but apparently, I do?

Maybe running a makeup company isn't going to be as hard as I thought. My phone vibrates in my pocket. Straightening my leg, I reach into my pocket to fish it out.

UNKNOWN NUMBER

Just what the fuck do you think you're doing?

Recognition slams into me.

Livvy Blake.

The devious minx somehow got my number and is now texting me. Well, I guess that means I can have a little fun with her now.

ME

> Ms. Blake, it's wildly inappropriate to be messaging me on this number.

The little grey dots appear in an instant and I can almost feel her anger vibrating through the phone.

I quickly save her name into my contacts.

MS. BLAKE

> No, it's not, you potato head. *potato emoji*

A grin pulls at my lip. I've never been called a potato head before.

ME

> I didn't think our level of acquaintance had progressed to name calling . . .

Livvy Blake has some bite and I'm loving the thrill it's giving me to watch her reaction when I mess with her.

"Who are you talking to?" Becks eyes me, no doubt noticing the complete shift in my mood.

"Livvy."

MS. BLAKE

> It's not name calling if it's true. Why did you send that email?

> **ME**
> I send many emails. You'll need to be more specific.

She sends through a photo of my email from earlier today about the product launch with her perfectly manicured finger flipping me off in front of it. I click my tongue to the roof of my mouth.

"What's so funny?" Becks tries to take my phone from my hands, but I quickly pocket it, annoyed, not wanting to share our little conversation with him.

"It's nothing. She is just talking about her Make Me video."

"Right." Becks nods, but he isn't buying my excuse at all. My phone continues to buzz in my pocket, but I leave it. I don't want to pull it out with Becks here in case he tries to sneak another look. I want to keep my relationship with Livvy kind of private. This little game with Livvy just became a lot more fun . . . more than I'd probably care to admit.

Zander and I meet our dad on the golf course. It's bittersweet, there will come a time when this isn't going to be possible anymore, so I take our golf days seriously while we can.

Zander is finishing up his stretching routine. From the direction of his stare, his attention is firmly set on the woman playing tennis on the courts next to the golf course. My playboy brother never seems to get the hint — not everyone is here for his pleasure. Although, I squint, something about the woman on the court seems vaguely familiar. She's a retired pro player.

Zander is probably going to get a hard-on when he realizes, if he hasn't already. My brother follows tennis like it's a religion.

"I will never get tired of watching women play tennis. They're much better than men. They prefer to actually play the game instead of just trying to send as many aces as possible down the line," Zander mumbles the tips of his ears turning red. His eyes follow the swish of a toned brunette's skirt as she pounces around the court, adding extra emphasis to the sway of her hips. Probably more for Zander's benefit than for the benefit of her shot.

"Zander," Dad grunts. "Quit ogling the tennis players. We're here to play golf."

"Is that . . ." Zander trails off. Yup, he has just realized that she is an ex-pro. "Fuck, I need to get my racket signed."

"Please don't get us banned from this place too," I grumble, slapping him on the back of the head. I don't think I can deal with having to drive more than two hours just to go to a 'local' golf course. Zander glares at me, rubbing the spot.

"You don't have your racket, jackass. Now let's play. Before they throw you out for fan-girling," I snap.

Dad snorts as his club makes a satisfied click with the tee. "It wasn't Becks' fault."

"We have a life ban, Dad. Our photos are on the wall with red sharpie *X's* on our faces." The apples pull tight on my cheeks.

"Becks had that one coming to him," Zander laughs as he places his ball on the tee.

"Try telling him that." I drawl, placing my club on my shoulder.

Zander takes his swing as my dad looks at me.

While my brother is trying to hit his ball, I open my Make Me DM before shooting a message off to Liv.

ME

Hey, Olivia Grace, I noticed you don't do brand collabs. Would you be interested in doing one with my friend's brand?

OLIVIA GRACE

Hey, Rachel. Thanks so much for the message and the follow! I don't do brand collabs, typically. I do accept PR. But those videos are usually just quick shows of new products being released. I am more than happy to do an in-depth try on and review of your friend's brand for free. I love supporting small businesses. Drop your friend's brand name and I will be happy to buy some products and try them in a Make Me video.

ME

Oh that's okay. She is happy to send to you. No need to buy.

OLIVIA GRACE

Well, your friend is super lucky to have you in their corner. What's the name of the brand?

Fuckkkkk. I leave the message on read.

"How is Glam Co coming along?" Dad not so subtly asks.

My eyes flick to meet his. I decided against telling him

about the *six months to prove yourself* clause — mostly because I don't want to upset him after getting his hopes up.

"That depends on who you ask," Zander blurts.

I slice him a glare, hoping to cut him off from finishing that sentence.

Zander meets my stare, not backing down.

Dad laughs, completely oblivious to the silent conversation between my brother and me. "Finally, we have the Blakes right where we want them."

Trading spots with my brother, I line my shot up just as Zander says, "I wouldn't say that, Dad. It seems the Blakes knew this day would come and now Ryder needs to prove he's capable." The sarcasm in his voice drips like toxic venom and completely throws my shot off.

Instead of the ball, I hit a nice lump of grass straight into the air. "Zander," I growl in warning. *Shut the fuck up or you will get my fist in your face.*

"What do you mean?" Dad's face turns ashen as he stares between us.

"It's nothing, Dad." I quickly try to calm the situation, but like a pot of boiling water threatening to spill over, Zander scoffs.

Not helping, dickhead.

"Ryder." The warning in Dad's voice should be enough to have me backing down, but I don't want to put this extra stress onto him — not now, not yet.

I don't take my eyes off Zander. My chest is rising and falling with each steady breath as I use the silence to convey that I want him to zip his overeager lips. He doesn't understand half the shit pushed in front of me because I'm the oldest. He will never know, and as much as I hate it, I also want to continue to shield him from it.

"Someone better tell me what is going on right now. Or I will call Simon fucking Blake myself."

I continue to hold my brother's stare.

"The Blakes knew about the clause this whole time and they were ready for it," he announces. He turns to address Dad fully. "Ryder has six months to prove to the board that he is worthy of being CEO or we lose Glam Co forever."

Dad swears and leaves us standing with the hot sun beating down on us.

"Fuck," I yell, throwing my golf club into the bag.

"He deserved to know, Ryder." Zander's voice is barely a whisper.

I can't even look at my brother right now. "He didn't need to find out like this," I reply, defeat heavy in my voice.

"Then how, Ryder? When he sees Simon at a charity function and he rubs it in his face that we finally got one over him? Or better yet when you let your dick win and you lose everything we have been working toward."

I don't bother with a reply.

"Ryder?" His voice is a plea, his breath coming in short pants. He knows he fucked up; but right now, he is the last person who deserves my comfort.

I follow my dad — needing to smooth things over.

"Dad," I call. My legs push harder, closing the distance between us, but he either doesn't hear me or chooses to ignore me as he walks toward the bar. "Dad," I call again, grabbing his arm.

"Tell me Zander made that whole thing up." His voice is as piercing as a freshly sharpened blade while his eyes reflect the hurt, he refuses to acknowledge.

I swallow the lump in my throat. My dad has only ever spoken to me like this once before. "I can't do that." I shake my head and release his arm.

Dad lets the comment sit in the air. He purses his lips. "Why didn't you tell me?"

"Honestly?"

"No, Ryder, please give me the dishonest version."

"This is why. I didn't want you to worry about something that you don't need to." I wave my arms in front of me, pointing between us.

"Ryder, everything you do is important to me. Every. Single. Fucking. Thing." Dad's cheeks turn red. "It's only ever been the three of us. We have never kept secrets before so why are you starting now? And with something that means as much to us as this?"

Running my hand through my hair, I try to calm the anger bubbling through my own veins. "I don't want to disappoint you, Dad. I promised you I will bring you Glam Co, and I will." I take a deep calming breath.

Dad wraps his arm around my neck and rests my forehead into his. "Of course, you will, son. I don't doubt that for a second. You will right this wrong done to the Fallingtons. I just hate that the Blakes always seem to have one up on us."

"They won't anymore," I promise, the words solidifying in the recesses of my bones. "I will do what I have to. I will get

Glam Co."

Dad moves away from me, the anger from before gone, a smile now gracing his lips. "I know you will, son." He pats my shoulder and makes his way into the bar to get a drink.

I blow out another steadying breath. I need to shake this attraction I have to Livvy before it costs me more than Glam Co.

She's a Blake, after all.

CHAPTER FIFTEEN

Livvy

Ryder Fucking Fallington. The name I've been cursing on repeat every half an hour for the last twenty-four hours. I'm not usually a swearer, but Ryder has turned me into one. I still can't believe he just imploded my whole schedule then turned around and took a day off work. Who the fuck does that after being all, 'I want the company' and 'I'm going to prove I'm the better boss' — blah, blah, blah?

Someone is shoveling horseshit as exotic moisturizer, and I am not buying it by the pound.

My desk has practically become a cheap, vibrating motel bed from the anger coursing through my system. How dare he go ahead and change our set schedule, and for no reason other than he thinks the price is too high. Maybe if he did some research on previous collections, he'd be aware of what our usual spend is. He would know that our cost on this collection is totally comparable. Apparently, *Mr. Forbes* thinks he knows better without opening a single report from Glam Co from the past three years. And makes monumental decisions like this and just expects us to find a new printer, with a snap of our fingers. The marketing team sets our collection schedule a year in advance, and for him to change the line up now so close to the launch date is an astronomical ask.

I have a damage-control meeting with Cohen in half an hour. If we don't supply a collection, we might just lose one of our biggest contracts with a department store. I can already feel an ulcer forming in my gut.

After clicking print on the last of the proofs I need to sign off on, I put all the documents in a folder and make my way to the conference room.

I open the door, "Of course," I grunt rolling my eyes at Ryder already sitting in his chair.

Why doesn't it surprise me he knew about this meeting? At this point, I'd guess he's monitoring my emails or something.

"Morning, Killer," his tone is too chirpy, it only irritates me more.

"Looks like someone bothered to get out of bed today," I snark. Already pissed off I can only speculate where his suddenly happy mood has come from. God, what now? Is he going to announce a whole brand name change?

Ryder sits back in his chair with his signature grin resting on his lips. "Thinking about me in bed now, Killer?"

I run my tongue along the back of my teeth, "As if." Of course, that's the only take away from my insult.

He winks at me. "As much as I love hearing you're thinking about me naked in bed — "

"What?" I gasp. "I never said that."

"And worrying about the thread count — which is a thousand, by the way. I like to have my bedsheets extra silky against my naked body — " he continues.

"Oh my god, stop," I interrupt him, cupping my forehead in the palm of my hand, hoping the ground will open up and swallow me whole. I'm already imagining the bulge of Ryder's arms when he is on top of me, pounding my brains out of me as I reach closer and closer to my O. My cheeks turn beet red and all I want is to sink down in the chair.

"Miss Blake, I would ask where your thoughts have gone but by the look on your face, I think I can tell. "

My gaze snaps to his and I shake the stupid vision from my head. The man is clearly delusional. Where is he even getting this stuff from? I do not have a look. If anything, my face is a picture of disgust.

"I'll just go." Cohen chooses that moment to interrupt our exchange and announce her presence, her eyes darting rapidly between us.

"No — " I yell louder than I mean to.

As Ryder says, "I think that's for the best."

Throwing Ryder a glare over my shoulder, I speak directly to Cohen, "We need to go through this right now. Or we could lose the contract with Kosmedika." Then I look at Ryder. "Kosmedika is a high-end beauty service boutique which houses some of the world's luxe beauty brands. Glam Co is one of them."

"I know what Kosmedika is. They are one of the leading stores for beauty and skin care. They have just opened a new location in Havenville. You don't need to mansplain it to me," Ryder deadpans.

I lean back in my seat, cocking my head to the side, my eyes slowly dragging down his body. Well, at least he understands the importance of the company he is trying to screw over.

"More like Livvy-splain." Cohen jokes, eyes darting between us as she no doubt senses the thick tension in the air. She takes a seat on the opposite side of the table to Ryder and me.

Ryder's eyes harden, but I don't back down, holding his rigid gaze. Opening the folder I brought with me, I glare at him while handing Cohen the proofs. "Glam Co has been using the same printer for thirty years. We've never had an issue with them."

Apparently, until now . . .

Cohen nods. "Livvy's right. From what I understand, they are the only printing house that can do the foiling around the edges of our packaging — it's a part of our signature branding." Cohen points to the proof of our design with a fleur foiled edging. Or maybe this is Ryder's way of showing he has no clue what Glam Co signature lines are? In that case, perhaps I should leak a certain email to a few board members . . .

"Why aren't we updating this look?" Ryder doesn't even glance at the proofs.

"Because we can't just 'update a look' without talking to Kosmedika. They're our biggest retailer and an integral part of our marketing campaign — they like it this way. If we want to revise this then we need to bring the amended design to the Kosmedika buyer, and they have to approve it. Besides, IF they do approve it, they probably won't run it until next year," I stress.

Ryder rubs this forefinger along his lip as he appears to let what Cohen and I are saying, sink in.

"If, and this is a really big IF, we want to bring forward a change in design, we need to think about it for next year. We can't change our schedule for this year. It was set eight months ago." I know Glam Co like the back of my hand, evidently a heck of a lot more than Ryder does. If this giant fuck up is anything to go by, I might actually be able to beat him at his own game after all.

Ryder scribbles a note down and reaches his hand out for the proofs in my hand.

Sweat coats my palms, as I hesitantly hand him the proofs and watch him scrawl his signature.

"There — signed off."

My tense muscles finally relax, relieved. Crisis averted — mostly. We're going to have to do some serious groveling to the printer to make sure they can still get this out on time even though the proofs are nearly a week late.

Sensing the urgency, Cohen grabs the signed-off proofs and leaves.

I push the chair back and stand.

"Oh and, Livvy." Ryder's voice has me stopping the visible tension in his shoulders match my rigid muscles.

"Yeah?"

"Don't ever question me or my whereabouts in front of employees again." The cold venom in his voice makes me physically recoil as he pushes past me, leaving me standing there gaping at his retreating back. Quite frankly Ryder Fallington can go fuck himself.

After kicking my heels off, I let my stocking-clad feet relax into the fluffy carpet in my office. The stiffness of my heels making my feet ache.

'You need to make the board realize he isn't capable of running a makeup company,' Kendall's words repeat in my head. Given today's display, we're well on our way to proving I'm the better fit. Remember you're a shark, Livvy — start acting like it. A wicked idea springs to mind, as my computer dings with a notification from Make Me. Huh? A new comment from a video I posted two months ago. *Weird. But also, not out of the ordinary.*

> **RACHEL FALLOUT**
>
> GIRRLL, THIS LOOK IS INSPIRRED. I NEED MORE RED-LIP LOOKS.

I stare at the screen, blinking rapidly. Rachel Fallout, this is the new follower who messaged me about her friend's cosmetic brand. When I asked her about the brand, she never replied. Which was kind of creepy. I wave off the hairy feeling settling in my stomach. I make it a point to reply to every single Gracite — no matter how weird or strange their comments are. Even if it's just four red hearts, I'll still do it. After clicking reply, I start typing back:

> **ME**
>
> Thanks, gorgeous. I'm planning to upload a red-lip tutorial later this week. Be sure to click the bell so you will be notified. X

While my page is open, I do a quick check that the video I pre-uploaded is ready to go when my phone pings.

My eyebrows raise, and despite myself my core clenches. After how Ryder left the meeting, I was sure he was mad at me. Color me surprised, he's messaging me and something so left field.

> **RYDER**
>
> What made you want to start Make Me?

> **ME**
>
> Is this Ryder or has someone stolen your phone?

> **RYDER**
>
> I didn't know you're a comedian as well as Glam Co's R and D expert.

> **ME**
>
> I believe you're forgetting. I'm also the Co-CEO

> **RYDER**
>
> Trust me. It's not something I can forget in a hurry.

Make Me

RYDER

Are you planning to avoid my question?

ME

Depends, are you avoiding mine?

RYDER

You haven't asked one...

ME

Where were you yesterday

RYDER

Golfing with my brother and dad. We have this tradition, and I couldn't pause it. Not when my dad was having a good day.

Having a good day? What does that mean?

ME

I started Make Me because I have such a huge love for this industry. Nothing makes me feel more special than when I read a message from someone who has tried a technique of mine and found it's changed their life.

RYDER

I can imagine it would bring a lot of attention.

> **ME**
>
> It can. Like everything though you need to take the good with the bad. For the most part I try to block out the negative people. I love to do a lot of charity work with my skills. Around prom time I bring bags of new unused makeup to schools for girls and guys to be able to use and then keep and I run a giveaway to give two people from each school a free makeover. I actually don't post those looks ever. The people who win those are free to choose to do what they wish, but I don't use that as clout or to gain attention. I give back — it's a lesson my nanna really wanted me to learn. My nanna was my hero. Do you have someone you look up to?

RYDER

> My dad is my hero. He recently was diagnosed with MS. He used to be the strongest man in the world. Watching him have trouble walking upstairs now sucks so much. It's why our golf days are sacred to me.

A lump forms in my throat, he was golfing with his dad, that's why he missed work. Something tugs at my heart, and I rub the spot in my chest. Pancreatic cancer took Nanna. It was so quick but watching her deteriorate was one of the worst experiences. I miss her so much sometimes.

> **ME**
>
> Oh, I'm sorry to hear that . . . That must really suck.

Make Me

RYDER

More than I can put into words. A lot of the time I feel like if I don't do certain things, he won't be proud of me.

ME

I'm sure your dad is more proud of you than you realize. *love heart emoji*

RYDER

Are you close to your parents?

ME

No, not really. As the first born, I tend to shoulder a lot more than what my younger sister does. Which I suppose makes it harder on our relationship than anything else. My dad's favorite hobby is finding ways to pit us against each other. I wish Devin would spend less time looking for ways to hate me, and more time being a team with me. It would be nice to have someone on my team again.

I don't know what made me write that. This conversation has taken a turn down baggage lane and I need to lighten it before I burst into tears. I can't let our little session change my plans; he's just trying to find common ground but I'm not going to let that change my goal.

"Shit," I squeal at the time. I quickly pull myself together, I've been talking to Ryder for way too long. I put my phone on Do not disturb and turn my attention back to Glam Co work.

My devious little plan starts to formulate, I'm not about to let our conversation sway me from my goal. I pick up my discarded Louboutin pumps and wince as I slide my feet back into my new red-souled beauties. Fuck. Why are new shoes such a bitch to wear in?

Grabbing my sketch book, I walk into Ryder's office like I own the place — which I low-key *almost* do. If Ryder wants to create new packaging, that's exactly what's going to happen and I'm going to let everyone know exactly who came up with this *genius* idea.

"You know." I add an extra sway into my hips, tapping my pen to my lips and praying the wince of pain from each step doesn't show on my face. "I think you might be onto something." I stop on the opposite side of his desk.

Ryder's eyes track up and down my body before turning back to his computer screen. In a bored tone, he says, "You have a pen mark on your lip."

I freeze. He's just trying to get into my head. "N-no I dont?" I stutter.

Ryder doesn't take his eyes from the screen. "Just a lil." He circles his lips, and I begin furiously rubbing at the spot.

Shit. I pull the pen away from my lip to find the blue ink has dribbled down the side. Rubbing it on the back of my hand, I try to remove the pen mark. I just ooze sexy; I mentally roll my eyes at myself.

Ryder sighs, pushes away from his desk, and closes the little distance between us. He bats my hand away as he rubs his thumb along my bottom lip.

"Thanks." My cheeks burn. I continue staring at the spot

on the carpet like it's the most fascinating thing I've ever seen.

"No problem. You really needed the help."

I don't think I'll ever get over how humble this man is.

"And what's this about me being a genius?"

"I didn't — " My eyes snap up to meet Ryder's, currently dancing with mirth.

Ryder taps the tip of my nose with his index finger. "It's what I heard."

Batting his hand away, I roll my eyes and release a deep sigh. Why am I not surprised he heard that? "And the delusion hits a new level," I grumble under my breath and take a seat opposite Ryder's computer.

Ryder pulls his chair out and sits, loosely clasping his hands over his head. "One of these days you won't visit me for business." The corner of his lips twitch into the ghost of a smile, making me squirm in the chair under his heated gaze.

Clearing my throat, I open the sketch pad I brought. "I think you might be right . . ."

Ryder delivers me a cool, expectant expression.

". . . about the packaging. It's time we put a new spin on Glam Co."

"What made you change your mind?"

"I was looking back through the proofs in the email, and I realized they represent the old Glam Co. We need to usher in the new." I tap my pen on the sketch pad. "Let's figure out a new design and get some mockups of it."

Ryder's eyes light up, and I almost feel bad — almost.

"I was thinking the gold foiling is really dated." He grabs a box from our usual line and points to the areas he thinks could need improving.

My eyes narrow. "But we are known for the gold foiling."

"And I think the boxes are too chunky," he continues.

The irritation bubbles under my skin, making me itchy. I'm going to take great pleasure in sending these through to Kosmedika.

"And I think your forehead is too big," I reply, trying to rein in my sharp claws, but they are getting away from me.

"Livvy," Ryder says my name through clenched teeth.

I pout my bottom lip. "You're right, sorry."

"The color is so I'm-a-pre-pubescent-fourteen-year-old-girl-on-myspace."

My posture stiffens. "I didn't realize there was such a name for a color. I'm so glad we could get that vibe across though. I guess that's why most of our sales are to single white dudes in their fifties who live in their mom's basements." I want to flick his eyelid like an elastic band.

"Livvy," Ryder groans, his thumb and forefinger resting on the bridge of his nose. Clearly, I'm testing his patience.

Maybe I'm having a little more fun doing this than I should.

CHAPTER SIXTEEN

Ryder

This woman is beyond infuriating. "I thought you were here to talk about a new design." Grinding my teeth, I take a deep breath; I need to get my emotions in check before I say something I shouldn't.

"I am." She pouts her bottom lip.

I blow out a less-than-calming breath as my phone beeps and Cecelia's voice comes through the loudspeaker. "Ryder, I'm ordering you sushi for lunch; it should be here soon."

I don't even think twice before clicking my finger on the speaker. "Make that for two." Livvy isn't going anywhere in a hurry.

She tosses her hair over her shoulder. "A little bit presumptuous, aren't you?"

"I can see this is going to take a while and I think it would be rude for me to eat my tuna roll in front of you," I reply.

"What if I don't like sushi?" She quirks one eyebrow.

My skin tingles, I'm beginning to love it when she

challenges me. "You can watch me eat two tuna rolls in front of you then." Clicking the button, I add, "Cecelia, please make sure you order whatever Livvy's favorite dish is too."

With lunch now taken care of, I return to the reason she walked through my door. "I'm all good with having a teen line. I've seen the proposal you sent your dad. I actually think we should get one — we're missing out on a huge part of the market."

From the Glam Guide Cecelia gave me, it's clear there are a few areas Glam Co could expand on. I'm not a makeup guru like Livvy, but from the small amount of diving I've done into Glam Co, we're neglecting an opportunity here.

"Do you really think so?" she asks.

I don't miss the hopefulness in her voice or how she hides her shaking hands under my desk.

I nod. It's actually a brilliant idea.

Livvy's eyes are like a window straight to her soul.

They light up over everything I'm saying. "Before we do the teen line we need to rebrand with fresher packaging."

A smile splits her lips. "Agreed." She nods.

My phone buzzes as the screen lights up with a notification from Make Me.

Olivia Grace has released a new video.

Quickly pocketing it, I look back up at Livvy, hoping she didn't see anything.

"Your bed buddy missing you already?" The snark in her voice is unmissable. Is that jealousy I'm sensing?

Rolling my palm over my mouth, I use all my willpower to resist the urge to snort. If only she knew whose message I was looking forward to. "I think we should change to the cylinder look too," I continue, deliberately ignoring her comment. I hide my laugh when a dark look passes across her face as I resume outlining different changes I'd make and Livvy writes them down.

"I think that should do it," she announces, putting the finishing touches to the sketch. "I just need your signature." She flips the A3 sketch book around, leaning over the table and pushing her glorious tits directly in my line of sight.

My mouth starts to water when I get a peek of her black-lace bra. The distinct scent of jasmine and soft lilies wafts over me. It's the scent I've come to know as Livvy, and my dick becomes instantly hard from it. Discretely, I adjust myself under the desk and use the art pad in Livvy's hands as a distraction. Livvy has perfectly sketched what I had in my head. Without thinking, I grab my pen and sign off on the rough sketch.

"Hey, man, have you seen my girl — " The sound of a guy's voice interrupts us.

Livvy and I turn toward the source.

"Kyle." She jumps up, her cheeks flashing pink like she is embarrassed to be caught in the same room as me.

"Kyle?" I repeat, eyeing the guy. 'Kyle' looks like the poster boy for the Polo Ralph Lauren summer collection.

"I didn't realize you were in here." Kyle's lips thin as he surveys me and the room.

Kyle didn't realize I was sitting in my own office? Clearly a smart one.

Turning to my schedule, I flick through the notifications but don't find anything about an upcoming meeting — and I haven't seen him in the office before. *Why is this fucker in my office staring at Livvy like that?*

"Nice to meet you." I stand and cross the distance to Kyle in a few strides. "I'm Ryder Fallington, the new CEO of Glam Co."

I offer my hand, but Kyle looks down at it and back up and me.

"You've probably heard of me. Kyle Edwards, I'm interning over at Faluccino Investments."

I tuck my hand into my pocket and purse my lips. "Can't say I have. The intern program is very intense there, most don't make it. Good job getting in."

Kyle's lips pull into a sneer, I must've hit a nerve. Clearing my throat, I glance between Livvy and Kyle — the tension in my office is becoming thicker by the second.

"How do you know Livvy?" I ask.

"We've been on a few da — "

Livvy is cut off when Kyle replies with, "I'm her boyfriend."

"Boyfriend?" She gasps.

At the same time, I say, "Boyfriend?" My eyebrows hit my hairline as I flick my eyes up to meet Livvy's.

This guy is Livvy's boyfriend? This is the guy Livvy goes for? He looks like he would spend more time worrying about the seams of his shirt being ironed straight than anything else. He oozes try hard vibes. Most importantly, Livvy has never once mentioned her boyfriend.

"Sorry, I didn't realize Livvy had plans with you. Otherwise, I would have scheduled a meeting," I say, not really caring if I've ruined their lunch date.

"Why are you here, Kyle?" Livvy asks, her eyes darting from Kyle to me. An irritated look passes over her face before she plasters on a fake smile. I've known Livvy only a short time, but I can tell the difference between her real smile and this one. This one is completely devoid of the shadow of a dimple in her cheek, and her eyes are missing their sparkle. If he really meant a lot to her, wouldn't she be more excited he's interrupting her workday? From her expression, she's as surprised to see him here as I am.

"I have an hour spare, and I came to see how things were progressing in the office. You know, because you messaged me the other night and I was at lacrosse." He folds his arms over his chest.

"Lunch is — " Cecelia pushes her way past Kyle, the brown, recyclable bag with *Dear Kyoto* stamped on the front in her hand. "Kyle." Cecelia smiles, but it seems forced.

I'm not the only one who doesn't like Polo Boy.

"Thanks, Cecelia." I grab the bag from her.

She nods and quickly leaves.

Sensing the pissing match Kyle is wanting to have, I turn around and place our lunch on the desk before eyeing Kyle over my shoulder. "You're welcome to stay for lunch. I only ordered for two though."

His nostrils flare. For some reason annoying him is more fun than it should be.

Kyle reaches out, grabbing Livvy around the waist, making her teeter on her high heels, causing her to tumble into his chest. She stiffens in his arms and puts her hand against him, like she's trying to add space between them. Not what I would expect a loving couple to do.

"Maybe we can meet for dinner later?" Livvy places a quick, sterile kiss on Kyle's cheek and attempts to remove his arm from her body. "Ryder and I have a few more things to discuss, so we're probably going to just eat while we go through everything."

Kyle nods, his hand touching the curve of Livvy's ass through her skirt in a possessive gesture. He gives it a generous squeeze. My eyes focus on the movement. I grind my teeth together, confused at the weird spike of jealousy coursing through my veins.

"Don't be late, Olivia," he whispers in her ear, loud enough for me to hear, and turns to leave, her eyebrows pulled down in confusion. "It's a quality people don't like."

What a fucking moron. I'm almost surprised he didn't lower his zipper and piss all over Livvy's leg. He really wants to make it clear Livvy is his. *Livvy can be as late as she wants, if you truly loved her, you would know that's just Livvy,* I bite my tongue to stop the retort from escaping. It's not my place to step between Livvy and whatever relationship she has with *Kyle*.

A strange look passes across her face. "Ummm, that's Kyle."

"I got that," I say, casually leaning against the desk and crossing my arms over my chest.

"He doesn't usually visit me in the office, but I'm guessing we're due for a '*relationship*' talk soon." She motions around the room, letting the statement waft away. From the blasé way she refers to Kyle and their relationship, I don't think it's as serious as Kyle thinks it is.

"Or maybe he was making his claim on you known."

"Don't be silly." She waves me off and takes her seat, diving straight into the bag from Dear Kyoto. "Trust me. Kyle is too interested in himself worry about who is interested in me."

"Looked like you and Polo Boy were pretty cozy to me."

"I wouldn't say that. I don't even consider us dating, I don't know where he pulled that boyfriend crap from," she laughs.

I let that comment slide. Kyle's hand on Livvy's ass suggested they're more than PG.

Livvy pulls out a plate with sushi ōmakase all cut up in a nice, neat row. "Dear Kyoto is kind of my favorite restaurant."

"Mine too," I confess as I take my seat.

Livvy places another tray in front of me and she makes up a soy sauce and wasabi mix in between us to dunk our sushi in. After snapping my wooden chopsticks, I pick up a sushi and dunk it into the soy mix.

"Kyle hates Dear Kyoto; he only goes when I pretty much beg him to," Livvy admits, dunking her own piece of sushi before placing it in her mouth.

"Sucks to be him," I grumble as I swallow another piece. "He's probably too busy wondering what position to fuck you in, to worry about food."

Livvy's eyes widen as she chokes on her food. I lean over the desk and pound on her back. I didn't expect her to be so surprised. I hand her a bottle of water. She continues to gasp and sputter after taking a sip.

After a few calming breaths, she says, "He doesn't — " She tries to buy more time by popping another two pieces of sushi into her mouth, causing her cheeks to expand. Swallowing she chokes out, "We don't," her cheeks turn that adorable shade of pink.

"Fuck?" I finish for her, curious why she is all of a sudden being so shy.

She gives a small nod, her cheeks turning from pink to sun-ripened-tomato red.

"Why the fuck not?" The sushi I just ate rolls in my stomach. I quickly recover. "Are you saving yourself for marriage or something? Because I can respect that."

"No." She shakes her head. Polo Boy acts like he wants to fuck her, and she isn't saving herself for marriage. What the fuck is wrong with this dude?

"Do you not like sex?" I can also respect that.

"What. Me?" she snorts. "No. I love sex. I'm still craving my birthday 'O'. It's ummm Kyle . . ." she grunts.

I cut her off with my laugh. Livvy is a knockout. Polo Boy must be hiding a huge secret if he doesn't want to be with his girl.

"Don't laugh." Livvy chews on her bottom lip, abandoning her chopsticks on my desk.

"I'm sorry." I rub my hand over my face. "I'm not laughing at you. Polo Boy must be stupider than I thought."

Livvy blinks a few times. Her brown eyes shutter with hurt, and I continue, "If you were my girl, I wouldn't be able to do anything but fuck you on every single surface. In every single position." I dip another sushi into the soy mix, my eyes boring straight into Livvy's. "Morning, noon, and night." I pop the little roll into my mouth as a shudder goes down her spine, her eyes glazing over. The grin I've been holding back breaks through my lips. "What was it this woman at Club Trix said to me?" I click my fingers, recalling what she said and adding my own spin to it. "I look hot in a suit, and I fuck even better in one."

Her cheeks flame red as she slides down in her seat. Now I officially know Polo boy isn't really going to be a challenge, and Livvy Blake is ripe for the taking.

CHAPTER SEVENTEEN

Livvy

I squeeze the remaining juice of the lime into my gin and tonic before throwing the carcass into my glass. There is nothing better than a gin and tonic on a Saturday afternoon. I give my drink a quick swirl and hand Kendall hers before relaxing back on the leather couch, celebrating the start of my little devious plan to remove Ryder from Glam Co.

"I can't believe Kyle told Ryder he's my boyfriend," I grumble, taking a sip. The anger I thought would evaporate is now burning an ulcer in my guts.

"He wishes." Kendall snorts.

I kind of have to agree with her — the whole knuckle-dragging behavior was less sexy and more annoying.

"And what the fuck was with him grabbing my ass in the office?" I ask, irritation causing me to pick at my manicure. He really made me feel icky when he did that, and honestly it wasn't cool at all.

"Yeah, that's really not sexy. There is a time and a place,"

Kenny agrees.

"I thought it was some mistake until he squeezed my ass cheek. I've been waiting months for him to make a move, and he chooses my workplace to do it? The weirdest part is, instead of turning me on, it only annoyed me. It was like he completely undermined me in my place of business and overshadowed my career with his own." A shiver goes down my spine, making the hairs on my arms stand. Our relationship is going to hit its end sooner rather than later, and I don't think I'm sad about it our families be damned.

"Kyle situation aside. We should celebrate, to the plan let's-get-Ryder-to-fail," Kendall says, taking a sip from her glass. She is incredibly proud of my ingenious new packaging stunt.

"And the gin and tonics we're drinking now is just for funzies?" I giggle. I'm already halfway to drunks-ville.

Kendall rolls her eyes. "Drinking G and T is always for funzies, duh."

My phone buzzes with a notification. An excited flutter passes through my chest at the message from Ryder.

RYDER

I saw your post for the paws4acause walkathon.
Do you have any pets?

Strange question to ask. But with the G and T buzzing through my system, I quickly type back.

ME

Is someone stalking my Instagram?

I open the app and see a new follower RyderFEO, I click

on the account and no surprise its private. I tap on the follow back icon.

RYDER

> I don't think I can get around this one. I may have been...

There is something so different about the Ryder who I talk to on the phone and the Ryder in person. It's almost like our little conversations are the real Ryder, and I kind of like getting to know him in this format.

ME

> I do. I have a little fur baby, MoMo. She is the light of my life.

RYDER

> Is someone an avatar fan?

ME

> You mean my makeup prowess isn't enough of a secret power?

RYDER

> So not air then?

I snicker.

Kendall looks at me, her brows pulled down in question. "Is that Anders again? Why doesn't he use the group chat?" she grumbles, thinking she's missing out on some secret conversation.

"No," I reply, my thumbs moving along the screen.

ME

My star sign says otherwise.

RYDER

Evidently.

ME

What about you?

RYDER

Defo not in the air tribe. That only leaves fire, water, and earth . . . Guess.

ME

I don't know why but I'm getting some serious Azula vibes from you.

ME

HAHA. Although so many people ask, I sometimes just say yes.

"What has you smiling like that?" Kendall asks.

"Oh nothing." I shrug. "Just read a funny comment on Make Me."

RYDER

What kind of fur baby is she?

CAROLINE MASCI

ME

> She is a Jack Russell, who has an affinity for my roommate's designer shoes and rolled-beef chews.

RYDER

> That's sacrilege!

ME

> You have no idea . . . Do you have any pets?

RYDER

> Nope. I've always loved dogs though.

ME

> Kendall says she prefers cats. But I've seen her sneak dog toys home when I'm not looking.

RYDER

> Sounds like Kendall is incredibly patient and really loves you and your dog.

ME

> I don't know, Kendall changes her opinions easily. Right now she's on a man hiatus and between you and me — we are hitting tipping point. I don't think I can handle another rerun of Bridgeton.

RYDER

A man hiatus – that sounds serious. Are you standing in solidarity with your best friend?

ME

Heck no. A man hiatus is the dumbest thing I've ever heard. Especially if you're not healing from a bad breakup – because ooft man hiatus are a must then. I mean power to her and wanting to be single and all shhh. Don't tell her I said that.

RYDER

Don't worry. Your secret's safe with me.

That makes two secrets I've now divulged to Ryder. Shit.

"How about we go to Club Trix?" Kendall asks, sitting up abruptly and spilling the rest of her drink over her hand.

Closing my phone, I look at her. "How about no?" I don't want to go to that place ever again. Especially not if I'm going to have to sit in Ryder's VIP booth.

Kendall pouts. "You're no fun."

"I disagree. I'm loads of fun."

"I know. Just ask Ryder. I can't believe you submitted those designs," she laughs.

Kosmedika are going to be so pissed that Glam Co, under Ryder's direction, has gone ahead and changed the packaging without telling them, and they will go straight to the board with this issue.

"Shhhh," I laugh. "Ryder has no clue I submitted them, and he won't until Kosmedika get the delivery with the new boxes."

"You really are an evil little genius." Kendall's eyes light up.

"If you didn't come up with that great idea, I never would have thought of it."

"And it's only just the beginning."

She's right. Operation make Ryder look incompetent in front of the board is now underway. Submitting the new packaging designs is only just the beginning. Winking at Kendall over the rim of my glass, I vow; I will keep Glam Co and I will get my teen line.

I open the front door to my parents' house, and call, "Hello?" but the place is still and empty. Weird. I need a curling iron for filming tomorrow and Devin messaged and said I could borrow hers. She told me she left it in my room which is convenient since her door is closed, and it sounds like she's — groaning? Even though I don't make that sound often enough, I definitely know it when I hear it. She's… having sex. I gag.

Wonder which dumbass fell under her spell now.

"Right there," call's my sister's breathy voice. I shudder. I need to block my ears before they bleed. The only thing worse than not getting any, is listening to your sister getting it.

"You're such a beast today," she groans.

"You know how game days do that to me," rumbles the not so deep male voice.

I frown. My sister isn't seeing anyone. Well, not that she's told us anyway. But from the sounds of it, her secret relationship has been going on for a while. Gross. A shiver goes down my spine. Now Kyle is going to be all 'Let's double date.' I trip up the last stair, catching myself against the railing.

A few minutes later the door bursts open. Devin stares at me in shock — she didn't expect me to come by a bit earlier than she asked. "Liv." Her knuckles are turning white from how tight she is holding the robe.

The guy snorts, and the hairs on my arms raise.

"She wouldn't even know how to touch my cock."

What the actual fuck? That voice.

Sticking my foot in the way, I stop Devin from trying to close the door, causing her to slam it into my toes, but the pain doesn't register.

"I touched her ass the other day in front of Fallington. You should've seen the jealousy on his face. I even gave it a squeeze — he went wild. She has nothing on your ass though, baby."

Pushing past Devin, I find Kyle standing in the middle of her room buttoning up a pair of jeans. His cheeks are red and ruddy from the exertion, gross. My body is still rooted in place, completely frozen.

"Liv, it's not what you — " Devin sighs.

"Don't." I hold a finger up to her over my shoulder. I can't listen to her lies right now.

Kyle freezes, his green eyes snapping to meet mine. "Olivia," he breathes, his face going from red and sweaty to white as a ghost.

I guess I am a ghost though — of bitches past, present, and future.

"How long?" I grit out, my eyes burning from the onslaught

of tears, but I will myself to blink them away. I will not show these two how much they've hurt me. I can break down later.

Devin reaches a hand out but lets it fall to her side before it can touch me. The only nice thing she's done for me — I couldn't stand to have her touch me right now.

"Has it been the whole time we've been dating?" I ask the question but looking between the two of them, I already know the answer. "Did you even really like me?" My voice has taken on a deadly calm. My fingertips tingle from the rollercoaster of emotions racing through my system, my chest rising and falling rapidly with short breaths. I'm guessing — from the way he knew nothing about me and took even less notice of my likes and dislikes — no.

The thick silence in the room only makes my head spin more. I don't take my eyes off Kyle.

He snorts a laugh. "Olivia, how could anyone like you? You're just too much. No man wants a woman who can do his job. No man wants a woman who earns more than him. Look at you — you're too bossy and neurotic," he sneers, his eyes turning to steel, the physical hit of every single word landing perfectly.

The waft of misogyny almost chocks me.

"Do you really think you will ever find anybody who will appreciate you for more than the fact you're a Blake, a potential stepping stone to FF Group, and everything that comes along with the Elites?"

I rear back like he's slapped me. I thought Kyle was a walking green flag, that's why my parents were pushing me in his direction, and with his uncle being on the board of

Glam Co it was only going to strengthen our family ties, but I guess I was wrong. Being threatened by my success is beyond laughable. My eyes slowly slide down Kyle, my top lip curling in disgust, as I question what I ever found attractive about him. His words are like a knife cutting small slices into me.

I meet my sister's gaze, and the knife wounds become a deep incision. I cast a glance down but there isn't any blood. The wounds being inflicted on me right now are way worse than anything visible. I didn't think our relationship had hit this level. Sure, Devin and I have had our differences, but this is on a whole new low.

My sister's face mirrors the hurt in mine. She quickly wipes away a stray tear. Is that truly what she thinks of herself — that she is only worth as much as her last name or her connections to the elite? I suddenly feel something I've never felt for my sister before . . . pity.

Ignoring Kyle, I stare at Devin. "Is that truly what you think of yourself? People only care about your last name and connections?"

"Do you know how hard it is to be your sister? Everyone always gravitates to you. Livvy is so smart; Livvy is so determined. No matter what I do, I'm always just Livvy Blake's little sister." She can't even meet my eyes as her cheeks turn red and her top lip quivers.

My anger cranks up a notch at her gaslighting me because I work hard. But I know these words aren't just her own. They sound exactly like the things my dad says when he pits her against me. Too bad she used dumb logic to get back at me instead of turning her anger toward the person who really deserves it. I don't just waltz into a room and expect everything to be handed to me — I work my ass off for it. The fact my sister doesn't see how hard is a kick in the gut.

"And what, you've been sitting here, fucking each other, laughing about me behind my back? Oh, poor Livvy, she is such a naïve idiot. You're my fucking *sister*, Devin!" My cheeks become heated, my breaths shorter as the phantom hand starts tightening around my throat and cutting off air.

"It's not like that," Devin answers.

I don't take my eyes off her. "No?" I glare at her. "Please, tell me, what is it like?"

"We just — "

"You know what — I don't want to hear it," I cut her off and storm into my old room, kick a discarded pillow on the floor, and grab the curling iron from my makeup table.

Fuck this shit. Fuck Devin. Fuck Kyle. Fuck MEN. PERIOD.

Fuming, I stomp down the staircase and slam the front door behind me. I open my phone and dial Kendall's number.

It's Saturday night. Our plans have changed — we're going to Trix and getting wasted on shots. She better get on board, or I'll be there alone.

"Babe?" Kendall answers the phone on the second ring.

"Get yourself slutted up, bitch. We're going to Trix." I end the call and make my tires squeal in the driveway, no doubt leaving a nice mark behind.

FUCK MEN.

I don't even bother to go for a dress, instead opting for a lacy, black corset top and mini, faux-leather shorts with thigh-high leather boots. The amount of skin I'm showing I would normally consider to be obscene, but tonight I don't give a damn. I put another coat of gloss over my already glossy, red lips. Rachel was right; red lips do look amazing.

"Girl, you've come to play." Kendall whistles at me as she casually leans against the bathroom vanity.

I smack my lips together with the cherry gloss Ryder liked — it's become my new favorite gloss.

"You mean I don't play every day?" I eye her through the mirror with one eyebrow raised.

"Oh no, Livvy, you do. But tonight, I think you might just have the entire male population professing you the new queen of causing premature ejaculation."

I stare at her, a smile playing on my lips. "Good." Smoothing my hair with wax, I make sure not a single strand comes loose from the stick-straight high ponytail. This look hinges on my hair and my lips.

I've officially entered into my villain era.

I quickly snap a photo and upload it on my Make Me page with the caption 'Full tutorial to come this week'. I press post, and a few seconds later my phone dings with a notification.

Rachel Fallout replied to your photo
Rachel Fallout: Just wow.

I smile to myself and close my phone. On the last two videos I've posted, Rachel has been the first to comment. She is quickly becoming an uber fan. It's cute. I tap the heart, liking her comment.

"Ready?" I ask, peeking my head out of the bathroom.

Kendall is adjusting the strap of her bag over her shoulder. "Yep, Uber will be here in five." She grabs one of the two shot glasses on the counter behind her. It's my third one since I found *them*. THEM. The fact there is even a *them* makes my stomach roll and should annoy me more than it does. Heck, I should be mourning a guy who I effectively spent three months of my life in the 'talking phase' with. But I've not shed A. Single. Fricking. Tear. I'm more annoyed over the time I wasted with Kyle. Kendall has spent the whole time since I told her celebrating. Kyle is finally out of the picture.

"For now." She hands a shot glass to me. "To your villain era."

"To my villain era." We clink the glasses and take the shots.

Since I came in through the door, Kendall hasn't even asked me what happened. I just regurgitated what I'd seen. That was it. She didn't even make me feel sorry for myself. She just poured the shot and asked me what I was going to wear, and that was how our epic night started.

"Uber's here," Kendall declares.

"Let's get lit." I whoop, opening the door. I've already decided I'm not coming home unless I feel like the floor is going to hit my face and everything is nice and calm. I'm almost hoping we do see Ryder and his friends at the club.

Club Trix is absolutely packed. The DJ has some deep bass beat pumping through the walls. Kendall motions to the bar, and we push our way through the thick crowd, finding the only available space. Kendall quickly signals the bartender. We need liquor and we need it now. Without thinking, I start searching over my shoulder, my eyes zeroing in on the VIP area, searching for one person in particular. I roll my lips together and quickly look away when I find it empty.

"Becks said they aren't coming tonight," Kendall whispers in my ear.

When exactly did my friend ask that particular question of Beckham Jones?

"I wasn't looking for them," I yell over the music, deep down knowing I was.

A male arm lands on the bar beside mine, making me almost jump from the close contact.

Warm breath blows against my ear. "I really hope you don't have a boyfriend waiting for you at home because I need to change that."

A shiver goes down my spine, as the citrus scent wraps around my senses. He's here.

CHAPTER EIGHTEEN
Ryder

I need a hobby. Something to take my mind off Olivia Fucking Blake. I stare down at my phone at the photo she just posted on her Make Me page. I can actually hear angels singing. Those shorts. The lace bra — which leaves absolutely nothing to the imagination yet enough to make my imagination run wild. Those godforsaken red lips. Is she trying to kill me? I quickly type my comment. I know she isn't dressing up like this for Polo Boy, this has Livvy Blake dressing for herself written all over it. A low burn tingles in my gut, what the fuck did he do to her?

"I think someone just got sent the chick equivalent of a dick pic. A tit pic." Becks throws the tennis ball at my pec, causing it to bounce off.

"Fucker," I groan, glancing down at the red spot forming on my chest and then back up at him. "That's going to leave a mark." I close my phone, chucking it on my bag by the chain-link fence. "You're just salty because I am clearly beating you, bro."

I grab my T-shirt from the waistband of my pants and dab the sweat dripping down my face. We've been out here so long, the outdoor court lights are turned on, illuminating the night sky in an artificial glow. I tuck my shirt back into my pants and pluck the spare ball sitting against my thigh in my shorts. I run my fingers over the ball, bouncing it on the ground three times, lowering my heart rate before throwing it in the air and serving it straight to Becks. The top spin on the ball proves too strong, and Becks misses it completely.

"Ace," I call, pretending to mark a tally in the air.

We both know I don't need an air tally. I won the last match, and Becks keeps demanding rematches. Becks flips me off. Even though he doing a great job of hiding it, he's getting annoyed.

I bounce on my toes, loosening the adrenaline coursing through my veins, before lining up my next shot.

Zander left this morning for Japan. FF Group have a major trade deal going down and it will be Zander's first one he's handling on his own — not that he isn't ready for it. Dad prepared us our whole lives to take over FF Group. But you don't get to where I am without being a type A person who needs to know what the fuck is going on at all times. I've been checking my emails every ten minutes to see if Zander has finished the presentation, only getting more agitated that my inbox is flooded with bullshit I don't care about and not a reply from him. Playing the waiting game is killing me — my two options to get rid of all this pent-up nervous energy is fucking or fighting. Since fighting is off the table and fucking some mindless chick is about as appealing as having my dick waxed, Becks threw in another form of physical exertion — one he thought he was going to win at.

I send another serve straight down the line. "Nothing but net, baby," I whoop.

Becks grumbles something under his breath, it sounded like "cheater."

"What was that?"

"Hang on," Becks calls, jogging over to his stuff. He grabs his phone and smirks, his thumbs furiously typing on the screen before he throws his phone down and lets it land heavily on our clothes.

"Figures," I snort. "You're raging on me for tit pics, and you have a whole fucking contact list of them."

Becks stops short. "Doll would never send me that. Besides, she was asking if we're going to Club Trix."

"Doll?" I ask. He's never mentioned a *Doll* before.

"Kendall Fordham. You know, Livvy's best friend," he deadpans.

Straightening, Man hiatus Kendall Fordham? I wonder if Livvy knows her best friend has secretly broken that little pact. I blurt, "Since when did you start fucking Kendall?"

"What?" Becks eyes meet mine before turning back to his phone. "That's gross, bro. We're just friends."

Somehow, I missed the part when my best friend became BFFs with Kendall. My brain stutters to process everything Beck's unloaded. My man whore of a best friend has a friend of the opposite sex, and not just anyone — Kendall Fordham, the best friend of my supposed enemy.

Shaking my head, I hold up my hands, wiping everything Kendall and Becks related aside. "Wait, Livvy is going to be at Club Trix tonight?"

Livvy is going to Club Trix looking like a wet dream brought to life and I'm sitting here hitting a ball around the court. Fuck that.

"Yeah," Becks huffs and rolls his eyes, repeating himself a second time. "Doll wanted to know if we were going. I said no, you're too busy learning who the superior tennis play is."

"Four–zip, bro. I think we know who the superior tennis player is. Besides," I grab my shirt from my pants again wiping my face, "I could use a drink."

I've never showered so fast in my fucking life; the ends of my hair are still wet, making them curl slightly.

"Are you ready?" I call to Becks.

"Yeah," he replies, slipping his foot into his Tod shoes.

The uber's already waiting for us by the time we leave my apartment.

With a curt nod to the bouncer, we bypass the long line waiting to get into the club and head straight in.

"I think — " Becks yells over the music, but I don't let him finish.

I know where I'm going. The crowd melts away around me as I zero in on my target, waiting by the bar. The photo she posted is a crime for the injustice it did to her in real life. She is a goddess. Her dark-brown locks are pinned straight and glowing under the strobe lighting, creating a halo around her.

I place my arm on the bar beside hers, caging her in, a small smirk touches my lips as her body jumps at the closeness of mine.

Leaning down, I whisper in her ear, "I really hope you don't have a boyfriend waiting for you at home because I need to change that."

She takes a sip from her gin and tonic, turning her head slightly so her lips almost touch mine. "The only thing waiting for me at home is an overeager Jack Russell and my vibrator."

My mouth falls open. "And what about Polo Boy?"

"My vibrator is three times the size of Polo Boy, and at least I know how to use it." She spins in my arms, taking another sip from the straw, her eyes never leaving mine.

I snort. "Trust me, Killer, I know exactly how to use mine."

She tips her head to the side, surveying me through her dark gaze, the corner of her lips turning up in a seductive smile. "Don't take it personally, but I won't take your word for it."

"That's okay." I wink, closing the distance between us and pressing my body to hers — getting to feel her deliciously soft, warm curves against my chest. I run my nose down the column of her throat before pulling back and whispering in her ear, "I've always been better at show rather than tell."

Livvy moves her head to the side, giving me more room. "I can't imagine you as the studious type." Her voice is breathless.

"Imagine, baby. I wasn't just studious; I made honor roll."

Livvy finished her drink and clinks the empty ice around in her glass.

"Polo Boy out of the picture for good?" I ask. My fingers dig into the cheap wood on the bar, waiting for her to answer.

I need to hear her say yes.

Placing the drink on the bar top behind her, she quirks an eyebrow at me. "What, no VIP booth tonight?"

"That's not answering my question."

"He was too beige for me. I seem to only be interested in red flags."

I take that as a yes.

"Are your other friends going to meet us here?"

"Nah, I thought we could pretend to be normal for tonight. Like Glam Co doesn't exist, or that we're not a month into our six months' probation. You're just Livvy and I'm just Ryder."

"Perfect." She replies as I grab her hand and pull her through the crowd, so we can dance among the throng of thriving bodies.

"What about Kendall?" she calls over the music.

Looking over my shoulder, I spot Becks with Kendall by the bar downing a shot. "She's with Becks, by the bar," I reply, and Livvy's shoulders relax. She can break away from her friend without worrying about her.

Livvy trails behind me, her body moving slowly to the beat of the music as she walks — until I hit the center of the dance floor and spin her into me. She comes willingly, placing one hand on my chest while the other trails through my semi-dried hair. She feels so right against me. How can the woman I'm supposed to hate so much, feel so right?

Her hips moving in time to the music create a hypnotic rhythm. Her hands grab her tits, giving them a generous squeeze, as her hungry eyes bore into me. My dick instantly hardens. This is a side of Livvy I never would've expected; it's like she's let something loose in her tonight and it's blowing my fucking mind. I wrap my arm around her waist and pull her flush against me, not even allowing air to pass between our bodies.

"Please tell me this means you and Polo Boy are done." It isn't a question because I'm banking on the answer being yes.

Livvy's eyes meet mine. "We were never really together, so how could we be done?" she answers.

I nod, a smile splitting my lips.

I guess that's why Livvy has decided to leave the sensible girl behind in favor for the vixen who is currently in my arms. I knew Polo Boy was a fucking idiot, for him to fumble the woman in front of me is a crime, even if she is a Blake. I cup her jaw in my palm, trace my tongue along the seam of her lip until she opens for me so I can possess hers.

CHAPTER NINETEEN

Livvy

I can't believe I'm kissing Ryder fucking Fallington. Not Ryder Fallington the guy who is trying to take Glam Co from me, but Ryder Fallington — the guy who picked me up after I tripped over his bike. The guy who let me put lip gloss on him; the guy who I am starting to have feelings for. The guy who I'm somehow spilling my secrets to, and know they are safe.

My lips part, allowing him to continue to ravage me as our tongues duel, in a lip teasing, teeth-biting, earth-shattering kissing.

Ryder cups the back of my head in his giant palm, opening my mouth to him. My body ignites with a fire like I've never felt before and I have a feeling the only one who can put it out is the man who is running his finger along the crease where my butt meets the top of my thigh. I suddenly regret wearing shorts — even though I look fire in them — they are really cutting off access. Digging my nails into his muscular shoulder, I hook my leg around his waist, needing to feel the friction of him all over me. Sensing what I'm after, Ryder moves his hands to grip my ass, acting like a weight causing my clit to make delicious contact with the ridge of his hard dick.

He breaks our kiss. Both our chests are rising and falling rapidly from the lack of oxygen and lust coursing through our veins. "Come home with me," he whispers.

"Okay." I nod. As if I was going to say no.

Ryder releases his grip on my ass, and my leg falls to the floor like it's made of jelly. I don't know how I'm going to walk toward the door without tripping over them.

"But I have to tell Kendall we're leaving." I don't want her to worry if she can't find me at the end of the night.

Ryder pulls his phone out and types something before whispering in my ear, "Don't worry. Becks said he will take her home."

The Uber manages to get to Ryder's place in minutes. My body is still hot from the club, and it doesn't help that I'm tucked against Ryder's warm, hard frame. His hands don't seem to stray from either caressing the underside of my boob in my lace bra or rubbing slow circles on my waist.

Ryder pauses at his apartment door and turns me around to face him. "Are you still good to do this?" he asks, surprising the shit out of me.

"Yes." I nod.

Ryder bends at the knee and runs a trail of hot kisses down my throat. "No regrets, Killer. Once I open the door, you're mine."

"No." I shake my head, causing Ryder to pull away slightly,

his eyebrows hitting his hairline in surprise.

"No?" he repeats.

"I belong to me, but once you open this door, you just get lucky enough to be able to appreciate it."

Ryder throws his head back and lets out a laugh that goes straight to my core, making it pulse. God, he has such a deep rich laugh, I want to hear it all the time.

"What am I going to do with you, Liv?" He lets the question sit in the air.

Slowly slipping the third button through the hole on his shirt, I peek at him from under my lashes. "I'm hoping you will fuck me," I say, wishing my breathy voice isn't coming off as desperate as I am for him to open the door to his apartment.

Ryder must be on the same wavelength though, like he's read my mind, he pushes the door open.

"And what kind of man would I be to ignore a woman's request?" Ryder lifts me up, and I wrap my arms around his shoulders as my legs automatically find themselves in a lock on his hips. Ryder tucks his hands under my ass, holding me firmly against him.

My mouth drops open as I scan his penthouse apartment. It didn't escape my notice that the Uber dropped us off at the *Elite* tower. The best apartment building in the whole of Cheshire Shore. Kendall and I live in *Exclusive*, which is by no means a bad building, but this tower — the waiting list for an apartment is generational. It's home to some of the most expensive residences in the whole of Cheshire Shore. My second cousins, Sof and Leo, live here too, a few floors down.

A perk of being a part of the founding five families. From

the internal elevator, Ryder's apartment splits over two levels. *Holy shit.* This place is something out of architecture digest.

Ryder's giant strides, we are in his room in a few steps. Suddenly, I'm tumbling out of his arms onto a soft bed.

Fuck. Ryder's right.

His sheets are soft.

"I want to ask what happened to you tonight to make you change your mind."

"Polo Boy has been screwing my sister the whole time," I mutter, my hands finding their way into his hair and bringing his lips back to mine.

"We don't mention his name in here," Ryder growls. "But he is one stupid fucker to let an amazing woman like you go."

"I think that's your cue to make me forget then."

"With pleasure." He smiles down at me and lifts his half-unbuttoned shirt over his head before covering my body with his. His lips are everywhere as his hands expertly undo my lacy corset bra and let the straps fall down my arms, letting it fall from my body. Ryder's tongue peeks out, wetting his bottom lip before he takes my nipple in his mouth. I groan.

Fuck that feels good. I arch my hips, searching for the friction from his rigid, hard cock.

Ryder tweaks my other nipple into a stiff peak before swapping his hot tongue tracing a path from one breast to the other and taking it into his mouth. I tangle my fingers in his hair, tugging on the strands as he continues to work me into a frenzy with the attention he is paying to my nipples. Abandoning my breasts, his tongue drawing a slow line down my chest, dipping into my belly button before reaching the top of my leather shorts.

His eyes bore into mine as his fingers draw the zipper of my shorts down. "Next time, ditch the shorts."

"But then my look wouldn't be anywhere near as fire as it is now," I muse, a giggle escaping me at the tight line of Ryder's lips as he struggles to undo the concealed button on my shorts. I reach out and bat his hands away before undoing it and shimmying my hips out of the shorts. "No panties?" he muses.

"Do you think I would let a panty line ruin this outfit?"

I lift my heel onto the bed and go to unzip my boots, but Ryder stops me.

"The boots stay on." His voice is thick and gruff like he swallowed gravel.

I lift my eyebrows, "Kinky," I practically purr, running my tongue along my teeth.

"I haven't even started my fifty-shades mode yet." Ryder winks at me.

That's the only warning I get before he dives between my thighs. He slides one finger into my already slick passage before adding a second one, curling his fingers, hitting the right spot with each pass eliciting a deep moan from my chest.

"Baby, you're soaking me," he grunts before replacing his fingers with his mouth. His voice is like ecstasy. With slow deliberate licks, he continues to tease me into a frenzy. Before biting down lightly on my clit.

"Fuckkk," I scream becoming lightheaded, loving the feel of his mouth on me. He moves away just before he can give me exactly what I need. My body becomes a craving pit of need to release. I pull at the stiff peaks of my breasts before moving my hands to tug on the strands of his hair, dragging Ryder's mouth to mine. "Are you going to just sit there and tease me or are you going to fuck me?"

He chuckles lightly, "Such an impatient little Killer," before shutting off any further conversation with his lips. Ryder's mouth doesn't leave mine as he reaches into the draw and pulls out a foil packet. He rolls the condom down his thick, veiny cock — a bead of pre-cum already forming on his head. I lick my lips, hungry at the sight.

Ryder covers my body with his and my legs slide around his waist. Staring into the chocolate depths of his eyes, my gaze is held by his as the tip of his dick nudges my entrance. My skin flushes hotter as a hiss escapes my lips as he continues to ease his way in. It's been a while for me, and my body is letting me know, everything in my head empties except for the sensation of him filling me. Ryder stills as he bottoms out, giving my body a chance to adjust.

"Look how beautiful you are while taking my cock." His voice husky with pent-up need, the muscles on his neck straining as he holds himself still, waiting for me to give him the go-ahead.

I move my hips against his, testing the feel. The low hum of my 'O' is already thrumming in my veins. "If you don't move soon, I think I might explode."

"We wouldn't want that." Ryder hooks his forearm under my knee, opening my hips wider and giving him more room as he starts thrusting. The new angle slides him deeper inside me, hitting all the right places.

"Whose cock are you made for?"

A low moan escapes my throat, encouraging Ryder to go harder. He keeps pumping into me with shallow, hard thrusts.

"Yours," I reply and reach down, circling my fingers around my clit, the extra stimulation enough to set me off. I clench around his dick, Ryder releases a grunt from deep in his chest.

"That's it, baby," he groans. After batting my hand aside, he pinches my clit between his fingers, and it causes sparks to fly through my system.

"Oh god," I chant on repeat as I come harder than I ever have in my entire life.

After a few more pumps, Ryder grunts and follows me over the edge. He falls beside me, careful not to crush me under his weight.

My heart pounds in my throat and my breaths come in short, sharp pants. I feel like I've just run a marathon. Only instead of being exhausted, I'm completely refreshed and renewed.

I swallow, trying to add some moisture into my seriously dry throat. "Wow," I mumble, still catching my breath and batting away the wild strands of hair that managed to get loose from my updo.

Sometimes having sex with the bane of your existence isn't so bad. Especially when he takes pleasure in ensuring your mind is blown.

Ryder trails his lips down my arm. I don't think I'm going to get much sleep tonight.

My body is deliciously sore, I note as I turn the jet shower off. I rest against the marble tiles, letting hot water ease the ache in my muscles — not that I want the tingle to leave. I kind of like it.

Ryder's towels are just as soft as his bed sheets. After drying myself off, I wrap the towel around my body while I search through Ryder's walk-in closet for a shirt. My outfit from last night is still laying discarded on the floor, but I need more coverage than a lace corset bra and high-waisted faux-leather shorts today.

Staring at the rows of illuminated shelves, my mouth falls open, I suddenly need to convince Kendall to redo our closet. Maybe we could knock the wall between our rooms down and form a super closet, which would still be smaller than this one. Ryder's is literally the closet dreams are made of.

I grab his discarded shirt from last night and inhale his scent before quickly doing the buttons up. I make my way down the long hallway — it seemed much shorter last night — my toes sinking into the plush carpet, following the sound of clanging pans.

Rounding the corner, I find Ryder in the kitchen.

"Morning," he calls, not even looking over his shoulder. He is busy making us breakfast at the stove, his grey sweatpants hanging dangerously low on his hips and his beautiful chest bare. *Shit, my kryptonite.* I thread the final button through the hole, making sure I don't flash him as I walk into the kitchen.

I clear my throat, crossing one leg over the other, suddenly feeling incredibly naked and self-conscious even though his shirt hits mid-thigh. "Morning," I reply, heat touching my cheeks.

Ryder looks over at me as he places a cooked pancake on top of the small stack beside the stove. "I hope you like pancakes," he smiles, making my heart stutter.

"Love them." I return his smile and take a seat at the counter, as Ryder slides two pancakes onto my plate before adding to his. I drizzle maple syrup on mine, my brain working into overdrive. The only thing more awkward than after-sex small talk is awkward morning-after small talk, and the rate this is heading, I'd rather face thanksgiving with my dysfunctional family.

"Hey." Ryder takes a seat, resting his warm palm on my bare knee. "I hope you're not regretting last night."

I blink at him. Oh shit, he's misreading my silence.

"No." I shake my head, my eyes fixed on my toenails.

He crooks his forefinger and lifts my chin, so my eyes meet his concerned stare. "Are you sore?" Worry causes his lips to thin. The amount of care he is showing me makes my heart quiver.

"A little," I admit. "I'm just" — I blow out a slow, calming breath — "nervous, I guess. I'm kind of out of practice, especially with morning-afters."

Ryder rubs his thumb along my inner thigh, and the soft touch instantly calms my nerves.

"This isn't the morning after. We're still just Ryder and Livvy having breakfast." He takes a bite out of his pancake. My eyes stay glued to the column of his throat, working with his swallow.

"Why do you call me Killer?" I ask. The question has been

burning a hole in my brain since I first heard him say it.

The tip of Ryder's tongue peeks out, swiping away the leftover maple syrup. "I can see in your eyes you have fire and determination — a killer instinct; you didn't take the shit I dished out when I first met you. It's attractive as shit."

"Most men don't like women with ambition. It makes them feel weak," I mumble, pushing a piece of pancake around on my plate. "Kyle didn't."

Ryder snorts. "That's because Kyle is a dumbass."

Ryder is right; Kyle *is* a dumbass, but I'm stupid for letting him in. Ah, the stark difference twenty-four hours has made to my perspective on men. Being told my only worth is in my last name by one guy and having another practically cheer me on for being independent and going after what I want. It's giving me whiplash.

Ryder stabs another piece of pancake before placing it in his mouth and removing the fork with a grin. "I'm not like most men, Killer. I like a woman who has fire, intelligence, and goes after what she wants. A woman who doesn't take my shit. I like a challenge."

"I would guess that's why you have your sights set on Glam Co."

"Nu-huh," he tuts. "No Glam Co talk, remember? Just Livvy and Ryder."

I raise my eyebrows at him, I can't resist. "I hope you stay true to your word about liking a challenge, Mr. Fallington, because I don't plan on losing Glam Co anytime soon — to you or your magical dick."

Ryder snorts. "Yeah, my dick is pretty magical, isn't it."

"And you're clearly very humble." I roll my eyes.

Ryder looks at me. "Tell you what, how about we keep this whole you-and-me thing separate from Glam Co?"

"Separate how?" I eye him from the corner of my eye, not really sure what he is proposing here but my curiosity is piqued. I load my fork up with pancake and shove it in my mouth. A moan escapes my lips.

Ryder looks at me with hooded eyes. "Keep that up and you won't get to finish breakfast."

After grabbing another forkful of pancake, I stare at him as I lift it to my mouth and release a loud moan the moment the maple syrup touches my lips.

Ryder rests a hand on my bare thigh and cautions, "Don't tempt me, Killer," his voice more animal than man.

"Nuh-huh, big guy," I tut. "Sore, remember?"

Ryder pouts his bottom lip.

"Now tell me again how you plan to keep Glam Co separate from Livvy and Ryder?"

Ryder takes another bite of food. "At work we are Fallington and Blake, here though we are Ryder and Livvy. It won't matter what happens at Glam Co."

"Are you asking me to be your secret girlfriend?" I've had enough of that with Kyle, and I'm not really interested in being that for Ryder too.

CHAPTER TWENTY
Ryder

"What? No." I shake my head. Somehow, I'm butchering this. I'm usually the levelheaded person. Fuck, I've conditioned myself to be. But when I'm around Livvy, all that conditioning goes out the door. She makes me lose my mind, more so than any woman I've ever been with before.

Last night was something else and having Livvy under me felt so right, watching her come alive from my touch. I got to be in the presence of the real Livvy — the one I've only seen glimpses of in our messages — and she was intoxicating. "I just meant let's not allow Glam Co to stop us from exploring where this could go."

I'm not ready to let Livvy walk out the front door, and go back to fighting over Glam Co.

Glam Co means too much to both of us, and I wouldn't ask her to just hand it over, but I also don't want to lose whatever this is.

Livvy stays silent for a beat. "Okay." She smiles, and I lean forward and press my lips against hers. But she stops me with her palms against my bare chest. "Don't think I'll go easy on you just because you have a magical dick," she warns me. "I'm not going to give up Glam Co without a fight."

"I wouldn't dream of it."

Climbing onto my lap, she brings her lips down on mine, sealing our little deal with a kiss. She pulls away after a few minutes, breathless. "Why the butterfly?" she asks.

My brows scrunch in confusion and I scratch the stubble on my jaw, trying to process what the fuck she just said when all the blood is currently pumping into my dick.

"Butterfly?" I ask.

"You know, the tattoo on your thigh." She touches the spot, and the thick fabric of my pants feels non-existent against the warmth of her hand.

"It's actually a dragonfly." I smirk. "And I got it because I lost a bet with Becks. He has the matching one on his thigh."

"But didn't you lose the bet?"

"Oh I did, but he bombed the next one and it only seemed fair we match."

"Do I want to know what the bet was?" She quirks her brow, her eyes sparkling with humor.

"Let's just say it involved shaving foam, bandages, and laxatives." I laugh, shaking my head remembering it.

"Oh god," she croaks.

Livvy and I spent the rest of the day lounging around just being

Livvy and Ryder. She even convinced me to put on *Gossip Girl*, and after binging half a season's worth of drama, she finally left, still wearing my button-down shirt and her thigh high boots. She looks better than last night.

I can't remember ever having a day like that — just relaxing with a beautiful woman, no pressure or pretense. Just being. I didn't think about work or Glam Co or my dad's illness once the whole time. There is something about Olivia Blake that makes me forget about the outside world. With her, I don't feel I *need* to be *the* Ryder Fallington, chairman of the Founding Five Group and heir to the Fallington fortune. I can just be me. The guy who loves cooking because it's a release on his soul. The guy who can't sit on a couch without socks because that is weird. The guy who suddenly realizes binge-watching a series *without* Olivia Blake curled against him — giving him a running commentary of outfits and her outtake on relationships — isn't as appealing as it once was.

But now I'm alone again, my responsibilities have waited long enough. I open my computer and check to see if Zander sent through the email I've been waiting on, breathing a sigh of relief — it's finally sitting in my inbox. After scanning through the document to make sure he hasn't missed any crucial points to present to the investors, I type back my email before turning my attention to Glam Co.

We have a board meeting in a few weeks' time. It will be the real test for both of us and the first time the board will be assessing our competency. I plan to be on top of my game, especially because it will be around the release time of Glam Co's new dry shampoo. Opening the hair section in the

Glam Guide Cecelia sent me, I look up the meaning of dry shampoo. Contrary to what I thought, it's not shampoo for people with dry hair but used instead of washing hair. After clicking on the 'new launches' folder, I do some research into the upcoming production and product schedule. Glam Co has a range of haircare products, so this is hardly a new zone for the brand. But this product has different packaging and a new and improved formula — or so the campaign states.

A knock at my door interrupts me. *Livvy?* When I open the door to find it's not Livvy, disappointment is my first reaction.

Shit, I need to lock that down.

"Becks." I nod at my friend letting him in.

"Were you expecting someone else?" He cocks his head to the side, raising a brow, clearing wanting me to let slip about last night.

"Just my Uber Eats order," I reply casually, closing the door behind him.

"Is that what they are calling eating pussy nowadays?"

"Like you can talk. You count it as one of the five main food groups." I snort and take a seat at the kitchen counter where my computer is still open.

Becks makes himself comfortable on my sofa, throwing his legs on the coffee table and his arms over the back. "Are you going like that?" he asks, looking down at my grey sweatpants and bare chest.

"Going where?" I don't turn away from my computer, knee-deep in the 'new launches' folder and noting down certain things in my calendar.

"Our movie date with the twins who work in the office on

the floor below FF Group."

Shit. I completely forgot about that. Becks organized this 'double date' a few weeks ago because he was interested in one twin, but she wouldn't go out if her sister didn't have a date and Becks volunteered me.

"I can't go anymore. Ask Henley or Rome, or better yet, I heard Leo was interested in one of the twins – take him."

"What?!" Becks jumps up from the couch. "No, no, no. You can't bail now — this is our only chance with them."

Leaning back in the chair, I run my hands down my face, going out with anyone other than Livvy makes my stomach sour. "We have our first board meeting in a few weeks and it's about the launch of the product Livvy organized."

Becks' mouth pops open. "Oh," he says, the implications clearly sinking in. He fishes his phone out of his pocket and sends off a quick text. "Done," he says, coming to sit beside me, "Leo is going to take them out."

"I need to make sure this launch gets fucked over somehow, but everything is kind of already set in place. She's accounted for every detail — production, suppliers, distribution. She's even allotted for warehouse space for overflow. Not to mention the PR campaign. Look, it's all here." I click through the sub-folders that were in the dry shampoo product launch folder. It's impressive, the level of detail she's gone into — it's almost at the standard of how I would do it.

"What's the product?"

"Dry shampoo," I reply.

Becks stares at me, blinking, his face as blank as mine no doubt was a few minutes ago. Referring to the bible, I point to the dry shampoo description and hand it to him. It seems Livvy needs the board's approval for it to go into production, as the current reviews on the old formula aren't too promising. But it still sells, so there isn't a strong justification for a large overhaul.

Becks reads the description twice. "What if you mess around with the formula of the product? It shouldn't be too hard put it bit of blue coloring in it, turn everyone into a smurf. Shampoo is runny enough, mixing a bit of coloring in shouldn't be too hard."

I slap him on the back of the head. "It's dry shampoo, dickhead. It's not runny."

"How do you know?"

He's right. I'm just taking a guess here.

I quickly google dry shampoo and triumphantly show Becks the screen.

"It's a spray, surely, we can mess something up here? And look," he points to the screen. She has a small sample run scheduled for testers to show the board.

A smirk touches my lips at the golden ticket staring back at me. I track my tongue along the roof of my mouth; it's not a bad idea. It won't cause serious damage to the product, but it's enough to make the board question what the fuck Livvy was thinking.

"I don't think blue coloring will work." After shaking the can of dry shampoo, we got delivered with *Amazon one-hour delivery*, I spray some in Beck's hair before running my hands through it. It will be really obvious if people are spraying blue straight onto their heads.

How the fuck can we screw around with this before Livvy demonstrates the product to the board?

"Why my hair?" he groans.

"Because it was your idea, therefore, you volunteered as tribute."

Becks glares at me. *"Fuck you,"* he mouths in my en suite mirror.

I flip him off. "Thanks for your offer, but you aren't my type. You don't like to take orders in the bedroom."

Becks flips me off, and I laugh.

"Coloring won't work," I sigh. I haven't got much experience with products manufacturing in this area and sabotaging it requires a whole new level of understanding of these products.

Becks looks at himself in the mirror. "It's a cool idea. What if instead of food coloring we got, like, blue powder?"

Turning the metal bottle over in my hand, I scrunch my eyes at the ingredients list, everything ends in an 'anol' making me regret not doing chemistry past junior year. When a stroke of genuineness hits me, I slap Becks on the back. "What if we add some itching powder to it? That way when it's sprayed, everyone will be scratching their heads like crazy and it just might be the clincher I need to show the board I'm the better fit."

"Yeah, can you imagine how annoying that would be to anyone that sprays it," Becks agrees.

I send an email straight to manufacturing to avoid Brynn, the head of product development, catching wind and potentially flagging our additional new ingredient with Livvy. I word the email to sound like I've already received Brynn's approval for a potential Halloween product, so manufacturing won't question it. They will only manufacture a small sample run of ten cans with the updated formula ready for the board meeting.

"With this little tweak, there is no way the board will sign off on the production of retail stock. If it can't go into production, it won't go out for pre-order with Glam Co retailers. The product will be dead in the water before it even begins," I gloat.

"And since Livvy can't show the board a reformulation, they will turn to you to see how you can make this product dominate in the market." Becks admires the email. "Genius," he whispers.

Genius indeed.

Two weeks later, production has left a message to say my 'sample' bottles are ready to collect. I make my way to the lab area of Glam Co to meet Brynn for my samples, in the building behind our offices. I've never been here before and I make sure not to look like I have no clue where I'm going because my plan hinges on Livvy not knowing I have tampered with the dry shampoo formula.

I wander down the really long corridor. Everything in the area is sterilized by the filtered air circulating and the bright UV lights, killing any germ or bacteria that could possibly be growing within this space. Through all the windows, people in white lab coats — their hair covered in special nets and masks on their faces — are busily filling bottles of Glam Co products. I kind of regret never asking for a tour of the place.

It's extensive and well set out with laboratory facilities.

Scanning the labs, my mouth goes dry when I spot her. She's talking to one of the employees, helping to pull the lever on a machine down before grabbing the pressed product. They laugh and Livvy does this weird elbow high-five with the employee as they load the machine up to do another product. As well as creating and formulating new products, Livvy happily sits on the production line. Livvy throws her head back, her face glowing with laughter at whatever the person beside her said. The pulse at the base of my throat spikes. It's the Livvy effect.

She wasn't lying when she said she lives and breathes Glam Co.

"She is the heart and soul of Glam Co. The staff love her, she's never afraid to step into the lab," someone says behind me before I get a tap on the shoulder, "Mr. Fallington." I turn to find an older-looking woman standing there. Brynn — according to the stitched name on her coat.

"Yes." I give her a tight, smile, clearing my head of the Livvy haze. "Pleasure to meet you," I say and extend my hand to her.

"Glad to see you finally found the time to come down to the production area. I'm Brynn, the head of product development." Her tone is short and straight to the point as she takes my hand in her limp one and shakes it.

If I cared what my employees thought of me, the gesture probably would bother me. But I learned to stop giving a fuck about people opinions a long time ago. "I can see there is a lot here I need to get across. Glam Co has been a bigger learning curve than originally expected, but rest assured I will have it down in no time."

I flash her my usual smile, but the woman returns it with a blank stare and starts power walking in the opposite direction — not caring to check if I follow her. "Learning how products are made is just as important as reading the sales reports in the ivory tower across the road." She stops at a closed door before inserting her key, unlocking the door to her office and turns to face me.

Why do I feel like a toddler being scolded? My gaze drifts between the small, plain cardboard box sitting on the edge of the desk and her unimpressed face. *Fuck*, a chill skids down my bones. *She knows.*

She's going to tell me the samples have been tampered with.

"These are the samples you requested." She hands me the box and I wait for the big 'but' to come. "We adjusted the formula as per your instructions and added the new ingredient you requested."

"Great, much appreciated," I reply. *Fuckkkkkkk.*

Brynn blinks. "I saw on the email that I supposedly signed off on this potential Halloween product?" she asks, making me freeze in place. Brynn is more across her production schedule than I gave here credit for.

Thinking fast on my feet, I reply, "Yes, about that . . ." I grab the box and try to think of an excuse that doesn't involve 'I'm trying to make Livvy look bad in front of the board.'

Brynn's lips thin. "I know this is a new environment for you. But there are procedures in place. Next time, I would prefer to be consulted before you send emails to production." She crosses her arms over her chest.

"Noted," I reply, turning on my heel and high-tailing it out of her office.

CHAPTER TWENTY-ONE

Livvy

Deep breaths in, Livvy. I stare into my bathroom mirror, adjusting my shirt. The silk fabric forms a cute bow at the base of my throat. It's just femme enough for me without compromising the corporate look. After tucking the ends of the shirt into my high-waisted pants, I loop my Dolce and Gabbana belt through. And make sure to scrape off any stray hairs MoMo left behind. Not that I give a shit, but it won't really look good in front of the board. And one of the board members absolutely detests pets. I ran through each of the members in my head again, out of the six board members, there is only two women, four men. One of whom is friendly with my dad and Kyles uncle – I absolutely don't count that as a win in my direction, if anything it's more of a hindrance.

After swiping my signature red lipstick across my bottom lip, I smack my lips together twice and nod at myself. "Breathe, Livvy," I say again.

I need to keep a lid on my nerves. This board meeting is

a big deal. It's the first time they will be assessing me against Ryder for Glam Co CEO. No pressure or anything.

Changing the formula for our dry shampoo was my idea a few months ago. I could see the sales were going down against our competitors and there is no better way to revive a product than to give it a new and improved formula. The board is going to love the new formula — I just know it. I spent months with Brynn going over possible adjustments. I wanted to add a hair-growth factor — meaning our new formula actually helps stimulate the follicle, giving the user a healthy growth instead of the product clogging the base of the hair and building up on the scalp.

My stomach gives a horrible twist, and my throat starts to close up. *No, no, no.* I dig my nails into the palm of my hand, craving the bite of pain to keep me grounded. This is not a good time to have a panic attack. Staring at a spot on the carpet, I focus on getting my breathing back to normal. I need to be at the top of my game for this meeting.

I can do this.

I'm Livvy Fricken Blake.

I live and breathe this dry shampoo — well, since I revived it. I'm so confident in this line, I told Brynn to go ahead and run the lot from the sample batch and not even bother to wait for the feedback from the board.

"They will love it," I repeat to myself, resting my hand on the marble countertop and taking in deep lungfuls of air. "They are going to love it." After a few more pulls of air, my throat starts to loosen, and my stomach relaxes. I checked the formula twice myself before sending it to Brynn, making sure it was perfect before she ran the sample batch.

Kendall hands me my coffee in a to-go cup. "You got this." She winks at me.

I take a sip of the coffee and my guts immediately gurgle with a pre-warning of an emergency-evacuation drill. Maybe I shouldn't drink this just yet. I wouldn't want to accidentally shit my pants because I drank too much coffee on an unsettled stomach. *Lucky, I opted for black suit pants and not hot pink like I'd originally planned.*

"Fingers crossed," I reply, my tongue feeling too big for my mouth.

"Please. You've taken a product that was okay and turned it into something amazing. I mean, to add growth serum is innovative. They would be stupid not to see that."

I nod because Kendall is right. It is innovative. That's me — innovation plus.

"Thanks." Blowing an air kiss, I grab my work bag and leave. With my teen line hanging in the balance, I'm not willing to chance anything. I need to be innovative when it comes to Glam Co.

Walking into my office, I'm greeted by the plain cardboard box on my desk with *Dry Shampoo sample* written on a sticky note. Perfect. Brynn must have brought them up for me. I need to send her a thank-you email later.

After tucking the box under my arm and grabbing my agenda, I make my way down to the boardroom at the end of the hallway, my confidence rising with every step. Everything is already going so smoothly; it must be a sign the meeting will go just as I planned. I tuck a piece of hair behind my ear and push the doors open. A little of my anxiety eases — I'm the first one here, and I go about setting up the room. I take my time setting the sample bottles in front of the chairs the board members will occupy. I also add a card which outlines the changes I've made to the product and how it will be beneficial.

Once satisfied with the presentation, I take my seat to the right of Ryder's chair and wait for the others to join me.

Ryder is the first to arrive. "Livvy." He nods, his eyes surveying the table and making me sit up taller in my chair. Taking the empty seat next to me, he leans into me and mumbles, "Impressive," his hot breath tickling my neck and inadvertently I cross my legs.

"Glam Co," I say, reminding him we aren't to discuss pleasure when we are doing business.

"I was talking about the presentation, but the shirt works too."

My cheeks flame. I need to calm myself down now for a completely different reason.

Fucking Ryder Fallington.

Slowly, the board members file into the conference room, taking their seats. I offer smiles to each individual person. But the warmth I'm used to receiving from them is carefully masked. Luana is the last member to take her seat. I use that as my cue and stand.

No time like the present, Livvy, you've got this.

"Thank you for coming. I'm so excited to share with you the launch of our new formula for our dry shampoo." I pick up a bottle and my lips pull into a frown, but I quickly recover. The bottle feels a little heavier than I expected. I wipe it off as my nerves. "As you all know, our dry shampoo is a fabulous product but in the last few years it's fallen a little flat when compared to others on the market. I decided it was time to revamp, improve, and renew this once fan favorite." I make sure to have eye contact with everyone around the table, including Ryder who is staring at me with an impassive face. "In order to do that, we have created a world-first dry shampoo infused with hair-growth serum."

A few of the board members look surprised, turning to each other with interest.

Yes. I mentally high five myself. *See? Piece of cake. You got this.*

"In front of you, I have placed a flyer with the main ingredient changes. Flyers similar to this will be available in all our retail stores as part of the display and in store promotion. We have a six-week promo planned with Ulta and Sephora where we hope to become the number one seller in hair care. We're going to hit this product really hard; we have enlisted more than fifty influencers across fifteen countries." I hold my bottle up. "I've taken ten bottles from our production line to test out here and now. If you would all like to try your samples." I motion for everyone at the table to use the shampoo. There's a genuine smile on my lips as each member of the board pull off the lid and shake the bottle — that is, except for Ryder. "Don't you want to try it?" I ask.

"Of course. I'm just taking it all in. I've never used dry shampoo myself. I don't know how it works."

I straighten my spine, staring between the board members and Ryder. He just admitted he didn't know a Glam Co product in front of the board. Shouldn't that be a giant red flag? Why is no one scribbling this down in their notebooks? *Hello?* On the scoreboard of Ryder vs Livvy, I think I'm up by, like, two at this point.

The sound of a hiss draws my attention to the board members spraying their hair with the product. So far, everyone looks really happy and excited about it, which is great. After shaking my own bottle, I spray my hair too, waiting to smell the jasmine I had Brynn infuse it with. I scrunch my nose. *That's not right.* It smells like the gym after teenage boys have had a sweat session. Chairs crash against the floor as the board members start screaming and violently scratching their heads. Eyes wild, I stare around the room. My own head is beginning to burn. What is going on?

"Oh shit," I groan, scratching my head and trying to relieve the itch. But it's only making it worse. I don't understand how this happened. I went over the formula with Brynn multiple times. We tested it on a few members of staff in the lab before even submitting the trial formula. No one had an adverse reaction.

Except for today.

Shit. This couldn't have gone worse if I'd tried harder. Everyone is itching their heads — except Ryder.

My eye narrow on him as he casually leans back in his chair without a care in the world.

"I've never used dry shampoo, but is this normally what happens?" He asks so casually the hair on the back of my neck rises. He is way too calm in a room full of screaming people. Almost as though he knew this was going to happen. But that's impossible as he just admitted he has no clue what dry shampoo even is. So that must mean Brynn and I stuffed up on the formula or my dad was right — we can't add growth serum. Maybe the pressure in the bottle had a negative reaction and caused this?

"My hair," someone yelps.

"It burns," another groans.

"My scalp is on fire." That is definitely Luana shrieking.

"Quick, everyone, get into the emergency showers in the lab." I try to remain calm, but at this moment calm is so far out the window it's not even funny. Without knowing what has caused this reaction, the only course of action is a decontamination shower.

Pulling my hand away from my scalp, I pray I don't see chunks of my hair in my hands. So far, so good. I don't think I will be able to hold in the tears if we all lose our hair.

I follow everyone out of the boardroom and down to the Glam Co lab emergency showers. After saying a particularly sad goodbye to my favorite pair of Yves Saint Laurent heels, I dump them in the 'destroy' bin. Anything that is considered 'contaminated' gets destroyed, it's the rule. I jump into the shower and try not to stare at the other almost-naked bodies surrounding me. Thank God we all still have underwear on, but I am regretting my choice of white lace today. The only thing keeping up the small amount of modesty between us are ten-inch-long brick separators. *Freaking hell, this is awkward.*

Ryder steps in behind me, using the same shower head as

me. I'm surprised to find him in the showers. He didn't spray himself, but I guess he needs to maintain appearances and show the board he used the product too.

Sensing my questioning gaze, Ryder offers, "I wasn't sure if being in the room meant I was contaminated." He leans across my shoulder, not even hiding the fact that he's brushed my nipple on purpose and grabs the decontamination shampoo from the hole in the brick wall. My nipple, the traitorous bitch that she is, stands to attention at the small touch from Ryder. I mentally curse my stupid body. Ryder, though, smirks — clearly noticing my nipple through the white-lace bra — and tweaks the tiny peak, making me both gasp from pleasure and shock.

"There are other showers you know." My voice is way too breathy. I try to keep my voice low hoping no one can hear what is happening in this stall.

"There are," Ryder muses, squeezing shampoo onto his hand. His eyes flick down to meet mine. "But you're in this one."

"This is a business shower," I remind him, my eyes scanning the hard ridges of his body. My view is pretty spectacular. Ryder bumps me with his dick, now fully hard as he puts the shampoo back on the shelf. His body acts like a shield, covering us and his giant hard-on from the rest of the board members.

"Isn't that just a shame?" he whispers against my cheek before rinsing the shampoo out of his hair. "I would love nothing more than to push you up against the wall."

My core tightens, wanting nothing more than for him to do that too. Shaking my head and needing to cool off, I walk away from the shower, decontaminated and more than wet enough.

I need to figure out what the fuck went wrong with the dry shampoo before it costs me Glam Co.

CHAPTER TWENTY-TWO

Livvy

Tightening the belt on my fluffy pink robe with Glam Co stitched into the breast pocket, I pace my office for the umpteenth time. I grip the ingredients list of the dry shampoo as I wrack my brain over what went wrong. Thankfully, no one lost any hair. But to say I'm persona non grata with the board would be an understatement.

I rub tight little circles across my forehead, trying to alleviate the impending migraine. This is not good. I formulated this product. I have a degree in cosmetic science. I spent months with Brynn working on the reformulation. Up until this morning, I was confident in my skills. This dry shampoo mini launch is proof of how very wrong I was.

A knock at the door interrupts me.

"Who is it?"

I'm really not in the mood for anyone.

"Devin." My sisters voice has my muscles tightening. Of all the people who could walk into my office, she is the last person on my list of who to anticipate.

I roll my lips together, telling her to go away on the tip of my tongue but opt for, "Come in," instead. She opens the door and takes a hesitant step into my office and closes the door behind her. Tucking the paper under my arm, I stare at her, she's here to ask how I am, so why the fuck has she come? She seems nervous, her eyes darting around my office to the floor — anywhere but at my face.

"Devin." I say snapping her out of her perusal.

"Hi," she whispers.

"Hi," I echo, still trying to process what she is doing here, especially after what happened the other night.

I'd resolved myself to only see her on special occasions — Christmas and Thanksgiving — when I can get shit-faced and pretend she didn't betray me. I cannot stand to see her and Kyle without wanting to punch both of them.

"Nice office," she mumbles.

I know. I earned it, I want to reply, "What are you doing here?"

"I umm — " She starts to explain but stops short. "Why are you in a robe?"

Narrowing my eyes and blowing out a sigh, "My clothes got contaminated."

"What happened?" A look of genuine concern masks her face. She studies cosmetic chemistry and knows anytime you need to take a decontamination shower, something really bad has happened.

A sharp, "Why are you here?" leaves my lips as I cross my arms over my chest and take a seat behind my desk.

"I wanted to apologize," she blurts, and I scoff, not believing for a second that's something my sister is capable of.

"For sleeping with the guy I was dating? For getting caught sleeping with the guy I was dating? Or for being an all-round shitty sister?" I rattle off.

"Livvy," Devin sighs, her shoulders dropping.

"What?" I reply, sitting up in my chair. "You can't blame me for wanting clarification." I clench my fist under the desk.

Devin's cheeks redden with embarrassment. She fiddles nervously with the bottom of her top. After clearing her throat, she says, "I'm sorry for it all, okay?"

Rolling my eyes, I release a sharp breath, and half-heartedly reply, "Sure," and run my tongue along the roof of my mouth.

It's not that Kyle was blatantly cheating on me with my sister that hurts. He was a bag of dicks, and I stupidly dated him for two months too long thinking it was the right thing. I knew Devin and I were never going to be the kind of sisters who share everything — we have always been pitted against each other. If anything, it should have pushed us together to unite against our dad. But all it's done is drive us further apart and to a level I didn't think she would stoop to. If accepting her stupid apology means her leaving my office quicker, I will just sit here and smile.

Although, I can't be too mad. If anything, she did save me from wasting my time with Kyle.

"Did you really mean it?" she whispers, rocking on the balls of her feet.

"What? That I accept your half-assed apology?"

"That I'm worth more than my last name." She wrings her

fingers together in front of her.

A shiver causes goose bumps to light my flesh. There's uncertainty in Devin's voice — like she believes I would only say such a thing to make her feel bad instead of knowing it to be true.

"Of course, I do. You have so much to offer the world — whether it's being a part of Glam Co or being your own person. Why settle for some dipshit telling you what you are and aren't allowed to be?" I swallow, biting the inside of my cheek. My throat feels thick as my advice to Devin sinks in for myself too.

"I ended things with Kyle." She breaks through the silence. "I just wanted to tell you you're right. He is an asshole. I don't know why I didn't realize it sooner." She picks the skin on her fingers and wipes away a lone tear.

"I guess you aren't totally to blame in that department. I should've seen through his Polo Boy façade and the way he was so obsessed with the FF Group too."

"Polo Boy?" Devin asks, tilting her head to the side, the ghost of a smile on her lips.

I snort. "It's Ryder's stupid nickname for him."

Devin's lips part as a quiet laugh escapes past them. "You know, that's kind of funny."

I nod. "Just, whatever you do, don't tell Ryder you find him funny. I'll never hear the end of it." That man definitely does not need an ego boost.

Devin muses, "You're going to make a great CEO. You are the lifeblood of this place."

"Thank you." My eyes become misty as tears threaten to fall at my sister's words — mostly because today has been shit-tastic and the idea of me becoming CEO is even further away than ever before. Having the support of my sister is a lot more meaningful than a piece of paper telling me I'm worthy. All I've ever wanted was to have my sister by my side and remove this wall my parents constructed between us as a way to pit us against each other. Standing, I cross the room, the imaginary wall between us starts to crumble for the first time in our lives. Devin and I are seeing eye to eye. Glam Co isn't just a company. It's our legacy.

I embrace her. Devin stiffens at first, but after a moment, her body relaxes as she hugs me back tighter. We haven't hugged in years; it feels strange and yet so familiar to have her in my arms.

"How about we start over?" she whispers into my hair, her voice broken and hoarse. "I need my sister in my life."

"Me too." I nod, tightening my hold on her.

Me too.

Sitting at my desk after Devin has left, my spirit feels renewed and warmth spreads through my body. Devin saying I'm going to make a great CEO, today of all days, was something I needed to hear. My head becomes dizzy with the rush of endorphins and my chest is lighter than it has been all week.

The board is going to need a hell of a lot of convincing after this little slip up, but I can do it.

I dial Brynn's number; I need answers, and I need them now. The phone rings out. I try dialing again but have the same issue. Frowning, I place the phone back on the receiver. Brynn must be in the lab or something. She rarely answers her phone anyway.

Making sure the belt on my robe is secure — I don't have any panties on thanks to the contamination shower — I make my way down to the lab, strategically avoiding any possible Marilyn Monroe moment in my robe.

At the lab, I find Brynn in her office. *Strange.* If I wanted to let the bad thoughts win, it's almost like she's been ignoring my calls. "I tried to call but the phone kept dialing out?"

"I'm really, really sorry," Brynn cries hysterically.

"Hey." I rush to her side, wrapping my arms around her shoulder. "What happened?"

"I d-d-d-didn't know," she hiccups.

"Know what?" I stare at her in confusion, but she continues to cry.

"Is this about the board meeting?" I ask.

She nods, wiping the tears with the heel of her palm. I grab the Kleenex box from the corner of her desk and hand it to her. She pulls out a bunch and blows her nose before throwing them in the bin.

"It's not your fault. We need to relook at the formula. We knew there was going to be teething pains, especially doing something so new. I was actually coming to talk to you about it. Do you think the ingredients had a reaction in the bottle?"

"No." Brynn shakes her head and stands, her eyes glassy and puffy. She grabs a box identical to the one that was waiting for me on my desk this morning.

Rolling my lips over my teeth, I look at the box then at her. "Brynn, you left the box on my desk this morning. There is no need to pull another sample from the line. We know it's a failure."

Brynn's eyes meet mine, downcast and ashamed. "No, this box here is your sample box."

"What are you saying?" I stammer. "Do we have a breach in security?" I feel the blood drain from my body. This is a much bigger issue than just a reaction gone wrong. Glam Co has never had a problem with security in the past. But if someone purposely tampered with the product, we would have to go into a lock-down mode and investigate just what else has been touched.

"No. The sample you provided the board was made by me."

I stare at her, blinking, waiting for her to elaborate, but all she does is let the air between us sit and become sour. "Spit it out." I rub my temple, my patience thinning.

Brynn blows out a deep breath. "Don't get mad — "

I cut her off, "Nothing good ever comes after those three words."

"I made those samples with an adjusted formula because Ryder asked me to."

The announcement hits me like a cement truck, and I fall heavily in the chair she just vacated.

"What?!" I squawk.

Mad is an understatement. I'm fucking furious.

My hands shake at my sides. My vision dances with flashes of red hues as a rage like I've never felt pulses through my veins.

"He wanted me to add itching powder to the formula. He said it was a potential idea for Halloween, and it wouldn't go any further than him."

"Let me get this straight." I rest my forefinger and thumb on the bridge of my nose, trying to calm my rapidly beating heart. "You let Ryder change the formula, knowing it would create a product that could be dangerous, and had me serve it to the board."

She nods.

FUCKING RYDER FUCKING FALLINGTON.

"That's not all," she whispers, her voice barely audible.

"Oh please" — I give a sarcastic laugh — "tell me how this could be worse."

"We have already shipped out a thousand boxes with Ryder's ingredient change."

I stare at her, the muscles in my body becoming rigid. She's right. This is worse. "I'm sorry," I state. "It sounded like you just told me you shipped sixty-thousand units of dry shampoo infused with itching powder." I want to laugh — I really do — because not only is this the most colossal fuck up ever in the history of Glam Co, it happened on mine and Ryder's watch.

She swallows hard. "No, you heard correctly."

I plaster on a fake smile, the sarcasm dripping from my teeth. "Why would Ryder sign off on that — it would cause an issue for the whole brand and that would directly impact Ryder."

"He didn't. There was a miscommunication with the guys in the warehouse. Ryder's email was passed through, and production ran the whole line instead of just a sample run."

"We need to stop that truck," I announce, walking out of Brynn's office. It's not just me who has their name on this one though — Ryder is the one who asked for the ingredient change.

I've never been in such serious damage control in my entire life. I don't care if I have to shoot the tires out at this point, I need to figure out the truck's route before the stock gets unloaded and hits the shelves. "Can you find me the tracking and contact details for the delivery truck and message me the second you have it."

"Before you go — " Brynn calls.

I freeze and turn to look at her over my shoulder. I don't think I can handle hearing more bad news right now.

"The lip plumper sample is ready."

"Oh." The second reason I wanted to come down here — my lip-plumper sample, I was going to scour that formula next to make sure we don't have another bad reaction on our hands. Although at this point, it's a sad consolation.

I've been waiting for Brynn's schedule to lighten before she could finally get it ready. Glam Co doesn't have the product yet, and I haven't even put any of the necessary documentation in the 'new launches' folder — mostly because this is still very much in the testing phase. Well, it's more like I mentioned the idea to Kendall, who loved it, and slid into Brynn's emails with a 'plz make this' and the formula I created. I just need a small sample batch to see if it will work.

Whether Ryder is running Glam Co or not doesn't mean the company should stop turning. We still have new products to create.

"Did you happen to make one in red?"

"Yes." Brynn smiles, handing me three samples of lip plumper; one clear, one a light pink, and one in my favorite shade of red that Glam Co makes.

Ravage me.

"Perfect." A sinister smile graces my lips at the three samples in my hands.

"Be careful. I know we discussed making them extra hot to see instant results — but I decided to add even more of the heat factor to create extra volume. That way we can work backwards, depending on your feedback."

"I have a feeling these are going to be perfect," I muse, leaving Brynn's office feeling lighter than before.

Whether or not they are perfect for Glam Co, I don't know. But my meeting today was completely destroyed, and these lip plumpers are just the thing I need to extract my revenge on a certain dark-haired CEO.

CHAPTER TWENTY-THREE

Ryder

The image of the board screaming for their lives plays in my mind like the best movie I've ever watched. I didn't expect that kind of reaction when I told Brynn to modify the formula with itching powder. Sure, I anticipated people to start itching but not within five seconds of it touching their scalps — and screaming like they'd been doused in hellfire? That was just pure gold.

I almost feel bad for Killer. I can see how much time and effort she put into the product. After reading the flyer she gave us with all the points of adjustment and how they will fit into the market, there's no doubt she's actually really good at her job.

The only problem is there can only be one winner at the end of our six-month time frame, and I intend for it to be me. "Of course, I won't let the reformulated dry shampoo go to waste. It is a brilliant idea, after all. I'll tell the board I fixed the issue; with some extensive testing, the product release will go ahead as scheduled. I'll look like the hero."

"Bro, that is genius." Zander's smiling face shines in my phone.

When I got back to my office after the decontamination shower, I wasted no time Facetiming my brother even though it's two in the morning in Japan right now. I knew he would be just as proud of what happened in the meeting as I am.

"You should have heard the screams. It was like something out of a Tim Burton movie." I give a soft chuckle.

"Most importantly, though, it all happened in front of the board. There is no way they're going to pick her over you — especially if she just barbecued their hair follicles."

"It was totally worth the decontamination shower," I tell him, remembering the curve of her soft ass against my dick.

The decontamination shower was worth it for more than one reason.

"Who gave you the idea to put itching powder in the dry shampoo?" he asks.

"Becks."

Zander laughs harder. It's a very Becks idea to come up with.

"I was going through the launch schedule and saw the board meeting was attached to this product, and he thought about sabotaging it. The decontamination shower was a bit of an overkill, but I couldn't come out and just say, 'Oh, don't worry. It's only a bit of itching powder.'

"I'm just glad it worked out. I'm surprised you pulled it off you failed chemistry, and it's clear Livvy Blake knows how to fuck with a Bunsen burner. Who would've thought?"

Biting the inside of my cheek, I try to tamp down the unexpected anger Zander's words create. Livvy isn't just an unexpected piece of ass. The idea that my brother thinks of her that way kind of annoys me. Losing Glam Co has nothing to do with Livvy, explaining that to Zander is turning out to be another story.

"I told you," I reply, taking a deep, steadying breath. "I won't lose Glam Co to Livvy. Tell me how the meeting went with FF Group." I change the subject, moving it as far away from Livvy and Glam Co as possible.

Livvy storms down the corridor to the office opposite mine, muttering to herself something that sounds like 'Stupid Ryder and his stupid, magical dick,' a sultry smile plays across my face. My office neighbor could use a visit.

"Where did you get clothes from?" she asks me the moment I walk in.

I glance at my slacks and button-down shirt. "My house?"

She snorts. "Figures. You went home to get changed."

"No, I keep a spare set of clothes in my car, Killer. What kind of an image would it be for the boss to walk around in a robe all day?" The spare set of clothes in my car wasn't a fluke — I always come prepared. Today just happened to work out well with the decontamination shower.

"Not to mention I'm utterly naked underneath the robe," she grumbles like it's a bad thing, tightening the cord. "Now, there's a good look for a CEO."

The offhanded remark has me unmoving; a tingle moves

over my chest as my eyes devour her body. "You're naked under there, Killer?" If we were anywhere but at the Glam Co office it wouldn't bother me, but the idea of Steven from finance catching a glimpse of Livvy in her robe irks me. That fucker is creepy.

"As the day I was born." She wags her hips from side to side, causing her robe to open and flash me her perfectly waxed pussy.

"Ah," I clear my throat, my brain frozen. But I'm glad I'm blocking the doorway because I don't want anyone else to get a view of her magic pussy — bar me. Closing the door behind me, I fish my phone out of my pocket and send Cecelia a message to bring up the clothes I left at her desk for Livvy.

We stand there staring at each other in silence until Cecelia knocks on the door a few minutes later. Opening it just enough, to allow her to stick her hand in with two coat hangers dangling from her fingers. I protect Livvy from having someone accidentally catch a glimpse of something Livvy isn't sharing.

"Thank you," I murmur to her, taking the coat hangers before closing the door behind her. "Here." I hand a less-than-impressed Livvy the change of clothes.

"Boy, you move quick — already hiring your own personal assistant now?" She rests her hands on her hips, her cheeks glowing with built-up anger.

This morning's board catastrophe has keyed her dislike of me up to a new level. With her lips pulled down and a slight flare in her nostrils, her fierce look is adorable. Not to mention she's still in the robe. "No, but I do intend to promote Cecelia in a few weeks. She's wasted talent as a receptionist."

"She is — I'm glad you think so too." Her response is sharp and terse and yet I don't miss the subtle underlying compliment. Livvy takes the pair of high-waisted pants and button-down shirt from my hand and pushes past me to the en suite bathroom adjoining her office. With a stealthy sleight of hand, she slips a tube of my favorite red lipstick in the pocket of her robe.

A few minutes later, Livvy walks back into her office, swiping her lips and making them glisten with red lip gloss. She stalks toward me like a cat on the prowl, eyes zeroing in on their target, and I'm the lucky fucker in her sights. There is something about red lips on Livvy that has become my kryptonite. She closes her office door and the distinct sound of the lock snipping in place gets me three different kinds of excited.

"Livvy?" I ask, staring at her with raised eyebrows, but she stays pressed against the closed door. The rosy outline of her nipples peek through the silk blouse. Fuck, I chose well. Livvy forgot to do an extra button because her full tits are front and center, begging me to explore the soft skin. Tilting her head, she continues to stare at me, rubbing her lips together. The gloss she has on is almost making her lips look bigger–is that even possible?

Finally, she pushes off the door and takes a few measured steps toward me. "I've been thinking of the perfect way to say thank you," she whispers, her voice breathy and light — it goes straight to my dick.

My lungs feel like they've turned to ash. "For what?"

"For not rubbing the dry shampoo in my face," she sighs as she comes to stand in front of me.

I swallow the thick lump in my throat. "What kind of a man would I be to rub that in your face?" I reply, my mouth drier than the Arabian desert.

Livvy stops directly in front of me, her hands resting on my chest, and I'm really grateful she locked that door because I don't think I could handle an unexpected interruption at this point. I struggle to take a breath in, my lungs have shriveled up like a collapsed balloon. She kneels in front of me, her hands going to my belt and her fingers working to deftly unhook it.

"You don't have to." My voice is a horsey rasp.

But I really hope she does.

She flicks her eyes up to meet mine under her heavy lashes, "I want to."

Livvy Blake is going to be the death of me.

As if my pounding heart needed another reason to send more blood to my dick — it turns to granite in my pants. My eyes stay focused on her lips, the red gloss hypnotizing me. I've never really been much of a gloss guy but with Livvy's lips — that's about to change.

The sound of my zipper falling sends a shiver down my spine. Livvy's hand sneaks into the opening of my pants and wraps around my pulsing dick. My head falls forward and I stare at her with wide eyes, watching her small hand wrapped around my hard cock. Something about this take-charge Livvy is not what I expected, and it makes my cock jump. Livvy runs her hand up and down my dick, twirling her wrist when she gets to the end and making my eyes roll into the back of my skull.

A knowing smirk graces her lips, and I want to kill every single guy she has practiced on before me whilst simultaneously thanking them. With her free hand, Livvy tugs my pants down, letting them pool around my knees, keeping me fixed in place. My cock stands at attention, saluting her, the tip already beading with pre-cum. Livvy's tongue darts out and licks her lower lips prepping for my cock, and my dick jumps again.

That color is going to look so good smeared over my cock.

I'm glad she decided to keep her hair down. I gently run my fingers through the strands at the base of her scalp before cupping the base of her head. The greedy little thing takes that as an invitation and dives right in. Her tongue swipes the bead of cum straight off the head of my dick before sucking it back into her mouth, savoring the taste.

My lungs struggle to inhale as my balls draw up tight. This is a new level of torture, but I will willingly sign myself up for it every single day for the foreseeable future.

Livvy guides my dick into her mouth, taking me in her throat until I hit the back. Slowly, she pulls her lips away, as her red lip gloss leaves a trail in their wake. Closing my eyes, I wait to feel Livvy's mouth again. A few seconds pass and I look down. Sitting back on the balls of her feet, Livvy stares up at me with wide, innocent eyes as her cheeks hollow out.

My dick starts to tingle, and I give a soft grunt. My hands tighten in Livvy's hair. I try to encourage her on, but her eyes flash as they hold mine.

"Livvy?" I ask, my dick starting to burn like a godsdamn inferno. "Why is my dick burning?"

She bats her eyelashes and tilts her head to the side — she has the innocent act down. "What do you mean?" she asks.

I give another grunt as the burning in my dick increases. Not in the if-I-don't-have-you-I-will-cry sort of way but like someone is barbecuing my dick with super-fire seasoning. I try to remain calm, but the strangled gasp that escapes me makes my voice sound a few pitches higher than it is. "Why does my dick feel like it's on fire?"

CHAPTER TWENTY-FOUR

Livvy

"Oh no," I use my most convincing gasp, and stand. The lip plumper Brynn created is incredibly potent if my own lips are anything to go by — I can't imagine the pain Ryder must be enduring.

"Livvy," he grunts his teeth gnashing together, as a bead of sweat pools along his temple. "There's something really wrong."

My eyes widen at the sight of his dick swelling.

Oh yeah, Brynn has nailed this one.

I hold back a smirk. "Wow, you really are a show-er AND a grow-er. No wonder I was so sore with that snake in your pants."

Ryder doesn't say anything. His eyes just widen as he looks up at me in panic. Grabbing the lip gloss from my pocket, I swipe on another coat before lifting the bottle to eye level and letting out a fake gasp, "Oops." I cover my mouth with my hand. "I mixed up my lip glosses."

Ryder's eyes go comically wide, and I resist the urge to

laugh out loud. My plan to extract a little revenge on Ryder for the dry-shampoo clusterfuck has gone off perfectly, better than expected.

He screwed around with my product, sabotaged my launch; now I'm going to show him just how amazing our products can be with the right formulas.

"I had Brynn make up a sample of lip plumper. It's a product I have been thinking about adding to our line. I was ready to share it with the rest of the product development team and I wasn't sure which direction to take it. You know, like, make the ingredients cooling or heating? And with so many lip plumpers on the market, I wanted it to stand out. I told her to make it extra spicy so we can see instant results."

Ryder scrubs a hand down his face.

Hmm, maybe there could be a new market for this. If the discomfort is tolerable, that is.

Ryder's nostrils flare and the muscles around his eyes tighten. "Can you please just give me the SparkNotes version of this story? Is my dick about to fall off or not?"

I take more pleasure in the panic in his voice than I should. "Not," I reply. "At least, I don't think so?" I let the question hang in the air, Ryder's face becomes incredibly red, the muscles in his neck stiff and tense. "I mean," I continue, enjoying this way too much. "The last time Brynn made samples for me, they caused everyone to come down with a bad case of invisible lice and we all had to take decontamination showers. So, her track record on creating products that won't cause bodily harm is kind of lagging." I school my face to feign concern, adding in that touch of girly innocence.

"Livvy."

My name is a strangled gasp on his lips.

Shaking his head back and forth rapidly, "It wasn't — " he slams his jaw shut, the muscle ticking in the corner of his cheek twitching.

I stand slowly, cocking my head to the side and lift my eyebrows, "What was that?" His internal debate growing louder by the second.

"Brynn didn't make a mistake," he lets the pained words escape with a hiss.

"She had to have. I have a degree in cosmetic chemistry. I promise you none of those ingredients would have caused that issue."

"She added itching powder," he replies, gasping for air as he clings to his throbbing manhood.

Another laugh threatens to break free from my throat. "Why would she do that?" I trail my finger in slow circles over his chest.

"B-b-b-because I asked her to."

I rear back, needing to add some space between our bodies. If I wasn't ready to throttle the guy, I would applaud his genuineness. "Are you telling me you sabotaged my product to make me look bad in front of the board?" Keeping up the innocent act is a challenge.

Ryder swallows hard.

Gotcha.

"Yes."

"Well, I hope the sabotage was worth it. There was a mix up with production and sixty-thousand units of your formula are currently on their way to Ulta stores. Put that in your stupid honor roll."

"Fuck," Ryder groans, but I'm not sure whether it's from the pain in his dick or the fact that he has seriously fucked Glam Co over.

"On the plus side" — I tap my fingertip to my chin — "I think if you were to give yourself another shower, it should help with the burning-dick situation."

"Why didn't you say that a few minutes ago?" He bends, grasping his pants and pulling them up. But with the raging hard-on he currently has, they don't zip up.

"I mean, I could have." I shrug and grin at him. "But where would the fun be in that?"

Ryder opens my office door and cups his dick before storming down the end of the hallway, presumably to scrub his dick clean of our soon-to-be new product.

I can't wait to tell Brynn just what my thoughts are on the new product. I might get her to make some samples with the cooling affect as well — strictly for comparison reasons only . . . maybe.

With any thought of Ryder's dick firmly in a box, I turn my attention to what's important. I enter the tracking information of the truck and try to find its exact location or even a phone number for the driver.

"What are we going to do about the truck?" Ryder asks, striding into my office like his dick wasn't just on fire a few moments ago, his business mask back in place.

"How do you know I wasn't bluffing?" I cross my arms over my chest and sit back in my chair. The self-righteous path I decided to take is really blowing my confidence into overdrive.

"Because you wouldn't joke about something so serious." He meets my gaze.

Still riding on the high of busting him, I meet his gaze, the heat simmering in his brown eyes with my own. "You're right — I wouldn't."

Glam Co and the six-month deadline mean too much to me to tank the whole brand with a batch of dodgy dry shampoo bottles. Apparently, the same can't be said for Ryder. *Figures.* He doesn't care if there is no brand standing at the end of six months. He just wants to be declared the winner — even if it's the winner of nothing.

We let the silence sit like a heavy weight in the room until finally Ryder collapses under it.

"How are we going to stop the truck?" he asks, resting one arm on the back of my chair and the other on my desk, caging me in. citrus scent completely enveloping me, casting a spell on my sense.

I quickly shake that shit from my head, remembering who put itching powder in my freaking samples drying all those lovey-dovey urges straight up.

"I tracked the route and the driver's navigation on the way up to my office from the lab. Luckily, the faulty product isn't far out from the warehouse. I haven't had a chance to contact the driver yet." I scribble the number Brynn sent through on one of my personalized 'From the desk of Livvy Blake' sticky notes — it's the small things — and hold it up to Ryder. He quickly takes the number and leaves, setting to work fixing up his giant fuck up.

"Thank God," I whisper, relieved as I watch the little blue

dot tracking the truck turn around and make its way back to the warehouse seconds before Ryder walks back into my office. Arguably the biggest crisis to hit Glam Co has been averted. No thanks to Ryder.

"Livvy?"

I minimize the screen before swiveling in my chair to face Ryder. "Yeah?"

"How long is my dick going to stay big for?"

I smirk as my eyes fall to the noticeable bulge in his pants. I shrug, "I don't know. A few hours maybe." There isn't really a handbook on these things. At least, not one I've read. And I don't really want to ring Brynn to ask her because *that* conversation would just be too awkward.

Ryder nods and makes his way to my door before closing it and clicking the lock. "Then maybe we should take advantage of it. Don't you think?"

"What?" My voice cracks a little. "You can't be serious?" My eyes go straight to the bulge in his pants and a jolt of excitement pulses through my core.

"Oh, I'm deadly serious, Killer." A seductive smirk pulls at his delicious mouth.

"I don't know. Won't that be messing up the whole Fallington–Blake, Ryder–Livvy thing we have going on?" My panties are soaked from the suggestive look in his eyes.

"Nope. Besides, aren't you curious to see how this plumper shit works?"

I roll my eyes — because fuck yes! "Only if you promise to be really quiet."

Ryder makes his way to my desk before lifting me up on

the edge and fitting himself between my legs. "Again, with the fucking pants," he groans, making me giggle.

My hands instantly wrap around his shoulders as my legs find their perch around his waist. I start undoing the buttons on his shirt, needing to feel more of his skin under my hands. I manage to undo all the buttons in seconds, and Ryder throws his shirt somewhere in the room — I don't care and mine is quick to join his. Ryder's hot mouth finds my nipple as his fingers undo the button of my pants.

"What can I say?" I lean my head to the side, giving him more room to trail hot kisses down my throat. "I love a good power suit."

"That you do, Killer." His words are scorching against my skin before he makes his way to my lips for a hungry kiss.

There is something about me being laid out on my desk like this with Ryder on top of me, knowing we could get caught at any moment, that makes it so much hotter.

"Huh?" I gasp when he breaks the kiss.

"I think your phone is ringing, Killer." He looks at me, as the faint trill of my phone sounds again.

I couldn't care less who is calling right now, it could be the damn King of England inviting me to dinner and I still wouldn't answer. "Leave it," I gasp, struggling to suck down the oxygen I need to breathe. I'm almost positive my body will burst into flames if Ryder doesn't put his tongue back on me.

"Here." He hands me the phone.

"No," I breathe at the flash of my dad's name on the screen. "There is no way I'm answering that right now. Let it go to voice mail."

Ryder eyes me with a smirk as his thumb clicks on the green 'answer' button and he makes a show of hitting the speaker.

Shit, what a fucker.

Taking a deep, steadying breath, I grab the phone from his outstretched hand. "Hey-YAH," I nearly scream as Ryder decides at that moment to move his tongue to my aching core, sliding it along my slit deliciously slow.

"Livvy — " My dad's worried voice blares through the phone " — is everything okay? You sound out of breath."

Yeah, Dad, just peachy. I currently have a guy going to town on me like licking my core is the last thing he will do before he's sent off to war. Oh, by the way, the guy in question is the one who is trying to steal my birthright right out from under me — but it's cool. He has an amazing dick, so it's totally worth it for the orgasms he's giving me.

That might be seen as inappropriate, so instead I go with, "Sorry, I was in the middle of filming, and I couldn't find my phone." Ryder chooses that moment to bite down on my clit, causing me to nip the heel of my palm to stop from screaming out.

"If you were filming, you could have just called me back.

Ryder's eyes flick up to meet mine.

I mouth, *"Don't stop."*

He smirks up at me as he inserts his finger, making my eyes roll into the back of my head. "So wet," he murmurs loud enough for my dad to hear.

"What was that?" Dad asks.

"I didn't hear anything," I reply, lifting my leg getting

ready to kick Ryder — only to have him catch my leg and rest it on his shoulder, opening me up more and giving him much better access.

Yep. I am definitely going to kill Ryder Fallington.

CHAPTER TWENTY-FIVE
Livvy

It's official Ryder is the master of distraction. His thick fingers continue to pump in and out of my aching core as his lips skim my thighs, moving higher and higher up with each pass. As much as I want him to stop, I think I will die if he does. I can already feel the low thrum of my orgasm building. Shit. Shit. Shit. I need to end this call ASAP. Something tells me Ryder wants to ensure that it's impossible to be quiet when I come.

"Was there, umm — " I bite my lip to stop the groan building in my chest from releasing itself. "A reason for your call?" I hope my voice doesn't sound as choppy to my dad as it does to me.

"I was calling to see if you could tell me how you went with the board today. You know, the all-important product launch?"

"Oh yeah," I mumble, and Ryder pulls back, giving me a moment of reprieve to focus on the call — or so I thought.

Instead, he unzips his pants, freeing his hard — and I must

say plumper — dick from the confines of his pants. I become hypnotized by the movement of his hand gliding up and down his hard cock. A low moan escapes my lips, and I quickly slap my hand over my mouth. I hope my dad didn't hear that, because I have no clue how I can explain that one away. I shouldn't be surprised; half the board probably rang him with the splendid news the instant they dried themselves off.

"I don't think I need to remind you how important showing your competence is. And now with Kyle and your situation changing, it doesn't look great," he continues.

"Mmhmm," I reply, only half-listening to my father's passive aggressive attempt at chiding me for something that wasn't even my fault, as Ryder reaches for a foil packet in his pocket and sheaths himself.

I know what's on the line — I know how much this little mishap has put me behind in the boards' eyes. But right now, I really don't care.

Ryder glides one hand up my thigh as the other guides the head of his cock over my entrance. And I'm done — this call has to end. Right the fuck now.

"Sorry, Dad, I kind of have to go."

I end the call just as Ryder slams his dick inside me, I scream into my closed fist as white-hot pleasure shudders through my body. His chest grazes against mine as he leans over, letting my phone fall onto the floor, not caring where it lands. I reach my hands up, curling my fingers into his dark locks and pulling on the silky strands with the tempo of Ryder slamming into me.

Who says imploding your life is a bad thing when you get

railed like this?

"Oh god," I moan. The change in angle from his new, enlarged dick hits me right on a spot that has me flying with angels.

Freaking Hell, this feels good.

"God wouldn't be able to do this to you, baby." Ryder increases his speed, and I have to agree with him. My legs tighten around his waist as I creep closer and closer to my impending, earth-shattering moment.

Until finally — like a match to a flame — I detonate.

"Ryder," I call his name, tugging harder on his hair, my whole-body quivering and shaking with my release. Ryder follows me, grunting, his whole body stilling — his hands are on either side of my head and his face hovers over mine. Our lips brush lightly as the post-glow bliss takes us both.

"I really hope you hung up the call before you dropped your phone," Ryder says after we catch our breaths.

"Me too," I laugh, internally cringing at the thought of my dad hearing me get my world rocked by Ryder.

His eyes flick up to mine, his brow softening. I see the real Ryder when we're like this. Both our facades have been dropped. We can just be ourselves without the masks we need to keep in place in order for our families to get what they truly desire — Glam Co.

Ryder presses a kiss to the corner of my mouth before helping me get dressed. We have exactly three minutes to be in the warehouse before Barry arrives with the truckload of faulty product.

"We'd better hurry." I indicate the clock sitting on my desk.

"I knew I could make you come just before the truck arrived." Ryder smirks as I slide off the desk, slapping my ass.

For once, I'm happy to not deflate his ego. I make extra sure to put a seductive sway in my hips. Since Ryder is already looking, I may as well give him something to appreciate. "Hopefully, next time you don't need to be so quick." I wink at him. "I'm a two-orgasm kind of girl."

Ryder snakes his arm around my waist, pulling me against his chest and dropping his hot lips against my neck. "Two orgasm kind of girl, huh? And what kind of asshole would I be to not oblige a woman of her needs."

Tilting my head to the side, I bite my lip and try to stop the smile — but I'm doing a hopeless job of it. "A big one."

Screwing Ryder could easily become my new obsession.

After the most exhausting day ever, I just want to get home, order Thai takeout, open a bottle of wine, and relax in a bubble bath in that exact order. Between the three orgasms Ryder so generously gave me–he had to prove that he could go above and beyond the minimum quota–and throwing away sixty-thousand units of faulty dry shampoo, I'm so ready to put today behind me. Oh, let's not forget I put a giant 'X' against my name with the board after that disastrous product demonstration. There's no way I can even tell them it wasn't my fault without looking like a petulant child playing the blame game. Yep, today has been a real keeper.

My heavy footfalls make the short walk from our garage to the apartment seem like I decided to wear weights around my ankles during a yoga workout for how hard each step was. I need to regroup; the little packaging change I made is nowhere near the itching-powder-in-dry-shampoo level of payback necessary to show the board I'm the better fit.

Not even your idea of payback is as good as Ryder's — see why the board is already choosing him over you? The dark voice in my head returns. Shaking my head, I try to ward it off.

Finally reaching my apartment, I feel the sting of annoyance when I can't find my keys. Juggling three bags, I fish around trying to locate the stupid thing before Mrs. Dylan decides to open her door and ask how I'm going. That's the last thing I need today. How can one stupid key play hide and seek so well? My heart pounds in my chest when the handle jiggles behind me. My patience is already worn today, I just need to catch a break.

I breathe a sigh of relief as my fingers grasp the sneaky little piece of silver and I shove it into the handle so fast, I nearly break the lock. I open the door a sliver and slide my body inside just as Mrs. Dylan exits her apartment.

"Phew." I lean against the closed door, gripping it for dear life, my chest heaving with deep pants.

"Aaaahhhh." Kendall fake coughs.

Startled, I drop my bags, and wince when my laptop thunks against the ground. That one hurt. Kendall is standing by the kitchen counter, staring at me wide-eyed mid-pour. My eyes flick to Becks, frozen in place opposite Kendall, his hands cupping the wine glass she is pouring into. Clearly, I've interrupted something. Too bad I literally could give zero shits.

"Ohh, wine, gimme." After dumping my bags at the door,

with a few quick strides I reach Beck's and grab the glass out of his hand. Because yes, I am at the will-punch-you-in-the-eye-if-you-look-at-me-for-longer-than-twenty-seconds mood.

"Livvy." The warning in Kendall's voice evident.

I ignore her, drinking the whole glass in one satisfied gulp.

"Bad day, huh?" Becks guesses when I hand him back his now-empty wine glass.

"Understatement of the century," I reply, wiping the escaped droplets of wine from the corner of my mouth with my wrist.

Kendall's eyes bore into mine; it's becoming clearer by the second I've interrupted something. "Why are you wearing different clothes?"

Rolling my eyes, I take a deep calming breath, "I refer you back to Becks' statement." I motion for her to pour more wine into Becks' glass. Kendall fills the glass up again while I kick my shoes off, leaving them near my discarded bags. Becks hands me the glass. I eye him out of the corner of my eye. As much as his BFF has a great dick and knows how to give orgasms, it doesn't mean he is totally in the clear here.

"I've never seen that top before. Can I borrow it tomorrow?" Kendall asks.

I snicker. "The reason you haven't seen it, Kenny" — I flop down on the couch — "is because it's not mine. Who's up for Thai food?" I effortlessly change the subject as my stomach grumbles in agreement. Two glasses of wine on an empty stomach is not going to pan out well for tomorrow's Livvy. I open Uber Eats app on my phone and choose our go-to Thai restaurant. Leaning on the back of the couch, I ask, "What do you guys want? Fair warning, I'm in the mood for pad Thai and I'm not sharing."

Becks and Kendall share a look.

"What?" I ask, glancing down at my shirt and hoping I didn't mismatch the buttons after the third time Ryder ravished me.

And I've accidentally been flashing everyone my nipples all afternoon.

"Didn't you get my message?" Kendall asks.

I blink. The subtle 'you weren't supposed to be home yet' message becoming clearer by the second. "Clearly I didn't."

"We're going out for dinner."

I blow out a huff. "Fine." I don't really want to go out and, ya know, mix with people, but if Kendall wants to eat dinner out, I can mope about later on. "Give me ten minutes. I need to grab a fresh pair of panties and retouch my makeup and I'll be ready."

"Let me rephrase that, Becks and I are going out for dinner." Kendal points between the two of them, not extending her fingers to me.

Shouldn't there be some sort of code against this?

"Well then I guess there is no need for me to put some panties on now is there?"

Becks chokes out a strangled gasp, and Kendall pats him on the back while he continues to cough up half-swallowed wine.

"Besides." Kendall's eyes soften. "I figured you would have been out celebrating the win with the board today."

"Ask your dinner date how well today went. I'm sure he

would have known about it before I even did."

Kendall's eyebrows scrunch. "What? What does Becks have to do with dry shampoo?"

Becks at least has the good sense to look a little sheepish.

"No, not Becks so much as his best friend there sabotaged my launch by putting itching powder in all the bottles. I had the board test the shampoo and it led to us all standing in the decontamination showers."

Kendall throws her head back and laughs. When she sees I'm not laughing with her, she quickly sobers. "Oh wait, you're serious?"

"As four-week pube growth on the night of a hot date."

Becks cringes. "That's serious."

Kendall looks between Becks and me. "Maybe I should cancel dinner." Being the wonderful friend she is, she's willing to give up her plans — especially when they involve the enemy's best friend to stay with me and help me decompress.

"No, it's fine. I kind of want to call Devin anyway." Guilt draws across my stomach; I don't want her to change her plans for me. It's not her fault Ryder managed to make me look like a fool in front of the board.

Kendall's jaw drops. "You want to call Devin? What the fuck happened today?"

Leaving the couch, I liberate the wine bottle from the kitchen counter. They really don't need to drink the rest of this if they are going out — me, on the other hand? I have a nice, hot bath calling my name.

"Too much, Kenny. Too much," I call, closing the bathroom door behind me.

CHAPTER TWENTY-SIX

Livvy

I send Devin a message letting her know I'm here as I open the car door, letting MoMo jump out from her little doggy seat before attaching her leash. Getting up at this ungodly hour on a Saturday should be a crime, but Devin believes in early morning meditation and energy-reset shit. We're really taking this whole starting-over thing seriously, and after the shitty week I've had, some fresh air and early morning sun is the perfect medicine — or so Devin says.

DEVIN

Running late.

Of course she is. I tuck my phone back in the pocket of my yoga pants and tighten my grip on Momo's leash. There is no way I'm moving from the shield of my car, not when I know dad's home.

I haven't spoken to him since our phone call right before Ryder blew my brains out. I know our next encounter will be even less pleasant, and the bar on the last one was already set low. While I wait, I scroll through my notifications on Make Me from the video I uploaded last night. Hundreds of people comment the same thing: 'Where's Ryder?', 'Bring back Ryder.' I roll my eyes — *Ryder isn't everything* — and close the app without replying to anyone. The Ryder effect is in full swing, and I don't have the energy to respond with 'Ryder is an asshole.' It's safer to just be radio silent.

"Livvy." My dad interrupts the rabbit hole I'd found myself in.

My muscles tighten as I stand upright, priming themselves. "Dad, shit," I mutter, placing my hand on my pounding heart. "How did you know I was here?"

"The security camera sent a notification." He points to the camera, which has a direct view of my car.

Apparently, I'm not so lucky. His scowl confirms just as I'd suspected, I cue myself for the barrage of questions.

"Where's Mom?" I ask.

"At the country club. She's taken up playing tennis. I'm about to meet her."

I notice the tennis bag hanging off his shoulder, but I take time to delve deeper into his appearance. His cheeks are ruddier since the last time I saw him, emphasizing the wrinkles on his face which have become deeper. His collar is askew and lifted at the back, like he has grabbed an old shirt from a pile on the floor. A heavy shadow covers his usually clean-shaven jaw, and dark-purple circles line his under-eyes.

"What are you doing standing out here?" he asks.

Well at least he didn't say, *Who were you screwing while on the phone?* Small wins.

"I'm waiting for Devin. We're taking MoMo on a walk."

Hearing her name, MoMo gives a small bark and wags her tail like she is agreeing with me.

Dad's lips thin. He isn't at all impressed by my presence. I try not to let it sting, but it doesn't work. "Shouldn't you be at Glam Co, focusing on new products?"

"Dad, it's Saturday," I remind him.

"And you had a colossal issue with the board this week. You can't become complacent. You need to revise all the formulas of the products you are planning to present to the board next time. You can't make the same mistake twice."

"Dad," I huff. "There is nothing wrong with my formulas. Ryder sabotaged my samples to make me look incompetent in front of the board." My mood takes a dive. I'd finally gone a few hours without thinking about that meeting, only for him to just bring it up again.

He doesn't miss a beat, "Olivia, I *am* disappointed in you. You let a Fallington make you look like a fool in front of the board."

"I'm aware," I try and fail to keep the snappiness from my voice, Momo gives a growl beside me. "And I can't tell them it was Ryder, because it will only make me look like I'm blaming him for my product failure." Like a stacked deck of cards, my patience is about to crumble. It's not like I can go to the board either, because it will look like I'm making excuses for my failed product. And if I know anything, it's that a good leader doesn't make excuses.

Dad holds his hands up in defense. "Don't take out your bad mood on me. It's your teen line that won't go ahead if you don't gain control of Glam Co."

My knuckles whiten as the soft leather of Momo's leash bites into my palms, but I welcome the pain.

He's only telling you the truth. The dark voice uses my dad's words as fuel to ignite itself. *You can kiss your teen line bye, bye, and the legacy Nanna left behind. All because you know — deep down — you will never beat Ryder; he is so much better than you.*

"And Derick is not too happy about how you behaved with Kyle, what were you thinking breaking up with him?"

"He wasn't right for me dad. I shouldn't be with someone who doesn't love me the way I want to be loved." My dad's nostrils flare, I guess my answer wasn't what he wanted to hear.

I almost weep with relief at the sight of my sister bounding down the staircase, finally my reprieve. *I can do this; I am enough*, I tell that voice in my head. *I will do anything it takes to ensure Glam Co is mine.*

"Are you ready?" Devin clears her throat, cutting through the staring match between Dad and me. Devin's eyes dart between us, her face full of concern as she pushes past Dad and interlocks her elbow through mine, I give her a shaky smile.

"Yep."

"Thanks for waiting." She makes sure her voice is louder than necessary, clearly ending any more conversation.

"I'll see you later." I give Dad the polite acknowledgement even though I definitely don't plan on seeing him later.

He just grunts in response.

"I'm sorry," she whispers, as we watch dad get into his cart and drive off down the street. It's barely audible and if I wasn't concentrating, I would've missed it. Devin has finally seen the pressures I'm under, and I'm not entirely unhappy that it's helped bringing us together.

"What was that all about?" Devin asks as we wait for the gate at the end of the driveway to open, dad has already zipped through with the cart.

"Apart from Dad deciding the Blake legacy will live and die by every decision I make in the next six months; he was having a meltdown over the board meeting this week." My throat closes, not really wanting to talk about how much of a failure my first solo board meeting was, as we take off walking down the street toward the giant park in the center of the neighborhood.

"What happened at the board meeting?"

I try to gauge whether she is being real or just teasing me. By now, I'm sure that everyone has heard about what happened at the board meeting. She's been at college and doesn't really catch a lot of Glam Co gossip. Heck, even my high-school chemistry teacher sent me a message asking me if I forgot the lesson on endothermic reactions. Well, joke's on her because while dry shampoo is a literal endothermic reaction, no one's scalp froze.

Devin just blinks.

She really must be out of the loop. "I nearly made the whole board bald with my new dry shampoo." I proceed to recount everything that has happened between Ryder and me, including how Kendall told me I should try to prove Ryder unfit to the board. At the moment, that plan is failing and hard. It's a long walk and we have more than enough time.

"Frankly, I don't understand the big deal. So what if the

Fallingtons have come back and decided they want a piece of Glam Co? It's not like they don't really deserve it."

"True. But if the Fallingtons get Glam Co, it means that we would probably lose it. I've worked my whole life to be a part of Glam Co. I don't know what I'll do with myself if I don't have it anymore. Dad will disown me if I fail him. You know — "

"No one makes a fool out of Simon Blake," Devin finishes my statement.

"Exactly," I mutter, rolling my eyes.

Devin stays silent, mulling over everything. "Well then, I guess it's in our best interests to ensure you keep Glam Co." She clicks her fingers together. "Hey, what if we see if Sofia will help us out with a bit of pay back?" Sofia Faluccino is loosely related to us and her family also happen to be members of the FF Group.

It's not public knowledge that the Blakes and Faluccinos are connected, because we don't really run in the same circle or share the same friends. The Faluccinos are a part of the founding five families after all.

"Yeah . . ." Any mention of FF Group has the hairs on my arms standing on end. After the Fallingtons left Nanna's sister at the altar, she found love with Mario Faluccino and they had Donato and Carmelina. Sof's dad and aunt.

"Didn't she mention something about Donato getting Leo to step up more with FF Group?" Devin is already typing away on her phone, a wicked grin tracing her lips. "What if we fuck with FF Group a little? Leo and Sof are always up for a joke."

I swallow the lump in my throat. "I don't know," I reply.

Make Me

It's one thing to defend Glam Co, but going after FF Group seems a little too drastic.

Devin stops walking. "Liv." She shows me her phone opened to Sof's contact and her latest thread of messages.

Do I do this? Do I release this weapon in our arsenal?

Then I remember the screams from the board members after Ryder screwed around with my presentation. Gripping MoMo's leash tighter, I nod. He's not the only one that can get a bit of enjoyment out of this.

"Do it," I tell her, making Devin smile as her thumbs furiously type.

Nothing is safe from the Blake sisters.

Devin pockets her phone.

Is that it?

"Now let's talk about payback for the board-meeting fiasco." My sister flashes me a wicked grin, and for once I am happy to be on the other side of it.

With a little extra pep in my step, I walk into my office with Devin's payback plan tucked safely in my bag. I try to look as inconspicuous as possible, or at least like I'm not about to get my revenge on Ryder Fallington while I set phase two in motion. A little plan I devised myself thanks to Ryder and his addiction to his morning brew.

We have another board meeting today. Due to the presentation fail, the board has concerns and wants more frequent meetings. *Goodies.* My plan is to pretend like I have something vital to discuss and there is no time to get coffee —

hence why I already organized it. *It's genius.*

I close my door with a soft click and quickly dial Cecelia's number.

"Can you please bring me up two coffees and make mine with oat milk?"

"Sure thing," she replies before ending the call.

A few minutes later, Cecelia arrives with said coffees in recyclable cups. "Here you go."

"Can you please close the door? Thanks." I take the coffees from her and place them on the desk.

"That one has the oat milk and that one is Ryder's usual order." She points to the drinks.

Of course, she knew I was ordering for Ryder. Sometimes I have to remind myself that Cecelia and I have worked together longer than her and Ryder — she sure does act like she is in Ryder's pocket lately.

"Perfect." I smile and grab the foil packet from my pocket. I pop out four laxative tablets. It may be overkill, but I really want him hugging the porcelain throne — so to speak.

"Ahh, what are you doing?" she asks, staring rapidly between my hand and the cup.

I shrug. "Adding laxatives."

"Why?"

I wiggle my eyebrows, "To spice up life." *Why else? Duh?*

"More like you mean to make Ryder shit like a landslide?"

I resist the urge to laugh out loud as the visual crosses my mind. "Oh darn, did I put those in Ryder's coffee?" The remorse in my voice sounds fake even to my own ears. "Oops." I smile, mixing Ryder's coffee with my finger before licking it.

She giggles. "Did you just lick your finger from the laxative-laced coffee?"

I stare up at her with wide eyes. "Oops." This time I do mean it. I quickly chug half of my two-liter motivational water bottle, blowing through my half-day total in a few deep gulps. *This is why I leave the evil genius stuff to Devin; she wouldn't do something as stupid as dose herself with laxatives when she is dosing someone else. Hopefully that will dilute whatever laxative I accidentally ingested.* I very unsteadily convince myself, trying to use reverse psychology, mind-over-matter crap crossing my fingers it will work, or else I'll be joining Ryder in the bathrooms.

"I don't know how comfortable I am knowing you will give this to Ryder."

I run the tongue along the back of my teeth. A couple of weeks ago, she wouldn't have cared whether I gave Ryder a drink laced with laxatives or four tablespoons of cinnamon, and today she is all worried about her conscious like it should matter. "He got to you, didn't he?"

It's bad enough the Ryder effect has taken control of my Make Me audience, now he has taken Cecelia too.

Cecelia pouts, not able to meet my eyes as she curls absent strands of hair behind her ear.

"What did he get to you with?"

"First-edition, signed Sarah Franetico books."

I blow out a short whistle. "That man is evil. Who can say no to a first-edition, signed book series? It would be like someone offering me a 1990 straight-off-the-runway Chanel dress. He really went for the big guns." Cecelia is a giant Sarah Franetico fan, so much so she has managed to make it a personality trait. "How about this. He will never know you brought the coffees. In fact, we haven't even seen each other this morning? Hmm?"

After a few seconds considering it, Cecelia nods. Pretending to button her lips, she leaves my office door open, so I can see Ryder walk into his office a few moments later. My plan was nearly derailed by a simple stir of my finger. My stomach gurgles, and I pray that it will hold out long enough for me to watch Ryder experience the effects of his coffee.

Left hand, I remind myself, picking up the two cups.

"Morning." I smile at him as I walk into his office.

Ryder flicks a glance at me and smiles as he finishes doing up his tie. He kiss on my cheek, making my knees wobble — the gesture is so sweet and tender.

Left hand, I continue to remind myself. *The plan doesn't change.*

"Morning, Killer."

"I brought you coffee." I hold up the two cups and go to hand him the one in my right hand.

Left hand, I scream at myself.

I quickly pull my right hand down and hand him the one in my left hand. "Sorry." I smile. "This one has oat milk in it. You know how I can't handle dairy." I take a sip from my drink.

"Thanks Baby." He takes the cup from my left hand before sipping it.

"Hmm, this coffee tastes different?" Ryder muses after a few more sips.

"What? Different? How?" I rush out, trying to keep my mask of indifference in place as I wrack my brain, to remember if I picked up the flavorless laxatives and not, like, raspberry delight or some shit.

"The beans taste like more of dark roast. Maybe they've changed beans." Ryder takes a few more sips.

I watch him keenly over the rim of my own coffee cup. "Yeah," I agree. "It does taste a little more bitter than usual." NOT.

Satisfied he has ingested enough coffee to have the desired effect, I nod. "Well, I'll catch you in the meeting." I blow him a kiss and make my way to the boardroom down the hall, keeping my head down and trying not to draw any attention to myself.

CHAPTER TWENTY-SEVEN

Ryder

Livvy saunters out of my office like her ass is on fire. It's weird behavior, even for her, but I put it down to nerves over having another board meeting. I take another sip of my coffee; nothing beats my morning coffee.

I grab my things and stroll into the meeting room – I know it won't start without me. I'm pleasantly surprised to find Livvy sitting in her spot — the chair next to mine — not that I would admit it to Livvy, but I kind of like having her so close to me.

Slowly, Livvy Blake has consumed me, more than Glam Co should be. After the six months is up, I'm intending to keep Livvy on, her ideas for the company will only strengthen our position in the market. Although, if I'm honest with myself, it isn't only for Glam Co why I want to keep her here, working with her is slowly becoming the best part of my day.

I take my own seat and wait for the last two members to walk in before starting the meeting. "Thank you all for attending. I'm going to open the floor for Livvy to take todays agenda."

"You what?" She stares at me, her eyes comically wide in surprise. If I wasn't mistaken, regret flashes across her gaze.

"I'm giving you the floor…" I deadpan, my brows pulling down in a furrow. Her agenda is open, and I can see the first bullet point – the bullet point I included before sending to everyone– her teen line. "As you can see from the points listed today the most crucial is planning new expansion and Livvy has put forward formulas and specs on a teen line." I nod at her, taking a sip from my cup.

Will I regret showing the board Livvy is incredibly competent? No, because she is exceptional. It's also great optics as far as I'm concerned for the board to witness how I plan on expanding the product line.

"Yeah — " The word is a tentative whisper like she is hoping she didn't mishear me. "Shit," she glances down at her agenda, heat blazing over her face.

She seems like she's about to collapse, it's another sign I've come to notice from Livvy when she's overwhelmed or nervous in a situation. I allow her a few moments to compose herself, "Livvy wants to expand Glam Co into the teen space, and having looked at the figures, I can see why. Glam Co is missing a lucrative market."

The crimson slowly bleeds out of her face, as her blown pupils slowly return to normal. I want to reach out and cup her face, push a strand of hair behind her ear, but I can't, not only will it completely undermine her right now, but we also agreed we wouldn't do anything to interfere while we are at work.

"Have you started formulating the line?" I direct the

question at her.

Livvy had no idea I was going to bring this to the board today. I'm pretty sure she didn't think I was even paying attention when she told me about her plan for her teen line. But after the dry-shampoo disaster, I felt the timing was right for this. Me bringing this to the board doesn't have anything to do with Livvy or her magical pussy. It's about what's best for Glam Co's profit line.

Something inside her snaps and her professional mask slips back into place. "Yes, I have started formulating. I want to start the line with some simple skincare, moisturizer, cleanser, mud masks, serum, toner, and jelly under-eye patches. Because who doesn't love under-eye patches? They're very on-trend right now with the teen market." She sits a little higher in her chair as she flips to a heavily scribbled page in her notebook.

A few of the board members nod to each other, murmurs of agreement sound around the table.

It drives her to continue, "As far as formulation goes, I need to add a few tweaks before I'm ready to get samples from Brynn, first round results are here." She hands a technical sheet around. "But overall, I've spent a long time curating the line and it's an underpopulated market — "

A sudden burning sensation ripples across my guts, followed by a sharp sting that makes me keel over and groan, "Oh fuck," interrupting her.

"Ryder is everything alright?" she gasps, causing every single board member to stare at me, with mixed expressions of bewilderment and confusion.

"Fuck, fuck, fuck, fuck," I chant. Heat racing up my

neck to my face, sweat breaks out on my forehead right as another cramp grips my abdomen, doubling me over. Standing abruptly, my stomach gurgles, the contents already liquidizing in my body.

Oh shit.

"I'M NOT GOING TO MAKE IT." I eye the exit, cupping my ass yelling unintelligible lines to anyone who crosses my path. I know this feeling, and it's not going to end well if I don't get to a bathroom. Not even caring about the destruction I leave in my wake. Sweat beads gather around the nape of my neck and my ass clenches and unclenches with every step I take.

I'm going to make it. The five words are almost a prayer in my mind.

In a move my high-school football coach would love, I twirl and narrowly miss crashing into Sal from IT. That would've ended in a shitty disaster, pun intended. With an offhanded "Sorry," over my shoulder, I continue down the hallway whilst already undoing the zip on my pants.

Tears of joy spring in my eyes at the sight of the bathroom door. *Nearly there.* My stomach does another twirl, increasing the burn in my ass. After bursting through the bathroom door, I don't even bother to check before jumping into the first available cubicle. In one fluid motion, my pants are down around my ankles and my ass touches the cold, porcelain rim just in time for the explosion of crap to evacuate my ass. What the fuck just happened to me?

The bathroom door opens, and I cringe, hoping my shoes aren't recognizable because I can't help the noises pouring from my body.

"Ryder," Livvy calls.

"Livvy," I growl in warning. "For the love of God. Please go away," I plead, sweat beads rolling down my neck. I don't want her here for this. "This is the men's bathroom." I fucking hope it is.

"Ah, no, it's not." Livvy laughs. "The men's bathroom is next door."

I dab at the sweat near my temple with a piece of toilet paper. "Livvy, I know what I saw when I came in."

"Yeah, you saw 'Glam Girl' because 'Glam Guy' is next to it."

"Shit," I groan. I swear I went into the correct room.

"I'm joking, Ryder."

With those two words, I relax as much as my quivering muscles will allow. "Not funny."

"Are you okay, do I need to get the first aider?" she snorts, holding in her laughter.

"NO." A sharp pain stabs my lower gut. *I'm not going to make it.* Zander is going to have to take over, because I'm going to be found dead here very soon.

"Well, if you say so…" Livvy trails off before gasping, "Do you think it's corporate espionage?"

Espionage? What the fuck where did that come from?

"My coffee is the only thing I've had this morning," I grunt as my stomach rolls again. *Someone fucked with my coffee.*

"That's what happens when you use the same coffee shop every day."

"Livvy?"

She didn't.

"Oops, did I accidentally add laxatives to your coffee instead of sugar?" Livvy's too-sweet voice sing-songs.

She fucking did.

"Oh fuc — " My words are cut off by another explosion of crap.

Fucking Livvy Blake. "Did you just come in here to mock my pain?"

I'm going to be stuck here for the rest of my life.

As much as I want to throttle her for putting fucking laxatives in my drink, what's happening in my stomach is highly embarrassing and overrides everything else.

"Not just to mock your pain, per say. I wanted to see if you might need something like . . . some water . . . your phone . . . toilet paper . . ." Amusement colors her voice.

"Why did you do it?" I whimper, clutching my quivering stomach.

"I needed to even the playing field in front of the board."

"And you thought making me shit my pants in front of them was level enough?"

"Well, I wasn't going to lace the board members' coffee, now was I?" she drawls as her deep-brown painted toenails appear in the slot under the door.

"Well played. Level enough now?"

"We're just getting started Fallington. Don't go backing down on me now. You said you're up for a challenge."

I click my tongue to the roof of my mouth, pride swelling in my chest. I expected Livvy to cower after the dry-shampoo incident. But if today is proof, she truly is a worthy opponent.

She sticks her hand under the door, a small tablet perched between her thumb and finger. "Here."

"Don't take this personally, but it might take me a while to trust anything from you ever again."

"That's probably wise," she agrees. "Consider this a peace offering then. It's an Imodium and should help with your current . . . issue."

Ha, that's an understatement.

I eye the tablet like it's going to explode at any given second. "Why the sudden change of heart?"

"You brought up my teen line to the board. You probably wouldn't have heard as you ran out of the room screaming at people to 'Move or get shit on,' but they loved it and want me to send through more information before we can really consider adding such a large line into the brand. We might even change the name, so it's not related to Glam Co, since we're branching out into a new market."

I take the tablet from her fingers, and swallow it dry, almost choking on it. A bottle of water appears under the door, I hesitate for a moment. I'm hoping she didn't lace it with Viagra or something so I will be stuck here shitting my brains out with a raging boner, but reluctantly accept it.

My phone buzzes with an email. I reach into my breast pocket in my jacket and pull it out and scan the email. The subject line has me clenching my jaw, this can only be the result of one person.

I clear my throat, testing to see if she's still here with me. "Livvy."

"Yeah?" Her shoes come back into view.

"Why is Kosmedika threatening to pull the line because I've submitted a packaging change?" My voice is deadly calm like a cobra right before it's about to strike.

"What was that? Oh sorry, I think Cecelia's calling my name. Got to go." Her hurried footsteps click against the tiles. "Don't forget to wash your hands," she reminds me before the sound of the door shutting echoes through the empty bathroom.

Fucking Livvy Blake.

Half an hour later, I've finally stopped shitting liquid. But I'm still not ready to risk leaving the cubicle. I'm leaning against the back of the toilet when my cell buzzes in my hand.

LIVVY
How's the *shit emoji* situation?

ME
On what scale?

LIVVY
The laxative scale, I suppose.

ME
And what would that be?

LIVVY
4

The blood drains from my face. She's doused me with four laxatives. No wonder I feel like I'm fucking prepping for a colonoscopy.

> **ME**
> YOU GAVE ME 4 LAXATIVES!

> **LIVVY**
> No, I diluted 4 laxatives. Since you didn't finish your drink, I would say you probably had two and a half. Max.

Two fucking hours I was stuck on the toilet with Livvy's random messages to keep me company. It took a good hour, after the Imodium, before I started to feel better. Although not enough to want to be more than a few steps away from a bathroom. Livvy has been cautiously avoiding me, which is probably for the best because when I get my hands on her I plan to bend her over my knee and return the favor with my handprint on her ass cheek.

"Livvy." I walk into her office holding my butt cheeks tighter than usual.

"Well, if it isn't the Shit-E-OH himself." She looks up from her computer, grinning from ear to ear. "To what do I owe the pleasure?"

"Stay away from my morning brew, woman. This is betrayal in the highest order." I wag my finger at her. There is a lot of things I can tolerate in life — messing with my morning coffee is not one of them.

I hold my phone in the air. "Want to tell me why Kosmedika is threatening to pull our line because of a change in packaging?"

"Our line?" She questions, eyebrows raised.

Closing my eyes and rolling my head over my slumped shoulders, I blow out a harsh breath. "I've had a shit morning —"

Livvy starts laughing. "Pun intended."

My eyes narrow, as I glare at her. I roll my tongue along my teeth, praying for the patience to not take this infuriating woman over my knee. "I now need to have a call with the buyer and explain why these designs were submitted with my signature on them."

She sobers, but a tiny smirk plays on her lips. "That sounds serious."

"What design changes are they even talking about?"

"I have no clue?"

I would believe her innocent act, but the way her cheek twitches tells me she is the reason I have received this email. Anyone else may not notice, but I don't miss a thing concerning Livvy Blake.

"Kosmedika is a huge client." She picks a piece of invisible lint from her top. "Wouldn't want the board to hear you have accidentally messed up on the same day you pretty much pooped your pants in front of them."

I narrow my eyes at her. "The better question is what the fuck did you submit to Kosmedika?"

"Me?" She clutches her chest, attempting to bleed innocence into her act, but failing miserably.

"Yes, you," I growl, getting tired of this game.

"I didn't do anything, but you might want to check that sender address." She winks at me — fucking winks at me.

I rub my throbbing temple. My crappy day just got worse.

CHAPTER TWENTY-EIGHT

Livvy

With Devin's genius plan, Ryder officially ruined the board meeting. Practically shitting himself in front of the board is nowhere near the level of screw up I suffered–but Ryder running out on a very important meeting made us almost even. News travels fast — the staff are now giving him a wide berth every time he walks into a room. I titter and mentally high-five myself for the third time today. And I finally got to present my teen line. Today, honestly, couldn't get any better.

Grabbing the things I need for the self-care video I plan to film tonight, I dance around my office.

The only person who will be happier for me right now is Kendall. I can't wait to get home and tell her what happened today. I can already hear her laugh. My phone chirps with a message. Thinking it's Kendall, I'm pleasantly surprised when Devin's name flashes on my screen.

DEVIN

How did it go?

ME

He ran out screaming.

DEVIN

LMAO I knew a laxative would be great.

ME

. . . 1 laxative????

I swear Devin told me to use a couple of tablets, and we all know a couple is code for three or four, RIGHT?

DEVIN

Ya why?

ME

I may have used 4.

DEVIN

Oh my tits. The guy will never leave the bathroom . . . ever.

Devin's message only adds to my already happy mood, our relationship only improving by the day. My stomach gives a grumble, informing me it's time to go home.

I'm testing a new mud mask that requires oil for activation for Make Me, I've already done a video on my first impressions, but I want to try the mask with Kendall before I show others on my channel how it works. I go over my planner for the next video I will be filming, trying to see if I have room before my collaboration with Glam Co comes out.

The way Ryder always pays particular attention to my lips every time I have red lipstick on has me scheduling a red lipstick try on video. I already know which products I'm going to use; I've set aside five different red lipsticks and two liquid lipsticks — one is my personal favorite.

I tap the pen against my chin, toying with the idea of asking Ryder to be a part of the video. My Gracites have spoken, and loudly, and they want to see more of Ryder. But I don't really want to share my audience with him — they're my Gracites, after all. It's important for me to deliver what my audience wants — even if that does mean Ryder Fallington.

I gained half a million followers just from the unboxing PR video alone.

ME

How do you feel about filming another video with me?

RYDER

Ms. Blake if I'm going to keep filming, I think I need to be getting some sort of credit...

ME

I'm taking this as a yes. And no, your ego does not need any more stroking.

Make Me

RYDER

Well, if we're going to talk about stroking, then I definitely have a suggestion...

"Kenny," I call, the moment I open the door, my dinner hanging between my fingers.

I made sure to order extra for her. It's my night to cook, and unless she wants food poisoning from under-cooked chicken breast – takeout is a better option.

"You'll never believe what happened today." Resting my foot against the door, I unclip my keys from the lock, expecting to find Kendall waiting for me — but I'm met with silence. "MoMo," I call. My little fur baby scampers into the living room. "Hi, sweet girl." My face lights up at her wagging tail. "Is Kendall home?"

She just barks and sits by her food bowl. I'm taking that as a no.

Leaving the food on the bench, I kick my high heels off and change out of my work clothes into my comfy sweats. I tie my hair up in a messy bun and go in search of Kendall.

ME

Yo, dinner is getting cold. Where you at?

The grey dots appear.

KENDALL

Soz, babe. Stuck at work — boarding emergency flight to Paris.

I push out my bottom lip, looks like it's just me and MoMo for dinner. Must be a serious emergency if she's having to go to Paris.

After refilling her kibble, I kiss the top of her head and sit at the countertop ready to dig into dinner. Alone.

How fun.

I dip my fork into the saucy noodles just as a soft knock sounds at the door. All I wanted was a peaceful evening, but I suppose living next door to Mrs. Dylan, that's not entirely possible sometimes. "Mrs. Dylan, I'm not swapping dick stories with you aga — " I cut myself off. It's not an overeager Mrs. Dylan standing on the other side but Ryder blinking rapidly, his mouth opening and closing like a fish gasping for air. Subtly, I cross my arm over my chest, hoping he doesn't see my nipples salute him through the thin fabric of my top. "Are those?" I stare at the bouquet of flowers in his hand.

"Peonies," he replies, regaining his composure.

"No way." I grab the flowers before stuffing them under my nose and inhaling the floral scent deeply. He must've noticed I love peonies after Anders grave them to me.

"Who is Mrs. Dylan and why does she swap dick stories with you?"

"Shhhhh," I whisper-hiss, looking over his shoulder and hoping Mrs. Dylan isn't Beetlejuice and magically appears at the mention of her name. She is supposed to be visiting her sister at a retirement village in Florida, but that lady is always popping up at the most inconvenient times. Yanking Ryder inside the apartment, I double-check the hallway before closing the door as quietly as possible. Beetlejuice incident avoided.

"Can we just circle back to the swapping dick stories?"

"It's nothing." I wave him off. "Our neighbor is in her seventies and suffers from being dick drunk, and she will take it anyway she can get it — living vicariously through us included."

Ryder whole body shakes with a deep, rich, floor-vibrating laugh. He even wipes a tear from the corner of his eye. "It took a while to get there, but boy was that worth it."

"Yeah," I gripe. "She is a real firecracker. Next time you see her, I'll be sure to mention her days as an international model, she loves to share her stories." Needing to steer this conversation away from my overactive neighbor, I circle back to the fact he just randomly showed up at my door with my favorite flowers. "How did you know to get peonies?"

"Oh please. I don't need to break out the three words, eight letters to know that you, Killer, are a peony girl."

It makes my stomach knot in a delicious way. "And you brought flowers because . . ."

"Because I'm proud of you for showing the board the teen line."

"What?" My words are barely audible. Even after I made him poop for two solid hours? He's still proud of me.

I can't remember the last time someone said they were proud of me. A weird, warm sensation creeps its way through me. Damn. If I thought my stomach was knotting before, my knees have gone ahead and joined the wobbly party.

"I'm also mildly offended you don't remember our filming date."

I crush the flowers to my chest to stop myself from

reaching for him. "I didn't mean tonight."

Don't ruin this Livvy.

"Maybe I was hoping to see you tonight?"

"Would you, umm like to stay for dinner?" I rasp.

"Yeah," he replies, his throat bobbing, "I would."

This almost feels like our first unofficial date.

MoMo barks, breaking our stare. "MoMo, this is Ryder."

My little fur pup walks up to Ryder and promptly sits beside his leg, demanding he show her his hand so she can sniff him before allowing him to pat her. Which Ryder does, while I put the flowers in a vase. Ryder picks up MoMo, smiling when she licks his chin with her seal of approval, and that makes me feel all kinds of things I haven't since I was sixteen staring into my first boyfriend's eyes when he said, 'I love you.'

Dinner was surprisingly easy. We ate on the couch with our pad Thai nestled in our laps. Ryder seems completely at ease with the casual setting, something that surprised me. I caught him sneaking peeks at my chest at least a dozen times but decided not to call him out on it. In fact, I made sure to stretch a few times, pushing out my torso, just to mess with him. I had to hide my smirk when he crossed his legs, covertly trying to adjust himself in his pants. When MoMo jumped on his lap a minute later, causing him to double over, I smothered my laughter with a cough. For an almost first date, it was kind of perfect.

After packing away dinner, I get ready to film.

"I have a new product to test out. It wasn't exactly what I

had in mind for our video, but if you're open to it? I was going to test the product with Kenny." Ryder and MoMo turn to look at me. It's kind of comical, MoMo just met Ryder a few hours ago and now she is sprawled across his lap while he relaxes on the couch like they're best buddies. I almost feel betrayed by the way she is hanging off him, whimpering if he stops patting her.

Me too, girl, me too.

"That's going to be difficult with her and Beck's being in Paris."

My eyebrows shot up. Wait?! Becks is with her? I'm definitely going to have to have a chat with her about this.

"Are you interested in trying it?"

"You're not going to turn me into a smurf with blue dye, are you?"

I giggle at the mental image. "No. Though don't tempt me."

Ryder places MoMo on the couch next to him, and stands, a small smile playing along his lips, "Well then, where do you want me?"

My chest constricts, secretly loving that he's so willing to help me with my Make Me videos.

I spend a few extra minutes making sure I like the set up in the bathroom before I get Ryder to sit down next to me. "Ready?" I ask him before clicking play on the camera.

"I think so."

"It's just a self-care video — nothing too tricky. The vibe is extremely relaxed like the PR video we did. I'm kind of excited for this one. We will be trying this mud mask." I hold up the box with the mud. "It's from a small business, and I love testing products from small businesses on my channel." I shrug and adjust the product box to make sure it's visible in the shot.

Ryder snorts. "I feel I should get paid by the brand too."

"Oh, this isn't a paid partnership." Turning to look at him, I continue, "I bought it myself; the company came up on my TikTok and after looking into the brand's background a little bit and the product itself, I wanted to try it."

Ryder stares at me and an emotion crosses his face, but it's gone before I can work out what it means. "That can really help blow a small business up, you know. You have a shit-ton of followers; the kind of exposure this could generate is huge."

"Yeah." My cheeks heat. "That's what these platforms are for though, right? To help share up-and-coming brands and their products with people who value and trust my opinion."

Ryder stays silent for a few minutes. I wring my fingers together, waiting for him to say no or get up and leave, but he just nods his head and says, "I'm ready."

"Great." I smile and lean over, undoing another two buttons on his shirt.

Ryder looks down at my hands on his shirt. "Ummm, what are you doing?"

"Giving the people what they want," I reply, waggling my eyebrows.

The tips of Ryder's ears go pink, and we both burst out laughing.

Finally happy with the look, I press play, my influencer mask in place the moment the red-light flashes on my camera. "Hi, Gracites, welcome back to my channel. I'm so excited for today's self-care video, and we have a special guest." I pull Ryder into the shot. "You spoke, and I listened — Ryder is back."

"Hey, guys." Ryder awkwardly waves his hand into the camera.

"Ryder, have you ever used a mud mask before?" Lifting the box, I show the product to him.

"No." Ryder shakes his head, a little smirk pulling at the side of his mouth.

"Looks like I'm about to pop your mud-mask cherry then." My eyes glimmer with humor.

Ryder pokes his tongue in his cheek. "I didn't know we were popping cherries on this channel," he laughs.

I smile. "Only makeup ones." My eyes stay locked on Ryder's. "This mud mask is super cool. It comes in a DIY kind of way. You get the purple clay." I hold up the glass container with clay. "This clay is amazing. It's only found in one location in the world. It's known for its anti-inflammatory properties and it's great at tightening pores and detoxifying the skin. You also get the mixing bowl, the spatula, and the oil." I continue to pull the things out of the bowl and hand them to Ryder to look at.

I grab the headband I always use when I am doing my skincare routine and the fluffy one with bunny ears for Ryder. I don't warn Ryder before yanking it over his head and adjusting it to fit around his hairline. The look of shock and horror on his face is ridiculously adorable. My ovaries actually burst at the sight of this big, tough, CEO-guy wearing a bunny headband. I offer him my best 'you're awesome' smile, and his face softens in response.

Standing between his legs, I cleanse his face. Then I add the drops of water to the tablespoons of clay and oil and mix it around whilst talking to the camera about the consistency and feel of the product.

"What are your thoughts so far, Ryder?" I ask as I swipe the first stroke of the mud-filled spatula on his face.

"Is it supposed to feel cold?" his warm handsrest on my waist, imprinting the skin. The tips of his fingers brush the curve of my ass, and in my thin sweatpants the heat of his fingers send a burst of arousal through my body.

"Yup. Then it will start to feel tight on your skin as it dries."

"Here, let me." He takes the spatula and mixture from my hands and starts applying it to my face. My pulse thumps against my throat like a bass guitar from how lightly he touches my skin. His eyes never leave mine, as he dips the spatula back into the mixture.

I sink into his touch, my throat feeling thick and dry at the same time.

Ryder places the spatula and the finished container on my bathroom countertop. "All done," he whispers, his eyes all sexy and hooded as they drop to my mouth.

"I think I'm falling in love with you," I blurt, biting my lip the moment the words leave my mouth.

A small grin blossoms on his face, "'Bout time," he replies, making me bristle.

Here I am laying my heart out and he is just . . . glad? Could he honestly be more of an asshole?

Crossing my arms over my chest, I growl, "Excu — "

I'm cut off by Ryder cupping his hand around my neck, his thumb resting on my cheek, completely ruining my mud mask. "Because I have already well and truly fallen in love with you, Olivia Blake."

CHAPTER TWENTY-NINE

Livvy

Ryder is in love with me.

"Seriously!?" My working brain cells collapse — the smart, witty Livvy going with them and instead replacing her with this fan girl who can't think past '*he said he is in love with me*'.

Ryder snickers, "Yeah, seriously," seconds before his lips crash onto mine.

"Wait." I pull back, tearing my lips from his. "We need to turn the camera off." There is already going to be some serious editing needed, and I don't want to accidentally make a spicy video at the same time.

"Good idea. Sex tape will come next time."

I click the button just as Ryder lifts me up, and my legs instantly wrap around his waist as he walks us to my bedroom. His lips trailing a hot line down my neck.

My back hits the bed a few moments later, and Ryder wastes no time climbing on top of me. His hands go under my shirt, pulling it over my head.

"No bra," he muses, a smirk on his face.

"Yeah, lucky we have to refilm that video because I just realized my nipples would've been completely showing."

"They are beautiful nipples," he whispers before taking one in his mouth. "But I'm not ready for anyone else but me to see them."

I moan while his fingers continue to pluck and tease the other one. I tug on his hair, and Ryder lifts his head. I giggle at the bunny headband still in place, the mud mask — a mixture of mine and his now — lining his neck.

I tug the headband off his head, as he pulls mine off. "We're totally going to need a shower."

Ryder wiggles and lifts his top off. "Good. I plan to get you nice and dirty."

Hooking my legs around his waist, I flip us, so he is now underneath me. Ryder's hooded eyes stare up at me with heat and mouth slightly open at the maneuver I just pulled off.

I grin. "What? Do you think it's just you who has moves in the bedroom?" I wiggle my hips from side to side and along his rock-hard length.

"Livvy likes taking charge in the boardroom and the bedroom — you're my dream girl."

"Dreaming about me there, lover boy?" I roll my bottom lip along my teeth, peering down at him.

"Every day since you told me to get my own damn coffee."

"You know you're absolutely about to get laid, right?" I pant.

"Trust me." He flashes the panty-melting smile at me.

"I know." His hands settle around my hips before giving a squeeze, urging me to continue to move my hips, adding the perfect amount of friction against me, setting the bundle of nerves alight. I throw my head back and moan, needing to have less layers between us. Sensing my need, Ryder's hands slip under the waistband of my pants, cupping my ass and curling his fingers in the crease between my thigh and ass.

After lifting myself up on my knees, I raise one leg, then the other, letting him slide my sweats down my legs before discarding them on the side of my bed. I trail my fingers over his bare chest and down the ridges of his sculpted abs, as desire clenches my core. Ryder releases a pained breath as I undo the button and zipper on his chinos. His fingers find their way into my core, teasing my clit.

"Fuck, fuck, fuck," I whisper, all my nerve endings lighting up.

"So wet," he murmurs. "So ready for me."

"Always," I reply, licking my lips, needing him inside me, but not wanting a barrier between us. "I'm clean and on birth control."

"Me too." He conveys exactly what I'm hoping.

Grabbing the base of his dick, I slowly sink down; we both moan the moment I finish taking him in all the way to the hilt. I love the fullness of having him inside me — the length of him hitting me just the right way.

"I don't think I will ever get used to this." He exhales a sigh as I start rolling my hips.

"What's that?" I pant.

"Seeing angels every time your magical pussy wraps tightly

around my cock — like you're the perfect fit, designed just for me and only me."

I roll my hips, testing the feel of him inside me. *Heaven.* I do it again, this time baring down, pushing him even deeper. I gasp at the sensation; he replies with a small thrust.

Leaning my hands on his chest, I change the angle, making him hit the perfect spot that makes my toes curl.

Ryders eyes heat and his lips part as he starts to thrust his hips, causing me to moan harder. He's building the momentum, getting me closer and closer to my impending orgasm. Ryder gets harder inside me, swelling and stretching me even more, telling me he is close too. It's too much and not enough all at the same time and it makes me desperate. The room fills with heavy pants and moans. After a few more thrusts, I contract around him as lights dance across my vision. We both groan as we come together. I fall on top of him, completely spent and panting, in pure, unadulterated bliss.

We agree to redo the video at the office, hoping it will help us to keep our hands off each other. Although as I wipe the steam from the shower screen so I can get an unobstructed view of Ryder soaping up his hair, I'm almost tempted to join him. But the ache between my thighs holds me back. The three times last night and again in the shower this morning have caught up with me. If I don't give myself a break, I will be walking funny at work — heck, I'll already be walking funny.

"What are you smiling at?" Ryder pulls me out of my train of thought.

"Just imagining what everyone is going to say in the office today."

"About what?" he asks, closing the water off.

"I took your advice and added a little blue dye to the shampoo bottle — now you have a slight case of smurf-itis." I plaster a devious smirk on my face when his head comes into view behind the shower door, towel around his waist.

"You didn't." His face falls, and I roll my eyes.

"Okay, I'm lying. I didn't." I laugh as he lifts me up on the counter, caging me in with his arms either side of my hips. "Stop. You're getting me wet." Laughing, I try to wiggle out of his grasp.

At this rate, we're going to be seriously late for work.

"Hmmm, I like getting you wet." He buries his face in my neck, the wet strands of his hair dripping over my towel-clad body.

"You, Ryder Fallington, are nuts."

"About you," his voice rolls down my spine.

"And sappy. You're going to give me diabetes." My hand comes down, slapping his butt, causing Ryder to bite my neck before rolling the spot with his tongue. "You better not give me a hickey," I groan. "We still have to refilm that video."

"Baby, I told you if you were mine, I would make sure the whole world knew it." He scans the room. "And would you look at that? You're completely and totally mine, Olivia Blake." He says, moving my panties aside and slamming into my already slick passage.

Thank fuck for my pill because otherwise Ryder would have just got me pregnant.

I meet Brynn in the lab ten minutes after our scheduled time, which I blame solely on Ryder. I may have caved and let him rail me on my bathroom counter so hard I have a bruise on my butt cheeks from the force of hitting the edge over and over, but hey — feast or famine, right? A few weeks ago, I couldn't get the guy I was dating to so much as let me give him a blow job, and now I have sex on tap. I'm not complaining. Though I really need to practice my Kegels and maybe invest in some sort of anti-chaffing cream.

"Hey, hey." I knock on Brynn's open door, smiling like I just got laid. *Oh wait . . . I did.*

Since the board gave me the green light to gather some samples for the teen line, I emailed Brynn to let her know we need to get started on it before someone talked to my dad and change their minds.

Brynn pushes herself away from her computer. "What's got you glowing today?" She offers me a questioning gaze, but I say nothing. She raises a brow and grabs her lab coat from its hook by the door.

"I tried this new mud mask last night, and I can say I think it's made my skin literally glow," I offer up as a distraction from further scrutiny.

"And the hickey helps too."

"Oh, shit," I groan as she winks at me, clearly catching me red handed. I thought I color-corrected the hickey enough to not show under the concealer.

Fucking Ryder.

"Here," Brynn laughs as she grabs something from the shelf next to her. "Give this a go." She hands me a green-base foundation we benched a little over a year ago because we found it didn't really work as well as we wanted and needed to reformulate, but I've been focusing on other projects.

"Thank you." My cheeks heat as I take the foundation from her, hoping she doesn't connect the dots and figure out exactly who left their mark.

"I'll meet you in the lab." She pats my shoulder and pushes past me, leaving me there to fix up any traces of lip print left. I pull my phone out of my pocket and send Ryder a message.

ME

> I just wanted to let you know the hickey is cute, but my love language is more words of affirmation . . .

An evil little giggle rumbles out of me. Ryder's in a very serious but boring meeting with the finance team at FF Group, no doubt sitting there talking about numbers and figures.

RYDER

> I worship the fact that you are my woman, and your pussy is a literal glove around my cock.

He did not just say that.

Clutching my phone to my chest, I glance at Brynn from the corner of my eye, making sure she can't see the screen. My face is literal blazes of fire. When I'm positive no one is looking, I pull my phone away from my chest, a smile playing on my lips as I type back:

ME

And what if I were to say I prefer acts of service?

RYDER

Five minutes. My office.

ME

Sorry, baby. I've got a teen line to make. x

RYDER

Offer still stands.

I start to type back *enjoy the blue balls* but quickly delete it, leaving him on read instead. I grab my coat from the hook and walk into the lab. Thoughts of Ryder Fallington taking over my brain.

CHAPTER THIRTY

Ryder

Who knew the woman I've been taught to hate, has slowly become the one person who I can't wait to be around. Sitting through a finance meeting with a giant hard on from Livvy's text message had me wanting to give her a special kind of payback. One that I spent the better part of the morning thinking about.

My phone burns in my pocket — I need to know if she is still with Brynn in the lab. Today I have a full-on day with FF Group, every time I finish a meeting, I have another one starting in two minutes. My skin itches with excitement, the fast pace stoking the raging fire in my belly. I'm stuck at the FF Group offices until later this afternoon where I have another meeting with Glam Co.

Derick, one of the board members, has managed to squeeze himself into my agenda — even though I purposely keep shifting his meetings. Derick hasn't stopped talking about how his conservative visions for Glam Co don't see a woman at the helm. *Prick.*

I peer at my watch and blow out a frustrated breath. Thirty-five minutes and counting. "Well, thank you for the call and for raising your concerns," I say for the third time, but it seems Derick — no matter how many times I try to shake his call — isn't done sharing his annoying tirade against the Blakes.

He continues to drone on and on, his arguments sounding more misogynistic by the second. I bite down hard, causing my teeth to grind. It's much easier than punching the asshole in the face after hearing him talk about Livvy this way. I scratch my jaw, debating with myself if I should ping Cecelia on Teams and get her to rush into the room, claiming an emergency. If only that would be enough to get him to end the call.

I scrub my hand over my face. I'm rubbing my temple with my thumb to ward off the headache that's slowly building — this motherfucker is literally making my head throb — when Livvy slips into my office, making sure to close the door quietly behind her.

My heart stutters. Fuck how much did I miss her today?

Leaning back in my chair, I bite my lip as I rake my eyes slowly down her perfect body, made just for me. "Yeah, I completely agree," I reply, not giving a shit what Derick said.

He continues to express his grave concerns for Glam Co if we don't do something to drastically improve its image.

Livvy's smile is full of desire and promises as she closes the distance between us. I swivel my chair around at her approach, widening my legs and inviting her to stand between them. Derick's voice hums out as the buzzing in my brain grows. I groan internally when Livvy drops to her knees in front of me.

My dick becomes hard as granite in my pants. Livvy runs her hands up and down my thighs, getting higher and higher with each pass.

"Fallington."

My name snaps like an over-stretched elastic band.

"Derick," I strangle out, my vocal cords struggling to work.

"Are you listening?" he asks, as Livvy pops the button on my suit pants and pulls the zipper down. She releases my throbbing cock, all while staring up at me submissively from her spot on the floor between my knees.

Never has anything been more seductive than this. This vision of her will be burned into my brain for the rest of my life.

I swallow and reply with, "Yeah." *Not at all.*

"I've been observing your leadership style — it's clear you know how to run a company of this size and have the potential to make it as big as L'Oréal . . ."

I don't hear the rest of his words as Livvy wraps her red lips around my cock and moans like it's the most delicious lollypop she has ever tasted.

Livvy hollows her cheeks, taking my cock deeper and deeper until I hit the back of her throat. My hand finds its way to the base of her neck, urging her on. She continues to suck and lick her way up and down my cock, worshipping it.

"My nephew Kyle and I have had an in-depth conversation. The Blakes at the helm of this place doesn't bode well. Your vision for Glam Co is one we're buying," he continues. "And with the vote coming up soon . . ."

The rest of his tirade drowns out as my blood rushes through my ears. I'm focused solely on Livvy's mouth.

Livvy adds her hand, wrapping it around my base and squeezing. My eyes roll back into my head. If this is her version of revenge, I will take my punishment again and again.

"Derick — " My voice sounds like chewed up gravel. My fingers weave into Livvy's silky tresses, tightening my hold. "I have to go." I press the end-call button.

I let out a growl — my only warning to Livvy that I'm taking control. I start fucking her face, watching as a trail of Livvy's spit lines the corner of her mouth to her chin.

"I think I can get around this form of payback, Killer."

I shudder as Livvy swirls her tongue around my tip. I'm close to bursting from the ache in my balls and the tingling creeping up my spine. "I'm about to come, Liv. If you don't want to swallow, you don't have to," I warn her.

Livvy stares at me from under her lashes, digging her nails into my thighs. She draws me deeper into her throat and swallows me down in one large gulp.

It takes me a few moments for the high to ease off. I've never come so hard in my life.

She sits back on her haunches, wiping the corner of her mouth with her finger. Her eyes never leave mine as she inserts the tip of her finger between her lips, licking every last drop of me, a small, satisfied smile pulling at her lips. "Baby, I think that almost makes us even," she says, standing up and placing her hands on the arms of my chair, caging me in.

"Almost even how?" I ask, playing dumb and cocking my head to the side.

"It wasn't your dad on the phone." She smiles that perfect smile that makes my heart skip a beat and thud back in my chest.

I scoff and hand her my phone, eyes boring into hers. "Dial the number."

I've never backed down from a challenge before and I'm not about to start now.

Rescheduling the rest of my afternoon meetings, I get ready to help Livvy refilm her Make Me video. I never thought I'd be excited to film a video, especially about makeup and skin care. But with Livvy, I'm actually looking forward to it.

I have a few pressing emails to answer before I plan to fully switch my computer off and focus on her. Olivia Blake is really bad for my work ethic — if we weren't coming up to the vote soon, I would care even less than I currently do.

"What do you do with the videos before you post them?" I ask, leaning against the door jam and crossing my arms over my chest as she hooks the screen up behind her desk.

"All the raw material goes onto a USB, and I edit each video before uploading it to my channel."

"Interesting," I murmur, pushing off the door and filing that little tidbit of information away in my brain.

"If you say so." She shrugs, finishing with the preparation for the video. It's amazing how effortlessly she transforms her office from workplace to inviting studio.

Did she delete the last video we made, or does she still have it?

I don't have the faintest clue what's involved in editing, but it's clear from what I've seen that she puts a lot of work into each video. I take my seat next to her before placing my suit jacket behind me and rolling up my sleeves. This might get messy, and I want to be prepared. The tip of her tongue darts out, wetting her bottom lip as she pays particular attention to my forearms. I give her deceivingly sweet smile knowing that my forearms are a weakness of hers.

This video has a strong potential to go down the same path as the last one — not that I'm complaining.

"I've already reviewed the footage from last night. Minus the part sex-tape we made, I think if we just go through putting on the mask again, I should be able to cut what I have and mix in the new part ready for tomorrow's upload. Then we need to film the next video."

She pulls out six lipstick tubes all with distinct red bottoms.

My lips part. I swallow, my throat feeling extremely dry. "Please tell me you need help trying these on. I think we need to do a kiss test for them."

Fuck, the only thing hotter than Olivia Blake is Olivia Blake in red lipstick.

Livvy's eyes shine. Leaning forward, she whispers in my ear, "The title of the video is going to be 'Which red can withstand the kiss test?'"

Fuck yes.

"Why don't you put one to the test now?" I wrap my hand around her throat and pull her closer to me, ready to kiss her still slightly swollen lips.

"Nooo, we can't ruin my filming schedule." She whispers keeping her lips a breath away from mine.

I pout dramatically, coaxing a giggle from her. She places

a quick kiss on my lips and pulls away. "I can't keep falling for your wicked ways. You're turning me into a sex fiend. All I think about when I'm around you is when you are going to rail me next."

"And the problem is . . .?" Glad I'm not the only one feeling like my body craves hers more than air.

Livvy laughs. "Let's get back to filming, big guy. I've got a lot of people craving their #therybereffect fix."

"The Ryder effect?" I ask. I've seen the hashtag on a few of Livvy's videos, but I don't really understand what it means.

"Yep, that's what my Gracites have so kindly dubbed you." She waves a finger in the air. "Something about you putting them all under your magical spell."

"Really? Your Gracites are under my spell?"

We change back into our clothes from yesterday to make the edits work.

"It's not hard to see why. You've got me completely under your spell."

I lean forward and fuse my lips to hers. "Right back at you, Killer." I release her lips so she can methodically place the mud mask ingredients on the desk before preparing it with the drops — the same as she did last night but this time minus the explanation part. "Can't forget the bunny headband." She winks, pulling the headband from the bag on the floor.

My stomach clenches and my dick twitches as visions of last night swirl through my head. "Not the bunny headband," I whine but lean forward, letting her put it on me. Livvy could get me to do just about anything with the curl of her finger, and I'm starting to think she may know it.

She presses play on the camera and starts talking. I get lost staring into the animation of her face; how alive she looks when she's explaining why she loves the product.

"Ryder," she calls my name, snapping me out of the trance she put me under.

"Hmm?" I blink slowly, trying to remember what she said.

Livvy giggles. "I asked if you have ever worn a mud mask before."

"As a matter of fact, I have." Just last night, but I conveniently leave that part out.

Livvy starts mixing the mud mask in the bowl and she sends me a heated glance, no doubt remembering last night too. "And how did you find it?" she asks, a slightly seductive tone coating her voice.

"Now every time I think of a mud mask, I get this hard-on." I lean forward and kiss her pouty lips, unable to help myself.

Pulling apart, Livvy whispers against my lips, her voice light and full of humor, "That's going to get edited out."

"Shame," I reply.

Livvy finishes applying the mud mask to my face and turns to put it on her own before pausing the camera. Her lips slam down on mine the moment the red light stops flashing, claiming me.

About time.

"Fucking on company time — I don't think the board will be too happy to hear about that." My brother's voice sounds like a nail on a porcelain plate — irritating.

"Oh shit." Livvy jumps away from me, her eyes comically wide, while I stare at my brother's face.

"Zander," I growl, impeccable timing as always.

"I would ask why you haven't been answering your phone, but I think from this little image here" — he circles his hand in the air, gesturing between us — "I know why."

I turn my phone on and curse at the five missed calls and sixteen messages. You would think after the first call he would get the hint — not Zander. "So, you decided to show up here?"

"We had a major backer of FF Group pull out; Dad's currently locked in a meeting for over an hour. So yeah, excuse me for showing up to see where the fuck you have been," he barks.

"What?" The blood drains from my face. *Fucking fuck.*

My brother is pissed and rightly so. I've been way too distracted by Livvy, and now FF Group — the company my family have spent their lives building — is falling down.

I stand abruptly and the chair crashes into the green screen Livvy had set up, tearing a hole in it. *Shit.*

"Go," Livvy whispers. "I'll take care of everything here."

Pulling the bunny headband off my head, I bend and dot a kiss on her cheek. I take off in the direction my brother went, but not before stopping in at the bathroom to remove this mask. I can just imagine what my brother would say if I got in his car with this shit on my face.

CHAPTER THIRTY-ONE

Livvy

Four messages. Ryder hasn't responded to a single one. He's reading them because the little 'read' signal keeps popping up under each message. But for some reason he won't reply, and it only increases the level of my anxiety. Did I go too far?

Putting my focus into finishing off editing our video, I add segments of us before filming my final opinion on the mud mask and uploading it ahead of release tomorrow.

"I have the signed-off samples." Cecelia barges into my office, and I welcome the distraction.

"What samples?" I ask, my eyes flicking away from my screen to the cardboard box in her hand.

"The samples for the Olivia Grace collaboration with Glam Co."

I blink.

"The upcoming collaboration you've had in the works for months . . ." she continues.

"Oh shit . . . that." I completely forgot about it. With everything that's happening with the board vote, I've taken my eye off the upcoming-release-ball so to speak. I'd been looking forward to this collection for months, but that was before my life was turned upside down by Ryder Fallington.

"Yeah, that," Cecelia laughs, dropping the box on my desk.

My stomach flutters. This is my second collaboration with Glam Co, and I'm hoping it will do as well as my previous one. And give me some much-needed bonus points with the board.

"Thanks." I smile, tearing into the box, the excitement of seeing my collaboration sending an adrenaline rush through my system. "Do you know if there is another samples box?" I stare back at the lipsticks and frown; it was supposed to be a full range, minus foundation and concealer.

"Oh, and there is also this." Cecelia hands me a folded note before leaving my office and closing the door behind her.

I don't bother opening it, expecting the note to be from Brynn — probably specs on the lipsticks. Given the collaboration is already set, reading her notes seems a little redundant.

Tipping the box upside down, I let the lipstick tubes roll out. I suck in a sharp breath; the rush of oxygen makes me dizzy with excitement at the *Glam Co X Olivia Grace* labels. I don't think I will ever get tired of seeing my name on Glam Co products — like ever. It's a small steppingstone to me potentially getting my own line. If I can bring in high sales with my collabs, it will show the board that I can promote my teen line and get the same kind of sales — thus lowering the risk for Glam Co to produce such a new line.

Something catches my eye on the bottom of the lipstick tubes. Where it should say 'Gracites' — the specific color I designed for this collaboration — says 'Killer'.

What? Oh, no, no, no, no.

Each of the tubes I flip over has the same name. My collection is launching next week. The bottles are all labelled, packaged, and have already been shipped off to the warehouses of our biggest clients that are stocking this collaboration, with the incorrect name.

I grab the letter Cecelia left behind and instantly recognize the handwriting.

Can't wait to see the launch, Killer. xoxo

Ryder fucking Fallington.

He's single-handedly tanked my collaboration and put the teen line at risk in a big way. My stomach roils. This man is always one step ahead of me.

After snapping a photo of the box, I send a message to Kendall.

Her reply is quick.

KENDALL

Love the name, babe. Great choice.

Ahhh, someone has missed this whole point.

ME

Don't you remember the name we spent more than a month thinking about? The name that was going to entice all my Make Me followers to want to buy the product?!

Kendall heavily influenced this collaboration. Given she is a marketing whizz, we put our heads together to come up with names that my Gracites would gravitate toward. My phone chirps with a message from Kendall.

KENDALL
TBH I like the change. Glad you decided to go with it. It's edgy x

I didn't decide to go with it — it has been thrust upon me.

After locking my phone, I toss it carelessly on the desk. Yet another person has fallen victim to the Ryder effect.

I ping Cohen on Teams since she is the person in charge of the collab between Glam Co and Olivia Grace.

ME
Just received the collab.

Her reply is instant.

COHEN
I haven't sent the email yet. I am still ironing out a few details with Sara Jones.

I stare at my screen, completely confused. Of the three influencers Glam Co collabs with a year, Sara Jones is number three, slated for production end of the year. Why has it been pushed up?

ME
Do we need new formulations for Sara?

Am I being sly? Abs-o-fricken-lutely. I can't outright ask

her where all the proofs are without looking nosy as shit. But since I deal with the tweaking of formulations, I can 'pretend' that is my interest.

I groan at the shrill tone of an incoming Teams call.

"Hey, Liv." Cohen's face comes into view.

Why couldn't this have just been a message?

"Hey, Cohen." I scrub my sour mood from my face, adjusting the thick-framed blue-light glasses farther up the bridge of my nose.

"I wanted to call you because I thought it was going to be easier than Teams messages."

AKA this could have all been put in an email, but I wanted to see your reaction when I spilled the beans.

Cohen shuffles paperwork and clears her throat. "We have had a few changes to the influencer lineup. We decided in our last meeting to not do so many influencer collaborations and instead focus more on Glam Co as a brand rather than as a collaborating partner."

Crossing my arms over my chest, I sit back. "And when was this meeting held?" *I certainly don't remember getting a calendar invite.* I quickly click through my emails, seeing if I missed the e-vite.

"Last week," she says, completely unruffled and like she didn't just drop a massive bomb on me.

I run my tongue along my teeth. This particular fuck up has a certain *warm day on the Amalfi coast* smell to it — Ryder.

"I'm guessing that means we only have the two collabs then?"

"Yours and Sara's." She nods.

I grab the lipstick tube and hold it up to my computer. "I just received the box with the lipsticks. They look… well, I'm surprised. I'm still waiting on the pallets and highlighters."

Cohen nods, dipping her tea bag into her mug before tying the string off on the handle, really making sure to draw out her response. After taking a sip of her drink, she replies, "We decided to keep the collabs smaller and cut the pallets. They are Glam Co products at the end of the day."

My eyebrows shot up, silence hums between us. They might be Glam Co products, but I designed them, I Livvy Blake hold the IP. Did I just hear her correctly? Surely, she didn't just say that my collaboration, which last year brought in nearly a whole quarter's worth of profit in the first week alone has been cut to just a single shade of lipstick?

"And who is this 'we'?" I ask, already knowing the answer.

"Ryder, and he has the full support of the board."

I scoff. Why does this not surprise me? I hover the mouse over the 'end call' button. It takes everything in me not to press down.

"Did you not receive the email with the approval?" The sarcasm drops from her tongue like a leaky tap. Someone seems to have forgotten who exactly she's talking to. Ryder might think he has a bit of pull right now — but so do I.

"If I got the email, do you think I would be asking you this question?" I reply through gritted teeth.

"Oh, sorry about that." Cohen's eyes move around the screen just before the incoming email sounds. "There." She smiles. "Now you have it."

Something in me snaps, and I can't keep the venom from

my voice. "So, you're telling me, you and the board decided to support a decision to drop an entire collection that last year made Glam Co more than twenty-five percent of its annual profit and reduce it down to one lipstick? Am I getting that right, *Cohen*?" *The ass licker.*

Cohen visibly swallows. "Yes, the board wasn't happy about the cut, but they are interested in exploring new avenues for Glam Co," she replies.

"Maybe you should put that in an email," I grumble, rubbing my temple and already feeling a wrinkle forming between my brows from squinting.

I press delete on the email; I have no interest reading it now.

"Since you weren't aware" — Cohen clicks her tongue against the roof of her mouth — "I can schedule a meeting with Ryder and I, next Thursday, at the earliest. To go over the email *you* missed."

I make a few clicks on my screen. "Ohhh, Thursday." I blow a whistle through my teeth, pretending to look at a full schedule. "My schedule is kinda full. Why don't I get back to you with some dates?" I hang up the call before she can reply. I check our stock levels in the Glam Co system. Then I call Brynn to see the production schedule before putting on my lab coat and meeting her in the lab, but not before I send Sof a message. Seems Ryder needs to remember exactly who he's fucking with.

If Ryder thinks he can screw with my collaboration just because he can screw me senseless, he has another thing coming.

CHAPTER THIRTY-TWO

Ryder

Fuck. Fuck. Fuck. The small vein in my temple has been pulsing ever since my brother announced FF Group are in damage control. I pore over the reports I had Zander send through to me. I'm not finding a single fucking reason why Faluccino Investments might want to do this. Losing a major backer of FF Group is going to cause some serious issues.

My office door opens, and I know of only two people who would dare disturb me at a time like this.

"Did you bring the contract?" I ask, not even looking up from the document I'm reading. I had Becks run over the agreement the Faluccinos signed with FF Group before becoming an investor to see if there was anything we could use to persuade them to not pull their funding.

"Here." Becks places two glasses of scotch next to me, the F on the ice cube mocking me. I take the drink, downing the amber liquid in one gulp and place the cup back on the table.

Becks blows out a breath and takes a seat opposite me. "Now that that is out of the way," he sighs.

I drop the paper, lean back in my chair, and ask the question that is on my mind. "What the fuck happened?" I left FF Group running like a well-oiled machine. I was preparing Zander to run the reports before I read them and submit them to our shareholders.

Becks shakes his head, scrubs a hand over his face, and shrugs his shoulders. "I guess the shareholders got cold feet."

I run my hand along my jaw, inhaling a strangled breath. "I would believe you, but the Faluccinos have been shareholders of FF Group for more than fifty years. How could they just wake up one morning and 'get cold feet'? It makes no sense."

"Losing Faluccino backing won't cause that much of a dent in FF Group — "

"But it won't look great either," I finish for him.

"I pored over the agreement." Becks places the manilla folder on the table. I hand him his glass, and Becks throws it back in one swallow.

"And?" I ask, one eyebrow raised, letting the burn of the second glass of scotch hum through my already acrid veins.

"And if they decide to pull back, they can, and you can't buy any of the shares. The Fallingtons have hit their limit, according to the original agreement."

"Just fucking perfect."

"But I might have a way to fix this."

I stare at him, waiting for him to continue.

"I've been in talks with another potential investor for a few months."

"I'm listening."

"Anders Davenport."

Anders Davenport, as in Liv's childhood friend?

His name causes an unexpected spike of anger to course through me. My gut instinct is to flat out say no, but the fact that Becks is bringing his name up means he has been vetted thoroughly by him. Right now, though, I need to figure out why Faluccino would decide to do this before I can even look at bringing someone else into the company.

I pick up the phone and dial Donato Faluccino's number. If he wants to pull his investment, he can fucking tell me to my face.

"Hello, Sofia speaking."

Fuck. Sofia Faluccino — Donato's daughter who has a habit of monopolizing conversations. Why couldn't we get Donato's assistant?

"Sofia, this is Ryder Fallington." I use my full name, hoping she will get the hint I'm not interested in shooting the shit.

Sofia gasps. "Oh, Ryder, hey. What a funny coincidence. Leonadis was just talking about you. Are you guys still on for poker? It's your place this round, right?"

I massage my temple. Maybe I should have had Becks make this call. He has this way of making people not want to talk to him for long periods of time. It could have something to do with how he just shuts down small talk with 'one of us is making money in this call and it's not me' line which instantly has people doing what he wants real fucking quick.

"Sofia," I say, rubbing my hand along my lips.

"Oh, Leo just walked in. Do you want to talk to him?"

"What? No — " I say just as the line cuts out. My grip on the phone tightens until my knuckles threaten to pop through my skin. "Hello?" My voice echoes into the dead line.

"She hung up?" Becks asks, his voice way too light and full of the laugh he is holding in to respect the gravity of the issue unfolding in front of us.

I send Becks a scathing glare as I redial the number.

"Hello, Sofia speaking," Sofia's cheery voice chimes through.

"Sofia," I growl.

"Ryder?" she questions like we weren't just on the phone a few seconds ago.

"You hung up on me."

"Oops, yeah sometimes I get the hold and hang up button confused. My bad."

Yeah, your bad. I blow out the breath I've been holding, bite my tongue with the control I've spent years honing, and say, "Mistakes happen."

"Here's Leo," she laughs.

"What? Fuck, Sofia — " I growl, clutching the phone.

Becks throws his head back laughing.

I flip him off and whisper, *"Fuck you."*

"What's that? You want to fuck my cousin?" The gravelly voice of Leonadis hums through the phone.

"No, I don't," I groan. There is a reason I try to call these fuckers as little as possible. In typical Faluccino fashion, these two love testing my patience and make it a game amongst themselves.

"Why? Is my cousin not good enough for you to fuck?"

Leonadis mocks, acting offended, but I can feel the smile through the phone.

I groan. Despite the over baring act, Leonadis doesn't give a shit who fucks his cousin.

"I think my current girlfriend would have a serious problem if I were to fuck your cousin."

"Girlfriend?" Leonadis and Becks say at the same time.

I eye Becks as I reply, "Yes, girlfriend." Livvy has pretty much owned the label ever since she laced my coffee.

"Are you bringing her to poker night? Rome and Henley will be dying to meet her," Leonadis asks excitedly, making me snort.

"No," I reply flatly.

"Shame," Leo huffs. "I would've liked to meet the woman who managed to tame Ryder Fallington."

"Trust me, Livvy Blake is something else," I muse.

Leo pauses a moment before he blows out a loud whistle. "You sure she's your girlfriend?" he laughs.

The way he is asking the question makes me grit my teeth. "Her pussy is still fresh on my tongue. I would say yes."

Becks pours himself another finger of scotch, eyeing me the entire time. I motion for him to do one for me too.

"Fuck, Fallington," Leo snorts. "You always know how to make an entrance."

Becks hands me the glass.

I quickly down the contents and stay silent for a few heartbeats, letting the alcohol burn through me. I need to get this conversation off my girlfriend and back on track. "Leo. Why are you pulling out of FF Group?"

"What the fuck are you on about?"

I don't miss the feigned shock in his voice. I narrow my eyes and hit the speaker button, letting the phone fall from my fingers onto the desk.

"You know exactly what I'm talking about. I have a document signed by you right in front of me."

Leo laughs a deep, belly-aching laugh; my eyes flick up to Becks. He shares my grim expression. I'm starting to feel like I'm about to star in some new version of *Punk'd*.

Leo finally stops laughing. "Faluccino is not pulling from FF Group permanently. Just . . . for a few months."

"What the fuck? You can't just temporarily pull funds, Leonadis. We're not a fucking bank."

If he needs cash, he can fucking ask. FF Group can't just liquidate itself because Leo is feeling moody.

"Ah, I believe now is when I'm supposed to tell you, 'Don't fuck with my collaboration again, asswipe.'" He uses a high-pitched voice, mimicking a woman's voice.

What the fuck?

"You're pulling your shares because of Livvy Blake?" My vision clouds red. I motion to Becks to pour me another finger and one for himself. I run my hands through my hair, tugging on the strands, needing to feel the pain.

"Only for a few months," Leo replies.

"Why?" Becks cuts in.

"Becks, bro, where the fuck you been? Or did you get a girlfriend too?"

"Been around, cleaning up your messes. Or did *you*

forget?" Becks cocks his head to the side as he stares at the phone between us. Leo is notorious for leaving legal messes, and it's safe to say he keeps Becks very busy.

"Trust me, I didn't forget."

The phone beeps before Sofia's voice filters through the call. "Leo, Dad wanted me to ask you if you still want a grilled panini for lunch?"

This is my chance. "Sof, pass me through to your dad." My tone is more desperate than I would like. I need to talk to Donato so he can slap some sense into his nephew before the Blakes cause him to make a really bad decision.

"Ryder? You're still here? Do you want a panini too?"

I roll my head back and blow out a long breath. Becks barks out a laugh.

"Panini is fine, Sof," Leo says before the line cuts out again.

"Where's my panini?" Becks asks.

I punch him in the bicep, making him groan in pain and clutch the sore spot. *Yeah, like I give a crap.* "Leo," I repeat his name.

"Ryder," he replies.

"Do you really want the Blakes controlling you?" I growl out.

"Blakes don't control me. I just love fucking with you. Livvy giving me an excuse to do it is only icing on my cannoli."

"There is no changing your mind?" I ask, sounding hopeful.

"Nope. After this quarter's reports are released, Faluccino will be back to giving FF Group our full backing and taking up all our shares. I'll see you at the poker night. Catch ya, bro."

Leo hangs up, leaving Becks and I staring at each other.

If I wasn't in love with the woman, I think I would strangle her.

Storming into the Glam Co office, I'm on the warpath and my target is set on one brunette who loves wearing pant suits.

Becks and Zander are finalizing the remaining reports. We have spent the last few days drafting everything that needs to be submitted before the quarter ends because FF Group is a publicly listed company. But like Berkshire Hathaway, it's the kind of company you can't randomly buy a share in. Most of our shareholders are vetted by a board, and in order to buy in, there needs to have been shares released by current holders. Even then, it's only held between five families — the Fallingtons, the Crofts, the Faluccinos, the Jones', and the Venuccios. Looks like Becks is thinking of adding the Davenports to the group too.

Releasing quarterly reports with the company's progress is kind of a given. Faluccino deciding to release their shares is going to look really bad to the other shareholders and having Leo's assurance its only for a few months isn't really comforting. Donato will shit a brick if Leo lets this slide any longer than that and will make him give FF Group their full backing — if that's any consolation.

I stop at Cecelia's desk, which is now in front of our offices — after promoting her to be my assistant, we got some new admin girl in for reception. "Where is she?" I'm well and truly past the 'I can tolerate bullshit' mood.

Cecelia jumps. "She went home."

I slam my hands on the desk and roll my eyes. "Of course, she fucking did. It's just like Livvy to fucking leave at a time like this." I rest a hand on my hip and the other on the bridge of my nose. She is probably at home celebrating with Kendall.

"Ohhh, I thought you meant Cohen. Livvy's in the lab working on her collaboration with Glam Co."

"What?" I yell, making her jump again.

"She kind of got mad you culled her collaboration and so she's had the lab producing the remaining units."

I purse my lips. *Perfect.* I smile to myself as I walk down to the lab. My little Killer has no idea what's about to hit her.

CHAPTER THIRTY-THREE

Livvy

Placing the last of the *Glam Co X Olivia Grace* stickers on the eyeshadow pallet, I laugh to myself. Ryder thinks he can cut my collab just before launch. He seriously underestimated me. I place the pallet on the closest pile to me. That makes fifteen-thousand-nine-hundred and forty-nine pallets, half of the lot but at least it's something. Only one thousand to go.

I scan the room, as the staff place more finished eyeshadow pallets into cardboard boxes. At this rate, we will be finished by close of business today.

"We only have a few left." Brynn sidles up next to me, announcing the obvious.

If the room wasn't temperature controlled, the amount of sweat that would be pouring off my body would be enough to soak my lab coat through.

"It has been a godsend that Ryder has had to be at FF Group the last few days. Otherwise, I don't think we could have managed to get it done in time. The team has really rallied," I tell her. If Ryder had been here, it wouldn't have been possible to move the staff from their regular schedule to the one I whipped up to get all the units I need for my collab done.

Brynn places another finished pallet in the cardboard box.

A knock on the window causes us to jump.

My stomach gives a flip at Ryder standing there, his suit makes my mouth water. I didn't think I would miss his presence as much as I have these last few days.

He points to me and mouths, *"You."*

My heart slams against my rib cage, staring at the fire burning in his molten-brown eyes. *Oh shit*. I duck under the bench. My eyes flick to meet Brynn's nervous ones. We need to come up with an excuse for why I can't leave.

"Hey, Liv, I think there is someone who wants to talk to you," a muffled voice calls through the buzzing in my ears.

Guess we can rule out Ryder not seeing me.

Biting the corner of my lip, I peek back over the bench only to find Ryder now leaning against the window, his arms crossed. I don't think he's planning to leave in a hurry.

"Can I help you?" I ask, opening the lab door.

Ryder's eyes slowly trail over my body, making my cheeks heat. I quickly take the hair net off and stuff it in my lab coat pocket.

Way to look hot, Liv.

"Livvy, Livvy, Livvy," he tsks, sending shivers down my spine.

I blink my eyelashes rapidly, going with the play-dumb route. "Is there something I can do to help you? The offices are that way in case you are lost." I point over his shoulder. The lab isn't really Ryder's vibe — he is more the freak in the sheet's kind.

"Nope." He casually shrugs, burying his hands in his suit pockets. "What are you doing in the lab, Liv?" he asks after a few beats of awkward silence.

"Nothing?" I shrug, crossing one leg in front of the other, hooking my ankles together, and focusing on the way my sneakers are tied — I look anywhere but at his stupidly beautiful face.

Ryder closes the distance between us. He bends his knees slightly and tucks a strand of hair that has come loose from my tie, behind my ear.

I wet my bottom lip. My body is already thrumming with energy, just waiting for Ryder to turn the barely-there kiss into something more.

"You wouldn't happen to be making eyeshadow pallets for the *Glam Co X Olivia Grace* collab, would you?" he asks, his lips featherlight against mine.

I gasp and pull back. "Who told — " Then it clicks. "Cecelia," I growl.

So much for the girl code. The moment Ryder bats his stupidly gorgeous eyes at Cecelia and flashes her another set of signed, first-edition books, Cecelia switches sides quicker than a jumping bean on a tight rope.

"I run multiple billion-dollar companies, Liv. That means nothing happens without my knowledge or say so."

"Hmm, I guess that's why you just lost a major shareholder in one of your multibillion-dollar companies, then, or was that *your* say so?" I muse, unable to keep the smugness from my voice. I pat his cheek before placing a light peck on his lips. I finally have the upper hand, and it feels amazing.

Ryder growls, and it goes straight to my core making it pulse and tighten. I secretly love it when he gets angry. He must read the reaction on me. The anger on his face dissolves as a smug smirk tugs at his stupid mouth.

His stupid, but oh-so-delicious mouth. I suck some much-needed air through my nose and clear my throat.

"The board vote is only a few weeks away. Maybe if Glam Co is too much, you should just stay focused on FF Group." I pout innocently at him but follow it up with an obnoxious wink before walking away and holding in the laugh that threatens to explode out of me.

I have a Make Me video to film and a collab to launch.

Ryder thinks his name is on the wall and that means he can do what he wants, but Glam Co is my world, my legacy, my purpose, and I'm not going to lose it without a fight.

Devin, Kendall, and Sofia are waiting for me at Enoteca Ilaria to celebrate the successful launch of *Olivia Grace X Glam Co*, which sold out in three hours. I still can't believe it. Stick that where the sun don't shine, Ryder Fallington. I add another coat of lip gloss and check my makeup in the car mirror before blowing a kiss at my reflection. *I'm Livvy Fucking Blake, and no man, especially a fucking gorgeous one, is going to tell me what to do.*

Walking into Enoteca Ilaria, I find Devin already sitting at the table next to a strawberry blonde-haired woman, and a bottle of half-empty champagne sitting between them. "Looks like the celebrating has already started?" I interrupt.

"She's here." Sofia stands up and hugs me.

"Hey, Sof." I hug her back before separating from her embrace and Somehow, I went from being reserves around woman to having a group who support and cheer me on.

"Here you go." She hands me a fresh glass of champagne.

"Thanks." I take it from her. "But shouldn't we wait for Kendall before popping open the bubbles?"

Sof screws her nose up. "Who said we're only getting one bottle?"

I can't help the laugh that tumbles out of my chest. Faluccinos are famous for their alcohol tolerance, Sofia has the highest. She can drink us all under the table, especially her cousin Leo.

"To being hungover as shit." I raise my glass in a toast.

"To being hungover as shit." Devin clinks her glass against mine.

Sofia rolls her Mediterranean sea blue eyes and mumbles, "Weaklings," out of the corner of her mouth.

I'm already through my third glass when Kendall finally arrives. "Sorry, sorry, I got held up with a freaking launch emergency," Kendall groans. *"Emily in Paris* has nothing on what it's actually like to work in marketing."

"I have a way to fix that." I hand her a glass of champagne. "Numb the pain."

Kendall snickers and takes the glass from me.

"Sof was just about to tell us how she had Ryder begging on the phone for a second time." I dip a breadstick in the dip, nodding at Sof.

I don't think I will ever get tired of hearing how Sof and Leo cornered him. And the panini interruption? Pure, molten 24 karat gold.

"I've heard already." Kendall sips her champagne.

All eyes on the table stare at her.

"Heard how?" Devin asks, narrowing her eyes.

"Becks told me. He was pouting because the panini never showed up. I swear sometimes he is such a big baby," she scoffs.

"Becks? As in Beckham Jones — the most ruthless lawyer this side of Cheshire Shore is a big Baby?" Devin repeats slowly like the idea of putting those two things together sounds hilarious.

"He can be, especially when he is hangry." Kendall laughs and continues, "Sof, you really did a number on Ryder. Becks couldn't stop talking about how he could literally see the vein pulsating on Ryder's temple the entire time." She holds her hand up. "You go, sister."

Devin and Sof are silent, staring at Kendall with mouths slightly ajar and watching her swirl a breadstick in the eggplant dip before popping it in her mouth.

She pauses when she notices everyone is gawking at her. "What?" she asks, crumbs falling out of her mouth.

"Are you going out with Becks?" Sof asks.

"What?" Kendall sputters, choking on her half-eaten breadstick. Her eyes dart amongst us. "Why am I in the hot seat all of a sudden? We're just friends. Do you know Ryder told Leo that you're his girlfriend?" She throws me under the bus.

"Wait, what?" I gasp and turn to Sofia.

This is the first I've heard of Ryder referring to me as his girlfriend. We had that talk ages ago, but we haven't labelled each other since.

"You didn't say anything?" I question Sof.

"What? No." She lifts her phone and starts tapping away. "He didn't say that when I was on the line. Oh wait, hang on, Leo just said he defs said you're his girlfriend. And — " She scrunches her face, her cheeks turning red. "I can't repeat this."

"What is it?" Devin tries to grab her phone, but Sof holds it out of her reach as she reads another message from her cousin.

"Yep, nope. Sorry." She rolls her face in disgust and hands the phone to Devin, who takes it.

Her eyes scan the phone before she blows out a *pfft*. "Did he seriously say that?" she asks. "Because it seems like a Leo-exaggeration thing."

"Nope. It's a direct quote — word for word, apparently." Sof nods.

"Oh my gawd, give it here." I snatch the phone from Devin's loose grasp and read the message. Then I quickly lock the phone, my cheeks flaming hot.

Ryder is so dead.

I clear my throat, hand Sof back her phone, and tuck my arms in my lap. "So, Kendall, you're really only friends with Becks?"

Devin clicks her tongue on the roof of her mouth and gives Kendall that knowing look.

"Just friends," Kendall repeats, glaring at me, clearly unhappy that I've put her back in the hot seat. *Just friends who meet in Paris – no doubt.*

"Oh, my shit," Sof gasps, clicking her fingers. "Do you know where Becks is now?" she asks Kendall.

Kendall's brows furrow and she purses her lips. "Yeah, he is at Ryder's place. Why?"

"Does he know you're here with us?" Sof asks.

I twist my fingers along the stem of my wine glass, waiting to see where she's going with this.

"Yeah," Kendall replies, cocking her head to the side. She shares a look with me, clearly wondering the same thing.

"Perfect." Sof giggles, still on her phone.

"What're you doing?" Devin asks, peeking at Sof's phone from the corner of her eye.

"The man wants his panini order. Who would I be if I didn't deliver?" She giggles, her thumbs working like she is in a race, before throwing her phone down on the table.

"You didn't?" Devin gasps, picking up Sof's phone and showing us the screen.

Yep, she did. Sof just put in a massive panini order to be paid upon receipt — Ryder's receipt. "That's almost a thousand dollars' worth of panini."

Sof shrugs her shoulders, taking another sip of her champagne. "So, he has a Centurion AmEx for a reason."

"Will they even make that many without payment?"

Sof just smirks. "They will when they see I'm the one who made the order, and the address I'm sending them to. I'll call ahead and have them buzzed into the Elite tower too."

Our food arrives, and I signal the waiter before ordering a gin and tonic. I will probably regret mixing drinks, but that's a tomorrow problem. "You, Sofia Faluccino," I say as I take a sip from my gin and tonic, "are devious beyond your years."

She flicks her red hair behind her shoulder. "It's the lifetime of practice."

Clearly, she is humble too.

We've almost finished all the antipasto plates Devin pre-ordered — she really is celebrating our little win against Ryder hard — when Kendall's phone rings.

"Oh shit. It's Becks." She shows us the screen.

I don't mention the fact that there is a red love-heart emoji next to his name. *'Just friends,' alright*. My stomach drops as Kendall clicks on the answer button.

Things are about to get interesting.

CHAPTER THIRTY-FOUR

Ryder

I stare down at my cards before eyeing the rest of the table. My hand is shit, but I keep my best 'I will still get these fuckers to fold' face in place. The stakes of this game are high. The next gen of shareholders are sitting in my lounge room, each with more money — and even more to prove — than the other.

After Leo enjoyed screwing around with FF Group, I realized this game could be a good way to fuck with him a little for payback, before it costs FF Group more than just a shit quarter report. The Heir to the Venuccio empire and one-fifth of the FF Group shareholder. Rome sits opposite me with the cockiest grin, the tattoos gracing his arms peeking out from under his long-sleeved top. His family are big into shipping companies. Rome and his two brothers are shit at playing poker, but he has this godlike 'go big or go home' complex which I love playing on. He bets more than the average person's yearly income in a single round without batting an eye.

"Are we playing poker or what?" Rome announces.

"You call," Henley Croft says, squinting at the card. Henley is a hard fucker to track down. The Croft family owns Croft Racing. And most of the time, when Henley isn't following his F1 brothers around the circuit, he is partying on the Croft private island near Monaco. He is the ultimate OG playboy.

"I fold," Becks replies. Of course, he does.

I roll my eyes and Becks snorts.

For a guy who thinks 'going for the jugular' is normal, he plays poker like a drunk twenty-one-year-old chick who doesn't know the difference between clubs and spades.

"Me too." Anders Davenport follows, throwing his cards in the middle.

Since Becks is thinking of having him buy into FF Group, I thought it might not be a bad idea to have him at tonight's poker game.

Davenport is Leo's best friend — not that I can hold it against him, nor would I ever use Leonadis Faluccino as a guide for best friends. Or a gauge for good friends in general. But given Anders relationship to Liv, I can tolerate the guy a little more. I'm supposed to be Leo's friend and yet he didn't hesitate to fuck me over for shits and giggles.

"Leo?" I ask, staring at him with one eyebrow raised. The cheesy fucker hasn't stopped grinning since he walked into my place. It's unhinged.

After throwing a few chips into the middle of the table, his eyes meet mine as he says, "I raise you," goading me to meet his bet.

I snort at the chips he's thrown in. Chump change. "That

it, Faluccino?" I grab the same amount of chips and throw them on top of his.

"When's the food getting here?" Henley stretches on his chair.

"I haven't — " I start to say when a knock on my door interrupts us.

"I'll get it." Becks answers the door.

"You going to play or do you need a refresher on how to play, Rome?" I say waiting for him to put his chips in.

"Ah, Fallington," Becks calls.

I drop my cards face down and turn to him. "Wh — " I ask, but the word dies in my throat finding the delivery driver for Panuccio's Paninis standing at my front door with takeaway boxes stacked up to his waist and a very unimpressed expression on his face.

"Oh shit, you ordered Panuccio's! Bro, I fucking love the hot salami panini," Henley groans.

"Nah, nah, nah, the prosciutto is where the party is at." Rome shakes his head.

I stare at the driver. This must be some mistake — I didn't order from Panuccio's. The better question is how the fuck did he get up here? He's definitely not on the list.

"I have other deliveries to make. Can someone settle the bill already?" the driver grumbles.

"Yeah, I've got it." I stand, taking the bill from his outstretched hand. "What the fuck?" I yelp, gawking down at the total.

"Hey, Panuccio's," Leo laughs, grabbing a box from the pile. "Sof loves ordering from this place. It's her favorite."

It doesn't take me long to connect the fucking dots.

"Fucking Livvy," I growl, making Becks bark out a laugh and the delivery driver huff while checking his watch.

"Buddy, you need to pay for the order," he says.

I grit my teeth. I didn't order a thousand dollars' worth of panini, I want to tell him, but from the way he is looking at me, he doesn't give a shit.

"Here." Leo hands over a thick wad of hundred-dollar bills. "Tip's in there too."

The delivery driver takes the money and leaves the boxes of panini lined against the door.

"Yeah, we'll just carry it inside," Becks calls down the hallway to the driver's retreating back.

"Fallington, this one's for you." Chuckling to himself, Leo hands me the box he took but not before showing the other guys sitting around the table.

'Glad you like the taste of my pussy. You'll have to beg for it next time,' written in black marker.

I'm going to fucking kill her.

Becks has his phone out and he is already dialing Kendall — shocker there.

"Hello," her voice coos into the call.

I grab the phone out of his hand. "Give it here," I growl, so past the point of being nice. "Where is she?" My voice is more animal than human.

"Well hello to you to, Ryder." Kendall smiles at me through the phone screen, waving her fingers. She is trying to be funny, but I don't find her the least bit hilarious.

"Paninis are amazing," Leo groans loudly, causing all

the girls to giggle over the phone. As if I needed further confirmation, they ordered the paninis.

Sending a glare at Leo, which only makes him smile bigger as he takes another bite from his panini, I grunt, "Livvy."

The picture on the phone jumbles as Livvy takes it from Kendall.

"Oh hey, if it isn't my lover. Did you get my message?" She holds the phone a little too close to her face, giving me a great view up her nostrils.

Resting my thumb and forefinger on the bridge of my nose, I blow out a short, sharp, and completely uncalming breath. "Are you drunk?" I ask.

"As a skunk, who loves a monk, ready for funk," she continues to rhyme. *Ohhhh, she is tanked.*

"Does she mean fuck?" Rome whispers. I roll my eyes.

"I heard you wanted panini, and what kind of a girlfriend would I be if I didn't supply you with your favorite food?" She pouts.

"I don't need one thousand dollars' worth of panini," I grumble, but the anger is already turning down to a simmer. She is just too fucking adorable to stay mad at.

"Says you," Henley yells.

Whether she knows it or not, Livvy Blake will be the death of me.

Zander walks into my apartment like he owns the fucking thing, not giving a shit if I'm naked, showering, or even fucking on the counter.

"Come right in," I mutter, pressing the button on the coffee machine, waiting for the beans to grind while leaning against the marble countertop with my arms crossed over my bare chest.

Zander grumbles under his breath and slams the door shut. He stomps to my fridge like a moody five-year-old who's been told he can't eat chocolate before dinner and glares at me before opening my fridge.

I have a feeling that his mood today is because he wasn't invited to poker. I wanted to keep it as the next-generation family heads, so to speak. Each guy sitting in the room last night is being groomed to take over empires that have more CPI than the whole European economy. After the stunt Leo pulled, Zander was less than impressed when I told him he had to sit it out. Realistically, he should be thanking me. Last night cost me a lot more than the one thousand dollars at Panuccio's — and I lost two hundred grand to Davenport.

"What crawled up your ass and died?" I grouse, taking a sip of my hot coffee.

"Why the fuck is your fridge filled with Panuccio's?" Zander's face is all scrunched up as he stares in shock at the contents of my fridge.

"I hosted poker last night," I grunt, stating the obvious. I'm not really sure if the event that transpired can even be considered poker. But from the group text Becks set up and the amount of weird emojis coming from Rome and screenshots from Leo, I think everyone had fun.

"Of course, the game I wasn't invited to." He rolls his eyes before grabbing a panini and hacking off a bite.

"Oh, that reminds me. You're going on a date with Charlotte Croft next week." I click my fingers before tucking my hand in my sweatpants pocket and taking another sip.

"Why?" he asks, his mouth full of half-chewed food, throwing his hand in the air and sending panini pieces scattering.

I shrug my shoulders. "Because I won."

Zander scoffs.

"Hey, you should be grateful; would you rather have a box seat with Luca at sharks game?"

Zander's eyes nearly fall out of his head. "I thought you guys were playing poker not 'Let's set my siblings up.'"

"Pfft," I snort. As if we care about setting our siblings up. "We were. We just decided to make the round a little more fun."

Zander groans. "Why couldn't you win Annie or Allegra?"

"I don't think Becks would approve of you fucking his sisters."

According to Becks, his sisters are still virgins who don't even know the meaning of the word sex.

Ironic, coming from Becks.

Zander throws his head back and laughs. "I'm pretty sure Allegra has a higher body count than me."

"Don't tell Becks that." I finish off my coffee, my eyes narrowing in on my brother as he takes another panini from my fridge.

Anytime someone mentions Becks' sisters, he gets that weird look in his eye that makes him certifiably crazy. If I had sisters, I would probably be the protective, overbearing, older brother too.

My brother hacks another bite from his panini and my fingers itch with the need to get Livvy back for her little stunt.

He groans. "Panuccio's is on another level. It's got to be the mayonnaise." He pulls back the bread, staring at the mayonnaise slathered on the side.

He only adds fuel to the inferno already alight in my stomach with each bite he takes. It's not that I really care about the paninis or the money — it's that the little minx's points in this war of ours is adding up. She is pulling ahead, and I don't let anyone beat me. Not even my incredibly tempting and sexy new girlfriend.

The perfect idea hits me. After pulling out my phone, I send Henley a message.

ME

Yo, is one of Croft Racing's tow trucks in town?

His reply takes a few minutes, but when it comes through it has me snorting in laughter.

HENLEY

Didn't think you lost that much last night. Already needing help affording a tow?

ME

I have other plans for the tow.

HENLEY

Ew, keep the Croft equipment away from your sick fantasies.

I bark out a laugh. My fantasies are less mechanical and more manual.

ME

> I had other plans that involved towing a car, wiseass.

HENLEY

> We are at your service.

He sends *a bowing gif.*

I snort and send a quick message off to Cecelia.

Clicking my phone shut, I smile as I stare out my window. Livvy Blake is in for a fucking treat.

CHAPTER THIRTY-FIVE
Livvy

Blasting the radio, I sing at the top of my lungs — it really hits different at seven-thirty in the morning. I pull into the empty Glam Co parking lot. I have a full schedule today, and the extra time before everyone starts will help me clear my head. Ryder still hasn't made his move after the whole Panini-gate and I'm a little edgier than I would like to be. I made sure to pack my own coffee in a to-go cup just in case Ryder wants to take a bit of inspiration and add salt instead of sugar into my coffee or something.

I get to my office, the first thing I do is start my computer, click on my schedule for the day and wait for the slow connection to load. I get my notes and files in order so I can move from meeting to meeting with all the correct materials. There is nothing worse than showing up to a meeting unprepared.

When my schedule comes up blank, *stupid slow internet connection*, I grumble under my breath. Closing all the screens, I reboot my computer; I hate it when technology isn't my friend. Taking another sip from my coffee, I let it do its thing and scroll through TikTok and Insta before uploading a post of me and the girls at Enoteca. I make sure to tag them and add a few comments under my sister's post and Sof's.

Clicking on my schedule, I squint at the screen when it comes up blank — again. "What the heck?" I saw my schedule last night. It was full, barely five minutes to use the bathroom kind of full.

"Morning, Liv." Cecelia knocks on my office door before walking in and placing a pile of unopened envelopes on the edge of my desk.

"Morning, Cecelia." My eyes don't leave the screen. Clicking a few buttons, I try to refresh and find all my appointments and meetings that I know for a fact should be there. My brow furrows. Every single thing I try makes no difference. My schedule is still … empty.

That can't be right? Where's Cohen's marketing forecasting brief? The Kosmedika's meeting? The meeting with Brynn about the teen line?

"Everything alright?" Cecelia asks, her brows drawn down, matching mine.

"Actually" — I sit back and look at her — "I think there is something wrong with the server." I grab the phone and dial Sal's number, checking my watch. Lucky, I got to work really early and have time to deal with these problems.

"You got IT — Sal speaking."

"Sal, hey, it's Livvy Blake. I'm having computer issues. My schedule is coming up blank."

"Let me do a check on the system." Sal starts tapping away.

Covering the end of the phone, I look up at Cecelia. "Is there anything else?" I ask her.

"Livvy," Sal says.

"No." She shakes her head and takes that as her cue to leave.

"Livvy?" Sal repeats my name. "There is nothing wrong with the system. It looks like adjustments were made to the calendars early this morning, but I couldn't tell you specifics — only that the company calendar was accessed."

"Are you sure? My schedule was full last night and I'm looking at a blank screen."

"Livvy, I ran an update a few days ago to speed up the overall office connectivity. There are no faults showing, no bugs, nothing."

"Fabulous," I breathe and hang up the phone.

Just fricken fabulous.

The only people who should have access to my personal schedule are Cecelia and the IT department when there's an issue. And from the way Cecelia's eyes were darting, I think I know exactly why my schedule just cleared itself right up.

Jumping out of my chair so fast the thing spins, I storm across the hall to Ryder's office — his closed door be damned.

"Morning, Killer." He doesn't look away from his computer.

"How did you know it was me?" I ask.

"You're the only person who storms into my office when the door is closed without knocking." He leans back and steeples his fingers on the desk, and winks at me.

My nostrils flare as I cross my arms over my chest. "Here I was hoping it was the smell of my Chanel N°1 perfume."

"Did you just come in here to ask me about your perfume choice? Because if you'd like to come a little closer, I'd be happy to give you a full and thorough critique?" he asks, his smoldering gaze holds mine and taking the air from my lungs.

"I seem to be having some issues and I was wondering if I could borrow your computer."

Ryder rolls his chair away from the desk, inviting me to use his computer, *Oh, he's asked for it.*

Let's make this interesting.

I cross the room and sit right in Ryder's lap, making sure to wiggle my butt right in his crotch and biting down on my lip when he stiffens beneath me. Ryder's hands grasp my hips, holding me firmly in place.

His hot breath tickles the side of my neck, sending a shiver down my spine. I'm already lightheaded when he whispers, "If you wanted an excuse to sit in my lap, all you had to do was ask."

Trying to tamp down my raging libido, which just wants to tear Ryder's suit off and make good on what he said, I click on his schedule and find it stacked with back-to-back meetings. My skin flushes hotter when I read in between his busy schedule 'lunch with Liv'.

"Found everything you're looking for, Killer?" He places a soft, kiss against my neck.

"Oh yeah," I whisper, moving my head to give him more room. "It seems our schedules have been mixed up. But I can fix it." I click delete on his agenda, watching the whole thing erase itself and quickly re-add in our little lunch date. "There we go." Arching my back, I wiggle my hips again, feeling him become stiff against me. "All fixed."

He groans. His hands grip my hips tighter as his lips continue to trail down my neck. "Did you just clear my schedule, Killer?"

"Yep." I turn in his lap, curling my arm around his shoulder, pulling his bottom lip between my teeth. "Mess with my schedule, baby, and I'll mess with yours."

Ryder chuckles, he seems too confident for a man who just watched his day erase. My eyes narrow in on his lips as my fingers play with the ends of his hair at the nape of his neck.

Ryder leans forward, wrapping an around my waist, holding me in place on his lap as he presses the speaker on his phone. "Cecelia," he says, "please come in."

Cecelia knocks on Ryder's door before stepping in and closing it behind her. "Ryder, what can I . . .?" Her cheeks tinge pink at seeing me in Ryder's lap. I try to scramble off, but Ryder holds me in place with his signature shit-eating grin firmly fixed in place. "What's my schedule for today?" he asks.

She furrows her brows and asks, "Why?"

"Seems I have had some technical issues and I've lost my whole schedule."

"No worries." Cecelia nods and recites his whole day, even including lunch with me.

"I make two copies of my schedule." He bops my nose, only causing the anger coursing through my veins to bubble. Leaning in close to my ear, he whispers seductively, "Did anyone ever tell you, you're very sexy when you're mad?"

My core clenches. He totally did that on purpose.

"Ahhh," Cecelia clears her throat, but her eyes are on the

window. "Livvy, is that your car being towed?"

"What?!" I shriek and jump out of Ryder's lap and press my face to the window, looking to where my car is parked — or was parked. "Shit."

I scramble out of Ryder's office, not even bothering to call the elevator and running down the stairs quicker than I ever thought possible in my pencil-thin heels.

"Wait," I scream, waving my hands above my head and trying to flag the guy down. "Stop! You have my car."

The guy doesn't even look up. If anything, he pulls the brim of his cap lower as he finishes loading my car onto the tray of his truck.

"Hey, stop!" I scream bending over, trying to catch my breath when I finally reach the tow truck. "Why are you towing my car?" I pant.

"It's parked illegally," is the only reply he gives me before swinging himself into the cab of the truck.

"Parked illegally?" I repeat.

That's the most ludicrous thing I've ever heard. Glam Co parking spaces are permit zones. How the heck is my car parked illegally? I'm still trying to work out the cryptic reply when the sound of the truck engine roars to life.

"Wait. Stop!" I bang my hand hard on the side of the truck as it starts rolling forward. What the hell is going on? The truck picks up speed and I start waving my arms and screaming obscenities, but it's no use. All I can do is watch my car being taken away. As the truck slowly turns to exit the parking lot, the logo of the towing company comes into view. Croft Racing.

That isn't even a towing company! Where the fuck is my car going?

I quickly snap a photo and send it through to Devin and Sof.

Sof is the first to reply.

SOF

LOL. Wut if Croft Racing doing towing your car?

SOF

*is

DEVIN

Y does Croft Racing sound familiar . . .

Kendall then pops into the chat.

KENDALL

Croft Racing is Henley Croft — BFFL with Ryder.

Holding my phone tightly in my palm, my body vibrates with anger. Did Ryder seriously just have my car towed? Of course, he did. Why am I even questioning that? And he cleared my schedule as a distraction.

I glare at the windows, my eyes seeking one window in particular. Even though we have tinted glass covering the façade at Glam Co, I know he is staring right back at me grinning. I grunt under my breath and flip the bird up in the air, hoping he gets the message. My phone vibrates in my hand, with a message from Cecelia.

CECELIA
FYI you have a meeting starting in 5.

Oh shit. I scramble to get back to my desk. I need to grab my notes before I'm late to another meeting.

Seven phone calls, three voice messages, and five text messages later, I finally managed to get my hands on Henley Croft's phone number. It seems the Croft family don't just tow cars to the impound lot or so the manager of the Cheshire Shore impound lot so kindly advised me. No, the Croft family have their own freaking car yard, which is constantly monitored by security and needs special clearance to enter.

"I think you turn left up here?" I stare down at the maps on my phone, directing Devin to make the upcoming turn.

"Are you sure?" She looks out the window, her gaze mirroring the worry in mine.

It feels like we left civilization about five miles ago — all that's out here is open fields of nothing. I've never been this far out of Cheshire Shore. Heck, I didn't even know this was still considered Cheshire Shore. According to Google maps — it is.

I open the map and double-check the turn-off. "Yes, turn left then it should be on the right."

Devin makes the turns and stops in front of two massive metal gates that say 'Croft Racing' twisted in the metal across the top. Giant, thick trees line both sides of the driveway, completely concealing anything behind the gates. "We're here," she breathes.

I quickly type the same sentiment to Henley as the gate open moments after 'read' appears under my message.

Devin sends me a worried look before driving through the gates.

"Ho-ly," I breathe. We continue to follow the tree-lined driveway until a mega mansion comes into view. "I think you turn left," I instruct Devin, who follows the neatly graveled road away from the front entrance of the house to a barn-like structure leading off to the racing track.

Getting out of Devin's car, I stop right in front of the person waiting for us who I assume is Henley Croft. All six-foot-five, brown hair curling around the base of a cap which is flipped around, grey eyes, and the chiseled jaw of Henley Croft. While he isn't my type, I can definitely see his appeal.

"Henley, where's my car?" I ask, crossing my arms over my chest.

Henley shrugs his shoulders. "I have no idea."

I click my tongue against the roof of my mouth and blow out a frustrated breath. In case he didn't notice, my day took a swan dive off a cliff this morning and I just want to get my car so I can go home, eat chocolate, have a hot bath, wash my hair, and maybe cry into my pillow.

"Liv," Devin whispers in my ear loud enough for Henley to hear. "That's not Henley." She turns her phone screen toward me, showing me a picture of an older version of the guy standing in front of me.

Not-Henley smirks.

"What do you mean that's not Henley?" I whisper-yell.

"I'm Duke," he laughs, pointing at himself. "Henley's out

the back fixing up a Mercedes he towed in."

Rolling my lips over each other, I try to hide my embarrassment. But I think the heat flooding my cheeks is a dead giveaway.

"Well, well, well, if it isn't Olivia Blake," a deep male voice calls from behind Duke. Looking past the giant man, I see the older version of Not-Henley, an exact replica of the picture Devin showed me, walking or more like swaggering toward us.

"Well, well, well, if it isn't the guy who stole my car."

"Your car's safe, serviced, and refueled," Duke replies sweetly like the big giant teddy bear he is.

"Wow, that's so nice," Devin gushes, twirling a lock of hair around her finger as she eyes Duke from under her lashes. "Can you take a look at my car? It's making this funny noise."

"What? No, there — " I'm cut off when my sister pinches my side. *Ow, needy bitch.* I bat her hand away.

"Sure." Duke nods, following Devin to her car.

I turn my head to Henley, who is now standing in front of me. "How much do I owe you for the service?"

"For you? On the house. I sent the bill to Fallington." He wiggles his eyebrows conspiratorially.

I snort. I don't mind Henley Croft after all.

CHAPTER THIRTY-SIX
Ryder

"Loser has to pay for dinner," I say. Flipping the visor of my helmet down, I nod at Henley before revving the engine of my bike. Henley just flips me off, spins his tires, and leaves before the practice lights turn green. The cheating fucker. Doesn't surprise me. It's probably the reason why I have a bill for 30k for servicing Livvy's car tucked in my back pocket.

The Crofts have built a nice practice circuit out here on the outskirts of Cheshire Shore. Too bad Henley is about to lose on his own turf.

I take off after him, eating the proverbial dust his tires create, but I'm not worried — yet. Croft races cars, but the skill must be transferrable because he is whipping my ass on the bike, or so he thinks.

Coming up to the second turn, I steal the lead. After changing gears, I glide right past Henley, making sure to flip him the bird over my shoulder as I go. After the fifth lap, we come to a stop, me whooping and cheering and Henley shaking his head. Rome is standing near the finish line with a stopwatch in his hand. He shows the face of the watch to Becks, who nods, his lips set in a grim line.

Henley and I turn off our bikes. I'm quietly confident I've won, but I can't wait to hear the words out of his mouth.

"Well, who won?" I ask, my chest rising and falling rapidly from the adrenaline coursing through my veins.

Becks tsks and jumps over the barricade. "Just like I thought." He shakes his head.

"My last girlfriend came quicker than you two." Rome beats Becks to the punch.

Henley turns to me. "I guess that means you're stuck with the bill."

"That or Rome is a one-pump chump," I snort.

Not that it bothers me to pay Henley's bill — knowing Livvy's car has been serviced by one of the best in the business gives me peace of mind she is safe. But I still have to shake my head. I only asked for a tow, and somehow we ended up with a 10k bill. I almost think Sof had a hand in this.

Leo bends over laughing and patting Rome on the back. "No wonder she is an ex, bro. Don't worry. I think they have pills that can help with that. Just ask Annie."

"You keep my sister out of this," Becks growls.

"Are we going to sit here swapping stories or are we going to eat?" Anders cuts in.

"Sure we are," Leo replies. "Rome's buying. Wouldn't want to miss a chance for him to whip it out." Leo stares directly at Rome as he continues, "His credit card, that is."

Henley shakes his head before parking his bike in the bay next to a line of luxurious cars. From Paganis to Lamborghini Aventadors, you name it — the cars lining the Croft lot belong to each of us. I wait for the others to get in their respective cars before revving the engine of my bike. About time some of them ate my dust.

I arrive at Enoteca Ilaria before the others, shaking my hair as I remove my helmet. There is nothing sexy about helmet hair, although I do enjoy when Livvy runs her fingers through my hair to try and tame it.

Through the restaurant window, I spot Livvy sitting next to Kendall and Sof already seated. The sound of roaring engines drowns out my thoughts as the guys pull up behind me. I don't bother waiting for them. I lock my bike, unzip my leather jacket, and enter the restaurant before making a beeline straight for Livvy.

When I reach my girl, I lean down behind her and kiss her cheek while she takes a sip from her drink — knowing Livvy, it's a gin and tonic.

"I have a boyfriend." Livvy almost spits her mouthful of *G* and *T* out.

I chuckle as I strip off my leather jacket before hanging it over the chair next to hers. "'Bout time you start referring to me correctly," I mumble. Something about hearing Livvy call me her boyfriend makes me feel lighter than I have all day. Almost like the ache in my chest is starting to close up.

The sound of the guys walking in breaks up the moment we are having.

After pulling out the chair beside Livvy, I take my seat.

She immediately curls into my chest, laughing at something Leo just said, not afraid to show affection in front of my friends. I put my arm around her shoulder, claiming her, and take a sip of her drink. *Yep.* I shudder. *Gin and tonic. Yuck.*

Wiggling her hips, Livvy seals her body to mine, knees touching all the way up from thigh to hip, not leaving any space separating us. At this point, Livvy is half sitting on her chair and half sitting on me.

I'm tempted to just lift her up and secure her on my lap.

Running my tongue along the inside of my lip, I try to hold back the grin that wants to break through. I've never felt this connected to someone, like my soul has finally found its shadow — the perfect match that is the puzzle piece I didn't even realize was missing. I let my hand fall to her waist and tuck Livvy in closer to me, enjoying having her tight little body pressed against me.

"Ryder." Anders clicks his fingers in front of my face.

"Huh?" Blinking out of the Livvy haze, I stare at him.

"Bro," Anders laughs.

He has that dark laugh, which matches his dark personality. Anders and Ares Davenport aren't known as Dark Knights for nothing. *Dark Knights* is one of the games Ares developed before selling it for an absolute pile to Nintendo or Marvel or some shit. Ares made the game for fun — something to do while recovering from a broken leg — and in the process made his inheritance from the Davenport media empire just that little bit bigger.

"Our girl really does have your balls in her Dior bag," Anders continues, causing a growl to thunder under my breath.

Anders referring to Livvy as *ours* sets off the possessive beast inside me. Anders smirks, clearly knowing exactly what he is doing. *Asshole.*

Livvy wiggles her eyebrows. "I think I do a pretty good job of concealing them in this bag, don't you?" Livvy holds up her Dior saddle bag.

Anders continues to laugh. "Yeah, trust me, no woman is ever going to take my balls away from me and stuff them in a tiny bag."

Livvy points to her purse. "You sure? There's plenty of space in there for yours too."

"Hey." I give her ass a slap, running my tongue along my teeth as her cheeks turn pink from both embarrassment and arousal. "There is only room for my balls in your bag, Killer. Remember that."

Livvy leans up and whispers so quietly, only I can hear, "Save that for tonight. I have plans for you."

"Ooh, très kinky. Can I join?" Rome replies, popping an olive into his mouth and hitting Livvy with a seductive but playful smile — all white teeth and sparkling eyes.

For fuck's sake, he's actually serious.

I ready myself to bark out a solid, 'NO,' but Livvy beats me to it with her sharp tongue. "I think Ryder might get a little shy once he sees what you're packing."

"Ohhh, baby girl, there is a saying in Napoli, *once you go Venuccio you can never go back.*"

Livvy giggles.

I don't like the way the fucker is grinning at my girl; it makes me want to punch him in the face. And who the fuck came up with that saying?

"Is that why you can make them come in under a minute? Performance issues?" Henley deadpans from his spot sitting opposite Rome, causing the whole table to break out in laugher.

It doesn't seem to bother Rome though; he just pops another olive in his mouth and smiles. "It's called technique, but hey, I'm more than happy to give you some pointers if you're spending too long trying to find your girl's G-spot." Rome laughs as Sof chokes on her food.

Devin thumps her on the back as Kendall elbows Becks' side and whispers not as quietly as she thought, "Maybe you should get some pointers."

Becks glares at her, lifting his glass to his lips. "I didn't hear any complaints last night."

"If we ever break up, dibs on Rome."

"Baby, that's never going to happen." I tap her nose with the tip of my finger, jealousy curling through my body.

"Corny alert," Rome fake coughs into his elbow.

I grunt under my breath, making a mental note to punch Rome.

My dad hasn't called me into his office in a while. Even though the office Dad is referring to is my old one turned Zander's at FF Group, something about it makes me feel like I'm fourteen and suspended from school for the first time.

I get in the elevator and press the button for the thirty-first floor. I close my eyes and rest against the cool side, my head still thumping from last night. It was all going fine until

Henley ordered the shots.

Walking into the office, I find Zander and my dad already sitting down staring at me, Zander with expectant eyes while the skin on dad's cheekbones stretched taught with discontent.

Is this some sort of intervention? I bite my tongue. Nodding at them as I take the seat opposite my father.

"Ryder, you look like shit." Zander snorts.

Livvy offered to cover the dark circles under my eyes, but I refused. I can assume Zander is seeing right through my attempt at a composed façade.

"I'm fine," I reply. "Nothing a coffee can't fix." Using the need for a coffee as an excuse to not explain myself to Zander, I stand and walk to the machine. "Dad, would you like one?"

Dad nods. "Thanks, Ryder."

I press the buttons, even though this will be my fourth coffee in two hours. I'm hoping I don't end up running to the bathroom again. Livvy has made me question the motives of my favorite drink.

"How are things going at Glam Co, son?" Dad asks, while I hand him his coffee and place Zander's on the table.

"Not too bad. We have the board vote coming up after the fundraiser ball," I reply, grabbing my own cup and sitting back down.

Dad rests his walking stick in front of him. "I've been talking to a few of the board members. It seems they are pretty happy with you, more than they have been with the Blakes."

It's meant as a compliment and it's probably one I would have appreciated a few months ago.

I swallow the thickness clogging my throat. "Oh," I reply

— it's the only word that can get past my lips. The excitement I should be feeling suddenly seems hollow.

"I have to hand it to you — I was worried when Zander expressed his concerns about you falling for the Blake girl. Girls like that are a dime a dozen, but now I see the long game. Keep your friends close and your enemies closer." The way my dad smiles while referring to Livvy as just some random girl has me seeing red and clenching my jaw, making it tick.

Livvy is not just some girl; she is the woman I love. I'll be damned if he thinks of her as anything less.

"Livvy Blake isn't just some girl, Dad. She is so beautiful and brilliant, and she's the heart and soul of Glam Co. She is involved with every aspect of that company, from design to marketing, she's even in the labs formulating the product. And if the board can't see she is responsible for a huge part of Glam Co's success, then they're idiots."

My dad's brows pull together, as he remains quiet.

"Dad, I'm in love with her." My voice is controlled, respectful. "And I would appreciate it if you addressed the woman I love with the respect she deserves." I stare directly at him, making sure to send the message home.

Fuck with her, and you will be fucking with me.

"Oh," my dad replies the same way I did a few moments ago. "What does this mean for Glam Co?"

Zander looks at me, waiting to hear my reply.

"She means more to me than Glam Co if that is what you're asking," I say.

A smile graces his lips as he stands. "Well, son" — he places a heavy hand on my shoulder — "it's about time you found someone who means more to you than all this."

Relief washes over me. Having my dad's approval means more to me than I can actually express.

I look between my dad and brother. "In that case, I have an idea on how we can expand FF Group, but I wanted to run it past you first."

"Son," my dad says, lifting the hand with the walking stick and gesturing around the room, "we're all ears."

CHAPTER THIRTY-SEVEN

Livvy

I think I'm going to have to go to champagne's anonymous soon — if there is even such a thing? Kendall pops the cork on our second bottle, as a small burp escapes in my chest. Sof stands beside Kendall and adds flecks of edible gold into the glasses– because why not – as Kendall refills all our empty glasses.

"Now look who joined the bougie band wagon," Devin laughs, watching as Sof adds extra gold flecks into her own glass.

"It's called celebrating a girls' night in." Sof rolls her eyes and takes a sip from her drink.

"No, it's called being Liv's trial testers," Kendall replies, finishing the remains of the second bottle of champagne in her glass.

"You do know I need your HONEST opinions, right?" I reply, already feeling the tingling, light-headed sensation of too much champagne too quickly. I'm regretting my decision to handwrite my notes. Tomorrow I'm going to reread them and be like *why did someone say, 'My spirit color is blue freckles' and why did I feel the need to record it?*

"Drunk or not, there is no filter ever on this thing. What you see is what you get." Sof waves at her mouth, making Kendall snort.

I grab the samples for the teen line I had made for us to trial before I present them to the board. Otherwise, our get together this evening isn't going to go any further than eating the antipasto board Sof brought over and drinking more bottles of champagne, and I really need their advice.

"And that is why you are just perfect for this," I reply, lining the samples up on the bench. "The teen line so far has moisturizer, cleanser, serum, toner, and the jelly under-eye patches of which I have two varieties."

"Didn't you say you were wanting to do a mud mask too?" Devin asks.

She has put a lot into helping me create this line with me. The more she is having to do with the company, the more she is enjoying it, and I'm enjoying working with her. I'm looking forward to her joining the Glam Co team when she finishes her degree next summer.

"Oh, shit yeah." I click my fingers and find the mud mask in my laptop bag. "You guys will be the first to try this since Brynn just finished tweaking it."

I hand each of the girls their own personal spatula and hand towel.

"I love the texture of this." Sof holds up the serum.

"Yeah, and this makes my skin feel really clean." Kendall

points to the toner.

I nod and scribble down the notes as their comments continue to fly at me.

"And now" — I open the freezer — "the grand finale." I hold up the jelly eye patches that were in there. "I've made two potentials, but this one — I'm not sure if we should save it for the adult Glam Co line instead of putting it in the teen line." I swallow the lump in my throat, unsure whether I'm ready to show them this idea. It could be amazing, but it could also be a disaster.

My eyes scan the girls. They're all waiting for me to continue. I blow out the nervous breath I didn't realize I was holding. *Here goes nothing.* "I've been toying with under-eye patches that look like jelly but you freeze them and they become — for lack of a better word — ice patches. They literally dissolve into your skin while you're using them, instantly taking away puffiness, and they're moisturizing and are suitable for the sensitive eye area."

"WOW," Kendall whispers, staring at the open jar in my hands with eyes as wide as saucers.

"This is . . . genius," Devin replies, stuttering.

"I volunteer as tribute." Sof butts in, sinking her fingers into the jar. She grabs an eye patch out and puts it on her skin. "EEEEppp, it's cold. But after a crummy day, this would be a lifesaver," Sof moans, pressing them into her face.

"Yeah, that's why I thought these would probably be better used in the adult line, but I just couldn't resist playing around in the lab to make them."

"Yes, way better suited to the adult line," Devin replies,

putting her own pair on.

I help Kendall before putting a pair on myself.

"Oh, wow, Livvy. These are ah-ma-zing," Kendall croons.

Sof gasps. "You know what you should call them? Iced jellies."

I test the name in my head a few times, I haven't really thought about naming them yet, but it has a nice ring to it. "I like it."

"The board is going to wet themselves when you bring these to them." Devin plays with a patch in the palm of her hand, watching it slowly turn from a solid to liquid ready to be wiped away.

I snort. "That is, if it doesn't melt their faces off like last time." The bitter taste of the dry shampoo incident is still on my tongue.

"More like melt their brains with your diabolical genius," Kendall laughs.

Despite the compliments, I can't help the heavy sarcasm in my reply. "You make me sound like I'm the new enemy of Batman."

"Just don't let Ryder get his hands on your samples," she laughs. I smile when Ryder's name is mentioned. I'm glad we're finally at the laughing stage.

"Well, I did make him practically shit his pants in front of the board as payback. The poor guy can barely drink coffee anymore without being triggered. So, I think he will think twice before he touches another one of my samples."

"No one messes with Livvy Blake," Devin snorts.

The sound of another bottle of champagne popping pulls

me out of my Ryder-induced cloud. I turn to Sof, watching the white foam pour over her fingers clasping the neck of the bottle. "Another one?" I raise a brow. Regret will be hitting me hard tomorrow. I really need to lift my alcohol tolerance if I want to hang out with Sof more often.

"I think these products are going to knock the boards' socks off and they're going to give Glam Co one hell of a teen line." Kendall holds her glass out, and Sof refills it.

"Agreed," Devin inputs.

Heat touches my cheeks. "Thanks, guys." Warmth spreads through my chest, their confidence in me is humbling.

Two more bottles of champagne later, Devin and Sof left me with a few notes and a glowing review of the line.

My sweaty palms grip the computer before swiveling it around to show Kendall the presentation I've been working on for the board.

Adding the final touches to the slides that I am going to present on the teen line has my heart in my throat. I've poured hours into not only the presentation and the creation of the products, but also into the research for the line. And it all boils down to a fifteen-minute presentation. It's probably the second-biggest pitch I will ever make to them — right behind me wanting them to vote me in as the full-time CEO of Glam Co.

Leaving absolutely no room for error, I personally made each product myself and sealed them in the boxes with tamper-resistant tape that I found after a two-hour long Amazon search. There is no way Ryder is going to trick Brynn into adding any new ingredients or changing a sticker on the label. I'm not taking any chances with this one.

"When this slide show finishes, are you going to talk from cue cards?" Kendall flicks to the slide in question.

Surprise, surprise, it's the slide I'm most concerned about.
Damn, I just knew she would pick that one out.

"No, I was going to walk everyone through the diagrams." *Wait, should I be using cue cards?* I start to second-guess myself. I'm on the third draft of this presentation. I've long since memorized the stats and the figures in the report. My plan is to use the slides to prompt each of the points I have. And yet, staring at the slide right now with Kendall, it's like a toilet has flushed away all the words I spent so long putting together.

"Do you think it might be too clunky?" she asks, and it sets the second-guessing voice spinning in my head into overdrive.

There are three different graphs all on the one slide and it probably is a bit more on the technical side — not that they won't know what I'm talking about, but it could make the presentation stagnant and a little robotic.

Worried it might bore the board too much, I ask, "I could split it into two? That might help a little."

Kendall is already adding another slide into my presentation and taking one of the graphs and placing it on the new slide. "There." She stares at the slide. "I think that will make it flow much better."

I click on the following one. "And when I get to here, I will hand out the testers for everyone to try."

Kendall nods. "Good, yes, I think this is a key slide. Make sure you stare each member of the board down as you explain the main points."

"Oh, I plan to." I quirk one eyebrow at her. This is my final chance to prove to the board I'm the direction Glam Co should go in before the vote, and with my teen line no less.

"Let's do another run through."

"Sure." I nod. My phone screen lights up, pulling my attention away. My stomach bottoms out at Kyle's name flashing on the screen. *Why the fuck is he messaging me? And why all of a sudden?*

KYLE

Hey, I've seen you hanging out with Sof on Instagram. Do you think we could meet for a coffee? You, me, and Sof?

No doubt sensing my change in mood, Kendall asks, "What's wrong?"

"Kyle is asking to have a coffee with me and Sof." I swipe to clear the message, not even bothering to reply to the dickwad. I've also just found friends who aren't using me, and there is no way I want to compromise that by doing the same thing.

"Ewww, are you joking? Can that guy be more of a wanna be. He's probably having trouble with his internship and is just using you for help."

"Probably," I echo. I'm not going to grab a coffee with him and I'm not going to invite Sof. *"But also- creepy. He is still stalking my Instagram."*

Just seeing his name is enough to sour my happy mood,

and right now I need to prepare for my future. There is too much riding on my presentation.

"Let do this." I blow out a nervous breath, emptying anything Kyle-related from my mind. I give a nod to Kendall to ready the stopwatch on her phone and prepare for my second run through today. When we get to the new slide she created, I recite each formula down to the micromole for each ingredient.

Kendall smiles, giving me the thumbs up. *Nailed it.*

CEO of Glam Co, here I come.

There are not many ways I hate waking up, especially with Ryder sleeping next to me. An incoming call from my dad is high on that list though. Ryder's arm tightens around my waist, alerting me to the fact that he is awake too. Squinting at my dad's name on the screen, I let the phone ring out, mentally waving him off. I wait for the call to end; I will call him back at a more decent hour. Putting my phone back on the bench, I focus on Ryder.

"Morning, baby," Ryder mumbles against the back of my head.

"Apparently it's a really good morning." I giggle, wiggling my hips against his hard dick poking me in the butt.

Ryder grunts in warning before smacking my ass.

I slip my hand into the waist band of his boxers and wrap my hand around his hard length, using slow langued strokes to make him even harder.

"Livvy," Ryder breathes in warning, but I know exactly what I'm doing.

I flip over and lift my leg over his waist, enjoying the friction the new position creates. Ryder curls his finger into my sleep pants and starts teasing my slit, before moving to my clit. "Look how fucking soaked you are for me."

I moaned at the praise. My skin blazes with heat. It's so exquisite I don't want it to stop. "Only for you," I reply as Ryder pulls my sleep pants down my legs. His giant hands circle my hips, massaging the muscle of my buttock. I don't get time to adjust when he and drives deep inside me, plunging hard into my pussy with each upward thrust. From this angle he's even deeper than usual and it takes a few thrusts before the burn from the stretching stops. My fingers dig into the hard muscle on his pecks, as I circle my hips increasing the sensation, eliciting a grunt from Ryder. I cry out, my mind emptying of any thoughts except the delicious sensation of his cock pounding into me. I'm already so close to orgasm it only takes a few more thrusts before it hits me like a lightning bolt, with Ryder following me over the edge. I fall onto his chest into a boneless heap.

"Best way to wake up," he mumbles into my hair.

I don't even care about my morning breath. Arching my neck, I achieve the perfect angle to align our lips, "Couldn't agree more." I whisper, when my phone rings again. Annoyance flicks at me finding my dad's name flashing across the screen again.

"He isn't going to leave a message, is he?" It's a rhetorical question because I already know the answer and that is hell no — he is going to keep ringing until I answer. Rolling away from Ryder, I prop myself on my elbow and answer, "Hello?"

My voice is thick with a mixture of sleep and arousal.

"Olivia? What are you still doing in bed?"

"It's six-thirty, Dad," I reply.

"So? The Fallingtons have already doubled their income according to the stock market."

My dad's obsession with the Fallingtons has officially hit stage-eleven clinger.

Ryder shrugs and grins. We're both obsessed with Fallingtons –just for different reasons.

Ryder catches my hand before I can slap the grin from his face before turning it over and placing a warm kiss to the inside of my wrist.

"Did you just call me to talk about the Fallingtons?" I huff, his fixation annoying me.

"No, I called to ask why you are spending time on the silly teen line?" he replies, unaffected by my question.

I pull the phone away from my ear, counting back from ten. The lid I have on my emotions start to lift every single time he downgrades my teen line. "The board told me to go ahead and provide them with samples, Dad." I try to not let my thoughts turn down the dark tunnel just lapping up the self-doubt coursing through my veins.

"Derick mentioned on the golf course how much he really wants to see the continual presence of a Blake at the helm of Glam Co. I don't want to hear you're giving him reason to doubt that vision. He expressed his concerns about this teen line, so I'm telling you now-you need to drop it if you want to have a chance of being voted in."

Interesting, Derick isn't just expressing his concerns to my dad; he's frequently articulating them to Ryder too.

"I'll take your advice on board, Dad, but I have to get ready for work." I end the call and let my phone thump on my bedside table.

My eyes meet Ryder's; his eyebrows are raised.

With only two days until the Glam Co fundraiser, we are at the business end of proving ourselves to the board, who vote on the CEO next week.

Ryder tilts my chin up. "That's absolute bullshit, Liv. Your teen line will open up an entirely new area of the market to Glam Co." Ryder kisses the corner of my mouth. "I know I'm supposed to be the competition and he's your father, but that man is talking out of his ass."

"Thanks." I offer him a weak smile. As much as his words are comforting, I still feel like I've been punched in the gut.

"It looks like Derick is playing both sides of the fence," he quips, changing the subject.

My thoughts exactly.

I purse my lips, thinking over everything that has been said. Maybe Derick isn't as trustworthy as my dad thinks he is.

CHAPTER THIRTY-EIGHT

Ryder

My fingers dig into the soft silk of the tie, making sure it's perfectly straight. Somewhere in the foyer the rest of the guys are getting ready, and from the grumbling I hear from Duke, he's less than impressed to be in a suit. The man thinks a racing suit is the extent of a suit. I run my hand through my hair a final time. That guy is always complaining about something.

I still don't remember agreeing to all the guys using my place to get ready — no matter how many times Leo shows me the group chat where everyone all but decided we would catch the limo from mine because we might get another random food delivery.

Thanks, Livvy and her merry band of friends.

It's not like we aren't going to a ball with food — the plates alone were a 50k donation to the charity Glam Co supports and it includes a Michelin-chef-cooked three-course meal.

Nope. The guys are excited for another random panini

delivery. Figures.

"What? Too used to wearing those race suits you don't know how to tie a proper tie?" Anders jokes as I walk out into the foyer to find Henley adjusting the tie around Duke's neck.

"I know how to tie a tie, dickhead," Duke deadpans, batting Henley's hands away and trying to fix the tie himself. Zander is already pouring himself a drink, which I steal before he can lift the two fingers of scotch to his lips.

"Hey" he grouches, "that was mine."

"Get your own glass," I grumble, not giving two shits he is offended and downing the drink.

"Who do you think will be the first to bid on something stupid because they are so wiped?" Rome jokes.

"Definitely Zander." Anders nods.

"Second that," Henley replies, not looking away from his phone.

My brother actually looks offended that the group has singled him out as the lightweight. I wipe my lips with the back of my hand to cover the snort wanting to escape.

"No way," Zander scoffs. "My money is on Faluccino there." He lifts his eyebrows, tipping his chin toward Leo, who is busy taking 'candid' selfie shots against the window.

"Gotta get them for the gram, hey, brother?" Henley's tone is full of unshed laughter.

Leo laughs, "You're just jealous that you don't look this good in Armani." He pulls on the lapels of his perfectly tailored jacket. "Besides, there is no better way to start a feeding frenzy than to give them some food."

Anders rests his finger on the bridge of his nose and huffs

out a breath while Rome and Henley look at each other and mouth, *"Feeding frenzy."*

"It's his code for the ladies that are in his little black book," Anders finally says, answering the question for us.

Zander and I turn to each other with a WTF look. My gut churns with shame at Leo's words, all too aware that I used to be like that not too long ago, collecting panties and hotel room keys. Falling in love with Livvy has changed all that. My brother pours me another finger of scotch, which I gratefully accept before pulling my phone out of my jacket pocket and clicking on the group chat Leo created to exit the chat.

The Cheshire Shore convention center has been transformed to host the Glam Co gala, complete with a red carpet and photographers. I pose with the guys for the group shot and make my way inside looking for a particular brunette. I send a silent thank you to the gods for choosing her for me. Livvy controls the room the moment she enters in a floor-length, silken, cobalt-blue ball gown with a split all the way up to her hip bone and no suit pants in sight.

"I don't think I say this enough but fuck me — I am one lucky asshole to have you," I whisper, my arm coming around to clasp her waist before placing a kiss to her exposed neck. I love the way my hand splays over the open back of her dress.

Livvy swivels in my arms, and if I thought my dick was hard before, her closeness has it turning to granite now. I run my hand down her back and cup the curve of her ass, which is effortlessly displayed in her dress, before pushing our bodies together like perfect-fitting puzzle pieces.

"And to think I decided against my nice dress pants tonight just for you." She bops the tip of my nose with her finger before placing a soft kiss on my lips.

Yeah, no. That won't do.

Cupping the back of her neck and being careful not to mess up her hair, I drag her lips back to mine before placing a much more appropriate kiss on her mouth. "Thank fuck for no pants," I breathe against her lips when we finally break apart. My mind is already trying to calculate where the closest secluded place is.

"No fucking on the common floor." Leo pretends he is talking into a walkie talkie on his shoulder, but in reality, he is just talking into his own palm.

"Second that," Rome goads Leo, mimicking his motion.

"I swear it scares me that you two make serious decisions that affect millions of people's lives." Devin slaps Rome's shoulder.

Second that, I almost reply.

Devin closes the distance between us and whisper-yells, "Is that Duke?"

Livvy tries to subtly look over my shoulder to where Devin is pointing.

"Depends," I muse. "Does he have a tie that looks like it was put together by a five-year-old?" As much as the guy thinks he can tie a tie, he really can't.

Livvy turns back to Devin, and whispers back, *"Yeah, that totally is."*

"Yesss." Devin does a little dance.

I send a silent message to Livvy; she needs to spill what

happened when she picked her car up from the Croft hanger.

I spot Rome's brothers, Luca and Dante, standing off to the side talking to Charlotte Croft and Becks' sisters, Allegra and Annie. Luca has his arm hooked around his best friend Florence's hip. Looks like the whole gang has turned out to support this event. It's not like any of the Elite of Cheshire Shore would miss a chance to be seen at an event as publicized as this.

The sound of a man clearing his throat draws our attention to Livvy's parents standing in front of us.

"Dad, Mom," Livvy and Devin say at the same time.

The heat touching Livvy's cheeks would be cute if it wasn't for her Dad sending daggers in my direction.

"I guess the rumors are true, Derick and I are due for a chat," Simon reflects, his eyes searing a hole in my hand wrapped around Livvy's waist. "I'll see you girls inside." He eyes each of his daughters before turning on his heel and leaving.

"What rumor?" Devin asks.

"My relationship with Ryder maybe?"

"Wait, you haven't told him?" Devin looks between Simon and Liv.

Livvy raises her brows to Devin in an 'are you serious' way, but she seems to take the hint.

"Riiiiight, stupid question really. Of course, you didn't tell him."

"We'd better find our table," Livvy mumbles, watching the mass of people making their way through the open double doors.

Our tables, as it turns out, are on opposite sides of the

room. It seems the Blakes and the Fallingtons could not be seen at the same table for fear of hatchet burying. My skin feels tight being so close yet so far away from Livvy and not being able to thread my fingers through hers or run my hand along her side. Missing the way her body shivers from those little touches only makes this event drag on longer than necessary.

As the alcohol continues to pour, the conversations grow louder, the people laugh harder, and the night gets that little bit longer. The guy on stage drones on and on, but I haven't got a clue what it's about. Nothing makes for a great charity event like open wallets, and nothing opens wallets quicker than lowering inhibitions.

It doesn't help that Zander's sitting next to me and he keeps jumping up. His paddle waves wildly as he enters a bidding war with Rome for something else. For fuck's sake, Leo and Sof seem to be cheering my brother on. Why the fuck did I get stuck at the immature table? I huff out a breath. That is the third bidding war he has entered with Rome and the second he has lost.

My dad leans over and claps Zander on the back. "You'll win the next one, son," he tells him. His face is plastered with a smile.

The charity supports Ovarian cancer research — a cause my dad holds dear. Anything to do with charity, my dad is all for.

Livvy winks at me across the room. My phone flashes with a new message from her.

"Sold to Zander Fallington," the MC announces as my brother sits down with a shit-eating grin.

"Nothing but paddle, baby," Leo whoops.

"You do know he is trying to get you to overpay on this shit?" I tell him.

"Hey, I just won a hot lap with Charlotte Croft." My brother looks at me from the corner of his eye. "Trust me, Rome was never going to win that one." Looks like Zander's date went better than expected if he is trying to win her charity bid.

"Hopefully the hot lap will be on more than just a car," Leo jokes and groans when Zander punches him in the shoulder.

"Before we get to the next item up for bidding, we have a special presentation from the Blakes," the host cuts in. "Please, can everyone turn to the screen."

A projector screen is lowered, and I quickly type a message to Livvy.

ME

What's this?

LIVVY

No clue. I didn't make it.

There is the sound of feedback as a microphone is dropped near the stage. Hushed whispers float across the room as the lights dim and a video starts playing. I lock my phone, staring at the first video I ever filmed with Livvy — except this is the unedited version.

Ice floods my veins.

"I get that, Killer, but I mean with you working for Glam Co — isn't it a conflict of interest?" I say in the video, and my stomach drops. This cannot be good.

"No one knows anything about my involvement with Glam Co. I keep Livvy Blake separate from Olivia Grace," Livvy replies.

Anger flares inside me. What the fuck is this hack job? This isn't Liv's video. A new video cuts in of Livvy pointing to her products at a Kosmedika store from her previous collaboration with Glam Co.

"All this stuff is just literally Glam Co products with my name on the front and because my audience loves me, they pay the marked-up price."

The way it's filmed and the way the person has created this farce of a video portrays Livvy as being a fake influencer who is just trying to make Glam Co look good in order to get the board to favor her.

"I mean, I review super shit products and I manage to make sales skyrocket all because I tell my audience how much I love it — and I get paid to do it."

The video cuts out as Livvy is walking with her camera held up in front of her, touring the Glam Co labs.

Something about Livvy looks different — the Livvy on the screen isn't my Liv. She looks younger. From the fringe and blonde streaks in her hair, it appears this is really old footage.

"All the formulations I use are just a rehash of my nanna's, and I get all the credit for them."

My heart stops beating in my chest, this whole thing is intended to humiliate Livvy in front of everyone. The board members of Glam Co are all here. And if this was a member of FF Group portraying themselves and our company like this online, there would be no question in my eyes that they are unfit to continue work with us. I scan the area, trying to find the board members in the darkened room. This doesn't bode well for Livvy and her Glam Co image.

"She was a genius, and I've got her little note book which has heaps of her ideas. And no one knows I'm just using her work."

My eyes search the room for hers, trying to offer some form of comfort. Her face is a mask of control, but tears stream down her cheek. Seeing Livvy in pain causes my gut to clench.

The sound of the video keeps echoing through the space, but I don't take my eyes off Livvy. I couldn't even if I wanted to. She is my whole world, and her world is being torn apart — and so is mine.

"I will do anything I have to in order to get Glam Co and make sure my sister is left with nothing. She doesn't breathe this place like I do."

Devin's eyebrows draw down in anger before her mouth falls open like she can't believe what she is seeing, and her arm wraps around Livvy's shoulders. She doesn't believe this video for one second.

It's all lies.

Simon Blake is sitting back in his chair, completely unaffected by what is happening. Clenching my fist, I stop myself from punching the sorry son of a bitch. How could he be sitting there, watching his daughter be humiliated, and do nothing?

My eyes meet Sof's horrified ones. *Fuck, I need to do something.* Zander is shaking his head in disbelief, and Leo is staring at Simon Blake. From the look on his face, I have a partner in handing Simon his ass.

My dad places a hand on my knee, squeezing hard. "Son,"

he whispers.

"I didn't — " I start to say but get cut off as the video pans to a less than flattering photo of Livvy before Simon Blake's voice comes through the speaker.

"I never had any intention of having a stupid teen line. I just kept sending her on a wild goose chase. Sure, Livvy is my daughter, but she isn't really CEO material. But we have no other choice — a Blake needs to run Glam Co. Devin is too young, and now the Fallingtons want back in. It's just a disaster."

My eyes flick over to Simon, who is sitting higher in his chair. If I'm not mistaken, he almost looks . . . shocked?

Rage like I've never felt before rings through my ears at her dad saying those things. Livvy would make an amazing CEO. She lives and breathes Glam Co. Simon's voice bleeds out and text lights the screen.

<u>*'Do you really want a liar to run Glam Co?'*</u>

I cut my gaze to Zander, who is staring at the screen with wide-mouth shock. The screen shuts off and the host gets back on stage.

I search for Livvy but find hers and Devin's seats empty. Sof's seat is vacant as well.

"Ryder." Leo's tone is deadly low. "We know that wasn't you. You fucking adore Livvy, but we need to find out who made that video."

Running a hand through my hair, I say, "I have to fix this." I just don't have a fucking clue how.

My dad tightens his grip on my thigh, pulling my attention back to him. "Ryder, you need to get your woman."

"Go now, bro, before she thinks you're somehow involved

in this shit," Zander urges.

Standing, my chair catches on the carpeted floor.

I need to find Livvy, is the only thought that runs through my head.

I need to find my girl and tell her this wasn't me.

CHAPTER THIRTY-NINE

Livvy

"Shhh, it's okay," Kendall coos, rubbing slow circles on my back. I don't know how I ended up here. After watching the video, everything kind of became a blur. Devin tucks the strands of my hair that have fallen loose from my updo behind my ear as my stomach revolts for the second time and I throw up all those hateful things circling through my mind into the cold porcelain toilet bowl. *That video.* I never even said half the things in that video.

"Livvy, your phone is blowing up," Sof whispers, quickly turning it on silent.

She can chuck the thing out for all I care.

"Not helping, Sof," Kendall scolds her. My stomach clenches again.

"Oh my god." I finally get the raspy words out, my throat burning from overuse. "Oh my god." I sit on the cold, tiled floor, causing Devin and Kendall to shuffle back as the space in the small cubicle becomes tighter. "How could he do this to me?" Clasping my thumping head, the blinding headache starts to take hold. I look over my shoulder at the others, my eyes burning from tears that won't stop falling.

"Do you really think it was Ryder?" Devin's hushed whisper asks.

That video being released in front of everyone has ruined everything. The board will think I'm completely incapable of running Glam Co. Not even my dad believes I'm deserving of the Glam Co empire — why should the six people who decide my fate?

I just watched my future blow up right in front of me in a three-minute, brutally edited video.

Kendall and Devin share a whispered conversation which I try to listen to but my ragged breaths are too loud even to my own ears.

"We need to get her out of here," Kendall whispers.

"On it," Sof replies before leaving the bathroom and returning moments later with Leo.

I brace myself for some joke or witty remark, praying I can withstand his humor without bursting into tears again.

But Leo shocks me when he wipes a fresh tear from my cheek with his thumb. "Sweet girls shouldn't cry," he whispers, bending to pick me up in his arms — which I'm incredibly grateful for, because I don't think my legs could hold me up anyway. I wrap my fist in his jacket and hold onto him. Closing my eyes, I rest my head against Leo's shoulder.

I just want to get out of here.

"This way," Kendall says, followed by the sound of the bathroom door opening.

Anders is already waiting on the other side.

"Livvy," I hear Ryders voice, but I turn my face into Leo's chest. I don't want to see him right now. I need to process everything.

Ander's must be holding Ryder back. "She doesn't want to see you. Give her some time."

"She's my girlfriend."

"Yeah, and she's fucking hurting. Get your head out of your ass and think about her for a moment and give her some fucking time." Ander's voice starts to raise.

"Livvy, baby, please." Ryders pleading voice only makes more tears flow down my cheeks.

"You're safe now, Liv. We will get to the bottom of this," Leo says as we leave the building.

Sof and Devin insist on staying at our place, against Kendall's adamant refusal. After Leo deposits me on my bed, a fresh set of wracking sobs take over my body. At some point Devin slips into the bed with me, wrapping her arms around my waist and holding me while I continue to sob into my pillowcase. MoMo just curls herself into a ball under the blanket and every so often she nudges me with her nose, telling me she is here.

Time has become a blur of broken heart beats and shallow breaths.

Kendall periodically knocks on the door, asking if I want food.

I just shrug and pull the covers over my shoulder. Eating food seems irrelevant now.

I continue to stare at the rain pelting the window; the grey sky is overcast and dark like my mood.

Sometime later, Devin pats my shoulder and produces a bottle of water before urging me to sip from it.

When I shake my head, no, she huffs. "Livvy, if you don't want to eat that's fine. But you need to drink or else you will become dehydrated, and I really don't want to have to take you to hospital."

I stare at the water bottle like the liquid inside is poisonous and then into her face, shaking my head.

How could Ryder take it this far?

This goes beyond office sabotage. This is taking our friendly feud and making it public. And this has the potential to ruin more than just my career at Glam Co. Everything I've ever worked for is now hanging by a fraying rope, all because I fell for Ryder fucking Fallington. The man who made me believe in myself, who saw me as more than just Livvy Blake — but he saw the real me. I guess that was a lie too.

"Please," she pleads.

Like me, she is still wearing her dress from the gala. She hasn't moved from my side. Something tugs in my chest. I take the bottle of water from her hand and sip it before handing it back to her. She shakes her head and says, "More."

Three sips later, and Devin is finally satisfied I'm sufficiently hydrated. She takes the bottle from me.

"Happy?" I croak, my voice raw from being unused.

"Immensely," she replies.

I grunt in response and lift my bed covers high on my shoulder, staring out the dim window.

I must have fallen asleep because the sound of hushed voices wakes me up. Throwing the covers off, I sit up too quickly and rest my spinning forehead in the palm of my hand. I wait for the room to come back to normal before I stand.

MoMo is asleep in her dog donut by my bed, still guarding me. I give a small smile at her sleeping form, but the muscles in my face hurt too much to let it last for more than a few seconds.

Catching a glimpse of myself in the mirror, I quickly look away. The image in the mirror is not me. It's not the Livvy Blake of twenty-four hours ago, who couldn't wait to show the board the teen line she has spent nearly a year creating and perfecting. It's not Livvy Blake who, for the first time in her life, was in love with a man who made her heart stop.

No. The mirror is showing a woman broken with nothing.

This dress doesn't help, it's only bringing back awful memories I'm really trying to forget. I unzip the dress, letting it fall from my body before balling it up and throwing it in the trash. Well, most of it. The can is too small for my dress, but the sentiment is there. If it wasn't a total safety hazard, I'd light the stupid thing on fire here and now and watch it burn.

Cathartic as it may sound, I don't think Kendall would appreciate it if I accidentally set fire to our apartment. I won't be able to ever look at that dress without crying. After grabbing a pair of soft sweats and pulling them on, I open my door and step out into the living room.

"We can't tell her."

That's Kendall's voice.

"She's going to find out sooner or later. Wouldn't it be better coming from us?" Sof asks.

"This will crush her more than she already is. I just — " Devin's voice catches before she finishes her sentence.

"Tell me what?" I ask.

The hushed whispers stop abruptly when they see me. The three of them look at me with deep sorrow etched in their faces, full of pity.

Ugh. If there is one thing I hate in this world, it's being pitied.

"Tell me what?" I repeat.

"Take a seat." Kendall motions and vacates her seat, instead opting to stay busy by putting the kettle on. I sit down and stare right at my sister, waiting for her to tell me what this little intervention circle is all about.

"Tell me what?" I say again, my eyes boring into hers.

Devin swallows, her jaw working overtime as she seems to be searching for the right words. The silence in the room is nearly killing me with what-ifs.

I look at Sof and ask, "Are you going to tell me?" breaking the silence.

Kendall places a cup of tea in front of me and takes the seat next to Sof.

"Someone leaked the video online," Sof finally says, bursting the already taut bubble in the room.

I just nod, my numb body refusing to let the news penetrate the wall I've erected around my already fragile emotions.

Someone leaked that sham of a video — why doesn't that surprise me?

"And the stitches that are coming through aren't great. You've got a trending hashtag," Sof continues.

I've always wanted a trending hashtag. Too bad it's for the

wrong reasons. I should be more upset, should maybe burst into a fresh set of tears, but nothing comes. I'm so numb, my body just hums in an emotional overdrive.

"And it's made its way onto Make Me," Sof continues, her voice soft like she is talking to a frightened animal.

All at once, a giant influx of emotions registers in my body and my fight-or-flight instinct kicks in.

My Gracites.

My stomach clenches just thinking about them.

Ryder really wanted to make sure he completely fucked up my life, but I guess what would you expect from a Fallington? There is a reason our families have hated each other for a hundred years.

Just as quickly as the thought hits me, my mind shuts it down, protecting me from the devastation of what this all means, returning me back to numbness.

"We are doing everything we can to remove it. Anders and Ares keep taking down the accounts that post the video, but every time they do, another one posts it. But they have put a lock on people tagging your account, which is good." Kendall rushes to input.

I nod again. They're just words coming out of her mouth — they don't mean anything to me anymore.

"How many?" I croak.

Kendal lets out a long, loud breath.

My muscles tense as I brace myself for the bad news.

"Nearly three million," she states.

Fuck. It's like I've just been slapped in the face.

Three million followers lost in twenty-four hours.

Three million people who think I have let them down and deceived them.

Three million people believe I'm a liar and a fake — the exact opposite of what I stand for.

It's more like someone took a sharp knife and gutted me and strung me up with my own insides.

"We will get through this." Devin leans across the table, placing her warm hand on my ice-cold one in a gesture of solidarity.

I stare at her hand, not feeling an ounce of the comfort she is trying to give.

"If you say so." My voice is robotic and monotone, and I get up from the table and return to bed. My energy has been zapped from my system.

Tomorrow, I tell myself. Tomorrow I will let what Sof just said sink in. But right now, like water droplets on a smooth glass surface, it's all just sliding right off.

Tucking myself into my covers, I close my eyes. After the amount I've slept in the last twenty-four hours, I'm surprised I can sleep at all. But I'm just so tired. I close my eyes, letting the darkness be my escape.

Sunlight streams in through my open window. I slowly lift my eyelids. A small layer of crust clings to my lashes. My hand comes up to block out the onslaught of brightness, allowing my eyes to adjust to the light. Reaching over, I fumble around on my bedside table, searching for my phone but finding it empty. *Whatever. I don't need the stupid thing anyway.* I sit up abruptly, my heart racing in my chest as my slow brain wakes up. *I need coffee or I have no hope of getting through this blur.* After kicking the covers off, I make my way into the kitchen only to find the girls sitting around our island.

"Liv." Devin jumps up and hugs me.

Great, another intervention circle. What more could they have to say now? I was adopted this whole time? The university is going to revoke my degree?

Returning her hug, I inhale her scent. It grounds me instantly.

Pulling away from her, I look at the others. "Morning." My voice is chirpier than I thought possible. I click the buttons on the coffee machine and wait for my preloaded brew to percolate.

"Morning," they all reply in unison.

I find them staring at me. *Creepy.* After grabbing my coffee, I take the spot next to Kendall. "Dev, can I have my phone back?" I ask, taking a sip from my coffee.

"Of course." She hands it to me. "Ryder has been blowing it up."

I accept my phone from her, but my attention is held by what is on our kitchen counter. There are pieces of paper and open notebooks scattered along the bench. "What's all this?" I ask, staring at the array in front of me and taking another sip from my coffee.

"*This* is our game plan," Devin announces.

It's on the tip of my tongue to ask *for what* when a loud knocking sounds at the front door, making me jump in my chair.

"I'll get it," Kendall announces.

I pick up the paper closest to me. It's a scanned copy of the drafts for my formulas for the teen line. Staring at my handwriting, my eyes water. I thought I could do this, but maybe I can't — it's still too fresh.

My teen line has been doomed from the start. My dad literally set me up just to fail. A familiar mixture of crippling sadness and disappointment rears its ugly head, but this time some new anger is added into the pool. *At least I'm progressing through the stages of grief.*

Screw my dad, screw Ryder, screw Glam Co.

My gaze swings between Devin and Sof and back down at the piece of paper in my hand, I can't quite work out why they would take copies of my formulas if not to rub more dirt in my already gangrenous wound.

"She doesn't want to see you," floats Kendall's harsh whisper.

My shoulders slump. I'm hoping she is talking to Mrs. Dylan about the hot guy who dropped me off two days ago and not the guy who completely betrayed my trust in order to be voted in as CEO of Glam Co.

"Please." Ryder's broken plea echoes through the room.

The sound of his voice snaps something in me.

No. He doesn't get to be the victim here today.

After closing the distance, I grab the half-closed door from Kendall and sharply open it and pull up short. If I thought I looked broken, Ryder looks just as bad. He has dark circles lining his eyes, his hair is a tangled mess that stands in all different directions, and a generous shadow covers his jaw — and not in the sexy, five o'clock way. His brown eyes, the ones I could spend hours looking into, appear glazed and unfocused.

"Livvy," he breathes like he doesn't believe I'm standing in front of him.

I continue staring at him, not uttering a single word.

I can't. My mind has blanked out.

"Livvy," Ryder says again before wrapping his arms around my shoulders. The warm, Amalfi-coast scent I used to find such a comfort is only making me nauseous. I count to ten in my head, simmering down the burning rage coursing through my veins, before I push against his chest with all my might.

"Livvy, I know what you must be thinking," he says.

"Oh, and what would that be?" I reply.

"That I created that video."

I almost snort with laughter, crossing my arms in front of me. "Let me guess, you're here to tell me you didn't?"

"Livvy, you know I wouldn't." Hurt clouds in his eyes.

"You said it yourself; you would do anything it takes to get Glam Co. The Fallingtons have been hard done by the Blakes for over one hundred years, am I right?" I repeat the things he said six months ago.

God. It almost feels like a lifetime ago.

Ryder scoffs, "You're really going to throw that in my face? I said that months ago, before I fell in love with you."

"I never said half those things in that video, yet somehow they ended up recorded for everyone to hear," I whisper.

"I know, baby. With AI, people can make it sound like you said shit you've never said. They can cut and paste conversations and make it look effortless." He runs a finger down my cheek, drying the silent tears.

I stare at a spot on the wall past his shoulder, not able to meet his eyes — knowing the moment I do I will crumble into a sobbing heap. "How do I know you really did fall in love with me? It could have all just been a ploy, some masterful part of your giant plan." I swipe angrily at the hot tears that fall down my cheeks, annoyed at myself for crying in front of him. "And the worst part is, my credibility on Make Me has been shot to fucking shit. Not only have you won Glam Co — I now have nothing. NOTHING!" My voice cracks, but I don't care. I let my tears fall, wiping them when they reach my lip.

All those years I spent hours in front of the camera, building trust, has been whittled to nothing.

"If I wanted Glam Co just signed over to me, why would I bother encouraging the board to listen to your plan for the teen line and getting them to sign off on you making the samples? Why would I go to Kosmedika and get a contract for them to stock your teen line before it's even been shown? Why would I create a profile on Make Me to watch you thrive. Every single message I sent you was real. And it made me fall so fucking hard for you. You have become my reason to breathe. I don't give a shit about Glam Co or the Fallington-Blake feud. I give a shit about you, Olivia Blake." He runs a frustrated hand through his hair, clenching his jaw.

"Wait, what?!" I gasp.

CHAPTER FORTY

Livvy

My heart stops beating. He created a fake profile, which invaded my safe space. How do I know everything he's shared with me hasn't been a lie. A business move to get me to lower my guard. I now question every single moment we've had together. I stare at Ryder, blinking. My brain is processing the words he just said but my mind is unwilling to let the meaning sink in.

"No." I shake my head.

"I realized I didn't want to get to know you that way. It's why I started messaging you."

I mentally change the name around — Ryder Fallington. Of course. Rachel or Ryder started following me right after I posed the video of us doing the PR haul. Balling my hands into fists, I let my fingernails bite into the palms of my hands. I can't believe I didn't connect the dots sooner.

"You. You — " A hysterical laugh bubbles in my chest. Out of everything that has been dropped on me these last few days, this is . . . almost unbelievable. "Why?"

"I did it because I love getting to know you, Livvy. I am so fucking sorry. I've wanted to tell you for so long – but I didn't want you to hate me for it. Every single time we got closer, everything you shared with me – it became harder to tell you. I wanted to tell you. Fuck. I just didn't know how."

"And the whole boyfriend and girlfriend thing wasn't enough, apparently?" Sarcasm drips from my lips.

"You once told me; I have a Ryder effect. But that's not true. You have a Livvy effect, and I am one hundred percent under it. And I know everything you said was all truth and that's why I fell even harder for you. Because even as Olivia Grace, you are still one hundred percent authentically you. Livvy Blake."

Wiping the single angry tear that escapes the corner of my eye, I swallow the lump in my throat. "So, essentially faking wanting to know why I want Glam Co?"

"No. I genuinely wanted to know why you have such a love for Glam Co."

"You were literally sitting in the office next to me pretending to be someone else and messaging me," I whisper, wrapping my arms around myself.

"I was always myself, Liv. Just like you were," he repeats.

"Did you ever really love me?"

"What kind of question is that?"

The one I need an answer too.

The way his voice falters causes something to crack in my armor. "Baby, I told you about my dad's illness. Which no one knows about except a few select people. It's why he has stepped away from the public eye and makes rare public appearances. He came to the charity ball because we were there, and he wanted to show his support for us."

While I get that Ryder and I didn't have strong feelings for each other when we started this, my trust has been completely broken.

"Yes, it was what made me realize you and I aren't that different. The shit you go through, the burden of being the oldest to a high-achieving family, the way you just want to make your nanna proud — it's the same with me and my dad."

Clearing my throat, my eyes finally meet his. "We're not done with this fight, Ryder. Or should I say Rachel? You fucking lied to me and that is beyond not okay! But what's this stupid Kosmedika thing? That video – you are the only person who knew I kept my raw version on that USB."

"I promise you baby, it wasn't me, I would never do something like that to you. I believe in your vision for the teen line, and Glam Co more than I can express."

Did I hear him correctly that he already got a contract for my teen line? The Rachel Fallout thing kinda makes sense, especially the comments about the red lipstick. "I haven't even presented to the board yet; how could anyone know the details let alone get a contract. I'm supposed to do it this week."

"I went to Kosmedika and gave them a heads up."

I eye him through narrow lids. "Gave them a heads up?" I repeat the words because they sound strange even to my ears.

No one give Kosmedika a heads up. Not even the great Ryder Fallington.

Besides, he expects me to believe he went to the biggest

beauty store and got a blind contract without samples? We don't even have the board's sign off, and if I can't use Glam Co machines to make the products, my project is dead in the water. Something smells like a fish market before closing time and I am not buying by the pound.

"Yes," Ryder repeats, heat touching his cheeks.

That invisible hand makes a reappearance, gripping my throat with such intensity. *Ryder just sees me as someone who needs saving — not as his equal. He went behind my back and did this without my knowledge because he didn't think I could do it.* "I need space," I manage to choke out.

Ryder scoffs. "How is space going to make this better?"

"I just need time to think. My whole world has been scrambled and served back to me on a hot plate. I just" — I blow out a breath — "I need to refocus on what the fuck I'm going to do with myself, and I don't know if it involves you." My lips pull into a frown. Saying those words out loud turns my insides to stone.

Ryder gave me wings, and now it seems he has taken a pair of sheers and cut them off.

"Romeo without Juliet was just a man who didn't know what it meant to love. Juliet showed Romeo love makes life worth living."

I blink away tears. "Clearly, you didn't finish reading that love story. Because they both died in the end."

Ryder's phone rings in his pocket. He fishes it out and looks at the name on the screen. "I'm sorry. I have to take this," he grumbles, glancing between me and the phone. Then holds a hand up. "This isn't over — *we* aren't over, Livvy," he tells me before turning and leaving along the hallway.

I want to believe him, but my head and my heart are at war with each other. *Were we even really together?* I want to scream to his retreating figure and slam the door shut behind him. I rest my forehead against the cool wood. I need space to figure out what my life is going to look like now and Ryder just clouds my judgement.

I lift my head to see the girls standing behind me, eyeing me. At least they were all witness to the conversation, and I don't have to retell it, I don't think my shattered heart could take it.

"What?" I ask just as a knock sounds on the door behind me. Blowing out an annoyed breath, I open the door with, "Ryder, did you not learn no means no?" but find a wide-eyed Leo, Henley, and Rome standing on the other side.

"Well, I can't speak for Ryder, but I learned that meaning when my Nonna whipped my ass with a wooden spoon after I told her I liked Valentina's boobs when I was twelve." Rome places a hand on his chest, and I don't know why but I just burst into a fit of uncontrolled, crazed, delusional laughter.

Leo and Henley exchange worried looks with each other.

"I think she's broken," Henley whispers out of the corner of his mouth.

I take a few calming breaths. My abs hurt from the effort.

"Beyond words," I reply, finally catching my breath and motioning for them to come inside.

"Ohhh good. You're here." Sof jumps up and runs to Leo before wrapping her arms around his shoulders.

"You call — we come," Henley says, taking a seat at the

kitchen island on the opposite side to Kendall and Devin.

I stand by the door, my body not moving a muscle as Rome and Leo fill in the empty gaps. It's almost like they are getting comfortable.

"Are you ready to hear about our plan?" Sof asks as she takes her seat, staring directly at her cousin on the opposite side of the island.

My cheeks blaze when it becomes clear that everyone's eyes are on me, cornering me. Shifting from foot to foot, I swallow, hoping someone will cut through the awkward silence. Or will they continue to wait for me to do something?

"It kind of rests on you," Devin says, finally cutting through the tension in the room.

"What plan?" I ask, not moving a muscle and standing rooted in place. I stare at my friends in confusion, the fuzzy tendrils of hope licking at me.

"Our plan to launch Livvy Blake Cosmetics, starting with your teen line which I can't wait to try," Leo announces, and my jaw hits the ground.

Wait what? The fuzzy tendrils of hope bloom in my chest.

I jerk my head back, scanning the faces in the room while I try to process what has just been said. I open and close my mouth like a fish gasping for air before I can finally get my throat to work. "I'm sorry. It sounded like you just said Livvy Blake Cosmetics?"

"That's what I heard." Rome smiles, crossing his arms over his chest and confirming I'm not hallucinating from sleep deprivation or dehydration or even maybe caffeine withdrawal.

"Why?" I ask.

"Because we always try before we buy," Henley announces. "And from what we've heard, this teen line is kinda awesome."

What in the actual heck is going on right now?

These guys have just taken their crazy pills, or they've lost a bet. There's no other way to explain what is happening right now. "I don't want you guys to save me."

I'm a girl boss building her empire after all.

Rome snorts. "Bella, have you met yourself? Livvy Blake doesn't need saving. Besides, I'm in the business of making money and I love diversifying my portfolio."

"Are you just going to stand there or are you going to get your samples out?" Devin asks, pushing on my back.

My legs start moving as if they have a mind of their own, taking me to where I have the samples sitting on the desk.

Slowly, each of the guys lean forward and reach for my samples before opening them up and testing them out.

Watching Rome put a mud mask on Henley is probably up there with one of my favorite things I've ever seen. This heavily tattooed guy gently swiping paintbrush strokes on Henley's face while his hair is being kept back with a bunny headband. I can't believe this is actually happening.

"I like the smell of this." Leo holds up the toner. "It's not overpowering like some of the stuff Sof uses."

"It's not designed to not be heavily scented," I reply, while Sof puts a pair of iced eye patches under her eyes. They're by far her favorite thing, and probably mine too.

"This" — Henley grabs the eye patches from Sof after Rome finishes applying the mud mask — "is sick. Charlotte would shit herself if she saw these."

I snort my laughter. Something about the way brothers refer to their sisters in such a terrible way but would defend them to their dying breath warms my very cold, crusted-over heart.

"It's a shame Duke was busy today." Devin pouts.

"Yeah, Lottie and D are training. They have Monaco coming up," Henley replies, missing exactly why Devin is upset — and it has nothing to do with Duke not being here for this so-called master plan. But rather to do with the fact she has a really bad crush on Duke Croft.

"You see this?" Sof holds up the moisturizer before she proceeds to talk about the specific ingredients I used and the reasons why I used them. It's as if I'd just coached her on it instead of giving her a quick spiel a couple of weeks ago.

My heart takes a few big beats, and my chest warms with affection for her. She then nods to Kendall and Devin, and I get the feeling these three have put a solid plan together — it's not a desperate attempt to make me feel better. No wonder they have been so hushed.

Kendall pulls out her laptop and clicks play, and the slides I put together illuminate on her screen as she starts to deliver the speech I've been working on. When she gets to the slide we worked on together, she looks at me. "I think this would sound better coming from you," she says, giving me the cue to start talking.

Rome, Leo, and Henley give me their full attention, waiting for me to continue. I swallow down the emotion swelling inside me for my amazing, sweet, beautiful friends before I look back to the screen. Everything I planned to say sits brimming, ready.

Opening my mouth, and confidently recite the whole thing; I nod to Kendall, who clicks the tab on the next slide where I talk about the market and the different lines. I keep going until I finish the presentation, only to find the guys completely engrossed, hanging off my every word. I flick my gaze to Kendall, who nods and gives me a thumbs-up. I guess it went well. Rolling my shoulders, I sit a little higher in my seat.

"I'm in," Sof says.

"You mean we're in." Leo wiggles his finger between them, correcting her.

"Yeah, that." She waves him off.

Rome nods. "So are we."

I stare between Rome and Leo, not really sure what they are talking about.

Henley leans forward and hands me a piece of folded up paper. "Lottie wanted me to give you this. She is really excited to be a part of something 'more girly,'" he air quotes.

Gooseflesh speckle my arms, sending a shiver down my spine.

Is this really happening?

I grab the piece of paper and open it to find a business name registry. Livvy Blake Cosmetics, co-founded by the Crofts, Venuccios, Faluccinos, Blakes, and Fordham families.

"What about Anders?" I ask, causing the whole room to burst out in laughter. "What?" I ask, clearly missing the joke.

"Anders is a part of the Blake share. He is putting in a large donation to make sure you and Devin have controlling share." Leo is the first person to stop laughing and answer my question.

My mouth forms an '*O*'.

"See?" Devin kisses my cheek. "We don't need Glam Co. You've got us, and we believe in you."

"We know how much Glam Co means to you and that you designed this line with your family legacy in mind," Leo adds.

"But we just want you to know that we believe in you and these products, and you have another option in the future if you ever want to take it." Rome grabs another under-eye patch and lays it on his face, while Henley pumps more moisturizer onto his hand before rubbing it into his neck.

I nod at my sister and eye every single person at the table. Maybe my world hasn't imploded as much as I'd first thought. I still have to present to the board, but at least now I have a seriously solid plan for the future that I'm excited about.

So why does it feel like something, or should I say someone is missing?

CHAPTER FORTY-ONE

Ryder

Four fucking days. Four fucking days without seeing her smile, hearing her laugh, or watching the way her brow furrows when someone says something she doesn't agree with. Four fucking days and I'm done. I can't take another day without her. I didn't think my life was empty before Livvy stormed her way in. But if these last four days have been anything to go by, I definitely can't spend another single day without her in it. I need to get her back, but not until I fix this mess and get to the bottom of just who created that fucking video.

I've had Ares and Anders Davenport working whatever magic they can to try to contain the bloodbath that is happening on Make Me. So far, they have deleted two accounts that have anonymously posted the video and any possible traces of the video have been scrubbed from the internet, which Ares assures me is a much bigger task than I realize.

I don't care. I just never want to see the crushed look on

her face again, and that video is way on the top of my shit list.

Right below her fucking father.

What kind of a fucker says the shit he does? Whether or not he knew he was being recorded isn't an excuse. It's a slimy, pencil-dick weasel-excuse-for-a-father thing to say that shit about a woman becoming a CEO, but to say those things about your daughter? Simon Blake and I are long overdue for a little chat, and something tells me he isn't going to like a single thing I have to say.

My phone pings. Lifting it up, I find a message from Ares. I've been waiting on update for the past hour.

ARES
Check now.

My email dings with an incoming message. I click the link from Ares and watch the video before picking up my phone and replying.

ME
done.

ARES
BTW there was a lot I had to cut. I will be scarred for life.

I send him a couple of emojis, flipping him off, annoyed that he got to see private footage of Livvy and I, but knowing I need his help, so I have to keep my temper in check. Now that's taken care of, I can't wait for Livvy to see it.

"The paperwork has just come through." Zander walks into

my office at Glam Co.

"Perfect." I smile at him before taking the piece of paper from his outstretched hand. I don't even bother to read it; I just sign my name on the bottom and hand it back to him.

"Are you sure about this?" he asks, looking between my signature and me.

"More than anything," I reply, standing up and grabbing my suit jacket from the back of my chair.

The office has been chillingly empty without her here. Even the lilac smell of her Chanel perfume has faded. I didn't realize how much of an important part of my day Livvy was until she wasn't in it anymore. Her bright smile lit up the whole building. The way she would stop and talk to employees and ask them about their days is testament to the caring person she is. She isn't just the boss's daughter. She's Livvy Blake, the woman who invests time and effort into making this place a success.

And our little pranks. Fuck, I miss them.

God, I would take a laxative in my coffee any day if it meant she would stand in the toilet cubicle laughing with me.

I check my watch and frown at the time. Livvy still isn't here yet.

She is presenting her teen line to the board in ten minutes, and it's so unlike her to be late to even a regular meeting let alone one as important as this one.

I hope she didn't decide to back out. No. That's not Livvy.

Someone clears their throat behind me. I turn to find Cecelia with a coffee in her hands.

"Your order from Beanz Please has arrived." She hands me

the takeaway cup, leaving the second one still in the holder.

My stomach gives a quiver, and I question whether or not this coffee is laced with a Livvy special.

I glance at my coffee then to Cecelia. "What? I didn't order —"

Livvy runs past us, grabbing the other cup from Cecelia's hand. "Oh, perfect, my order has arrived."

The imaginary dots connect themselves. I just hope she didn't decide to double her dosage from last time. A small smirk twitches my lips, Livvy is back.

"Enjoy your coffee," Livvy says.

I hang onto those three words like they are my life preserver in a torrid drift. Hearing Livvy's voice, I finally feel like I can take my first full breath of air in four days.

"I don't know I might need to check it for laxatives," I joke.

"There's nothing in that one Ryder." She stares at me with such devoid attachment, the muscles in my jaw clench. "We don't do that anymore."

You look more beautiful than ever; I want to call out to her.

Space. She said she wanted space.

But she isn't going to get enough to imagine her life without me. I think getting down on my knees and declaring my undying love for her is the literal opposite of that.

In my office, I bin the coffee, grab my binder and notepad, and wait a few minutes until she hurries out of her office before slowly trailing her. Simon is sitting in one of the unused meeting rooms. I do a double take. *What the fuck is he doing here?* Rage boils over me at the sight of his face. Turning toward Simon, I get ready to kick him the fuck out of here. But I stop myself.

I don't want to ruin Livvy's presentation by being late. I will not wreck Livvy's day by putting this meeting off any longer because her pencil-dick of a father is in the building. No, I will deal with Simon Blake later.

Walking into the boardroom, I find the board members already seated and Livvy staring at me in wide-eyed shock.

I return her smile and take my seat next to hers. "I learned a long time ago not to accept coffees from you, Killer."

"Oh, I thought we weren't expecting you today," Luana says, gazing at me with her nose scrunched up.

"And why is that?" I reply.

"Because Livvy sent an email telling us you were experiencing another bad case of" — she clears her throat, her cheeks flooding with heat — "diarrhea."

My eyes bulge out of my head as a few of the other board members snort, trying to contain their laughter. My eyes stay firmly fixed on Livvy, who is biting her lip and attempting to play innocent. If I wasn't deliriously happy to be sitting in the same room as her, I would probably want to wring her neck for telling the board I'm sick with gut issues. But still, this is progress, and I welcome it any way possible.

"Well." I quickly recover. "It seems I've had a miraculous recovery."

"It seems so." Luana nods before grabbing her hand sanitizer and spraying her hands like the mere act of us talking about my phantom sickness could randomly wish it into existence.

I turn to Livvy. "Shall we get this presentation going?"

Livvy just nods and says, "We shall."

Taking my seat next to hers, I make sure to roll the chair

as close to her as possible. Not wanting to leave a lick of space between us, it takes everything in me to stop myself from reaching out to touch her, to lay my palm on her thigh under the table.

As the first slide pops onto the projector screen over our heads, I scribble on my notepad and flick it to Livvy.

I love it when a good girl knows how to play dirty.

Heat creeps up Livvy's neck. She tucks a phantom strand of loose hair behind her ear — the sole tell she's read the note as she continues to deliver the presentation, her voice only stuttering twice.

Livvy produces a cardboard box and cuts through the tamper-evident tape.

A bit over the top if you ask me. Especially because I would never fuck with Livvy's teen line. *Where did she even get tamper evident tape from?*

She hands each member of the board their own set of samples. Everyone is looking at the individual products with interest and pumping out moisturizer on the top of their hands, adding the toner onto a cotton round, or running the serum between their fingers.

That is except for Derick, who is looking at the products in front of him like they took a shit in his breakfast, his face scrunched up in distaste.

The hairs on the back of my neck rise.

Livvy continues the presentation, not paying attention to Derick. But I don't take my eyes off him. The other board members ask questions and scribble down notes based off Livvy's answers.

The same can't be said for Derick. His disinterest for her line is evident and borderline offensive. Derick scans the table, visibly growing more tense when he sees the board reacting so well to her products.

Livvy has put her heart and soul into this, and Derick couldn't seem less interested if he tried. With each new question Livvy answers without missing a bead, Derick becomes more pissed off. His attempt to seem bored and disinterested slowly melts away the longer Livvy talks.

Keep going, baby.

Oblivious to Derick's behavior, Livvy continues with her presentation. As the last slide pops up, she looks around at the impressed faces of the board members — except for one. Livvy's eyes catch Derick's, a shadow passes across her face. Her brows crinkle in confusion as anger flares in her eyes, but it is gone just as quickly when her eyes meet mine.

"You did it, baby," I mouth to her.

Her face relaxes.

"This line sounds amazing, and I agree it would be an asset to Glam Co," Luana says excitedly, and the other board members nod their heads in agreement.

Derick clears his throat. "Is this all you plan to bring to Glam Co?" he asks.

Livvy lifts her chin as she meets Derick's stare with fire burning in her eyes. "Not at all, but this is something I feel would be wonderful for Glam Co," she replies.

"Glam Co doesn't really need a teen line now, does it? I mean, if you look at the figures Ryder has provided" — Derick nods at me — "Glam Co is sitting pretty with a nice profit.

So why would we invest such a hefty sum into creating a line which hasn't even got a buyer for it?"

My knuckles tighten under the table at the sight of his smug-as-shit grin. Lucky for me, he has just given me the opportunity to wipe it right the fuck off. But before I get a chance, Livvy's eyes narrow.

As she transforms before my fucking eyes.

"No one is disputing Glam Co's profits are stable and we maintain a strong hold in the current market, *Derick.*" She spits out his name like it's sour on her tongue and leans forward in her chair, staring the piece of shit down. "But my idea of a successful future for Glam Co is to expand our *market* and actually see growth in the company, not just maintain what we have." She leans back in her seat, turning her body away from him and dismissing him like he did her. "And considering the products that generated the most sales and profit this year were all my campaigns, I think it might be a fair assumption I know a little more than you . . . in this area, of course." She says the last part like she is pacifying a toddler, and I have to smother my laugh behind my hand.

From the way Luana's mouth is twitching, it looks like she might be in the same position.

Livvy stares down Derick, goading him to answer her back. But he stays silent.

"There is already a contract for the teen line," I interrupt, biting back my own smirk as his grin slowly slip. "Kosmedika is committed to taking the line." I turn my attention to Livvy.

"Well, the hope is a department store like Kosmedika will be interested in the teen line and will want to take it on," Livvy tries to explain my vague point but misses the mark completely.

"There is no need to worry about interest, Killer. As of this morning, FF Group acquired Kosmedika. We have been watching it turn a nice profit for the last two years and we decided to add it to our portfolio."

I happen to have it on good authority that they are more than interested in Glam Co's new teen line.

"And the first thing they will be doing is adding your teen line to all stores as either Glam Co or Livvy Blake Cosmetics. Your choice, Killer."

CHAPTER FORTY-TWO

Livvy

All the bravado and anger that was burning through my veins moments ago when I faced down Derick-the-douchebag has evaporated, and in its place is pride. I can hear my nanna cheering me on. Tears sting my eyes. "Why?" I ask, feeling like I should probably be embarrassed we are having this conversation in front of the board of Glam Co. If he doesn't start talking, my mind will fill in the blanks and it won't be pretty.

Ryder holds my stare. "Because I want you to choose how you deliver your teen line," he replies, and my legs turn to jelly.

I grip the edge of the table so hard my knuckles turn white.

"You bought Kosmedika so the Glam Co teen line would have a contract?" Luana sounds as shocked as I am.

"No," Ryder corrects her. "FF Group brought Kosmedika because it is a great investment we have been watching for a while. Part of the stipulation of the FF Group takeover is that Livvy's teen line will have a contract." Then he turns to look at the board. "Whether she uses Glam Co for her line or branches out is her business. The contract at Kosmedika will stand either way."

My heart thuds at the base of my throat.

"Livvy, you have presented your teen line really well and we really love this concept and the formulations you have devised. You've given us a lot to consider. We will see you next week for the vote." Luana looks at the other board members, who follow her lead and exit after her.

Derick isn't far behind, reluctantly trailing his colleagues. His face is pinched in annoyance as he leaves Ryder and I alone.

"Did you really buy a chain of beauty stores?" I ask, sounding out of breath. I need to know he wasn't saying that in front of the board to sway their opinion.

He nods. "Babe, I would do just about anything for you."

It's the words I've been waiting days to hear. Suddenly, the floodgates burst open. "I need to go," I reply, abruptly standing and walking to the door with Ryder hot on my heels.

Even though I told Ryder I needed to consider a life without him, thoughts of him have consumed me every single second of the last few days. There is no way I ever could. He's become the most important person in my world, behind MoMo.

"Liv, wait. I have to show you something," he says just as we round the corner.

I halt. My dad is sitting in the unused room with Derick. *What the heck is Dad doing here?*

Ryder smacks into me — his hands quickly resting on my hips and keeping me in place — instinctively going silent when he recognizes what brought me to stop dead in my tracks.

Ryder's warmth at my back grounds me, helping settle my racing heart as we both listen silently to the conversation between my father and Derick.

"He bought Kosmedika's. So no matter what, that teen line will see the light of day," Derick says.

My dad picks up the moisturizer sample I gave to Derick a few moments ago, inspecting it thoroughly.

If I wasn't mistaken, he almost looks . . . interested? No, it couldn't be.

He pumps the moisturizer out, testing it on his wrist.

"The rest of the board were eating this thing up — can you believe it?" Derick continues, shaking his head and pointing to my samples.

"It's not bad. I can see why," Dad replies and shrugs. "If the board sign off on it then there isn't really much we can do. It will, at the end of the day, benefit Glam Co."

"Are you joking?!" Derick yells. "She will never sit as the CEO of Glam Co. I made sure of it."

My body freezes. The blood pumping through my body pools in my veins as a buzzing sensation burns through my skull.

Derick made sure of it?

That would mean he made the video — not Ryder.

Ryder places a kiss against my head and like an antidote to the poison spreading through me, my body calms.

Ryder didn't do it. Ryder didn't do it.

Those four words keep repeating in my head what my heart knew this whole time.

He keeps me plastered against his chest; my body melts

into him.

Ryder didn't do it.

Deep down, I knew Ryder didn't do it. But my head had covered up the truth by convincing me that if he could lie on Make Me as Rachel, then I couldn't trust him with this.

But the video — I just couldn't let my guard down and risk getting hurt again.

"What do you mean?" Dad asks.

A sinister grin passes across Derick's face. The hairs on the back of my neck raise in retaliation.

"Who do you think made that video?"

I suck in a sharp breath just as Ryder growls behind me; Derick just confirmed it.

"It was you?" My dad blows out a harsh breath, and if I'm not mistaken, there is hurt in his voice.

Derick snorts. "Please, like you didn't know. The way she broke up with Kyle, humiliated him. I couldn't let it stand. I overhead Livvy telling Fallington about the USB stick in her drawer. Then hearing you say those things about Livvy during our golf day was the icing I needed on that particular cake."

"It was you?" Dad says again, standing and putting himself face to face with Derick. "You took something I said because I was pissed off and made it into something else. I'm angry she is fucking Fallington and not focused on her work, especially after the dry shampoo issue. You told me that she wasn't doing her job, that she wasn't spending time in the lab creating new products." He picks up my samples. "But clearly, she is more than capable if she can produce products like this. Fallington isn't stopping her from creating. As for your nephew there,

Devin explained how he was screwing her while belittling Olivia. If you think that's who I want my daughter to be with, you are sadly mistaken."

I blink. *Devin told dad. She stood up for me.*

"Jesus, Derick," dad continues. "What more could you possibly have against Olivia that would warrant this? Why are you so determined to keep her from Glam Co's top chair? Is it just because she's a woman? Or she's a woman who has standards?"

Dad waits to hear Derick's reply, but his silence speaks volumes.

"Really? You're threatened by a woman being top dog, so you made a video about her being incapable pioneering Glam Co."

Derick smiles. "Just like you always told me, Simon. It's just business."

Dad punches Derick, sending him crashing into the chairs lining the table. It's almost unbelievable. "I've lost my daughters because of what you did, Derick! Do you understand that?"

"Dad," I gasp as Derick sits in a heap on the floor, holding his face.

My dad turns to look at us, frozen in the doorway, just as I step out of Ryder's grasp and our hiding spot.

"Olivia," he whispers. He hangs his head between his shoulders and says, "I'm sorry. I doubted you, and I doubted your vison for this line." He shakes his head, slumping against the table. "I'm so proud of you. But most of all, I'm sorry I stood in the way of you being you. Even if it includes Fallington."

Slowly, I take in his broken, grief-stricken face. The gravity of what he set in motion is finally weighing on him.

"Thank you." I stand firmly against Ryder. I didn't realize how much I needed to hear those words until I did. "I appreciate the apology. But I don't think I can move past this so easily. You doubted me, Dad. You made all the hard work I've spent my life putting into Glam Co meaningless. You've made Devin think she is worth nothing more than her last name, and you've made it clear your love and attention is conditional. You almost lost us our legacy, all because you believed someone else's lies. But most of all, you broke our trust."

"Security, please escort this man off the premise," Ryder calls behind me.

I turn as the two security guards lift the semi-conscious Derick. His head lolls forward, blood dripping out of his nose that my dad has certainly broken.

"I think it's safe to say, once the other members find out about this, your seat will be vacant, Derick," my dad says as they drag him out.

After Derick is escorted away by security, I turn to my dad.

"I don't expect you to forgive me for how I've behaved these last few months," he starts to say, "but I want you to know I'm really proud of you, Starfish."

"Thanks." I smile at him. I don't quite forgive him for how he's behaved, but the apology is a start. "Well, I need to get back to work." Turning I find Ryder casually leaning against the wall, I give him a tight smile and push past him. My mind is completely overloading with everything that's just happened.

He follows me down the hall and into my office before closing the door behind him.

"Is there something else I can help you with, Mr. Fallington?" I ask, taking a seat behind my desk.

"May I?" He motions to my computer.

"What are you going to do?"

"I have one more thing I want to show you." Ryder leans over and lifts me out of the chair before taking my spot and depositing me on his lap so fast it makes me squeak. "There," he sighs. "Much better."

A smile tugs at my lips, but I try to hide it.

Ryder still isn't one hundred percent forgiven . . . yet.

My eyes drop to his arm resting on my waist. I wiggle my butt, glancing at Ryder. "How do I know this wasn't just an excuse to get me to sit on your lap?"

"Trust me, Killer." Ryder winks. "It isn't." He reaches over me, his other arm brushing along mine and sending shivers down my spine.

My senses are immediately flooded with his signature Amalfi-coast scent. Something about being back in his arms is extremely comforting.

Ryder types a few buttons on my keyboard before my Make Me page fills the screen.

"Oh god," I groan. I have purposely steered away from this. Devin gave me a SparkNotes version of the comments, and from what's popping up on my home page, I think I made the right choice.

My chest constricts. All the hard work I've put into this account has just been significantly impacted by a single, stupid video.

Ryder hovers the mouse over a video posted this morning. I

try to pull out of his lap, but his arm holds me in place. "What? I didn't post that." I don't think I can handle watching another botched video of me.

Ryder looks at me and says, "I know — I did," and clicks play on the video of us in my bathroom talking. Ryder is asking me why I would bother posting about small businesses and not focus on just Make Me. The screen zooms in on my face. My eyes soften as I tell him the truth about how I created my Make Me channel to celebrate brands and bring awareness and try makeup and skin care. I didn't start being Olivia Grace on Make Me to make Glam Co even bigger.

'I created Olivia Grace to be closer to my nanna — sharing some of her tricks for applying makeup. I spent a lot of my childhood being the awkward little girl whose lips were too big and hair too frizzy, but Nanna helped me to see past that. She made me see beauty and embrace my own. '

My jaw falls open when it shows me in the lab laughing with Brynn. *How did he get that footage?* It's the complete opposite of the hack job that was done on me earlier. *'Livvy Blake lives and breathes makeup and skin care; she spends hours tirelessly looking for innovative new brands to show you. Not because she gets anything out of it, but to bring awareness to young girls and boys who don't have anyone else to teach them about skin care and makeup application. If you think Livvy is here for anything more than to create videos for love then maybe you should go back and watch them again. Her whole channel is dedicated to her grandmother, Grace.'* Ryder's voice-over continues, *'And most importantly, she has the most beautiful soul.'*

The video then cuts to Brynn and a few other members

of our lab staff, and finally there's an interview with Kendall, Devin, and Sof.

I gasp as the video ends with Ryder and me in my bathroom with mud masks on our faces. *'And I am so utterly in love with her — I couldn't imagine life without her,'* he says on the voice-over just as the video finishes.

My gaze meets his. I'm blinking to stop the sting of tears threatening to escape. "I'm sorry I doubted you," I whisper.

I click play on the video again. I don't think I will ever get tired of watching this.

Ryder cups my cheek, resting his forehead against mine. "I'm sorry I made you think Glam Co is more important to me than you are."

"Deep down, I knew it wasn't. But seeing that video, all I could think was that you were the only one who knew."

"It's okay, babe." Ryder dots a kiss on my lips. "You once told me your love language is acts of service. I hope I can finally show you love through me."

I pull Ryder's head to mine and fuse out lips together.

He is right. My love language *is* acts of service.

"I think it might be my turn to show you just how grateful I am," I breathe, my pulse thumping at the base of my throat.

Ryder runs his thumb along the pulse at the base of my neck.

Quirking his head to the side, the sparkle I missed so much is finally back in his eyes. "Oh," he whispers. "And how do you plan on doing that?"

"Like this," I reply, slinking down his body and kneeling on the carpet. I unzip his pants, his already hard dick springing free from the confines of his pants.

"Livvy," Ryder releases a pained groan as I grip this base of him and start licking the head like it's my favorite flavor lollypop. "You don't have to do this. What if someone walks in?"

I release him with a satisfied smirk. "They can either stay and watch or turn and leave," I reply before taking him all the way to the base of my throat.

"I think Livvy Blake has officially entered her villain era," he moans, threading his fingers through my hair and keeping pressure on the back of my head.

My panties flood, loving that he's enjoying this as much as I am.

"I entered my villain era a few months ago — I'm just leveling up." I continue to work his dick, alternating between sucking, licking, and stroking — torturing him until he loses his grip on control and coats my tongue with his release.

Ryder wipes the side of my mouth with his thumb, and I quickly grab it with my lips, using the tip of my tongue to make sure its thoroughly cleaned, not wanting to lose a single drop.

Ryder's eyes flash with heat as his dick starts to rise again, a low grumble sounding in his chest. "Fuck, Liv, what do you do to me?"

Letting his thumb go with a pop, I crawl up Ryder's body and place my knees on either side of his thick thighs. If I wasn't wearing panties, I would sink down, taking him inside me. A rush of heat to my core tells me just how much I adore that idea. "My villain era wouldn't be complete without you," I say, grinding myself on his already hard dick.

Ryder hooks his finger in the center of my lace panties and shifts them to the side before placing his finger inside my aching core. He smirks at me, finding me soaking wet. He removes his finger, and I whine, missing the contact.

"I'm glad you think so, Killer." He punctuates the words by thrusting into me, making me moan and tighten my arms around his shoulders.

Having Ryder inside me feels like home.

"So good," he replies, nipping my chin then taking my lips in a punishing kiss — slamming into me with a punishing pace that shows he is as desperate as I am.

I scream out; Ryder's hand covers my mouth as the other goes to the back of my neck, anchoring me to him as he uses his grip to force me down harder onto his dick.

"Who do I belong to?"

"Me," I pant.

"And don't you ever forget that Killer."

My world blows apart in the most explosive orgasm I've ever had.

CHAPTER FORTY-THREE

Ryder

"Explain to me why we are playing poker at my place again?" I ask the guys sitting around the table. After surreptitiously leaving the other chat group, I woke up to my phone going off with messages. It appears Leo kindly re-added me back in.

"Because you pussied out of the group chat. Ergo, you now host poker," Rome announces, chucking his cards down. They must be a really bad hand for Rome to be folding.

"Do three aces beat a straight?" Livvy asks, curling her hand in the stands of hair at the base of my neck.

"Oh shit, no," Henley grumbles, throwing his cards in the middle, followed by Leo.

Sof is squinting at her cards, the tip of her tongue poking out the corner of her mouth. She isn't folding; that's either smart or stupid.

Leo leans over and whispers louder than he should, "Just fold, Sof."

Clearly, Leo has fallen for it.

"Hey, you can't tell me what to do," she yells when he takes the cards out of her hand and throws them in the middle of the table.

And clearly, Sof is smarter than I gave her credit for.

"Was it something I said?" Livvy looks at me with her adorable eyes wide as saucers. I tighten my hand around her waist in warning. She knows exactly what she is doing — that innocent act isn't going to fool me.

"Livvy, you just gave the whole hand away." Becks rolls his eyes.

I mentally *tsk*. Poor guy, he has no idea what he's up against. Livvy's got him hook, line, and sinker.

Tilting her head to the side, she looks at Becks and asks, "How?"

"Because we now know what you have," he deadpans, throwing his own cards in.

I bite my lip to stop the grin as I show the guys, I don't have three aces or even a straight — I don't even have two cards with the same suit. Livvy was trying to psych them out and the only person she didn't fool is the strawberry redhead sitting beside us.

"Did you just hustle us?" Kendall gasps.

Livvy giggles. "Who me?" She points to herself. "Hustle, no." She shakes her head. "Getting inside your head, now that is a different story."

My Killer is vicious. I place a kiss in the corner of her mouth, the guys all groan.

"Can you stop fucking for five minutes?" Zander grunts.

Turning at the waist, I find him busy trying to beat Duke at some racing game playing on the TV. How did he even see that?

"Eyes in the back of my head, bro," he replies with a smart-ass remark.

"More like he can see your reflection in the glass," Duke replies, pulling a move that has Zander jumping up and yelling.

"Cheater!"

Devin snorts and slaps Zander. "Dude, way to tell everyone your body count is lower than your racing score."

"What the fuck is that supposed to mean?" Zander pauses his game, causing an outcry from Duke as he glares at Devin sitting in between them.

"It means you must not know what fucking looks like," Rome's younger brother Luca pipes up. "That's PG at best."

"G, if you were dating a Venuccio," Dante, Rome's youngest brother, replies.

"I gave more action to my second-grade teacher," Rome agrees, his face set in a grim line as he takes the cards and starts shuffling them.

"Are you talking about Mrs. Finotto?" Luca asks, clearly reminiscing.

"See, I'm not the only one who had a thing for teachers," Leo inputs.

Stroking Livvy's rib, I go over the conversation in my head to see just where it all went wrong — the guys are now swapping teacher stories.

Sof hits his bicep. "That was different. You were trying to date the principal when you were sixteen. Smart-ass."

"Least he didn't get kicked out," Becks muses. That story hits a little too close to home for him.

I roll my eyes, focusing on Livvy in my lap. Why did I agree to this again?

"Don't worry," Livvy whispers in my ear. "I won't tell them how much you love it when I play your dutiful student in my basic chemistry class."

My pants suddenly become way too tight; discretely, I shift Livvy on my lap, trying to give my growing cock a bit of room before it gets strangled. "You are being very naughty, Miss Blake," I whisper in her ear before biting her earlobe and making Livvy melt into me. I don't think I will ever get tired of watching the way her body reacts to my touch.

"Guys," Anders interrupts. "Please tell me you ordered from Panuccio's again?"

"Nah." Sof shakes her head. "Can't do the same thing twice."

"Besides," Livvy pipes up. "We gotta keep Ryder on his toes."

Watching Livvy try to work my coffee machine would almost be cute if she wasn't seconds away from smacking the thing and possibly breaking it. Crossing my foot over my ankle, I lean against the wall, taking in her long, toned legs peeking out from under my T-shirt I just know I'm not going to get back. It looks way better on her anyway.

"I want a double shot of expresso," Livvy talks to the machine like it's a new-age version of Alexa.

"It usually helps when you press the double-shot button," I tell her, pushing off from the wall and rubbing the sleep from my eyes. Running my hand through my hair, I try to shake the morning fog from my brain.

"Ryder." Livvy glares at me. "I've clicked the button enough times to have twelve shots of espresso sitting in my hands by now."

Resting my hand on her hips, I pepper her neck with kisses as I grab the cup and place it under the machine. I click on the interactive screen before moving it to the double shot setting. "Sometimes you just need the magic touch," I whisper as the beans start grinding, running my nose along her neck and inhaling her scent deep into my lungs.

"If you keep that up, we aren't going to make it to work on time and today is an important day in Glam Co history." Livvy punctuates each word with a wiggle of her ass directly over my thickening cock.

I bite my lip to stop the groan from escaping. "Oh, we're definitely going to be late now," I tell, her my hand cupping her bare pussy and teasing her clit with slow, deliberate circles.

Her thighs begin to shake as I continue to stroke her core before sliding my fingers inside. "No panties. Someone has been naughty."

"We can't be late." Livvy grabs hold of my wrist, thrusting my finger even deeper. "So, you're going to have to be quick."

I don't waste a second in lifting her on the bench, loving the way her legs immediately rest around my hips. After pulling the front of my grey sweatpants down just enough to free my aching cock, I line it up with her and slide it straight into her already primed pussy.

"Yesss," Livvy groans, while I continue to pound into her aching pussy, loving the way it grips my cock.

I lift her top up. Livvy takes the hint and pulls it off her shoulders.

My gaze locks on her beautiful tits, watching them bounce in time with each thrust. *Perfection.* Leaning down, I take one of her pebbled nipples into my mouth. Livvy's pussy tightens around my cock and her fingers thread through my hair, holding me in place.

I move my attention from one perfect breast to the other, using my fingers to tweak and pluck the nipple not in my mouth. Her nails dig into my biceps — no doubt leaving little indents behind — and Livvy throws her head back as she rocks her body in time with my thrusts. I feel her tighten around me, and after a few more thrusts she explodes, and I quickly follow her.

I have Livvy a second time before we finally manage to leave my place, more than twenty minutes late for work. Not that either of us really care.

The rumble of the engine cuts out. I turn to Livvy and ask, "You ready?" The loaded question sits in the car.

Unclipping her seat belt, she turns in her seat. "Ready to find out who the board have voted in? No. But I don't think I ever will be. Ready to beat your ass? Hell, yeah. I'm a Blake, after all."

After taking her hand from her lap, I drop a kiss on her knuckles. "There is a reason why Fallingtons have been wrapped around Blakes' fingers for over a hundred years."

Livvy huffs and flicks her curled hair over her shoulder. "It's our wit and charm, isn't it?"

Something like that. I chuckle to myself. "No matter what happens in there today, you and I are a team. Just Livvy and Ryder — not Blake and Fallington. This won't change us."

Livvy smiles at me, and says, "Agreed."

We walk into the Glam Co offices, our fingers threaded together. I only release Livvy's hand when she goes to grab her notebook from her desk and then I intertwine our hands once more.

"Ready?" I ask again when we reach the boardroom, my palm sweating against the wooden door.

Five generations of Fallingtons have led up to this moment. Six months of hard work. And one woman who is the unequivocal centerpiece of the puzzle that I didn't know was missing.

Livvy nods, the complete picture of cool, calm, and collected.

I push open the door to find the board members already seated, ready and waiting. *Here goes nothing.*

One chair is noticeably absent.

Livvy and I take our seats and wait for Luana to start talking. As chairperson of the board, she is the one who will deliver the ultimate decision.

"In light of recent events, the board has voted to remove Derick from his position. There will be a new appointment in the coming months, but for now we are here to discuss the election of CEO of Glam Co."

I give Livvy's hand a squeeze under the table.

Luana continues, "Livvy, the board has unanimously decided that we want to proceed with the teen line you presented. We all feel it will be an amazing edition to Glam Co — with you as the CEO."

Livvy stills.

I wait for the anger, for the disappointment, for the pain. But it doesn't come. All I feel is immense pride.

"Me?" Livvy sputters. "Are you sure?"

"Yes, Killer." I nod, squeezing her hand again and smiling from ear to ear. "You."

CHAPTER FORTY-FOUR

Livvy

"Thank you so much." I'm struggling to allow the news to sink in. They voted for me. I'm the new CEO of Glam Co. I keep repeating Luana's voice in my head. *They voted for me*. I heard her correctly. I'm going to usher in the new legacy of Glam Co. I reach for my nanna's book in my bag. I need to hold it.

"Why?" The question slips through my numb lips — I'm hoping she doesn't say that it's because of my Olivia Grace platform.

"Why not?" Luana asks, pulling me out of the celebration currently happening in my head. "You've proven that you share the passion and enthusiasm that is needed for Glam Co to continue to succeed. You understand the market and product development."

A sticky dread passes through me at Luana's words — a couple of months ago, Glam Co was all I could see. But after my friends pitched their idea, I don't think Glam Co is the only thing that should take my focus. Nanna would say 'Be brave, Livvy-bean. Anything you do is truly amazing because you are using something that no one else has — your Livvy magic.'

"My teen line won't be produced through Glam Co," I blurt. "If my being appointed CEO is contingent on my teen line" — I straighten my shoulders and stare into the eyes of each board member — "I will have to respectfully decline the position."

I never really thought about starting my own line, but having the backing of my friends, I realize how much I want it. I have spent over a year dedicated to this teen line. Glam Co is the Fallington–Blake legacy, but this teen line is mine.

"Livvy Blake Cosmetics will be launching my teen line," I announce. As soon as I've said the words out loud, a feeling of rightness comes over me.

Ryder moves his chair closer to me.

"This isn't a decision I make lightly; I wish to continue with my position at Glam Co. But I also want to have my own legacy." I look at Ryder — the smile from when Luana announced me as CEO is still firmly fixed in place, pride welling in his eyes.

"Our appointment of you is based on your merit, regardless of whether you would like to produce your own line. We are enthusiastic about a Glam Co teen line — whether it's the one you have created or a new one. But either way, Glam Co want you, Olivia Blake. And we would like you to consider joining the board, Ryder. You would be an asset to the company."

"I appreciate the offer. Livvy and I will discuss it," Ryder replies.

The board members nod and stand.

"We look forward to hearing your updates in the coming weeks," Luana announces and waits for the others to leave. "I'm incredibly proud of everything you've done, and I know you are going to take Glam Co into a bright new future." She pats my hand and follows after them.

Ryder meets my gaze, a smile splitting his lips. "Look at you go — you already have a fan on the board."

Ryder discretely types something on his phone.

"Apparently, I do."

Announcing my decision to the board of Glam Co and Ryder just seems so right. So real.

"Congratulations Ms. She-e-o." Ryder pulls me out of my daydream. He tugs my wrist, and I go willingly into his lap and drape my arm around his shoulder.

"Are you mad?" I ask him, needing his reassurance.

"Babe." Ryder puts his hand under my jaw and turns me to face him. "The board chose you fair and fucking square. You deserve this. How on earth could I be mad?"

"But what about your dad?" My mouth turns down.

"My dad said, and I quote: love is more important. Plus, now that FF Group owns Kosmedika, we've expanded our portfolio. So I don't think he can be all that sad."

A knock interrupts us. "Come in," Ryder calls.

Devin pokes her head through the open door, surveying the area.

"Do they have clothes on?" comes Zanders muffled voice, making Ryder and I both laugh.

"Yep," my sister replies, pushing the door open wider.

As my friends all pile into the boardroom. Kendall walks in last, holding a giant bunch of flowers.

"Oh, Kenny." My eyes go wide.

Kendall smiles and shakes her head. "These aren't from me. I'm just the glorified delivery driver."

Ryder takes the bunch of flowers from her and hands them to me. "What would Blair Waldorf do if she didn't receive her peonies on her special day?"

A gasp leaves me, my hands coming up to cover my mouth. "You remembered?" I lift the peonies to my nose, inhaling their sweet scent.

"Of course, I did." He places another kiss on my cheek.

Everyone is staring at me expectantly. My heart explodes from the amount of love pouring from my friends. "How did you all get here so quick?" I ask.

"Ryder pre-planned for us to all be here. He wanted us to congratulate you after the announcement," Kendall replies.

"And what if I didn't get the position?"

Leo pulls a bottle of tequila from behind his back. "We were going to do shots to numb the pain. Although, your man, here, was pretty confident you were going to get appointed."

As I stare up at Ryder, butterflies take off in my stomach.

"Never had a doubt," he mouths.

"Well," Sof asks, "are you going to leave us hanging?"

I blink, letting the silence sit in the room and enjoying the buildup. "The board appointed me CEO of Glam Co."

Everyone gives a cheer.

"But the next few months are going to be really, really busy for me — you know, with me becoming CEO of Glam Co. I just hope you guys are ready, because Livvy Blake Cosmetics is going to be launching this awesome teen line soon. I have it on good authority it's going to be amazing," I announce, and Sof and Devin scream before hugging each other and jumping up and down.

When they first brought up the idea of Livvy Blake Cosmetics, I was shit-scared. Through my Make Me channel, I've done a lot of collaborations, but I've never felt the confidence to build my own line. I just thought I would naturally progress into Glam Co. But the lightness in my chest at the thought of having my own line — it just feels right.

"Does that mean you've decided?" Kendall asks, her eyes widening.

"I have. That is, if you are all still interested?"

Leo pulls me into a hug. "You bet we are."

"I just specifically asked to be included in product testing because those eye patches are the shit! My skin is so soft and shiny from the moisturizer stuff," Rome inputs, grabbing Henley's hand.

"Dude, why me?" Henley stresses through clenched teeth.

"Shiny?" Kendall asks.

Becks snorts.

"Livvy, I'd really like a good hand cream. My hands get really dry and sore working on the cars," Duke says in that serious, quiet voice of his.

Devin's face takes on a look of concern and she comes over to him to look at his hands.

"Sure, driving is what is causing his hands to chafe," Henley coughs.

Duke sends him a glare, causing the room to burst into laughter.

Devin flicks her puppy dog eyes to meet mine. "This is a serious problem — look at the skin near his nails. Can you help me make a hand cream, Livvy?"

Rome's arm comes around my shoulders, squishing me into his chest. "Our girl can definitely help you, brother. Can't you, Livvy?" The look of complete confidence on his face warms my heart.

Ryder's chest rumbles. "My girl, Rome."

Rome just sends Ryder a shit-eating grin and whispers really loudly, "He's never been good at sharing . . . but pushing his buttons is really fun." He lightly kisses my cheek. "Congratulations, Bella. We're all proud of you."

"I vote we have Lottie as the face." Zander throws his hand up.

"Your vote is vetoed." Devin's lips flatten, and Zander flips her off.

Looking around the room, I can't believe this is now my life.

Six months ago, I thought I'd lost my legacy, my family was a mess, and work was the only thing that mattered. Somehow, the man I thought was ruining my life turned out to be the catalyst that changed everything. We're creating a new legacy together and a new family with our friends.

I cup my hand behind Ryder's neck and pull him down to me before resting my forehead against his. "Thank you for being my person, Ryder Fallington. For giving me my wings."

Ryder's eyes heat and soften. "You already had your wings,

baby. I just watched you fly." He whispers so only I can hear, "I hope you realize I'll never let you go."

Something about that statement makes me calmer than I have ever been, with the man who I was supposed to hate but couldn't stop loving right by my side.

EPILOGUE

Ryder

I hand my brother a beer as he swims up on a stupid, fucking, hot-pink inflatable flamingo.

"Thanks, big bro." Zander accepts the drink from me and paddles back into the middle of the pool, closer to where Devin and Livvy are floating.

Livvy blows me a kiss, which I return.

"I feel sick." Zander pretends to gag. Devin rolls her eyes and grabs the head of the flamingo. "Woah, that's a little too close to my dick," Zander says as Devin tips his inflatable over, causing him to end up in the water.

"Trust me," Devin says when Zander comes up for air. "I was nowhere near your pencil dick. And the flamingo isn't an extension of it."

The faint sound of my dad calling has me turning on my heel to find him, leaving my brother and Devin to bicker.

I pull my phone out of my pocket and answer the incoming call.

"Rome, to what do I owe the pleasure?"

We decided to spend the long weekend at our holiday house in Havenville, needing the mini-getaway after the events of the last six months.

"I know we're supposed to be meeting for lunch, but I've just received an email. Our acquisition with Deeter group isn't going as expected."

"Shit," I mumble.

"My sentiments."

"Send me through the details, we need to stop this from getting out of hand." I tell him and hang up the call.

"Dad, hi," I say, when I find him in the kitchen. "Did you just arrive?"

"Yes. Just in time to watch Zander receive an ass whooping, I see," he chuckles, motioning his head toward the giant floor-to-ceiling windows looking out on the pool deck. "I'm glad. It's been a long time coming for that kid."

"Oh yes. Trust me, you haven't even seen how Sof hands it to him. I actually think his ego deflated a little last time."

Dad gets a faraway look in his eyes; it usually happens when he's thinking about Mom.

"Ryder — " Livvy walks into the kitchen wearing a bathing suit cover-up. Her sunglasses sit on top of her head, pulling her hair out of her face.

Her presence pulls my dad from his memory.

"Livvy." He smiles. "I never thought a Blake would be so welcome into this house." He raps his knuckles on the marble counter. "But here you are. I think it's time we have a little chat and iron some things out."

Livvy and I share a worried look. I swallow the lump in my throat, not sure where my dad is taking this.

"You know my grandfather hated the Blakes? Probably more so than the original Michael Fallington after he helped build Glam Co. My grandfather used to tell us to spit in the face of any Blake if you meet one." Dad purses his lips. "A little uncivil if you ask me, but he had his reasons, I guess. He was in love with Stylas Blake's daughter, but Stylas forbade him from ever pursuing her. He believed Fallingtons were unworthy of the Blakes." He gives a sarcastic laugh. "Even though if it weren't for the Fallingtons, Glam Co would have just been the pipe dream of a really clever man."

Livvy clears her throat. "I'm guessing that is why the Blakes hand down the company to the next generation on their twenty-fifth birthdays."

"Yes. In order for Stylas to ensure his daughter didn't pursue a Fallington, he told her when she turned twenty-five, she would run Glam Co."

Livvy tucks her arms around herself.

Needing to comfort her, I reach out to her and pull her close to me.

She gives a shiver the moment her cold body touches mine. We wait for Dad to continue.

"From then on, it became about Glam Co. If the Blakes thought we were unworthy, we would take what was most precious to them. It became an obsession, a way to prove to the Blakes that the Fallingtons weren't just worthy — they were better."

Dad grabs his walking stick; with shaky legs, he stands and

shuffles the few steps to us. "Livvy, I want you to know, this feud ends here. Today. You two have shown five generations of Fallingtons and Blakes this company is complete with us together."

"Thank you," Livvy whispers.

"I've never seen my son happier. For that, I can't thank you enough. Just please, whatever you do, never bring me my coffee."

Livvy's eyes grow so comically large as she stares at me. "You told him."

I burst out laughing. "Babe, ruining coffee is sacrilege to my dad."

"Welcome to the family, sweet girl." Dad kisses her on the cheek then kisses me too and slowly shuffles out of the kitchen.

"I think this means our feud is officially over," Livvy whispers.

"I think so, and it was just getting fun." I pull her bottom lip between my teeth.

"Devin, why the fuck did you pull my pants down?" Zander bellows, jolting us apart.

Flicking my eyes up, I find my brother stark fucking naked out the window.

"Ahhhh, I see a dick," Livvy cries.

"Fuck, Fallington, you must be really fucking cold." Sof laughs as she and Leo appear on the pool deck.

"Or maybe he is just a grower," Leo replies.

"Devin, you're so dead," Zander yells, pulling his swim shorts back up and running after Devin's retreating form.

"Have I told you today how much I love you?" I dot Liv's

nose with the tip of my finger.

She thinks it over for a moment. "About six times, but it wouldn't hurt to say it again."

A smile splits my lips. "I love you, Olivia Blake. You complete my soul."

Livvy kisses me with fervor.

Five generations of Blakes and Fallingtons feuded for this moment.

So my sworn enemy could become my person.

My reason for breathing.

My world.

The End

Acknowledgements

It's tough to put into words just how grateful and thankful I am to every single person for picking this story up. I wouldn't be able to be doing this without you. It truly takes a village to publish a book and I can't thank every single person that has helped bring Make Me to life enough. To my parents, for loving and supporting me on this journey. To my brother who is literally my biggest supporter. To my fur babies, Rupert and Tilly for being the best lap blankies when I'm writing. To Harold – my princess parrot and your filthy mouth. To my younger cousins for reading the endless screenshots I send through at all hours of the night. Half the time I'm convinced if they weren't my own hype team, writers block would've taken me very early on. To my friends for supporting me – you guys stitch me together when I feel like falling apart. I can't thank you enough for all your help and advice you've given me. To Sali- what can I say other than thank you for taking me under your wing. I am so thankful and grateful I became your unicorn because you became my unicorn editor and friend. Thank you so much to my beta readers, Ellie and Lauren, you guys really helped this rewrite. To the team at Books n moods. Thank you for designing an amazing cover (and did you see that family tree?)

I had literal tears. It's stunning. Thank you so much to Ellie at Lovenotes PR – you have been a pleasure to work with and I am so happy to have you on my team. Finally, I will forever be grateful to all the readers, Bookbloggers, Booktokers and book reviewers, for taking a chance on the Elites of Cheshire Shore. Thank you so much for taking a second chance on Make Me.

About the Author

Caroline, the self-confessed spicy romance lover.

Embracing her unique perspective, Caroline strives to create love stories that captivate with both wit and profound emotion. Caroline crafts characters that resonate deeply, aspiring to champion voices and stories that are often overlooked in romantic comedies, adding delightful complexity and depth.

Caroline continues to enchant her audience with her unique blend of humor and depth, one spicy tale at a time.

Find me:

Website: www.carolinemasci.com.au

Instagram: @Author_carolinemasci

Tiktok: Author_carolinemasci

Join my Facebook Group Carolines Elites

Read Carolines other works here:

Elites of Cheshire Shore Series
Make Me
Love Me
Find Me
Coming Soon

House of Royal Series:
The Spare Diaries
Coming Soon

Stand-alone works:
Love at first Château.